JUDGE DREDD
YEAR TWO

An Abaddon Books™ Publication
www.abaddonbooks.com
abaddon@rebellion.co.uk

This omnibus first published
in 2017 by Abaddon Books™,
Rebellion Intellectual Property Limited,
Riverside House, Osney Mead,
Oxford, OX2 0ES, UK.

10 9 8 7 6 5 4 3 2 1

Editor: David Thomas Moore
Cover Art: Neil Roberts
Design: Sam Gretton, Oz Osborne and Maz Smith
Marketing and PR: Remy Njambi
Editor-in-Chief: Jonathan Oliver
Head of Books and Comics Publishing: Ben Smith
Creative Director and CEO: Jason Kingsley
Chief Technical Officer: Chris Kingsley

Judge Dredd created by
John Wagner and Carlos Ezquerra.

ISBN: 978-1-78108-596-7

Printed in Denmark

JUDGE DREDD
YEAR TWO

MATT SMITH
MICHAEL CARROLL
CAVAN SCOTT

ABADDON
BOOKS

WWW.ABADDONBOOKS.COM

Introduction

BORAG THUNGG, EARHLETS!

Welcome to the second zarjaz collection of prose stories from Judge Joe Dredd's early years, cunningly entitled *Year Two*. As the name suggests, we're now into 2081 AD, and these novellas establish a Young Stoney-Face that's making his mark on the mean streets of Mega-City One, and no longer quite the raw rookie that he was. Of course, being a clone of Eustace Fargo, the Father of Justice and creator of the Judges—engineered from the finest genetic material, and fashioned into a law-enforcement machine—Dredd was never going to be as wet behind the ears as other graduates from the Academy of Law, but he has a lot of expectation to live up to, and nothing, not even fifteen years in the toughest school on Earth, can quite prepare you for policing this violent, crazy metropolis.

A shadow looms over Dredd too in the shape of his corrupt clone-brother Rico, who despite being Joe's equal in so many ways, chose a darker path. The previous collection saw Rico still a Mega-City Judge, and using his ill-gotten gains through association with organised crime to fund a luxurious lifestyle.

In *2000 AD*, Rico's corruption was only glimpsed—the first full story of how far the Dredd sibling had fallen didn't come until the three-parter from March 2000 *Blood Cadets*—but prose has allowed the writers to explore the character and his relationship with Joe a lot more deeply. Indeed, Michael Carroll, who pens the first story here *The Righteous Man*, has also written an e-novella purely about Rico's time on the penal colony of Titan called *The Third Law*. By Year Two, however, Rico has been arrested and sentenced, the bloodline besmirched. How Dredd deals with this, and the impact it has on him, informs not just Carroll's book but the second story too, *Down & Out* by Matthew Smith.

The Righteous Man asks questions of Dredd in the aftermath of Rico's fall from grace—can he be trusted? They're cut from the same cloth, share the same DNA—who's to say Joe doesn't also possess that bad seed that could see him twisting justice for his own ends. Dredd struggles with these questions himself in *Down & Out*, opening with him being asked to express how he feels by a Justice Department psychoanalyst—and that's the problem. He *doesn't* feel—he doesn't know how, it was drilled out of him by his tutors. When he becomes cut off in notorious part of town, severely injured, escape impossible, he's haunted by the spectre of Rico, about what it means to be part of the bloodline, and what he must do to step up to restore honour to the Fargo lineage.

The press interest and publicity around the Rico case also plays a part in needling the Grand Hall, who frankly could do without the scandal, and indeed it is a journalist that travels to Titan to interview the ex-Judge who ends up bearing Dredd's niece Vienna. Scurrilous reportage forms the backbone of the story that rounds out this omnibus, *Alternative Facts* by Cavan Scott, which works in an on-point plot about a whistleblowing blogger alongside a murder case and several neat continuity elements. Enjoy, Terrans!

SPLUNDIG VUR THRIGG!

THARG THE MIGHTY

THE RIGHTEOUS MAN

MICHAEL CARROLL

**MEGA-CITY ONE
2080 A.D.**

One

"No way, Rico. I'm taking you in."

Seven words that marked the end of everything. They echoed through Joseph Dredd's mind as he watched a squad of more experienced Judges go into action.

Joe had already cuffed Rico's wrists and stripped him of his weapons and equipment, but no one was taking any chances. They put a second set of cuffs on Rico's wrists, two more on his ankles. A Med-Judge hit him with a heavy tranquiliser, then allowed him to topple backwards onto a stretcher.

Four street Judges carried him out of the block, another four walking alongside them, all with their Lawgivers already drawn.

As they carried Rico's barely-conscious body past Joe and toward a waiting H-Wagon, one of the Judges muttered, "How the hell do we know we got the *right* one?"

Joe ran his gloved hand over the back of his neck; it came away damp with sweat.

He glanced back toward the block. Inside, Virgil Livingstone was dead, face-down in a drying pool of his own blood. So far, the other Judges had only barely glanced at him. That made sense: a rogue Judge needed to be dealt with immediately, and Livingstone wasn't going anywhere.

Joe moved to follow the Judges into the H-Wagon, but a senior Judge stepped in front of him, palm out. "Not a chance, boy. You stay put—the chief's on the way to see you."

"Understood," Joe said.

They were all watching him, he knew that. He didn't blame them. He and Rico were identical, down to the names on their badges. Few of their fellow Judges were able to tell them apart.

Until they spoke, at least. Joe's voice was a little deeper, his manner more calm. Where Rico was talkative, Joe was taciturn. When they were together, one sure way to identify them was to see who spoke first in any given situation. Odds were, that was Rico.

Joe was the cold one. He was aware that some of tutors at the Academy had believed him to be too dispassionate to make it as a Judge. Once, during preparation for a training exercise to the Cursed Earth, he'd overhead Judge-Tutor Semple talking about him with Judge Ruiz: "Judges have got to be calm and assured, but this damn kid's a *robot*. He's good at what he does—the best—but a Judge needs empathy. Joe's about as empathic as a rock. You meet Rico, he asks you how things are going. Joe asks you what needs to be done."

Judge Ruiz had said, "Have to say, I prefer the latter. We're not here to be friends."

"At least you can have a conversation with Rico. You get the feeling that there's more behind those eyes than a law-book. Joe Dredd needs to learn how to *engage*, because right now his attitude is holding him back. Rico has friends who'd take a bullet for him; Joe has colleagues who are cautious around him. No Judge works alone. Joe will only become an effective Judge if he has the full support and trust of the rest of the Department."

So he'd tried harder to fit in with the other cadets, to join in their conversations and sometimes offer opinions even when he hadn't been asked. That hadn't been easy, and he wasn't completely sure that it was as important as Judge-Tutor Semple believed, until he realised that it wasn't just for *his* benefit; it was also for *theirs*. A suggestion here, a subtle prompt there, and soon Joe found that the other cadets were coming to him for advice. Only on judicial matters, of course; for almost anything else they came to Rico.

All those years in the Academy, a year on the streets... And it had come down to this. Rico had turned bad. Somewhere along the way, he'd strayed from the path.

Every cadet strayed to some degree, of course—that was only human—but most of them realised their mistake and turned back. Joe himself had experienced moments of doubt about the system, but unlike Rico he'd never chosen to subvert that system.

He'd put his doubts aside. If the Law was wrong—and it sometimes was—then the correct approach was to temper that error with justice and mercy. Rico's approach had been to say, "Drokk it," and do whatever suited him in that moment.

The H-Wagon rose silently and Joe watched it go, very much aware of the many Judges still at the scene of the crime.

Now, another senior Judge stepped up to him. Kimber was a tall, lean, fifty-year-old man sporting a non-regulation grey moustache. "Chief Judge Goodman is on the way, Dredd. Hand over your Lawgiver, daystick, boot-knife and utility belt."

Joe didn't move. "I'm under arrest?"

"Just hand them over."

"You didn't answer." Every other Judge present was now looking in his direction. Some of them already had their Lawgivers in hand, held pseudo-casually by their sides.

"I don't answer to you, Dredd. I've been on the streets since before you were mixed in a test-tube. So either you give me your weapons, or I take them from you. Trust me, you will *not* enjoy the latter option."

Another H-Wagon was approaching. The other Judges would never let him anywhere near the Chief Judge if he was armed. He unclipped his belt and handed it over, along with his Lawgiver and everything else.

Kimber passed them to another Judge, then removed a set of cuffs from his own belt. To Joe, he said, "Arms out, wrists together."

"Do you think I'll be any less dangerous wearing cuffs?"

Kimber regarded him for a moment. "All right. Your decision. If the chief won't see you like this, it's your loss. But you ought to understand that the word has already spread. You arrested your own *brother*, Dredd. That's not won you any new friends."

"He broke the *law*, Kimber. The only reason we *exist* is to uphold the law. If you're implying that I should have let him walk, then—"

"Shut the drokk *up*, you stupid punk! You think you're the only decent Judge in the department? That the rest of us are looking out for each other and to hell with the citizens? Rico was armed, he'd just gunned down a civilian, you had the drop on him, and you *arrested* him. Didn't even fire your weapon once. You were within the law to blow his drokkin' head off." He leaned closer. "He's a killer, and you protected him. *Now* do you understand me? If your brother kills again, that's on you."

CHIEF JUDGE CLARENCE Goodman dismissed the other Judges— they retreated out of earshot, but remained close enough to act should anything go wrong—and stared at Joseph Dredd for a full minute before he spoke.

During that time, he ran through a dozen opening sentences, but none of them felt right. In the end, he just sighed and said, "Stomm."

Dredd didn't respond to that. Goodman hadn't expected him to.

"Joe... When did you know?"

"Sir?"

"You know what I'm asking. When did you realise Rico had turned?"

"I... Sir, that's hard to say. I wasn't ever *sure*, but I had suspicions. On several occasions, citizens I'd never met before greeted me as though they knew me. Obviously they thought I was Rico. It's likely the same thing happened to him."

"But?"

"On three of those occasions, the conversations seemed to imply that they were low-level perps operating under Rico's protection. Without further evidence, that wasn't reason enough to question them, or even talk to him about them. Sometimes a Judge must allow some things to slide in order to—"

"Do please keep teaching me the finer points of the law, Dredd," cut in Goodman. "I'm only the damn Chief Judge!"

"Sorry, sir."

"Go on."

"Rico's been residing in an apartment belonging to a citizen who's currently out of the city. That's not against the rules. I checked out the owner. Everything Rico said was confirmed, and the owner himself was clean. He *had* been implicated in a body-sharking racket, but was cleared by subsequent investigation shortly before he relocated to Texas City."

"All right," Goodman said. "His apartment will be vacant, so he asks a Judge to live there while he's gone. That's not uncommon. It helps keep the Judges among the people as well as protect the apartment. There's even a tax-break the owner can claim for that."

"Sir, Rico was the investigating Judge in that body-sharking case."

"That's not proof of *anything*, Dredd."

Dredd glanced back toward the building. "The body of Virgil Livingstone is pretty solid evidence."

Goodman took a step closer to Dredd, his eyes narrow and his face grim. "Funny. I didn't know better, I'd swear that's Rico talking. There'll be a full investigation. Into *both* of you. You will return to the Hall of Justice. Once there, you will remain in your quarters under house-arrest pending the outcome of this investigation. Understood?"

"Yes, sir."

"I mean it, Joe. You are *forbidden* to engage in any judicial activities unless and until specifically requested to do so by a senior Judge." Goodman started to move away, then stopped and turned back. "Of the two of you, you were the one I had the most hope for. If you've let me down, I swear to *Grud* I'll..."

He couldn't finish the sentence. He felt like he'd swallowed a ball of concrete. His opponents were going to have a field-day with this. They'd been arguing against the use of cloned Judges for years, and now they had all the ammunition they needed to put the programme on ice for good.

Damn Rico. Always just a little too smug, too cocksure, for his own good. From the moment the kid learned that he was a clone of Judge Fargo, he'd thought of himself as special, better than the other cadets.

And he *had* been good, that couldn't be denied. Rico and Joe had been by far the best cadets the Academy had ever turned out.

From the moment they were removed from the accelerated-growth units—Rico first, then Joe—they'd been monitored every step of the way. For the first few years, at least. It was all on file; Goodman briefly wondered how much of that archived footage would become part of the investigation.

Goodman climbed back into his shuttle. Despite the situation, he had to suppress a smile as he recalled Joe and Rico learning to walk. They'd looked to be the equivalent of about five years old, but—fresh from the cloning vats—they'd been as weak as newborn infants.

Rico had been the first to walk, of course. Rico was always first. His chubby little legs had been supporting his own weight for a couple of days as he carefully made his way around the nursery, holding onto walls and chairs and anything that he could use to keep his balance, grinning and giggling as he grew steadier on his feet. For most of that time, Joe had sat in the middle of the room, just watching him.

Then Rico had cautiously let go of the chair, first with one hand, then the other, and took his first real steps.

Goodman had been watching. He'd spent a lot of time watching the twins, probably far too much time, he knew, but they were fascinating. He hadn't had a lot of experience with children, and had been captivated by the rate at which the clones were developing.

Rico had walked eight steps before collapsing onto his backside with fresh burst of giggles. Moments later, he was up again. Twenty-one steps. Third attempt, almost fifty steps before he fell. And then he got up once more, and never crawled again.

Joe had started walking the next day. He'd crawled over to a low plastic table—one of those ones with geometric holes and matching brightly-coloured blocks—pulled himself up, and began walking. He never fell, not once. It was as though Joe had learned from his brother's mistakes and avoided making them himself.

Where Rico led, Joe followed. That's how it had been throughout their years at the Academy. But it wasn't that simple, Goodman knew.

Rico had been the first to learn how to talk, but Joe had been the first to learn *when* to talk.

Rico had been first to challenge the Tutors on contentious points of law, but his brother had been the first to offer feasible solutions.

They were cloned from the same source, but they were far from identical.

As the Chief Judge's shuttle descended toward the Hall of Justice, that thought was his only comfort. *They're* not *the same man. They have embraced different aspects of their father, even though neither of them realise that.*

The investigation was going to turn over a lot of rocks that the Department would rather stay hidden, Goodman knew. Rico was guilty; there was no doubt of that. But the investigation wasn't really going to be *about* Rico. On the surface, yes, but beneath that... There would be questions raised about not just the validity of clone Judges, but about the competence of the people who had supported the cloning programme.

When he pulled the trigger, Rico Dredd hadn't just murdered that citizen Virgil Livingstone. He'd painted a target on the entire Department, and Grud knew that it was already riddled through with more than enough holes.

As Chief Judge, he was in the unique position to understand exactly how everything worked. Sure, from the outside, the Justice Department of Mega-City One was a solid, implacable force, but that was an illusion. When you got right down to it, the Department was made up of people, and people are fallible.

All of them. Every Judge had skeletons in the closet. Hell, even *Fargo*'d had them. All it would take was the right push at the wrong time, and those closet doors would come crashing open, disgorging their damning contents into the laps of their enemies.

If Joe Dredd isn't clean, Goodman thought, *if he has a single speck on his ledger, that'll destroy the cloning programme and everyone who supported it. It could rock the foundations of the Justice Department. And if we fall, the rest of the city will fall with us.*

Two

In the Chief Judge's office, Goodman sank deeper into his chair and read Joseph Dredd's case history.

On the whole, the Judge-cloning programme was not regarded as a major success. *The initial idea was flawed*, Goodman thought. *Judges aren't grown—they're built. A fifteen-year stint in the Academy was what made a Judge, not an artificial womb filled with Morton Judd's chemical soup.*

Sure, the accelerated growth had been a boon, but Judd's ultimate plan—to create fully-grown Judges already programmed with everything they'd need to know—was a very long way from bearing any fruit.

Goodman recalled telling Judd, "There are too many things that can go wrong. You're hurtling down a skedway at five hundred kph, then the slightest pot-hole can send you careening off-course. Slow and steady. That way, you actually reach the end of the road in one piece."

The sealed records listed hundreds of failures before the first viable infant had been pulled from the vats. Judd's people had begun crowing like they'd just beaten Grud at his own game, but

Fargo himself had cut them off. He'd looked down at the child and said, "This isn't a Judge. You made a baby. Any pair of horny teenagers can do that, and with far less time, effort and money."

The programme had continued, of course, because Fargo had had faith in Judd's vision. More vats, more embryos. The failure-rate dropped significantly, the accelerated growth continued to improve. The process reached the point where the subjects could be removed from their vats, rinsed down, measured for a cadet uniform and shipped to the Academy of Law within a day.

But they still had to be trained to be Judges. There was no way—yet—to accelerate that part of the programme.

Goodman had discussed this with Fargo and the other senior Judges many times. "The cloning programme saves us a little over four years from new-born to Judge... And this is assuming that at least *some* of the cadets will actually make it through the Academy and onto the streets."

The source DNA was no guarantee of a good Judge, even if that source was Fargo himself.

But the Dredds had been exceptions, no doubt about that. Right from the start, they had shown aptitude for life at the Academy.

Goodman instructed the computer to bring up some old video-footage of Rico and Joe. The first file showed them at six years old, receiving their first Lawgiver training.

Rico and the other cadets were excited at the thought of handling a firearm with live ammunition—their practice weapons were barely capably of raising a bruise at point-blank range—but Joe, as always, had been impassive.

On screen, to the amusement of the watching tutors, Cadet Wagner giddily ran around the room with two of the scaled-down Lawgivers, pretend-shooting at everything in sight. He arrested a chair for loitering and a door for "opening and closing without a permit."

Young Rico picked up his own gun and immediately began

fake-shooting at his fellow cadets: "Drop it, lawbreaker! Blam-blam-blam! You're down, Ellard! One through the heart, two through the head!"

While the other cadets had fun as they played with the guns—which the tutors encouraged, because a Judge should be comfortable and familiar with his or her Lawgiver—on the edge of the room Joe wasn't taking part. He had placed his gun into his boot-holster and just observed the others. But now, as Goodman watched, Joe crouched, drew and aimed the gun in one swift movement.

Goodman sat back. He reversed the video-clip and watched it again. Then he checked the video's time-stamp. *The first time Joe Dredd ever drew a gun. Six years old... And he was as fast then as I was in my prime.*

He skipped to the next video clip. Seven years old, simulated combat, live but non-lethal ammunition. This was a kidnap-rescue scenario, based on a real case where a gang of perps had kidnapped an entire school-bus full of nine-year-old girls.

The cadets steadily made their way through the mocked-up tenement block. Rico took charge. He silently instructed Gibson and Joe to advance through the darkened corridor, which they took one doorway at a time, leap-frogging each other, always keeping the cadet ahead covered.

A door opposite them was pulled open, and Joe immediately turned, aimed and fired, his low-impact round striking Judge-Tutor Semple square in the protective face-plate.

Semple called out, "All right, simulation over—shut it down!" The lights went up and the cadets gathered around the Tutor.

Semple raised the face-plate and looked down at Joe Dredd. "Perfect shot, Dredd. But poor judgement. Anyone want to tell him why?"

Cadet McManus said, "Sir, Joe fired instantly. Didn't wait to see whether you were a victim or a perp."

"Correct," Semple said. "Dredd, there was no way you could

have known. A Judge can *not* endanger the life of a citizen unless—"

Rico interrupted. "Sir, Joe made the right call."

Watching the screen, Goodman smiled at that. Rico always stood up for his little brother.

"How so?" Semple asked, a weary, resigned tone in his voice.

Rico turned to Joe.

Joe said, "Sir, the tallest of the kidnapped girls wouldn't even reach up to your shoulder. I could see instantly that you were an adult."

"I could have had one of the victims in front of me, as a human shield," Semple said.

"I aimed high, shot you in the face. If it *had* been a victim who'd opened the door, my shot would have passed over her head."

"What if I'd been *carrying* the victim? Holding her up so that her head was on the same level as mine?"

Joe said, "Sir... You clearly had a gun in your right hand. If you'd been carrying a victim, your left arm would have been occupied."

"So?"

"Then how would you have opened the door?"

Goodman closed the video-clip and stood up. Even now, he knew, a hundred Judges were poring over every aspect of Joe and Rico's careers. Reports were being compiled, statistics analysed, old prejudices dusted off in preparation.

Rico had been doomed by his own actions, as he should be. But Joe... Guilty by association, that was the approach some of the investigators were taking. They'd start with the assumption that Joe was dirty and do their damnedest to prove it.

Goodman's initial comment on the early reports urged caution: "Yes, Rico and Joseph Dredd come from the same stock, but a blacksmith can forge an iron ingot into both a dagger and a horseshoe. Same source, different outcomes. You don't destroy the horseshoe just because the dagger was used in a crime."

Some of the investigators had thanked Goodman for his input, and carried on with the investigation regardless. If they couldn't prove Joe's guilt directly, well, Joe and Rico were genetically identical. In the year they'd been on the streets there was certain to be at least one suspicious situation where there was no way to tell which was which.

Between the time Virgil Livingstone was killed and Goodman arrived at the scene, he'd already heard from three other members of the Council of Five, two basically saying "I told you so" and the third not-so-subtly suggesting they keep the mess under wraps: "This is ammunition for the fourth estate. If we don't keep a lid on this, they'll tear us all down."

Goodman's response to the latter had been firm: "Justice needs to be seen to be done. As far as the media knows, the investigation will be completely transparent."

As far as the media knows. Goodman mused on that thought as he stared out at the city. There was an unspoken understanding between the media and the Judges. *They don't push us, we don't push back.* There were times when someone in the press uncovered possible corruption in the Justice Department, but Goodman had learned that it was generally more effective to bribe their way out of the situation than use threats. And bribery could take so many different forms... A juicy piece of celebrity gossip could give a news outlet much higher ratings than the story of a Judge who'd turned a blind eye to his mother's unlicensed stamp-collection. A quiet word to the right sector controller could see a journalist's kids transferred to a better school. Sometimes all it took for a story to be buried was a hint that a network's rivals might find themselves hampered on the way to the site of the next newsworthy crime.

Every now and then one side or the other would test the boundaries, but it had been a long time since anyone had gone too far.

This, though, was different. The citizens loved a good corruption story, and once the press got their teeth into it, there wasn't much the Department could do to encourage them to let go.

Legally, the Department could shut down any story citing the standard public safety clauses, but they could only play that card so often before the press decided that the gag orders were an even bigger story, the old 'What are they hiding?' angle.

That was when the individual threats came into play. And in the few cases where even that didn't work, there was always the perennial stand-by: the hostile takeover of the media company by one of the Department's shell corporations.

Goodman looked out at Mega-City One, built on the scorched bones of the east coast of America, and he knew—*everyone* knew, on every side, whether they admitted it to themselves or not—that this was a dictatorship. It had to be. It was the only way to stop the city crumbling under its own weight.

The Justice Department always gets its way.

The citizens could rant, and resist, and even riot all they wanted, but ultimately it would make no difference. *Even the loudest protest is a whisper in a thunderstorm*, Goodman told himself. *And we're the thunder*.

DREDD'S QUARTERS IN the Hall of Justice were deep in the bowels of the building, a windowless three-metre-cube. It held little more than a narrow, rarely-used bunk, basic washing facilities, and a small pull-down desk-and-chair combination, at which Dredd was now sitting as he read his law-books.

He looked up as the door opened, and SJS Judge Gillen entered.

"Searching through the books for a loophole, Dredd?" she asked.

"No. What do you want, Gillen?"

"Your brother's a murderer."If she'd hoped to provoke a response, Dredd didn't oblige.

"You watched him gun down Virgil Livingstone and you did nothing to stop him. That makes you an accessory."

Dredd closed over his book. "Incorrect. Don't try to goad me into anger, Gillen. That's beneath you."

She sat down on the end of the bed, pulled off her helmet and rested it on her knees. "You don't have much respect for the Special Judicial Squad, do you?"

"I understand the need for the SJS. It wasn't so long ago that you offered me a job. I assume that offer has been rescinded."

Gillen nodded toward Dredd's law-book. "Open the book at random. Go on."

Dredd opened the book.

"The Law, volume eighteen," Gillen said. "Page?"

"Three-twenty-four."

"Three-twenty-four," Gillen said. "The importation of dried vegetable goods with particular emphasis on the risk of using said goods' natural sugars to create alcohol."

"A good memory doesn't imply a good Judge. You have a point?"

"My point is that I know the law, inside-out." Gillen ran her gloved hand over her close-cropped hair. "It's one of the reasons I've been appointed by the investigation committee to uncover evidence of your guilt. And I've been granted any and all powers necessary to do so."

Dredd nodded.

"Nothing to say?"

"I've never broken the law. That's going to make your job a lot harder."

"Dredd, I don't think you understand what's happening here. There are factions in the Justice Department who are anxious to put an end to the cloning program, and Rico has given them the only excuse they need. Some among them are even arguing that you're not truly human, that you don't have the most basic of human rights. Those particular Judges are not even talking about the investigation. They consider it *fait accompli* that the two of you will be terminated."

"And what do *you* think?"

"My opinion is that you're an unknown element, and in the SJS our job is to shine a light into the darkness. We are going to trace every second of your life from the moment you left the Academy. Same with Rico. The slightest hint that you knew what he was doing, and that's *it* for you. Game over, no second chances."

"If I had known, I would have arrested him sooner."

Gillen pushed herself to her feet. "That's exactly what I expected you to say."

"So what now?" Dredd asked. "I'm sequestered here until it's time to present my defence?"

"No. You don't *get* to present a defence. The investigation will take place without your involvement. It's also been decided that you won't be called as a witness against Rico, because there's no doubt of *his* guilt. Chief Judge Goodman, in his wisdom—or folly; I'm not yet sure which—has concluded that your skills would be put to better use on the streets. You're going to be tucked away in a sector you've never visited while the investigation takes place. You will be partnered at all times by a senior Judge who is known to us and is considered above reproach. Any attempt by you to interfere with the investigation, circumvent the law or to leave the city without authorisation will be considered confirmation of your guilt."

Gillen slid open the door. "Your transport is leaving from the eastern H-pad in thirty minutes. I suggest you use that time to gather your personal items and put them in storage, because the odds are you won't be coming back here." She looked around the small room. "Dredd, do you even *have* any personal items?"

Dredd indicated the law-books on his desk. "I have these."

Judge Gillen pursed her lips and nodded slightly. "All right. In that case, the transport leaves in five minutes."

Three

SECTOR 198 WAS known to many locals as 'the Sweats.' It was the only sector in Mega-City One bordered on three sides—north, south and west—by the Cursed Earth.

As the Justice Department transport approached the sector, the pilot—a fifty-year-old woman who'd spent much of the journey quietly singing to herself—looked over her shoulder at Dredd and the other young Judge sitting next to him, and asked, "So, what'd you two kids do to end up here?"

She turned back to the controls and said, "Must have been bad, whatever it was. I've been a pilot for four years, and I've ferried a lot of Judges just like you to this sector." A calculated pause. "Haven't yet brought one home."

She glanced back again. "That should tell you something. See, what happens is that they get Judges like you two who've wet the bed or whatever, and they stick them here because it's as rough as a gravel enema down there. This sector burns through Judges like matches in a rainstorm, you know what I'm saying?"

"I've read the reports," Dredd said.

The pilot laughed. "Kid, you're going to learn pretty quick

that reports are only words on a screen. They can't convey the *true* experience, y'know? The nuances, the *flavour* of a place. In this case, the flavour is a subtle blend of adrenaline and formaldehyde. You get me?" She pointed out through the cockpit glass. "That out there is a lake of piranhas and you're a prime cut of steak."

Dredd said, "You should focus on piloting the craft. Failure to give your full attention to a vehicle under your control is a serious offence."

"You think I don't know that? I'm a Judge too. And I could fly this pram with my damn eyes sewn shut, boy." She snorted a laugh. "You are *not* gonna last long in the Sweats, if you want my opinion."

"I don't," Dredd said.

The other Judge—female, mid-twenties, currently wearing only her uniform tunic and helmet—spoke for the first time since boarding the shuttle. "Why do they call it the Sweats?"

The pilot said, "Because it sticks right out into the Cursed Earth, and weather control is patchy. Sometimes in the height of summer they've gotta pipe in water from what's left of Lake Erie just so's they can spray down the old asphalt roads to stop them melting. Then you've got your muties on the other side of the wall. They cluster around the waste pipes and go fishin' in the garbage for anything they can sell or trade." She turned around to face the young Judges. "You ever smelled a mutie who's been up to his neck in warm garbage all day long? Well, multiply that by ten thousand, and that's a start. You feel like your eyes are gonna melt right out of their sockets. I heard of one Judge who was ambushed and torn apart by a bunch of crazies just so they could get hold of his *respirator.*" Another pause, then, "And it wasn't muties who did that. They were cits."

She adjusted the craft's orientation in preparation for descent. "But the muties do attack, too. Every couple of weeks they'll breach the wall somewhere. They get in, set a bunch of fires or they use their home-made bombs on a bridge or something. Then all the Judges come running and, whaddaya know, it was a decoy and the *real* raiding party is five klicks away and they're plundering a supermarket or a warehouse. On your left there is the sector's largest block, David Shires Con-Apt. Take my advice: you don't want to get to close to *that* place. Two hundred thousand cits or thereabouts. No one's sure exactly because it has the highest murder-rate in the city."

Dredd said, "*Eighth* highest."

The pilot said, "Thanks. I sure do love being corrected by a *child*. Whatever. Strap in. Touchdown in sixteen seconds."

Dredd had barely clipped his seat harness before the shuttle landed with an impact that he was sure must have stretched the limits of its landing struts' shock-absorbers.

"Get moving," the pilot said. "Doubt I'll be seeing either of you again. Try not to get killed on your first day." She flicked a lever on the control panel and the craft's starboard hatch hissed open.

A gust of warm, foetid air rushed into the shuttle like someone had just opened an enormous oven right next to them.

Dredd followed the other Judge down the shuttle's ramp onto a wide plaza in view of the local Sector House.

As the Judges watched the shuttle rise unsteadily but swiftly, the other Judge said, "Celia Montag, tech-division, sector eighty."

"Dredd, thirteen. What brings *you* here, Montag?"

"I'm a weapons specialist. There's a lot of old pre-war munitions coming in through this sector and the Judges here need my help detecting and tracking them. You?"

"You haven't heard?" Dredd asked her.

"No."

He started moving toward the Sector House. "You will."

* * *

"LET'S TALK, DREDD."

Rico Dredd raised his head slowly. Too slowly: Judge Gillen realised he was still under sedation. That might make this interrogation more difficult than she'd like.

In the heart of the Hall of Justice, Rico's cell was five metres by four—larger than his brother's quarters, Gillen noted—and utterly secure. Fourteen separate layers of security, from armed guards to impervious bars to scanners capable of detecting any foreign object more substantial than a human hair, would ensure that the rogue Judge would be around long enough to face his sentence.

"Sure," Rico said. "What do you want to talk about?"

Grud, they really are *identical*, Gillen thought. Except for the expression in his eyes, it could be Joe on the other side of the bars. "Your safety-net is disintegrating. Those files you gave us have proved very useful, but they won't save you. There's not a Judge in the Department who buys your story about infiltrating the mobs to take them down from within. Your old contacts are squealing under pressure; you really should have chosen them more carefully. We know about your part in the heist at the Kool Herc Infernodrome, about Madame Ozelle's brothel, your endorphium stash, the Quasarano family... All of it. But I want to know when it started for you. When did you begin to see yourself as above the law?"

Rico stood on the other side of the bars, chained hand and foot, the chains only just long enough to allow him to shuffle around the cell. It was not a dignified look, but somehow it only made Rico seem even more dangerous. "The law." He smiled. "The law is artificial. You have to understand that. You choose to believe that the city's laws are immutable, like the laws of physics. But they're not. They're... customs. Traditions that we cling to because they make us feel comfortable. We all know that murder is wrong because..."

Gillen watched him for a second, wondering whether the

sedatives coursing through his veins had dulled his thoughts.

"Well?" Rico asked.

"I see. You were waiting for me to supply the answer. I understand your point, Dredd. Collectively, we've decided that murder is wrong. In another society, it might be perfectly acceptable."

"It's acceptable in *this* one. We call it justice. You know how many people I've legally executed since I left the Academy?"

"I'm more interested in the ones you've murdered."

"Execution and murder, right and wrong, good and evil, order and chaos... They're just labels. Switch them around, and people will protest for a while, but pretty soon the new way will become the norm."

"Do you see yourself as good or evil, Dredd?"

He stared at her, unblinking. "Didn't you hear what I just said? Any label I apply to myself has no relevance; it's just a word, and words are not absolutes."

"You killed Virgil Livingstone."

Rico nodded. "That's true. Though that was not murder. It was unintentional. I was distracted."

"By your brother."

Another nod.

"Joe wanted a slice of the action, is that it? He saw that your life was better than his, and he wanted in. Things got out of control and Livingstone died."

"This is what you *really* want to know, isn't it? Whether Little Joe has started to see the light. You won't get that answer from me, Gillen. Walk away. Interrogate my contacts, pick over every second of my life. I'm sure you'll find something—an event, a decision—that you'll conclude is what made me the way I am. Perhaps you'll even be right. You'll understand the reasons behind every decision, every action. Go ahead. Learn to see the world through my eyes. Come back and tell me whether you think I'm good or evil."

"I already know the answer to that," Gillen said. "Every sociopath has their own justifications for their actions. In your view, you're right and anyone who opposes you is wrong."

"That's not an attitude exclusive to sociopaths," Rico said. "*Everyone* thinks like that."

"True. But you, Dredd... Standing there with that smug expression, trying to tell yourself that everything is going to work out in your favour, that you can take whatever punishment we decide to throw at you, that you're content with how things are and you're *not* boiling with concealed fury... Well, I know what's at the core of this facade. The nameless rage that constantly gnaws at your soul. It's the same rage that drove you to become the highest-scoring cadet to ever graduate from the Academy of Law. The rage that allowed you to justify every cruelty, every selfish act."

"And what is that?"

"It's *jealousy*. You despise your brother because you know that in every way—*every* way—he is better than you."

Rico smirked. "Oh, please. That's beneath you."

"Funny, Joe said the same thing. But my point is that he has no ego. That *kills* you, doesn't it? In the Academy tests, any time you scored higher than him he was happy for you. Even proud of you, in his way. But whenever *he* beat *your* scores, you worked your butt off to make sure you surpassed him next time. Joe didn't care about that. Still doesn't. He doesn't want anything for himself. I've seen the apartment you've been living in, Dredd. It's packed with luxury items, the most expensive food, all the latest high-tech entertainments. The only thing your brother owns is a set of law-books. That's all he needs, and all he wants."

"You believe that, Gillen, then you're not digging deep enough. Joe has his secrets, trust me on that."

"Save me some legwork, then. *Tell* me."

"Why should I do your job for you?"

Gillen looked around the cell. "What else are you going to do here? Just tell me this, Dredd... What was your ultimate goal? Suppose Joe hadn't been there this morning. Livingstone wouldn't have died, no one would know what you've been doing. So what was your *plan*? Accumulate a few million credits and retire from the Department?"

Rico didn't respond to that.

"You don't know," Gillen said. She moved back toward the door. "You can't answer that because you *had* no goal. You spent the past year corrupting the system and you don't even know why. You know what that tells me about you?"

"That I'm rudderless," Rico said. "That I just submit to my whims and can't see the big picture."

"No. It tells me you're incompetent. With your skills, you could have been a senior Judge within four years, heading a division within ten, Chief Judge by the end of the century. Instead, you traded all that for a top-of-the-range Taneasy lounger and drinks by the pool." Gillen placed her palm on the door's hand-plate. As it slid open she turned back to face him. "You're a drokkin' *idiot*."

Four

THE DOORS TO the public area of Sector House 198 hissed open as Dredd and Montag approached, but the left door stuck halfway.

Dredd said, "Hmph," and shoved the door the rest of the way.

"Yeah, that's not a good sign," Montag said.

Dredd glanced back at the clusters of dishevelled citizens waiting on the Sector House steps, then strode ahead of Montag into the building. The stench here was even worse than outside. Fifty citizens—at least—waited in broken lines against the side walls, most of them sitting on the floor because there was only enough seating for twenty. One woman was dozing, stretched out across four seats.

None of the citizens looked up to see who had entered. That told Dredd more about this sector than any report he'd read.

At the front desk, a Judge—female, mid-fifties, long grey hair tied into a pony-tail, badge-name Eisenhower—nodded at Dredd and Montag as they approached. "You made it, then." She slid a battered computer-tablet toward them. "Sign in."

Dredd pulled off his right glove and placed his hand on the tablet, and the desk Judge read his details from her own monitor. "Joseph Dredd, formerly assigned to Sector Thirteen. Reassigned to 198 for supervised duties pending the outcome of an investigation..." The woman sighed. "And so on. Thirteen, huh? Well, we *work* for a living out here, Dredd. We've got the same budget as any other sector of this size, and that's got to cover defending the wall and battling the weather and keeping the outposts safe. So all *this*"—she spread her arms—"might not be as clean and fancy as you're used to, but it's all we've got."

Dredd looked around. "Unwashed floor, cracked windows, aircon's not working, place is overcrowded... This is how you run the House, Eisenhower? What are those cits waiting for?"

"Most are waiting to be processed. Some are here because it's safer than being outside. The gangs can't get to them in here."

Dredd nodded. "Understood." He turned back to Eisenhower. "Am I logged in?"

"Yeah."

"Good. I want a full set of equipment and a Lawmaster. I'm hitting the streets in ten minutes."

"You have to wait for your supervising Judge."

"That's what the ten minutes are for." Dredd strode over to the dozing woman, and nudged her in the side with his boot. "You. Get up."

She pushed herself to a sitting position and glared at him through bloodshot eyes. "What?" She had scabs on her knuckles and old bruises on her arms and throat.

"How long have you been waiting here?"

"What's it to you?"

"Your answer will determine whether I throw you back out onto the streets. How long, and why?"

She stood up and sneered at Dredd. "Three days. I'm here 'cos the women's refuge won't take me in no more, which is 'cos of a fight that happened last time. And the time before."

"Fight a lot, do you?"

Another sneer. "I *defend* myself a lot. Not the same thing."

Dredd placed his hand on the woman's chin. She flinched briefly, then allowed him to turn her head to the side. "You make a formal charge against whoever gave you those scars?"

From the desk, Judge Eisenhower called out, "Her boyfriend. It's in the system. We'll get to it."

Still looking at the scarred woman, Dredd said, "Montag, you logged in yet?"

"I am."

"You're with me today."

Montag walked over to Dredd, stopped by his side. Softly, she said, "Dredd, I'm a *Tech*. I don't—"

"You do now. Take this woman somewhere quiet, get a fresh statement, check the records. I want everything there is in the files about her alleged assailant. Then you and I will go and pay him a visit."

As Montag led the woman away, a young man sitting cross-legged on the ground muttered something to his neighbour.

Dredd turned to him. "What was that?"

The man paled. "I, uh, I was just saying that some of us have been waiting longer than she has, but she gets seen first because everyone's scared of her. We've heard the stories about what she's like."

"I picked her first because she was taking up four seats," Dredd said. "Figured more of you might want to get off the floor. What are *you* here for?"

"I'm *innocent*. I was—"

In two steps Dredd was standing in front of the young man. "Didn't catch that. You might want to tell me again. Maybe choose your words more carefully this time."

"Caught shoplifting."

"What'd you try to take?"

"A pocket Tri-D set."

Dredd nodded. "Been sentenced?"

"Not yet. The Judge said—"

Dredd pointed over his shoulder. "Talk to Judge Eisenhower. She'll tell you where to find a mop and bucket. Your sentence is to clean every floor in the Sector House. Once that's done, you can go. Try shoplifting again if you're tired of not living in an iso-cube." He took a step back and looked at the rest of the waiting citizens. "Any of you creeps know how to repair an air-conditioning unit?"

A young woman tentatively raised her hand. "I used to fix the one at home all the time."

"Why are you here?"

"I got nowhere else to go. My mother threw me out, said that I have to find my own place or start paying my way now that I'm eighteen. And I can't pay my way without a job."

"Give Judge Eisenhower your details. You get the aircon in here working, the department will pay you the standard rate. I'll talk to your mother and make sure she understands her responsibilities."

Behind him, Judge Eisenhower said, "Dredd, you can't do this. We have a *system*. It's not perfect but it works."

"Clearly it doesn't." Dredd pointed to another waiting citizen, an older man wearing a torn, sweat-stained shirt. "You?"

The man looked down at his feet. "I owe money to a shark— her men chased me, I managed to get away and came in here."

"Three men, early thirties, fake-fur jackets with cut-off sleeves?"

He nodded. "Oh, Grud, they're still out there, aren't they?"

Dredd walked toward the entrance. As before, one of the doors only opened part of the way. "Eisenhower, see if any of those cits knows how to fix a door."

A minute later Dredd returned. "Need a Med-Wagon, Eisenhower. Three to pick up. Multiple lacerations and contusions. Fifteen years apiece. Promise them twelve if they squeal on their boss." To the older man, he said, "They won't bother you again."

The man nodded gratefully. "Thank you, Judge! You've saved my life."

"Glad to hear it," Dredd said. "One year in the cubes for dealing with an unauthorised money-lender."

A deep voice from behind Dredd said, "Who the *drokk* do you think you are?"

Dredd turned to see another Judge approaching him. She was female, in her late thirties, almost as tall as he was, with a wiry build.

From the side, Eisenhower said, "Dredd, this is Senior Judge Izobel Ramini. She's your supervisor."

Ramini stopped in front of Dredd. "I read the reports. Joseph Dredd. Brother's a killer, no one's sure about you. So they sent you to me for baby-sitting duties." She looked around for a moment. "Not here ten minutes and already you're upsetting the apple-cart. And I'm told you intend to take my new Tech out onto the streets. Montag has almost no combat experience. She won't last a *day*—"

"She will if she's with me."

Ramini leaned closer. "Don't interrupt me, son. Don't *ever* interrupt me. I don't give a dripping drokk if you were a hot-shot at the Academy. Here in my sector, you're just another rookie until I decide otherwise."

"Understood."

Her eyes narrowed. "I hope so. Let's see how good you are. What's the plan?"

Dredd nodded toward the waiting citizens. "Start clearing the backlog."

"We've got a lot bigger problems than *that* in this sector."

"Have to start somewhere," Dredd said.

"All right," Ramini said. "I'm your back-up for the night

shift. If I'm not impressed, you'll spend the rest of your time here working out duty rosters and indexing the evidence lockers."

GOODMAN UNCONSCIOUSLY CLENCHED his fists when the door to his office opened and Judge Hubert Badger entered.

"Good morning, Chief," Badger said. He was a dour twenty-three-year-old who'd never spent any real time on the streets. In his final year at the Academy he'd been recommended for a position in Strategies, and had worked there ever since. He had a vivid imagination for a Judge, which Goodman had always found unsettling.

"Badger."

"Been looking over the Dredd reports... Had some thoughts I want to bounce off you." Without waiting to be invited, Badger dragged a chair over to Goodman's desk and sat down. As always, Badger worked without notes, having committed everything to memory. "I'm told that the SJS are going around in circles trying to find evidence of the younger Dredd's corruption. So far, they've come up with nothing. It's been thirty-three days. Time to shut that down and put their resources to better use."

"That's not up to us, Badger. The SJS operates autonomously. You know that."

"Sure, sure. But a word or two from you might speed things up. Rico Dredd's scheduled to ship out to Titan on the next transport. I wonder if I might have a chance to spend some time interviewing him before then."

Goodman didn't respond to that one. He was all too familiar with Hubert Badger's grand plans and wasn't in the mood for any of them.

"Well?" Badger asked.

Goodman sighed. "Badger... We've been over this. No one but the SJS gets to talk to Rico Dredd. He is exceptionally dangerous, and the sooner he's gone, the sooner I'll be able to relax a little. Request denied. And for the record, any future similar requests *must* go through the proper channels before they reach this office, at which point they will also be denied."

"I can use him, Chief."

"I know you can. Just as I know that Rico can—and will—use you. And he's a lot stronger-willed than you are. Trust me: fifteen minutes in his company and you'd be signing up to be his second-in-command. Now, is that everything?"

"No. The other Dredd... he's been making waves over in Sector 198."

"Elucidate, please."

"In the month since his reassignment, he's accumulated nineteen official complaints about his behaviour."

Goodman nodded. "Sounds about par for the course with Joe Dredd."

"Sir, those are the complaints from other *Judges*. Complaints from the citizens are well into three figures. What the hell is he *doing* over there?"

"His job. Badger, I haven't seen *all* of those reports, but I have no doubt that there's not been a single instance where Dredd's judgement has been at fault. Am I right?"

"As it happens, you are. But, sir, Sector Chief Benzon has put in a request to keep Joseph Dredd on a permanent basis. A personal note, along with her usual request for a larger budget, says, 'If you've got any more like him, send them my way too.' Sir, I can't permit that. I have my own plans for Dredd."

Goodman toyed with an ornamental antique fountain pen on his desk. "Of course you do, Badger. You have plans for everyone. But most of your plans will never see the light of day... Every sector should be walled off from its neighbours for greater security. Put all Judges in plain clothes to keep the perps off their guard. Sector Zero. Ban education on the grounds that dumb criminals are less trouble than smart ones. Even your *better* ideas either haven't been practical or will take years to come to fruition. The Venusian penal colony, head-to-toe body-armour for the street Judges, the Land Raider project... I could go on." Goodman shook his head. "No, Dredd's too good a Judge to be taken off the streets, and he's our last viable link to Eustace Fargo. He stays where he is until the SJS either find some concrete evidence against him, or they conclude that he's innocent. Which I believe he *is*. Do you understand me, Badger?"

Without giving the younger Judge time to respond, Goodman added, "Half of the senior Judges are still calling for him to be put down just in case he turns out like Rico, three members of the Council of Five are trying to use him as proof that the cloning programme is more trouble than it's worth and should be terminated, *you* want to squirrel him away for one of your frankly implausible long-term schemes... And not *one* of you seems to have the intelligence to grasp the single most important thing about Joe Dredd!"

"And what would *that* be, sir?" Badger asked.

"No matter where you put him, the crime rates drop."

Five

SJS Judge Gillen waited on one of the landing pads on the roof of the Hall of Justice, watching a shuttle touch down. The craft's hatch opened, and Judge Joseph Dredd emerged. He spotted Gillen and walked toward her.

Forty-seven days had passed since his brother's arrest: the longest the brothers had ever spent apart.

Dredd stopped in front of her, and nodded. "Gillen."

"How's Sector 198?"

"Hot. Uncomfortable. Dangerous."

"So you're enjoying it, then?"

"Why are you here, Gillen? I was told that I wouldn't need a chaperone."

Gillen nodded toward the building's entrance. "Walk with me, Dredd." He fell into step beside her, and she glanced up at him. *Stoic, that's the word*, she thought. *Nothing gets to him.* "I heard you're breaking a few arrest records over in 198."

Dredd didn't respond.

"Sector Chief Benzon tells me you're one of the hardest-working Judges she's ever seen. I *know* Benzon—she doesn't dole out the praise too easily. Now, that's got some people thinking that maybe Joe Dredd is on the level after all. And others are saying that you're trying too hard, that you're hiding something. *Are* you, Dredd?"

They paused at the building's security doors long enough for the automated scanners to confirm their identities.

"I have nothing to hide," Dredd said. "But I understand why you're still looking."

Gillen walked ahead of him into the Hall of Justice. Even at this level, she could hear the murmur of crowds many floors below.

Ten minutes later, in the Hall's cavernous but rarely-used main courtroom, Gillen kept a close eye on Joseph Dredd as his brother was escorted through the hushed crowds.

Even though Rico was cuffed hand and foot, the six escorting Judges had their Lawgivers drawn and ready. No one was taking any chances. They led him to a chair in the centre of the room, and stepped back.

This was the closing session of the three-day hearing into Rico's case. Gillen had been present for every second of the hearing. Ten separate reports had been presented, compiled from hundreds of interviews with Judges, witnesses, perps and victims. Not one report had concluded anything but guilt on Rico's part.

Gillen leaned a little closer to Dredd and whispered, "Just so you know... There are eight snipers and twelve autoguns targeting your brother right now. And just about the same number watching you."

Dredd nodded. "I've seen them."

"As Rico's only living family member, you have the right to speak with him before the sentence is issued."

"Fine where I am."

"You sure? The odds are you'll never see him again."

"I'm sure."

A minute later Chief Judge Clarence Goodman entered, with little fanfare. Gillen admired that about the Chief; his predecessor, Solomon, had been the sort who expected everyone to stand when he entered a room.

The Chief Judge stepped up to his podium and waited a few moments for the room to settle, then nodded to one of his assistants. The assistant told Rico to stand.

The Chief regarded him for a second, then said, "Rico Dredd, on the charge of the premeditated murder of citizen Virgil Alain Livingstone, this board has taken your testimony, witness statements and the physical evidence into consideration."

Judge Gillen realised that she was focussing almost completely on Joe Dredd's demeanour, though she wasn't sure what she was expecting. So far, anyone unfamiliar with the situation would have been forgiven for thinking that Joe and Rico had never even heard of each other: he hadn't displayed any reaction.

The Chief Judge continued: "We have concluded that citizen Livingstone's death was unintentional, and on said charge this board finds you innocent."

All around Gillen, other Judges began to whisper: this was not what many of them had been expecting. She looked up at Dredd's face, half-expecting to see a slight smile. Nothing. Not the slightest flinch.

A voice from behind them said, "Jovis... Joe, is that *you*?"

Gillen and Dredd turned to see Judge Gibson easing his way through the crowd.

Dredd nodded to him. "Gibson."

As Gibson moved to stand next to Dredd, a lot of the other Judges nearby seemed to realise who he was, and began to subtly sidle away.

"So," Gibson muttered as he removed his helmet. "Poor old Rico. You doing all right?"

"Can't complain."

"You can't *complain!?* Joe, you *see* what's happening down there?"

Down in the centre of the room, the Chief Judge looked around with a slight scowl until the room settled back into silence. Then he continued: "But Livingstone's death was not unavoidable. Rico Dredd, you abused your position as a Judge for personal gain, and in doing so you put the life of citizen Livingstone—and countless others—at risk. A Judge's first duty is to serve the citizens, and in that duty you have failed."

"They're railroading him," Judge Gibson said. "Look at this drokkin' circus. You'd think he was the *only* Judge ever caught with his hand in the register! Joe, we have to do something!"

"No," Dredd said. "We don't."

"He's your brother!"

Dredd turned toward his old friend, and for a moment Gillen thought that Dredd was on the edge of losing his temper, something she was certain she never wanted to see.

But Dredd simply said, "He's a lawbreaker," and turned back to watch the hearing.

At the podium, the Chief Judge said, "Rico Dredd, this board finds you guilty of conduct unbecoming a Mega-City One Judge. Specifically, multiple counts of extortion and theft, and deliberate actions that led to the manslaughter of citizen Virgil Livingstone." He looked around the room. "If any Judge present has anything to say before I pass sentence, speak now."

Judge Gillen became uncomfortably aware that everyone present was now looking at Joe Dredd. Even the Chief Judge had turned to look toward him.

"Well?" Gibson whispered. "Say something!"

The seconds drew out and Joe Dredd remained silent and immobile.

The Chief Judge cleared his throat and the moment was broken. "Very well. Rico Dredd, you are dishonourably discharged from the Justice Department, and sentenced to a period of not less than twenty years' penal servitude."

Gillen half-expected an outburst from Rico, a tirade of abuse at the incompetence of the Justice Department, but there was nothing from him but that look of pure contempt on his face, the same expression he'd worn throughout the entire hearing.

The Chief Judge said, "The time for appeals, submission of evidence or pleas for clemency on any grounds has now passed. Clerks, file and seal the records—this hearing has ended. Escort the prisoner back to holding. The galleries are to be cleared, all Judges present return to duty."

After one last, brief look at Rico, and another at Joe, the Chief Judge strode out of the room.

As the guards escorted Rico after him, Gibson whispered to Dredd, "You are one cold-hearted bastard, Joe! Why didn't you say something?"

"Why didn't you?" Dredd asked.

Gibson glowered at him for a moment, then sagged. "You're right. He knew what he was doing. He deserves punishment. That's *another* one gone from the class of 'seventy-nine... A bunch of us are getting together tonight. Just an hour or two, to chew the fat and talk about the old times. You in?"

"No."

"Yeah, thought not." Gibson put his helmet back on, then patted Dredd on the arm. "Be seeing you, Joe."

Dredd and Gillen watched him go, then Gillen said, "Shuttle's waiting. I'll walk back with you."

"There's no need."

"I'm not offering out of sympathy," Gillen said. "I'm going to make damn sure you do get back on the shuttle. Rico's case is closed, but yours isn't."

"I understand that." He looked down at her. "But you're wasting your time, Gillen. You can't find evidence that doesn't exist."

"Everyone's guilty of something, Dredd. That's just human nature."

"Then what are *you* guilty of?"

"I'm not the one on trial."

Dredd began to walk away. "Nor am I."

"Yet."

Six

"HMPH," JUDGE MONTAG said as she followed Dredd and Ramini out of the ore-processing factory and into the warm, dry night-time air of Sector 198's south-side.

Dredd turned back to face her. "What's that?"

Montag unclipped the cartridge from her Lawgiver. "Just an observation. Outside of the shooting gallery, this is the first time I've emptied an entire clip."

Ramini pulled off her helmet and ran her hands through her sweat-drenched greying hair. "It won't be the last time." She looked back toward the factory. "Think we got them all?"

"We did," Dredd said. For the better part of a day, Dredd, Montag and Ramini had been tracking the organ-legger Wylie Quartermaine and his gang, resulting in a fire-fight at the factory. Quartermaine's people had brought heavy weapons: by Dredd's estimation, the damage to the factory was likely to run into millions of credits.

Ramini said, "I just hope to hell that whatever we recover from Quartermaine's funds is enough to cover the cost of this."

"It doesn't have to," Dredd said as he headed for his

Lawmaster. "Factory's owned by the Hanenberger family. They're billionaires—they can afford to personally absorb the cost of the damages. Their factory's security was weak. If it had been better, Quartermaine wouldn't have tried to hide out here."

Ramini followed him. "Hah. You've clearly never *met* the Hanenbergers, Dredd. They're the wiliest, most ruthless family in the sector. They pay the bare minimum, they cut every corner they can, and they skirt the edge of legality without ever stepping over it."

"So we move the edge," Dredd said. He nodded toward the bullet-riddled factory, where four teams of Med-Judges were now carrying out the members of Quartermaine's gang, most of them in body-bags. "Fences are three metres high... We draft a new law, effective yesterday, stating that for a building of this size security fences should be four metres minimum. Means the city's not responsible for their weak security."

"Yeah... It doesn't really work like that."

"It works like that if *we* decide it does."

"Not a chance," said Sector Chief Benzon the next morning. "I had the Hanenbergers' legal team chewing my ear off all night. They're blaming us, and they want compensation or they'll just pull out of this sector completely."

Ramini began, "Sir, let me talk to them—"

Benzon shook her head. "No. If the Hanenbergers pull out, we wave goodbye to a huge source of revenue, not to mention all the jobs that would be lost."

"You're allowing a corporation to dictate judicial policy."

"No, I'm allowing them to *believe* that's what's happening." Benzon glared over her desk at Ramini. "You, Dredd and Montag... you're being reassigned."

"Sir, working together, Dredd and I have made a significant impact on the crime statistics in the sector."

"I'm aware of that. But the Hanenberger Corporation is asking for greater security for their iridium mine in the Cursed Earth. They've got a town there, about five hundred people, pretty much self-governing. But both the town and the mine have been hit by raiders ten times in the past two months. In exchange for keeping their ore-processing factory in the city, they want me to give them thirty Judges. I can't spare that many. I'm sending them you three."

"*Just* us?" Ramini asked.

"Best I can do," Benzon said. "You'll work with their local law-enforcement, help shore up their defences. Right now we need the iridium and the Hanenbergers' support more than we need you."

THE TOWN OF Ezekiel had been established a little under one hundred kilometres north-west of Sector 198, in a natural canyon that allowed access to iridium deposits and provided some shelter from the Cursed Earth's ferocious radiation storms. The only safe way to reach the town from Mega-City One was in a shuttle: the stretch of blighted land between the canyon and the city was littered with the burnt-out, sand-blasted remains of a dozen Hell-Trek convoys.

But even flying to Ezekiel wasn't without hazards; experimental gravity-warping weapons deployed during the atomic wars had created huge, unpredictable aerial pockets of near-zero gravitation that impeded an aircraft's instrumentation and often carried fast-moving air-borne streams of detritus—rubble, dead trees, abandoned vehicles, truck-sized boulders—that had been whipped up by powerful magnetic storms. These regions, named 'death-belts' by the pilots stupid or brave enough to navigate them, had been known to last for months or even years before fading out, slowly depositing millions of tonnes of debris across the landscape.

Now, Dredd was looking down on a particularly large death-belt as the Hanenberger Corporation's shuttle passed the half-way point to Ezekiel.

"Spectacular, huh?" the pilot said to Dredd. "I've flown this route ten times and it still scares the crap out of me."

The pilot—Brian O'Donnell—was a couple of years older than Dredd. A large man with unruly red hair, weather-beaten skin and strong hands, he had been quick to point out that his primary job was Ezekiel's deputy sheriff. "I keep the town running. And we were doing fine until these raiders started showing up. They hit fast and hard, raid our supplies, sabotage the equipment... I don't know if they're new or just the same old guys who've always been around, but *something's* working them into a frenzy."

"What are your town's defences?" Ramini asked.

"Well, the canyon keeps a lot of the natural predators out," O'Donnell said. "Or it *did*. Couple of years back one of the seams ran dry, and this geologist the Hanenbergers brought out said it'd be easier and cheaper to blast the canyon walls than it would be to open a new mine." He let out a long sigh. "Pity about that geologist. I kinda liked her. I thought she might keep in touch, but she never returned any of my calls. Anyway... So we *used* to have these great big near-vertical walls a hundred metres high, with guard towers on top so we could see the Earthers coming. Now we've just got a fifty-metre watchtower in the centre of town. It's better than nothing."

"Earthers?" Dredd asked.

Montag said, "Colloquial name for denizens of the Cursed Earth. Anyone who doesn't live in the town or the Meg. Mostly mutants."

"That's right," O'Donnell said. "You been outside the city before, Montag?"

"Not since I was a cadet."

"Oh, right. The old hot-dog run, huh? I always thought that

maybe that was a way to make sure you Judges realised how cushy life in the city is compared to out here."

Dredd asked, "If you're the deputy of Ezekiel, who's the sheriff?"

"Alfonsa Hanenberger. But she's sheriff in name only: she mostly leaves the day-to-day stuff to me."

Three minutes later, O'Donnell dropped the shuttle through a gap in the death-belt's debris stream—the craft was rocked twice with the sudden loss and then regain of gravity—and then Dredd saw the town of Ezekiel spread out before them.

The walls of the canyon were almost completely gone. They had been stripped back layer by layer, and now the town was at the centre of a two-kilometre-wide cone made up of unnaturally accurate concentric rings, each about three metres high. Clouds of grey dust drifted and skidded across the geometric landscape, and if it hadn't been for the occasional building or vehicle, Dredd would have had a hard time figuring out the scale.

O'Donnell said, "Now, we've gone about as far as we can with the strip-mining, so it's all turned around again. Lately the pickings have been so slim that it's cheaper to go back to mining the seams. Could be why the Earthers are increasing their raids: they mostly kept away when everyone was working outside."

"Hold at this height," Dredd said. As the craft slowed to a hover, he examined the landscape ahead. "Raiders can only easily approach over land from the north and south along the canyon bed. Any reason you can't create barricades?"

"Because we need the roads clear. The trucks that take the ore away are *huge*, and their schedules are calculated to the nearest minute—any barricade will slow things down, and Hanenberger is a stickler for schedules."

Ramini said, "Turn us around three-sixty. Keep it slow and steady."

As the landscape rotated past the shuttle's cockpit, Dredd took note of everything. To the north, a huge array of medium-sized, identical hills: presumably spoil from the strip-mining. To the east, nothing but broken, dried land criss-crossed by drifting shadows from the debris-laden death-belts above. The view south-west was almost completely obscured by a dense, slowly rotating, ten-kilometre-wide dust-cloud.

"That's been there for about five months now." O'Donnell explained. "They don't usually last so long."

"It stays in the same spot?" Montag asked.

"Pretty much, yeah. It's safe enough, as long as you seal your vehicle's vents. You just can't see more than a few metres ahead. We get hit by smaller, more powerful storms from time to time. You ever been caught in a rad-storm, Judge? Without the right protection you're dead in seconds. I heard that there was this band of slay-riders heading for the Mississippi, couple of years back, and a sudden storm hit them. The only survivor was this teenage kid they'd taken. They had her tied up in the back of this old truck they used to transport their prisoners, so she was safe from the storm. But the slay-riders were exposed, riding on horses and grazelles and bullwolfs, a couple on motorbikes... She said that the storm hit them instantly, absolutely no warning. One second, clear skies. Next second, everything was dark and the riders were screaming. The storm didn't last long, but when it was over the riders had been skeletonised. Every speck of flesh and blood had been blasted away. You don't get that in the city, huh?"

"No," Dredd said. "Weather-control."

O'Donnell shifted the craft out of hover-mode and resumed the approach toward the town. "Exactly. *All* the mega-cities have their satellites working overtime to keep the elements out, makes sure it's not too hot or too cold. In the Meg you let the people vote on whether they want sunshine or rainbows or a gentle fall of pretty snowflakes. They think that's what the weather-control is *for*, don't they? They've no idea that it's about the only thing that's saving them from being sand-blasted, scorched, frozen or irradiated out of existence." He pointed toward the wide, slow-moving stream of detritus floating overhead. "Y'know, I heard that the weather-control satellites use the same gravity-distorting tech that created the death-belts in the first place."

Ahead, the small town was laid out in a simple pattern: three long north-to-south streets split by five shorter cross-streets. Though some of the buildings were old-fashioned wooden-framed structures, anything that had been constructed since the war was squat, not more than two storeys high, with small windows and tapered walls: "Best way to ride out the storms without too much damage," O'Donnell had told the Judges.

The shuttle touched down on a plaza in the centre of the town, where a small group of people was waiting in the shadow of a steel-framed watchtower. As O'Donnell was shutting down the controls, he said to Dredd, "Woman with the tricorn hat and the long coat? That's Alfonsa Hanenberger. She's the sheriff—self-appointed, of course—and she's pissed as hell that your Sector Chief has only sent you three, so best not to get on her bad side, yeah? Make a good impression."

"The others?" Dredd asked.

"The two women with the blasters on their hips are her bodyguards. Mercenaries. There's eleven of them in total. Most of them guard the mine. The three older guys are Hanenberger's advisors. Far as I can tell, their main job is to find evidence that proves anything she does is right."

Dredd, Ramini and Montag followed O'Donnell out of the shuttle and toward the waiting group.

Alfonsa Hanenberger was thirty-four years old, but had the mottled, wrinkled skin and stooped posture of a woman twice that age: her Justice Department files mentioned a rare hereditary skin-condition. Given that she was worth several billion credits, it struck Dredd as odd that she hadn't had rejuvenation treatments.

Hanenberger walked up to the Judges and looked them up and down, then stepped back and addressed Dredd. "Grud... you're a *child!* What the hell is Benzon thinking? How long have you been a Judge?"

"Seventeen months since I graduated from the Academy."

"Seventeen months? I got food in my fridge that's older than that! What am I supposed to do with a rookie Judge who still has diaper-rash? I've got bands of Earthers swarming down on my town and shooting the place up, and the city sends me two women and a Judge who's so wet behind the ears it's a wonder his helmet hasn't gone rusty."

Hanenberger's advisors chuckled at that, but it was obvious to Dredd that their amusement was forced. When the boss makes a joke, you laugh.

Hanenberger looked down at the Lawgiver in Dredd's boot-holster. "You ever even *fired* that thing? 'Cos out here, a man who doesn't know how to use his gun might as well trade it in for a shovel and start digging his own grave." She stepped back from Dredd and turned around, pointing to the top of a nearby building. "See that weather-vane? If you can't hit that from here, you're no use to me."

"I can hit it," Dredd said.

"As they're fond of saying around here, Judge, talkin' ain't doin'. Show me."

"No. Waste of ammunition."

Slowly, Hanenberger turned back to face him. "No? Judge, I *own* this town. You do whatever I tell you."

Ramini said, "We're here to help defend the town and keep the peace. Not to perform tricks for you, Miss Hanenberger. Your social status will have no influence on how we do our job."

The woman peered at Ramini through half-closed eyes for a moment, then nodded. "Glad to hear it. Last thing I need around here is another bunch of yes-men too scared to speak up if they see something wrong."

One of her advisors muttered, "Damn straight," and Hanenberger threw him a withering glance before turning back to the Judges. "All right. O'Donnell here is deputy sheriff, you follow his lead. Don't forget that you're not in Mega-City One now—we've got our own laws here in Ezekiel. Screw up and you're out." She turned and walked away, with her entourage following her to the largest building on the edge of the plaza.

O'Donnell approached the Judges. "*That* went well. Okay. I'll get you settled in. First thing tomorrow I'll give you a tour of the town and the mine, then—"

"We'll do it now," Dredd said.

"No, we *won't*. I went straight from a ten-hour shift to pick you up, so I'm due some down-time. Relax, Dredd. Put your feet up for the rest of the day."

"Where are our quarters?"

"I've cleared out space in my basement. It's not what you'd call five-star accommodation, just three beds, but—"

"It'll do," Ramini said. "We're going to take a look around."

"Not without me. Some of the people around here are liable to start shooting if they see Judges coming."

Ramini picked an arbitrary direction and began to walk. Montag and Dredd fell into step beside her. "We can handle ourselves."

"It's not you I'm worried about," O'Donnell called after them.

Ezekiel appeared to have been constructed on the remains of an older town; here and there Dredd spotted old moss-covered bricks and cracked paving slabs, and some of the town's older buildings had been constructed from weather-beaten wooden panels, patched and re-patched dozens of times. Windows were small and either shuttered or made from shatter-proof glass.

The streets of Ezekiel were mostly packed dirt; during the wet season, it would be like wading through a swamp.

The Judges reached the north end of the town without

encountering any people, animals or vehicles, but as they turned west toward the mine they heard two short blasts of a siren.

Montag froze. "I don't like the sound of that. A warning siren?"

"End of shift at the mine, is my guess," Ramini said.

Within minutes dust-covered citizens began filing out of the mine's entrance. Others—presumably part of the next shift—were lining up outside, and as each worker exited they handed their pickaxes and shovels to the next person in line.

"Efficient," Dredd said.

"Cost-effective, too," Ramini replied. "Check out the mine, Dredd."

As she and Montag walked on, Dredd stopped to watch the miners, mentally noting faces and distinguishing features. Most of them appeared to be normal, with perhaps twenty per cent showing visible mutations. One young man had a second, poorly-formed face on the side of his head, another lacked a nose or ears. A middle-aged woman who passed by was sleeveless, her arms covered in thumb-sized bumps, each bump containing something dark at its core, just beneath the skin.

While many of the citizens spotted Dredd and nudged their colleagues, the first one to approach him was a middle-aged bear of a man with a thick off-white beard and eyebrows like arctic caterpillars. "The heck is a Judge doing here?"

"Brought in to supplement the town's security," Dredd said. "Who are you?"

"Ishmael Stinnett. I'm the town's preacher. Have you been saved, Judge?"

"Not interested."

"That's not what I asked. In the end, the Lord Grud turns his big squinty eye upon us all, even Judges. What we do in this life is an audition for the next. Our lives on Earth are the box *containing* the cereal, not the cereal itself, nor the awesome plastic prize within!" Stinnett pinched the back of his hand.

"This flesh-cloak is merely the film canister that holds the unpleasant short, grainy travelogue that heralds the awesome all-star main feature! Do you understand? This human existence is but the clam before the storm!"

"The *clam?*" Dredd asked, even though he didn't want to be drawn into this conversation. "You mean the calm?"

"No, the clam! The oyster that holds the Pearl of Eternal Truth. 'Give unto others and be ye not shellfish,' sayeth the Lord, 'for, um, its flesh be-eth foul and slimy and looketh like unto a mighty lump of snot, yea, and such.' Praise Grud!" He reached inside his dust-covered jacket and pulled out a dog-eared pamphlet. "You should read this. I know you come from the city of the darned, but even you can be spared Grud's hefty wrath—even for the worst sinner there is always time to repent, except right at the end when it's too late. Praise Grud! Praise him!"

"Save your sermon for someone else," Dredd said.

Stinnett froze, and stared at Dredd. "I *said*, praise him!"

"Not today." Dredd resisted the urge to arrest the man for harassment and charge him with preaching without a licence, reminding himself that things were different out here. "Move along."

"The wrath of Grud be on you, Judge Dredd! He sees all, he knows all! He will smite the lawless!"

"Then Grud and I have something in common." Dredd walked away, still watching the other mine-workers.

The preacher called after him, "Big one's coming, Judge! You better know which side you're on! *Grud* knows, you bet he does!"

A dark-haired woman waiting to enter the mine said, "You'd do well to steer clear of Preacher Stinnett, Judge. Or if you can't avoid him, just agree with anything he says. It makes things a lot easier."

"Advice noted, citizen. You are?"

"Eloise Crow."

"You're a miner?"

She smiled. "Why, thank you for the compliment, kind stranger! It's just my youthful looks."

Dredd didn't know what to do with that. Obviously, she was deliberately confusing the homonyms 'miner' and 'minor' for humorous effect, but he wasn't sure why. She could be flirting, or just engaging in banter. Rico would have known the difference; he was good at that sort of thing. They'd been trained at the Academy of Law to recognise and resist attempts at flattery, but it wasn't an area in which Dredd considered himself an expert by any stretch of the imagination.

Officially Judges were forbidden from entering into romantic relationships, but that didn't stop some of them. And there were certainly members of the public who pursued Judges. That was something Dredd *could* understand: Judges were healthy, committed, and uncompromising. They were also—technically—unobtainable, and for some reason people are drawn to what they're told they can't have.

Rico had given in to his base urges and indulged in physical relationships, Dredd knew, and that was a sign of weakness, not to mention a potentially huge security risk. Even though the citizens should know better, Dredd himself had so far been offered sex on seventeen different occasions. Those offers had resulted in sixteen on-the-spot fines for attempted bribery and one arrest for assaulting a Judge.

When the class of 'seventy-nine were eighteen-year-old cadets, Ellard had taken Joe aside one day and said, "One of the others wants you. Physically, I mean. I'm not saying who. Just warning you, Joe. Don't go reporting this, okay? I'm just letting you know so you can watch out for it." Nothing had happened after that—at least, nothing Dredd had noticed—but it had troubled him a little, and he'd often wondered whether Ellard had concocted the story for personal reasons, maybe to unsettle him and throw him off his game. If that was the case, it had almost worked. Almost.

Now, Dredd looked down at Eloise Crow and wondered how he should respond, but he was saved from that dilemma by the arrival of a man of about Crow's age, who strode up to her and slipped his arm around her waist.

The man nodded at Dredd. "I heard we were getting some Judges. Good to have you here. I'm Travis Crow, Eloise's husband." He leaned a little closer to Dredd. "You want to watch yourself with some of these folk, Judge. They're not happy you're here."

"People with something to hide are rarely pleased to see a Judge," Dredd said, a little relieved to be on familiar territory once more.

Eloise said, "We have ways of getting things done in Ezekiel that might not sit well with you."

"Such as?"

She shrugged. "Hopefully you won't have to find out."

At the mine's entrance, a burly woman wearing dusty, battered body-armour called out, "Aaannnd... that's the last one! Next shift, you're up! C'mon, get moving! Ore ain't gonna mine itself!" She had a shotgun slung over one shoulder, and a pair of powerful-looking handguns on her hips, the same models as Hanenberger's bodyguards used.

The Crows nodded to Dredd once more, then followed their colleagues into the mine.

Dredd walked up to the burly woman. She was perhaps sixty years old, and kept watch on the miners as she greeted him. Past her, further into the mine, he could see at least four more similarly-dressed women.

"So you're the bump in the town's security. Just three Judges."

"Yes," Dredd said. "Who are you?"

"Santiago, mine supervisor."

"You're a mercenary."

She shrugged. "No law against that, is there?"

"Not out here." Dredd moved to step past her into the mine, but she put out her arm to stop him.

"No unsupervised access."

"Then supervise me."

Santiago called to one of her colleagues to take her place, then walked side-by-side with Dredd through the winding, low-ceilinged tunnel.

"Smooth walls," Dredd observed. "Cut with a laser."

"Right. This was an ore seam, the first one discovered. Hanenberger's father saw it, bought up the land. They used lasers to melt the rock and free the iridium at the same time, followed the seam right back." She rapped her gloved knuckles on one of the metal pillars lining the walls. "Support beams are steel, but back at the entrance they're cast from solid iridium. Worth a fortune—old man Hanenberger likes to give a good impression to prospective customers. Last thing we'll do before we shut this place down is rip them out."

They emerged from the winding tunnel at the top level of a seemingly bottomless cavern, over a hundred metres across at its widest point. The nexus of dozens of side-tunnels of varying diameter, the cavern was criss-crossed with walkways and platforms, ladders and gangplanks, crude elevators and suspended platforms, all strung together with thick ropes, cables and old scaffolding poles. Right now, between shifts, there were very few people to be seen, but it was easy for Dredd to picture the mine at its busiest, with hundreds of workers shifting tonnes of ore.

Santiago said, "This was a natural cavern. Hanenberger wasn't big on spending money, so once he found this and saw all the ore seams, he sold off the lasers and hired locals instead. Built up the town outside."

Dredd stepped to the edge of the platform and peered down into the darkness. "This was within the bounds of Mega-City

One, I'd shut the place down. I can see a hundred health-code violations without even turning my head. How many workers have fallen to their deaths here, Santiago?"

She shrugged. "*All* of them, I guess."

"What?"

"Anyone who falls down there isn't getting back up. It's about six hundred metres down, I'm told. Never been inclined to find out."

"Should have nets strung across the cavern every four metres."

"Maybe. But life out here is very different to the city, Judge. The Hanenbergers rule with an iridium fist in an iron glove. Don't let Alfonsa's pleasant nature fool you. When she gets worked up into a frenzy, heads start to roll."

"Not literally, I hope," Dredd said.

The woman turned to look at him for the first time. "Yes. Literally."

Seven

THE FIRST FIGHT broke out as the sun was setting, in the larger of Ezekiel's two taverns, the Brazen Hussy, a squat, single-storey building on the eastern edge of the town.

Ramini and Montag were resting in the Judges' makeshift quarters in the basement of Brian O'Donnell's house; Dredd had elected to take the night-shift.

He stood in the doorway of the tavern watching the citizens. Most were sitting in clusters of three or four and drinking what he took to be alcohol-based drinks—real alcohol was illegal in Mega-City One, but not out here. A few loners sat at the bar, staring into their drinks. One woman sat slumped face-down in a puddle of liquid, and a man sat with his back to the bar, apparently trying to look suave and desirable.

The barman—a topless, muscular man covered in tattoos— looked over at Dredd and called, "Hey, one of the Judges! What'll it be, Judge?"

"What'll *what* be?" Dredd asked, aware that almost every conversation in the large room had stopped and most of the patrons had turned to look at him.

"What are you drinking?" the barman asked. "First one's on the house."

"I don't consume intoxicants," Dredd said. "Just carry on about your business."

They were a strange group of people, Dredd thought. He'd visited much of Mega-City One, even spent some time in a mutant town during his cadet days, but this was something he'd never expected to see: mutants and normals socialising together, treating each other more or less as equals.

Nearby, an apparently normal woman was wrapped in an embrace with an obviously mutant man—he had panther-like paws instead of hands, with long whiskers protruding from an otherwise neatly-trimmed black beard. Next to them, two normal males were engaged in four-way chess with two mutant women. In the far corner, a group of mutants were playing darts while a human kept score.

The door opened behind him and he turned to see O'Donnell nodding at him.

"Thought you were going to take it easy," Dredd said.

"This is a *bar*, Judge. That's what we do here. The whole point of a bar is that it's somewhere to take it easy. Drink?"

"No."

"I'm astonished."

"Who's on duty tonight, O'Donnell?"

The red-haired man shrugged. "What do you mean?"

"Your town is being constantly raided. You must have look-outs posted. An early-warning system of some kind."

"Sure, we've got look-outs. We patrol the perimeters all night long, the watchtower is always manned, but somehow the Earthers keep getting in." As he spoke, O'Donnell began to make his way backward toward the bar. "Hanenberger's too cheap to shell out for an automated alarm system."

The panther-pawed man looked up and said, "Hey, Red, you mind what you're saying about Miss Hanenberger."

"Opinions are *free*, Esteban. You don't have to like it, but you can't stop me from saying it."

"A kick in the nuts is free too, O'Donnell."

O'Donnell sighed. "Seriously? Again?" He looked toward Dredd. "I have to lock this idiot up at least once a month. He gets drunk and starts to believe he can take on anyone in the room. He's never won a fight yet."

"I *can* take on anyone in the room!"

The human woman slid down from Esteban's lap, and quietly sidled away. Now unencumbered, the mutant rose to his full height, which brought him to a little above O'Donnell's shoulder. He held up his paws, displaying long, sharp talons. "I say we take this outside."

"I say you *don't*," Dredd said. "Threatening an officer of the law is an offence. Because I'm new here, you get a warning. Next time, I—"

Esteban struck faster than Dredd could react, his right paw slashing across Dredd's chest. Its talons sliced through the tough mock-leather of his uniform and snagged the chain connected to his badge, ripping it from his chest.

Another slash with the left arm, this one faster and aimed at Dredd's throat, but Dredd was prepared; he whipped up his right arm, and the talons tore four thin but deep strips across his forearm, cutting straight through to the flesh.

Esteban carried the movement through into a whole-body spin, ducked into a crouch. Before Dredd could even register what was happening, Esteban had set his right arm down on a small table and kicked Dredd with both feet, one striking him in the chin, the other ploughing into his stomach.

Dredd crashed backward into another table, smashing it, scattering its occupants and spilling their drinks.

He recovered quickly, shaking off the shock of the ferocious, unexpected attack. The panther-like mutant was now crouched on the table, snarling at him, claws out and ready to strike.

O'Donnell began, "Now, Dredd, don't—"

Still on his back, Dredd pulled the Lawgiver from his boot-holster.

O'Donnell jumped in front of Dredd, putting himself in the line of fire. "Dredd, no! We don't settle disputes with firearms here in Ezekiel!"

"Yes, we do," Esteban said.

"Well, we *try* not to."

Dredd tucked his feet under him, still aiming at Esteban, and stood up.

"Seriously, Dredd! He's a good worker and we need him!"

Esteban smirked. "You have no jurisdiction here, Judge. And there's no way a damp rag from the city could beat a real man in a fight. Me and Red here have *history*—any problems between us have nothing to do with you."

Dredd holstered his Lawgiver, then looked down at his chest. Four parallel cuts through his tunic, with blood-soaked flesh beneath.

"They're so you don't forget me," Esteban said. "You ever want any more reminders, come see me. I'll be happy to oblige."

"That's the last time you lay a claw on me, creep."

Standing next to Dredd, O'Donnell said, "Let it go. This is just his way of sussing you out."

"I thought you said he's never won a fight yet?"

"Right. He goes nuts, tears the place apart, and it takes eight or nine of us to bring him down. But we do, every time."

Esteban said, "Hah, he's not wrong about that." He smoothly climbed down from the table, and nodded to Dredd. "You didn't scream." He slowly extended one claw toward the wounds he'd made across Dredd's chest. "I think you're the first one I ever sliced who didn't scream, and I *know* it hurts. Maybe some of you Meggers are tougher than people say." He glanced toward O'Donnell. "If the woman Judges are as tough as him, could be we got a chance against the Earthers."

To Dredd, O'Donnell said, "The Earthers come in hard and fast. Used to be small numbers, three or four at a time, but lately they've started hitting us in groups of a dozen. Esteban here's our best spotter, especially at night, but even he can't be on duty all the time."

A woman approached Dredd from the side, holding his badge and warily watching Esteban. "Judge, you dropped this." Dredd thanked the woman, who introduced herself as Lauren Featherman. She was a mutant almost as tall as Dredd, with pale grey skin and solid blue eyes.

"Are you all right?" She tilted her head to the side a little as she examined Dredd's wounds. "Yeah... you might want to get those scratches looked at."

"They'll heal," Dredd told her. "Took my inoculations before I left the city."

"You can't walk around with open wounds, Judge. My sister Conra is a medic. Come with me, she's at the infirmary now."

"Lauren's right," O'Donnell said. "Best not to take any chances."

Dredd followed the woman out of the bar, and across the street to the one other building with a light burning above the door.

Lauren pulled open the door and called in, "Conra? One of the Judges needs your attention."

Conra's mutation was similar to her sister's. She greeted Dredd with a calm, professional manner intended to put her patients at ease; that immediately raised his suspicions.

The medic told Dredd to remove his gloves and armour, and strip off the top half of his uniform so she could get a better look at the wounds. "In no time we'll have you right as rain used to be... There we go. Careful with the right hand, those look nasty too... Oh."

"Oh what?" Dredd asked.

"Those scars... You've seen a *lot* of combat. Funny, I thought you were fresh out of the Academy. I've seen forty-year war veterans with fewer scars than you." She poked at a mark on Dredd's right shoulder. "Your armour should have stopped that one."

"That happened when I was a cadet."

"And this one here on your back?"

"Broke up a Juve brawl. Five of them were packing guns—I was too busy returning fire to see the one behind me with a crossbow."

"And that's a nasty-looking—"

"I'm not here to give you a guided tour of my scars, Featherman. Just clean the fresh ones and sew me up if you have to."

The doctor sprayed a cold, misty liquid on Dredd's wounds. "Give that a few seconds to seep in." She wiped at Dredd's wounds with a synthcotton pad and stepped back. "That and your inoculations should stave off any infections. I'd advise stronger body-armour if you intend to tackle Mister Esteban again. I'd say he's responsible for a good ten per cent of my work here."

As Dredd pulled on his tunic he said, "And the other ninety per cent?"

The doctor sighed. "Radiation burns, heatstroke, infected insect bites, animal bites, mining accidents, dehydration, alcohol poisoning, sand-burns, rabies, malaria, food poisoning, fist-fights, malnutrition... You name it, I've treated it."

Lauren said, "Out here we really are on the edge. The soil is practically dead, our drinking water has to go through a seven-stage filtration process, we're constantly under attack from either the wildlife or the damn Earthers, there's no respite from the heat... We have to stick together and support each other in spite of our foibles and oddities, because if we don't, the community will collapse, and without it we're dust. Miss Hanenberger knows that; that's why she stays here in Ezekiel instead of in the city. Here, she's able to keep a personal eye on her investment."

To the doctor, Dredd said, "Figure there's no point asking you if she's undergoing treatment for her skin-condition. Records say she's thirty-four, but she looks seventy."

"You wouldn't want me telling anyone *your* business."

Dredd nodded slowly. "Understood. Appreciate the work, doc. Send the bill to the Mega-City One Justice Department."

"For a few mils of detox spray and a couple of swabs? There's no charge, Judge."

He left the grey-skinned sisters and crossed the street back to the Brazen Hussy, where he found O'Donnell leaning against the bar.

"Sure you don't want a drink, Dredd?" O'Donnell asked.

"I'm sure. Anything happening here?"

O'Donnell nodded. "Crowd in the corner over there are getting a bit boisterous. They have a day off tomorrow, so we're likely to see some action tonight. Two of Hanenberger's mine security are scheduled to have tonight off, too. If they decide to come in here, we're definitely going to have to crack some skulls if we don't want to spend tomorrow morning digging holes."

Dredd was about to respond when a wooden chair sailed across the room from one side to the other, crashed into a table and scattered half a dozen drinks.

O'Donnell said, "And they're off." He turned to Dredd. "You want to handle this? And no guns, huh? A few good thumps should be enough to calm them down." A few minutes later, Dredd, O'Donnell and the barman were the only people left standing in the bar. Everyone else was on the floor nursing their wounds, or had long since fled. To the barman, O'Donnell said, "Give me a sapbeer, Maddox."

The tattooed barman scowled at him as he fetched a bottle. "A *whole* one? Wow. That sure makes up for the fact that no one else will be drinking tonight."

"Got to hand it to you, Judge," O'Donnell said to Dredd, "you don't let up once you get started."

"I'm out of cuffs here, O'Donnell. Find something to tie them up with."

O'Donnell opened the bottle of sapbeer and took a long sip. "Nah... let them go. All of them."

Dredd grabbed one of the unconscious men by the hair on the back of his head, and raised him up a little. "*This* one had a knife."

"I'm sure they *all* have knives, Dredd. He's just the only one who brought his into the game."

Dredd let go, and the man's head crashed back down to the floor. "What the drokk is *wrong* with you, O'Donnell? You're supposed to be the law around here!"

"And it's your expert opinion that these idiots should be locked up?"

"That's your job."

"Dredd, Hanenberger will have our knackers on crackers if we arrest everyone." He sighed. "You're not getting it, are you? Ezekiel is *her* town. She owns everything from the streets outside to the sweat under our armpits. You want to know why this damn town is always being raided? Because she won't shell out the creds for proper security. And you know why she won't do that, even though she's got more money than Grud's agent? Because she wants the people here too scared of the Earthers to leave. There's strength in numbers, and her numbers run into billions."

"Then why am *I* here?"

"Because for some reason even she doesn't understand, it's all starting to fall apart. The raids are getting more frequent, and more vicious, too. So Hanenberger figured that calling in a squad of Judges would help reset the balance. Instead, we got three of you. That's upset her more than she's letting on, I reckon. See, the Hanenberger family has a *lot* of influence in the city, and they're used to getting what they ask for. Sure, you're hard as nails and you know the city law inside and out, but here you're just a newbie who can't tell the difference between an actual criminal act and a few drunk miners blowing off steam."

Dredd considered that. Something about the town of Ezekiel didn't feel right. His instinct told him that there was something missing, and it took him a few seconds to pin it down. "O'Donnell, where's the local school?"

"We don't have a school."

"Yeah, thought not. Now tell me this... Where are the juves?"

"You mean kids? Don't have any of those, either."

"No children in the whole town?"

"No. Miss Hanenberger doesn't like kids. I figure that's because she got teased a lot when *she* was a kid, what with the way she looks. So part of the deal is that folks aren't allowed to settle here if they've got children under the age of eighteen. And if any couple here gets pregnant, they have to leave." O'Donnell shrugged. "Sounds strange, I know, but it makes sense when you think about it. Kids mean someone has to look after them, safety rules have to be more stringent, there has to be a school and a proper hospital and somewhere for the little buggers to play. But no kids means we don't get gangs of bored teenagers causing trouble. Believe me, *that* one is worth its weight in iridium. No graffiti, no joyriding, no bullying... The town where I grew up, the local cops spent most of their time dealing with all the crap kids bring to the equation."

"How can you expect the town to survive if there's not going to be a new generation?"

"We don't. The geologists reckon there's only a couple more years' worth of mining left here. Once the ore is gone, or not worth the cost of digging out, Hanenberger and her people will pack up and go. I heard she's already bought up a whole new stretch of land somewhere west of here."

"And the citizens?"

"We'll move on, too, I guess, unless we can find another way to keep the town going. It's all about the bottom line, Dredd. The Hanenbergers didn't get rich by investing in lost causes."

"Then why are they so desperate to defend the town that they called in Judges?"

O'Donnell leaned over the counter and found a fresh bottle. "They didn't. They called you in to defend the *mine*. As far as that wrinkled old bat Hanenberger is concerned, the people here are just assets. Disposable and replaceable." He popped the top off the bottle and raised it to Dredd in a short salute. "And that includes you, Judge. You get on her wrong side and she'll order her mercs to gun you down and not give you a second thought."

Eight

THE LAST TIME SJS Judge Marion Gillen had worn civilian clothes was the day of her fifth birthday.

She couldn't directly recall the event, but when she graduated from the Academy of Law, fifteen years later, her father had given her a photograph. "Look how cute you were... And *now* look at you!" he'd said. "My little girl is a Judge!"

After six months on the streets, mostly working in the city's southern sectors, she'd been called for a meeting with the Special Judicial Squad. Her initial fears that she was being investigated turned to surprise when she was told she had been nominated to join the Squad.

Even receiving the nomination had been enough for most of her friends to begin distancing themselves from her, and once she was accepted, they shunned her completely.

"No one likes the SJS," her supervisor had told her on the first day of trials. "And that's as it *should* be. In your first year, you will make more enemies than you ever imagined possible. And not just among the citizens. Good, upstanding Judges will go out of their way to hamper your investigations. At the very best, they will despise you. They will try to tear you down in any way they can. They will go after your family. If you haven't faced at least one assassination attempt by the end of your first year then you're doing something wrong. You have to be the very best of the best. You must know every letter of the law, and you must give full, unconditional commitment to the job, because anything less will result in your death."

The trials themselves had been infuriating, exhausting, demoralising. Twenty-two-hour days of studying, testing, training and evaluations. Every action and every decision Gillen had made since she joined the Academy was questioned and examined. Her Academy records were scrutinised to a level of detail that went beyond microscopic: every test answer was studied, every pause while *considering* an answer was a cause for suspicion.

She'd had to justify every arrest, fine or warning she'd issued on the streets, every interaction with other Judges, every round fired from her Lawgiver, every scratch or dent on her uniform. Her memories and emotions were probed and examined by Psi-Judges. Her knowledge of the law was tested over and over.

She was accused of being an enemy spy on four separate occasions, and subjected to rigorous psychological and physical torture in order to extract the truth.

And she had come through it all, passed every test, and was now one of the elite. The Judges who judge the Judges. One of the few final arbiters of the law in a city of eight hundred million people.

But today, as she walked along a shadowed street and hundreds of citizens passed her by without a second glance, she realised that to them she was nobody, just another face in the crowd.

She didn't like that she was unarmed—she *had* to be; if she was found carrying a weapon, everything would fall apart—and that made her uneasy.

The civilian clothing didn't help. She'd avoided anything too flashy or encumbering—no high heels, nothing too tight or too baggy, nothing that restricted her movements or obscured her vision—but she missed the familiar weight of her armour and helmet, the comforting sensation of the Lawgiver in her boot-holster.

Ahead, half-hidden in a doorway, she spotted the citizen she wanted. She'd spoken to him before, but was reasonably sure he wouldn't recognise her without a helmet or uniform.

He was pretending not to watch her approach as he chewed on a munce-dog, and didn't directly look at her until she was standing right in front of him. "What?"

"I've got message for you... From a mutual friend."

"Is that so?"

Gillen nodded. "It is."

After an uncomfortably long pause, the man said, "Who's this friend we both know?"

"Rico Dredd."

Another long pause, during which the man thoughtfully sucked at the end of his munce-dog, until he apparently realised what he was doing and pulled it out of his mouth. He brushed a string of saliva away from his lower lip with the back of his hand. "Rico. I heard he was dead."

"He's not."

"Well, I heard he *was*. I heard that his brother killed him over a bag of crawbies."

"I assure you, he's alive. But he got himself arrested, and he won't be around for long. He's going to be shipped off to Titan. That's one of the moons of Saturn."

"I know where it is," the man lied. "But I don't know who you are, or why I should talk to you."

"I'm Sadie. Sadie Butler. And you're Evan Qausarano. Rico's told me all about you. Said you're his friend. His *only* friend, apart from me."

Quasarano nodded. "Yeah, that's true. About me, I mean. You, I got no reason to trust."

"Rico stashed some money away, and he said it's no good to him now. He told me you and I can split it fifty-fifty. But you have to help me find it."

"How much are we talking about?"

Gillen had spent some time trying to come up with the ideal imaginary sum. It had to be enough to appeal to Quasarano's greed, yet not so much that it would raise any suspicions. If she'd told him that Rico had squirrelled away ten million credits, Quasarano would start wondering how he'd managed to get his hands on so much. "About sixty-two thousand," Gillen said. "Thirty-one for you, thirty-one for me."

He grinned. "What's to stop me from just taking it all?"

"Rico told me you're a man of honour—you wouldn't do that."

"Yeah, that's true. So, he's really off the streets for good, then?"

She nodded. "There's no way out. They have him locked up in the Hall of Justice. There's a thousand Judges in the way."

Quasarano jerked his head and started off along the street. As she fell into step beside him, he asked, "So, how did he tell you all this if he's locked up so tight?"

"He still has a few contacts in the Justice Department. Joe, for one."

"His brother? But they hate each other!"

"No, they don't. They're rivals, sure, but they're still brothers. You can't break that sort of bond. Joe managed to get to see Rico, and he passed on the message to me."

Quasarano seemed happy with that. "Okay." He held the damp, chewed end of the munce-dog a few centimetres in front of Gillen's face. "Want a bite?"

"No, but thanks."

"Okay. So... Why doesn't *Joe* just keep the money?"

"Well, because they're *watching* him, of course! They know that he's, you know, like Rico was. A good guy but not opposed to the idea of maybe looking the other way now and then, for a friend."

They reached a corner, and Quasarano stopped. "I get that. I had like a dozen Judges interrogating me about him. About both of them. They all wanted to know if Joe was on the straight-and-level. Kept asking me if—"

"If he'd ever taken any bribes," Gillen said, finishing Quasarano's sentence to help persuade him that she was on his side. "Yeah, same here. But I never met Joe before Rico was arrested, so I didn't know anything about that."

"Hah! You *think* you've never met Joe, but they're identical."

Gillen feigned surprise at the notion. "You have a point there."

"So, were you one of Rico's, you know, special friends?" He waggled his eyebrows at her. "If you know what I mean. One of his girlfriends."

"That's none of your business!"

"Ah, so you *were*. He must have thought you were *really* special if he told you where the money is. Where is it, anyway?"

"He never said exactly, just that you would know his best hiding places, and that there's no way anyone else will find it."

"Okay." Quasarano's brow furrowed for a few long minutes, his expression slowly turning from puzzlement to mild panic. Eventually, he said, "I dunno. I mean, there's lots of places, but I can't think of anywhere pacific."

"*Specific*," Gillen corrected automatically.

"Right. Maybe Joe would know?"

"Maybe, but he's not in the city right now. They sort of exiled him. You know? Keep him out of the way until they can prove whether he's innocent or guilty."

The young man laughed. "Oh, he's guilty all right!"

Gillen froze. *This is it*, she thought. *The pay-off.* "What makes you say that?"

"He's a Judge. They're all guilty of something. What's the saying? Power corrupts, and absolute power does too, but even more so."

Damn it! "But you don't know for certain that he's actually broken the law, do you?"

Quasarano nodded. "Oh yeah. He has, definitely. This one time, Rico was doing a deal with someone—I'm not saying who—and then things turned bad and some money didn't get where it was supposed to go. Spar— I mean, the guy Rico was dealing with—accused Rico of taking the money, but he swore he didn't. There was a witness who identified him, though. Rico figured that it was Joe who'd taken the money. He said he'd talk to Joe about it, and then the next day Rico turned up with most of the money. But not all of it, because Joe had already spent some."

No good, that's just hearsay, Gillen thought. *Most likely Rico stole the money himself and made up the story about Joe when he realised he'd been seen.* "You were going to mention Sparks Petrosky, weren't you?"

"No! Anyway, he's gone now. Spending the rest of his life in an iso-cube."

Gillen considered her options. So far, there had been no tangible evidence against Joe Dredd. A lot of rumours from low-lifes like Evan Quasarano, but nothing she could use to build a case.

Another dead end. She'd always known that Dredd was intelligent, if not particularly imaginative, but she hadn't expected him to able to out-smart her. He had covered up his actions with remarkable foresight.

The other possibility, which she didn't feel comfortable taking into account, was that he was innocent, that he had never broken the law.

That seemed impossible. Every Judge she'd ever investigated had done something against the rules, even if it was as minor as lying on an arrest report about the amount of force used to subdue a suspect.

But apparently not Joe Dredd.

No one is clean, she told herself. *Everyone is guilty of something. That's just human nature.*

Then Quasarano said, "Y'know, maybe my *sister* knows where Rico hid that money. They were close for a while, until he dumped her. That kinda pissed me off, got to tell you. Just outta the blue, he decided it was over."

Gillen knew this story. Judge Ernest Kenner, Rico's supervisor, had discovered the affair and warned Rico to call it off. Kenner hadn't reported it or made any note of it in his logs, but a colleague remembered a conversation in which Kenner told her that one of the young Judges under his guidance needed to be "set straight on a few things about how we interact with the cits." The process of elimination had narrowed the young Judge down to Rico.

But Kenner was dead now, the victim of a crime that would probably never be solved.

Quasarano said, "I lost a lot of respect for Rico after that. I mean, if he hadn't been a Judge I'd have pounded the stomm outta him, you know what I'm saying?"

"I do."

"And Stacie couldn't let it *go*, of course. She kept after him, calling him all the time and telling me to pass messages on. Until the day Joe came around and smashed her place up and threatened to blow her head off if she didn't leave his brother alone."

Gillen stared at him. "What? Is that true?" She had read all the reports on Rico's interactions with the Quasarano family, and this had never been mentioned.

"Yeah, it's true... Joe was all, 'He's my brother *and* he's a Judge, so you better forget about him or you'll end up in Resyk with no drokkin' head.'"

Gillen reached into the pocket of her long coat, and pulled out a small communicator. "SJS Control, this is Judge Marion Gillen. Round up the entire family of Evan Quasarano, Brendan Behan Block, immediately. Take them to the nearest Sector House, keep them separate until I get there."

As soon as Gillen started speaking, Quasarano had tried to run, but she had grabbed hold of his arm with her free hand and slammed him against the wall, pinning him.

Now, he was whimpering, repeating "You never said you were a Judge!" over and over.

"I never said I wasn't."

Nine

ON DREDD'S SECOND night in Ezekiel, the town was attacked by raiders.

A watchman stationed in a camouflaged hide eight kilometres south of the town—on the very edge of radio range—reported a column of dust approaching along the south road.

On the streets, O'Donnell assembled his guards: ten of them, plus Dredd, Ramini and Montag. "Could be another raid. If it is, we've got maybe eighteen minutes," O'Donnell said. "They'll split up into two groups, hit us from the north and south at the same time. Ramini, your team will defend the south, tackle the first group. The rest of us will take the north. Don't make yourself known until they're within range, then hit them hard. Ignore the outriders and take out the leaders first."

"No. Outriders first is a better tactic," Ramini said. "And we should take them down before they get a chance to split. If we don't, we've got two areas to defend. So we pick off the outriders first, that'll discourage them from splitting. Then we target the main group."

O'Donnell said, "Judge, don't undermine my orders. I'm the deputy here."

"I don't care." Ramini looked around at the assembled townsfolk. "I want the best marksmen up on the roofs of the southernmost buildings. That includes you, Montag. Target the raiders at the *rear* of the group, not the front, got that? Crashed vehicles at the rear makes it harder for the others to retreat; crashed vehicles in front gives them cover. Anyone own a motorbike?"

One young woman raised her hand, and Dredd recognised her as Eloise Crow, the woman he'd met waiting to begin her shift in the mine. "We have one. It's only an old Suzuki, but it works."

"Get it, bring it back here."

As Eloise darted away, someone else called out, "Why the hell should we follow *your* orders, Judgie? You're barely here a wet day! You don't know squat about our town!"

O'Donnell said, "He has a point, Ramini. We—"

"We've read your reports on the previous attacks," Dredd said. "You keep making the same mistake—letting them get away. The survivors tell their comrades the state of your town's defences. The raids aren't increasing in frequency just because the Earthers are getting more desperate, it's because they're wearing you down. They're winning."

"We don't *have* the resources to stop them all!"

"Just do what I *tell* you, O'Donnell," Ramini said. "And douse every external light in the town—we're not going to make it easy for them."

Dredd drew his Lawgiver. "Ramini, you're the best shot. You take the watchtower." He began to run.

"Where are *you* going?" she shouted after him.

"We need reinforcements." Dredd raced westwards through the small town toward the mine entrance, where three of the mine's guards had gathered.

The burly woman, Santiago, watched Dredd approach. "Another attack?"

"Looks like it," Dredd said. "How many of you are there?"

"Nine, including me."

"That'll have to do. I want two of your people to remain here, in case the raiders get past us. The rest of you come with me."

Santiago shook her head. "No. Miss Hanenberger gives the orders, not you."

A younger woman stepped out from behind Santiago, her hands resting on her guns. "You heard her, Judge. Walk away. We'll defend the mine; that's what we're paid to do. You want us to help you, take it up with Hanenberger."

Dredd glowered at them. "When this is over, we'll talk again."

FOUR MINUTES LATER, Dredd and Montag stood on the roof of the town's southernmost building. Next to them, Esteban was crouched, unmoving, watching distant hills that were barely visible against the starless sky.

"We could booby-trap the roads," Montag said.

Esteban shook his head. "*Lot* of people use those roads." He froze. "They're coming—I can hear them." He pointed ahead, to a gap between two small hills about a kilometre away. "There. Figure they'll split into two groups any minute."

Dredd drew his Lawgiver. "What else is out there? Any homes in that direction within two klicks?"

"Nothing. Just different types of dirt. Sometimes sand."

Dredd unclipped the communicator O'Donnell had given him from his belt. "O'Donnell, this is Dredd. Hold your fire until I give the word. Maintain radio silence unless absolutely necessary."

"Wilco."

"Tower, what can you see?"

Judge Ramini's voice came back, "It's raiders. Maybe twenty vehicles, most of them armoured. Starting to split into two groups. One coming right toward us, other's starting to head west. Their outriders are breaking off too, on bikes."

Dredd raised his Lawgiver and adjusted the scope. At this range, in the darkness, even the best marksman would have trouble finding a target, let alone hitting it.

For a few seconds, the Lawgiver's enhanced-light scope showed nothing but wavering darkness, then a blur appeared, growing steadily stronger. Smaller blurs moved off to either side.

Dredd tracked the one moving left and fired, his shot streaking out into the darkness. He immediately panned right, and fired again.

Esteban said, "Dredd, even *I* can't see well enough to—"

Out in the darkness, almost a kilometre away, something exploded. A second later, a scream from somewhere off to the right.

"Heat-seekers," Dredd explained to Esteban. Into the radio, he yelled, "Light them up!"

From every rooftop in the town, long-burning flare-rockets were launched. They arced over the Cursed Earth, exploding into light on reaching their apex, illuminating the scene.

A couple of the Earthers' vehicles were already turning back, but most remained on course for the town. All pretence at a sneak attack was cast aside: they gunned their engines and spread out, roaring over the rough ground.

"Montag, stay put and keep low. And conserve your ammo— standard shots unless you have no choice. Esteban, let's go."

As the other townsfolk on the rooftops opened fire at the raiders, Dredd swung himself down from the roof and landed next to Eloise Crow's old motorbike. It wasn't much compared to a Lawmaster, but it would be faster than being on foot.

Esteban jumped down next to him, landing lightly in a crouch.

"You know what to do?" Dredd asked him.

"I know." Esteban climbed onto the bike, kick-started it and sped back through the town.

Dredd turned back to face the approaching raiders. He had six heat-seeking rounds left, but resisted the temptation to release them in one rapid-fire volley aimed at the largest cluster of raiders. They would be more useful later on, and right now some of the raiders were close enough that he could pick them off with standard rounds.

Around him, the night air was filled with gunshots, engines and screams, but the raiders had clearly been rattled by the early elimination of their outriders and the use of flares.

As a lone armour-plated jeep broke ahead of the others and roared toward the town, Dredd darted across the street ahead of it, and disappeared into the shadows. A glimpse of a Mega-City One Judge should unnerve them.

Behind the jeep, a half-track truck was on its tail, followed by two Earthers riding what looked like a large, heavily-modified snow-mobile, one steering, the other shooting. Dredd aimed and fired at the snow-mobile's driver. The single-tracked vehicle wavered for a second, hit a furrow and flipped. It hit the ground upside-down, crushing both the driver and his passenger.

The half-track should have been his next target, but the jeep was blocking his shot. Dredd switched to armour-piercing, and put four shots into the jeep's shielded cab where he expected the driver to be sitting.

The jeep swerved and scraped against the tapered side of a building, and the half-track behind it was forced to veer around it, passing within two metres of Dredd's position.

He darted out behind the half-track, and saw that it was only armoured at the front: the raiders hadn't anticipated an attack from behind. Its rear bed was carrying six Earthers, all but one armed with rifles and handguns.

The sixth raider was hoisting a rocket-launcher onto his shoulder. The man spotted Dredd and yelled a warning to the others, but he was too late: Dredd opened fire with a high-explosive shell which struck the rocket-launcher at the same instant that the raider fired.

The explosion tore through the half-track with enough force that shrapnel embedded itself in the walls of the surrounding buildings.

Dredd didn't slow down. He raced toward the remains of the half-track, leaped over lumps of charred, twitching flesh and burning debris. The wounded, blood-drenched driver of the vehicle collapsed out of the cab onto the dirt, his handgun falling from his smouldering grip. As he scrambled to snatch it up, Dredd put a single round into the back of his head, and kept moving.

He sprinted along a cross-street, now illuminated by the burning wreckage of the half-track, and out onto the next main street, where he saw two of O'Donnell's men still on a rooftop, expertly picking off a team of Earthers as they raced toward the town on foot. Another Earther, a mutant who was more animal than human, rapidly loped toward their building from the side. As Dredd was about to fire, a shot from high above turned the mutant's brain into liquid.

Over the radio, Ramini's voice said, "Got 'im. Keep moving, Dredd. Armoured vehicles coming in."

Twin explosions from the far side of the town lit up the night sky and shook the ground, but right now Dredd wasn't in a position to investigate.

Further along the street, he saw O'Donnell lying in wait for an approaching hoverskid; the craft was completely enclosed in armour-plating, with only a few thin horizontal slots to allow the crew to see and shoot. O'Donnell fired two shots at the hoverskid and ducked back into the shadows. On the opposite side of the street, Dredd saw Travis and Eloise Crow hiding beneath a building's raised porch. As the hoverskid turned toward O'Donnell, they darted out—Travis was carrying a thick blanket over his shoulder. They both jumped onto the rear of the craft, then Travis scrambled onto its roof and quickly draped the blanket over the slots in the cockpit's armour, while Eloise jammed the muzzle of her gun into a gun-slot in the side and emptied the entire clip.

Eloise and Travis jumped clear as the hoverskid careened out of control, crashing into the side of an old wooden house. They ran back toward Dredd and O'Donnell.

"Could do with a few more like you two," Dredd told them. "Go with O'Donnell, check out those explosions."

As the trio darted away, running past the crashed hoverskid, Dredd went in the opposite direction. Into his radio, he said, "Montag? Status."

"Still here, Dredd. Esteban's on his way—I'm providing cover."

"Good. Watch your ammo and keep me posted."

As he approached the plaza, Dredd saw a group of four Earthers, on foot, racing toward O'Donnell's shuttle.

A quick volley of shots from the guards on the rooftops changed the Earthers' minds: most of them scattered, but one dove for cover beneath an old, out-of-commission digger. From that vantage point, the Earther would be well-placed to take aim at the guards on the roof.

Another heat-seeker would be of little use here: from this angle, the Earther was shielded by one of the digger's oversized wheels. But that also meant that the Earther couldn't see him. Dredd ran full-pelt toward the rusting vehicle. At the last second, he threw himself forward and landed in a face-down skid that took him past the wheel and face-to-face with the shocked-looking Earther.

"What—?" the Earther began.

"Good news," Dredd told him. "You're the one who gets to live." He grabbed the young man by the throat and jerked his arm up, smashing the Earther's head hard against the underside of the digger, then did it a second time, just to be sure.

Ten

DREDD HEARD BRIAN O'Donnell groan, and turned to see the deputy roll onto his side, clutching his head with bandaged hands.

"I'm *never* drinking again," O'Donnell said. He winced as he swung his legs off the bed and sat up, then saw Dredd. "Oh yeah, *now* I remember." He looked around the room, then sighed. "Dredd, what are you doing in my house?"

"Doc Featherman assessed your wounds, concluded you weren't seriously hurt. Minor lacerations and contusions."

"I see." He looked down at his hands. "I have no idea how that happened."

"One of the Earthers had an old pre-war grenade," Dredd said. "You got caught in the blast."

"I don't remember... We were running toward the DuFours building when..." He shuddered. "Oh crap. Why am I not dead?"

"Travis Crow pushed you—and his wife—out of the way. He was wounded, but Doc Featherman patched him up. Eloise is unhurt, aside from a few scratches."

O'Donnell stood up, wavered a little. "Feel like I've been head-butting a bucket of bricks... Any other injuries?"

"Yes," Dredd said. "Three fatalities. Lulu McCulloch, Sam Meenan, Oleg Schreyer. Some minor injuries. We're also low on ammunition. Scavenged what we could from the raiders, but it wasn't much."

"Oleg...? Grud, no... I've known him since we were kids—I'm the one who introduced him to his husband."

"I'm sorry for your loss, O'Donnell, but this is not the time for grief. We have to shore up the defences and get to training the rest of your people. Most of them are practically useless. McCulloch and Schreyer died because they didn't have the wits to stick to their cover. They—"

Dredd blocked the first punch easily, dodged the second, and caught the man's wrists before he could throw a third.

"You heartless son of a *bitch!*" O'Donnell yelled at him, struggling. "They were my friends!"

Dredd pushed him back down onto the couch. "Schreyer took a gas-powered harpoon through the neck. He and McCulloch were supposed to watch out for each other. Because Schreyer was careless, they *both* died." After a moment, Dredd added, "If it's any consolation, the harpoon severed his carotid artery and his spinal cord. He was dead within seconds."

"Shut up! Drokk you and your consolations, Dredd. If you'd let *me* run the defences, they'd all still be alive!"

Dredd resisted the urge to immediately correct O'Donnell. At the Academy, they'd been trained to deal with hysterical citizens. Often it was best to let them boil the fury out of their system. They'd calm down soon enough. Forcing the truth on them rarely helped; it only added fuel to their rage.

And the truth was that O'Donnell's idea to wait until the Earthers had split into two groups wouldn't have worked. This raid had been almost twice as large as the previous one, and the Earthers had been better armed. By being the first to open fire, the defenders had managed to scare off some of the Earthers, and unsettle the rest. Their plan of attack had been shot to pieces before they could get it off the ground.

Next time, Ezekiel wasn't going to be so lucky.

"Have you spoken to Fellegara?" O'Donnell asked.

"Schreyer's husband? Yes. He was distraught."

"All their deaths are on your hands, Dredd. You Judges had to do it *your* way, didn't you?"

"We can argue about this later. Right now, we have to prepare for tonight's attack. I want you working with us, O'Donnell, not against us. Understood? Your alternative is to spend the night in one of your own cells."

"They won't attack tonight. They'll need time to regroup. Couple of days at least. How many got away?"

"None of them. I sent Esteban out to track the stragglers; after the attack, we took your shuttle and hunted them down. We left one alive here in town. He's scared, just a kid, but he says that his group was just the vanguard. There's a *lot* of groups out there, from all over the Cursed Earth, and they're gathering. They'll hit us tonight, tomorrow night at the latest."

"How many are we talking about?"

"Kid says there's more than he can count. Could be hundreds."

O'Donnell pushed himself to his feet. "We need back-up, from the city."

"Ramini took the shuttle up over the death-belt. She was only able to get a partial message through... There's a rad-storm building between here and the city, and it's going to be big. The western sectors have got their hands full trying to prepare for that—they can't spare anyone." Dredd moved toward the door. "Much as you want to sit here and wallow, we can't allow that."

"I want to talk to that Earther. And *I'm* still in charge of security around here. I'm not going to forget what you've done."

* * *

CHIEF JUDGE GOODMAN looked up as SJS Judge Gillen entered his office. He shut down his terminal, and leaned back in his chair. "What can I do for you?"

"I'm bringing charges against Judge Joseph Dredd."

Goodman watched her carefully. He'd been expecting this a few months ago, but recently all SJS interest in Joe Dredd seemed to have dissipated. "You don't need my permission for that."

"I'm not asking for it, Chief Judge. Just letting you know as a courtesy. I know you've taken a personal interest in the clones. You considered yourself something of a mentor to both Joe and Rico... Which is why Rico's betrayal hit you so hard."

"Indeed?"

"And now Joe. Both of them corrupt. A one hundred per cent failure rate. My guess is that's the end of the cloning programme."

"Hmm... A tip, Gillen, from one professional to another. Try not to sound *quite* so smug when you're delivering news like that."

"You don't seem concerned."

"I'll wait to see the evidence before I believe that Joe is guilty of anything. Unlike the SJS, we don't start with an assumption of guilt and then go hunting for the proof to back it up. Well, not always. So what evidence *do* you have?"

"Joe threatened and intimidated a young woman with whom Rico had had a physical relationship. Several members of her family were present."

"And you can prove this beyond a reasonable doubt?"

"We've psi-scanned every member of the family. Their memories corroborate each other and are all the evidence we need."

"You're certain that it was Joe and not Rico who made the threats?"

"Rico was on-duty elsewhere at the time of the incident.

That's been verified by other Judges. Joe's location is unknown. We were able to determine the exact time of the incident from the Tri-D channel playing in their apartment when Joe arrived. So it could only have been him. It's not enough to send Dredd to Titan, but it'll put him in an iso-cube for a ten-stretch at least."

Goodman stood up from his desk, and walked toward the window. He stared out at the city, conscious that this was something he did every time he was perturbed. "You happy now, Gillen? You've spent months trying to pin something on him. This has to be a banner day for you." He sighed. "But like I said, you don't need my permission. You're here for a different reason. Other than to rub it in my face, that is. What do you want?"

"I'll have eight SJS Judges with me, and I want a squad of twenty-five senior Judges, seven fully-armed H-Wagons and full satellite support. I want the sky over the city empty when I bring him back, and the major streets closed off. I will need the full cooperation of every department."

Goodman laughed. "You want to shut down a city of eight hundred million people...? He's not a *monster*, Gillen. Judge Dredd is just one man."

"He has Ramini and Montag on his side. Even if they don't aid him, Sector Chief Benzon says it's unlikely they'll help apprehend him. Besides, have you *seen* Dredd in action?"

The Chief Judge considered that. "Good point. But if I were a betting man I'd lay good odds that he's not going to resist."

"So you'll pass the word on to your departments?"

"I will. When do you intend to make the arrest?"

"As soon as the current rad-storm between the city and Ezekiel dissipates. We'll split into four teams, move in on his location from all sides."

"Good luck with that. And do remember to have the cameras on all vehicles serviced, and make sure they record absolutely everything, because it's going to be entertaining watching you trying to justify this action to your superiors. Also, you might want to have a word with Accounts. Get an estimate of the cost of the entire operation." He turned back to face her. "Or... We could save all that time and money by employing a much simpler approach."

"Which is?"

"Contact him, tell him he's under arrest, and *ask* him to return to the city."

"That's ridiculous, Chief. He'd never comply with that."

"You really don't know Joe Dredd at all, do you?"

Eleven

DREDD AND O'DONNELL met Alfonsa Hanenberger on the streets of Ezekiel. As before, she was accompanied by her entourage of advisors and bodyguards.

"Mister O'Donnell..." Hanenberger said, nodding toward him. "We heard the commotion last night."

Dredd said, "We need to begin evacuation. The entire town. And your mercenaries are going to help." He glanced at Hanenberger's bodyguards. "Even these two."

The woman scoffed. "All because one dumb Earther told you a fairytale about his people gathering for an assault? No."

"It wasn't a request. Your mercs will help, or they'll turn all of their weapons, ammunition and equipment over to us."

"Then you don't comprehend the meaning of the word 'mercenary,' Judge. They are soldiers for hire. *Do* you understand the concept? If you want them to work, you have to *pay* them. But since I'm already paying them, you'd have to double or triple my rate to persuade them to work for you instead. I don't see that happening." She turned back to O'Donnell. "We are safe here, you assured me of that many times. Were you wrong?"

O'Donnell glowered for a moment, then said, "No. We're safe. But we're only safe because we take the appropriate precautions. If we become complacent, we'll die."

"The Earthers are savages, O'Donnell. Really little more than animals. Most of them can barely string a sentence together, let alone organise some sort of mass-march on our town."

"Talk to the prisoner *yourself*," Dredd said. "You'll find he's intelligent and literate. And desperate. Underestimating the enemy shows remarkable short-sightedness on your part. If you want us to defend this town, you'll let us do it our way."

"Your way got three good people killed," Hanenberger said. "Perhaps life is disposable in Mega-City One, but not here in my town."

"Then take a good look around," Dredd said. "Commit the town to memory, because if that kid is telling the truth, memories will be all that's left of Ezekiel. Now I'm telling you to prepare to evacuate or I will hold you responsible for the consequences."

One of Hanenberger's advisors leaned close to her and whispered something that Dredd couldn't hear. The woman smiled and nodded. "Judge Dredd, outside the walls of your city, you have no legal standing. You're not even the most senior Judge here. You can issue orders, but we're under no obligation to comply."

"For everyone else here, that's true," Dredd said. "But *you* are a citizen of Mega-City One. You'll do what I say if you ever want to return to the city."

The woman barked a short, harsh laugh. "I will *not*. Now, you go about your business defending—"

"You brought us in to protect the people of this town, that's what I'm going to do. You all follow my orders and there's a chance we'll survive. I told you about the rad-storm between here and the city. In the few minutes before she lost contact with the Justice Department, they told Judge Ramini that their satellites had picked up another storm, and it's a *lot* bigger. If the two storms meet, we are going to be trapped right in the middle. If we begin evacuating right *now*, we might make it."

Hanenberger regarded him silently for a moment. "No. We've survived the worst weather the Cursed Earth can throw at us... And so have the Earthers. If we leave, we're putting down a welcome mat for them. Then when we return, getting them *out* is going to be damn near impossible. They'd take over the mine, and that would be the end of this town."

"You're making a mistake, Hanenberger."

"My town, my mistake to make. You don't understand, Judge. You're a city-boy right down to the bone, but the people here are made of tougher stuff. You expect them to abandon everything they've worked for? Then you're a fool."

"WE HAVE ALMOST five hundred reluctant people to evacuate," O'Donnell told Dredd and Ramini. "It's not possible."

They were on the roof of the town's highest building, using binoculars to scan the horizon. Overhead, the sky was clear, but to the east, a kilometre above ground, a wide death-belt was slowly approaching. Dredd watched the slowly-tumbling rocks for a few moments. Sand, dust and other small particles tended to get whipped away from the death-belts by strong winds, but whatever strange, gravity-nullifying force kept the belt in the air seemed to hold on to larger objects.

"The shuttle can carry ten, at a push," O'Donnell said. "Fourteen four-wheeled vehicles, maybe sixty more. Even if we can persuade everyone to leave, that means evacuation will take at least seven trips just for the people and another three for the supplies they'll need. And we don't even know where we're *going*. There's no way we can make it to the city through the rad-storm, and even if we could, they wouldn't let most of us in."

"What about the trucks that transport the iridium to the processing plant?" Ramini asked. "They could carry everyone."

"They could, if they were here, and if Hanenberger allowed us to use them. Last I heard the trucks are just outside the city, waiting out the rad-storm."

"So you're saying that it can't be done?" Dredd asked.

"No, I'm *repeating* that it can't be done! We'd die out there. We've a better chance of survival if we stay. Lot of the homes here have basements, should be enough room for everyone."

Ramini said, "If the storm hits as hard as the experts in Mega-City One are predicting, there won't be any basements under the homes. There'll be tombs."

It was early afternoon, two hours since Dredd's confrontation with Hanenberger. On the southern side of the town, the diggers were carving a wide, deep trench across the town's entire south side, piling the excavated dirt high just inside the trench to create a barricade. Some of the Earthers' wrecked vehicles had been dragged into position behind the barricade to provide cover against any Earthers who succeeded in scrambling over it.

Esteban swiftly climbed up onto the roof. "We've got about half the town still refusing to leave. What are the chances that the storm will keep the raiders away?"

O'Donnell said, "Could be that they're coming *because* of the storm. They know we'll have to take shelter, that'll give them a free run of the town." To the Judges, he said, "They're better equipped to deal with it than we are. Most of them are muties already."

"What's that supposed to mean?" Esteban asked, then added, "Racist."

"It's not racist. It's just a fact. They're mutants. I'm not saying that they're bad people." O'Donnell shrugged. "Well, I mean, these guys *are* bad people, but not because they're mutants."

"Enough," Ramini said. "We can't hide from the storm and protect the town from the Earthers at the same time." She turned in a slow circle. "Hell with the town—it's just buildings. Let the raiders take it. We're evacuating everyone to the mines."

Esteban said, "Hanenberger won't permit that."

"She won't have a choice," Dredd said. "The mines will provide shelter from the storm, and the iridium ore will shield us from some of the radiation. Get your people to start moving in the supplies." He walked to the edge of the roof. "I'll deal with Hanenberger."

DREDD FOUND ALFONSA Hanenberger in her home, the largest house in Ezekiel. She greeted him on the porch, along with her advisors and ever-present bodyguards.

"The mine is off-limits to anyone but me and my security people," Hanenberger said.

There was a slight cough from behind her.

"And my advisors," she added. "We're going to seal the entrances and ventilation shafts, wait until the storm blows over and the Earthers are gone."

"The raiders are not the problem," Dredd said. "I told you already: there's a storm coming."

"This is the Cursed Earth. There's *always* a storm coming. You're not getting it, Dredd. This is *my* town. My family owns everything you see out there. The buildings, the mine, the land itself. So out here *I* am the law, not you. You were brought in to help defend my property against the Earthers, not to defend the people. If you're not going to do your job, then why don't you just drokk off back to Mega-City One and leave us be?"

One of the advisors leaned close to Hanenberger and whispered something. She nodded, and looked back at Dredd. "I rescind my request for help from the Justice Department of Mega-City One. You and your friends will get out of my town immediately. You're trespassing... My people here have every right to gun you down."

"The right, perhaps," Dredd said, "but not the ability."

She stepped closer to Dredd. "Before the storm cut off all comms with the city, last thing *we* heard was that the SJS are coming for you. Did you know that? They won't get here before the storm, but they *will* get here. They're building a small army, Dredd, just for you. If you're lucky, you might even end up on the same ship to Titan as your brother." She smiled. "Didn't think we knew about that, did you? You've forgotten how powerful my family *is*, I think. We're powerful because the right people are afraid of us. Look at me: I have four homes in the city and I can come and go as much as I like. *Me*, Dredd. What do you think of that?"

Dredd looked down at the woman's wrinkled, loose-hanging skin. "So that's not just a skin condition. You're a mutant."

"I'm a *Hanenberger*, and that's more important than any radiation-triggered twist of genetics. We Hanenbergers look after our own. My people at the mine have orders to defend my property with extreme prejudice if that becomes necessary. Now, get out."

THE FIRST EARTHERS to arrive at the barricade were an old man and a young woman riding a thin black and white horse. They were stopped by Esteban and Travis Crow.

"Move on," Esteban called out. He and Travis stood either side of the makeshift drawbridge over the trench. "There's nothing for you here."

"My *brother* lives here," the old man called back. He climbed down from the horse and pushed back his hat. "I'm Abraham Stinnett, this is my girl Novena. My brother's Ishmael. Fetch him—he'll vouch for me."

A few minutes later, Dredd and O'Donnell accompanied the preacher to the barricade.

"That you, Ishmael?" the old man called. "Yeah, it's you."

Stinnett called back, "What you *want*, Abe?" To Dredd, he said, "Haven't seen this drokker in damn near twenty years."

"Storm's coming, Ishmael. A big one."

"We know that—we got eyes!"

"It's gonna be bad. Real bad. Remember the storm back in Oklahoma when grandma's whole town got wiped out? Badder than that. Much, *much* badder. I seen it."

"How can he know that?" O'Donnell asked.

"He's got the Sight," Stinnett said. "Always had. He can see down the road, sometimes. Devil's work, if you ask me."

"A psychic?" Dredd asked.

"Yep."

"Let them in."

Stinnett grabbed Dredd's arm. "No, don't. He's not been saved and that means he's not my kin anymore."

Dredd shrugged off the preacher and beckoned his brother forward. With some trepidation, the old man led his horse over the drawbridge. They looked a lot alike, Dredd noted. Same mid-brown skin, same wrinkles around the eyes, same pure-white hair, though Abraham was considerably more neatly-groomed than his brother.

The young woman, Novena, bore some resemblance to her father; she was covered in dust, thin to the point of emaciation, and her face was barely visible behind masses of white hair.

The preacher said, "Abe, you tell me that you've rejected the devil and then maybe we can talk. But if you're still curled up all cosy in his evil pocket, best thing you can do is get back on that horse and turn around. The Almighty Grud is merciful, but only up to a point, got that? He is kindness and wrath and fury and snuggliness all in one neat, easy-to-use package. Yea, verily, he is both consistent and contradictory at the same time, and yet not! Praise Grud! Praise his awesome musty scent which is like unto that great smell you get when you're digging fresh soil, for he is the creator of *all* things that ever were or ever will be, up to and including himself."

To Dredd, Abe said, "You see why I steer clear of this idiot? Our mother was a travelling faith-healer. Ishmael got all the belief and the showmanship, but I got the Sight."

"So I hear," Dredd said. "What have you seen?"

"There's a storm coming."

From the side, Esteban said, "You said that already. Judge, how do we know he's not a spy for the Earthers?"

"Or for the *Devil!*" the preacher shouted. "It is written that he will travel the land in human form, spreading lies and untruths and falsehoods and false witnesses and, um, big fat hairy fibs... and he shall ride forth on a mighty thunderous beast of raging poisoned *fire!*"

Everyone looked at the piebald horse, which was standing next to Abraham and gently chewing on the edge of his hat.

Dredd said, "Esteban, get this nut out of here." To Abraham, he said, "You, come with me. O'Donnell, find food and water for the girl. And the horse."

IN THE TOWN'S small jail, Judge Montag was guarding the prisoner. When Dredd and Abraham entered, the young man Dredd had captured during the last raid was sitting cross-legged in the middle of his cell, staring down at the floor. Montag was sitting nearby, sharpening her boot-knife on an old whetstone.

Dredd nodded toward the prisoner. "He meditating?"

"No, I'm not," the prisoner said. "There's a beetle here that keeps coming up out of the floorboards and then stopping, like he's thinking, 'Wait, *what* was it I came in here to get?'" He looked up at Dredd and smiled. "It's kinda cute."

Dredd asked Abraham, "This creep one of yours?"

"One of my what?"

"One of your people. Earthers."

"Judge, I don't *have* people. Only my horse. And my daughter."

"If you've got some sort of psychic abilities, scan this kid and tell me what's going on inside his head."

The old man frowned. "He's scared, but anyone can see that..." He walked up to the cell's bars. "Let me in, boy. It won't hurt... Just want to take a look around." After a few seconds, he pulled back and turned to Dredd. "He came with the vanguard. They were told to check out the town, test the defences. They heard there was Judges here, so they had to be sure."

"Doesn't prove much," Dredd said. "If you really are psychic, tell me how we caught him."

"He was hiding under a truck and you smashed his head up against the driveshaft, knocked him out."

Montag said, "Close. But it—"

"No, not a truck. Some kind of digger. Big, rusting... That enough for you?"

"It'll do," Dredd said. "So what brings you here to Ezekiel? You chasing or fleeing?"

"Little of both. When the storm hits it's going to be about as bad as you can imagine. We've got..." the old man walked to the window and looked out. "Reckon we've got an hour before it gets so bad out there that a fella won't be able to stand up in the wind."

Montag slipped her boot-knife back into its scabbard, and walked over to Dredd. "That can't be right. According to the weather charts we got from Mega-City One, we should have almost *four* hours."

The young prisoner in the cell said, "Okay... I think I wanna get out of here."

"Abraham, why only an hour?" Dredd asked. "There's barely a breeze out there right now. For a storm to build to its apex in such a short time—"

"I never said that was going to be the *apex*, Judge. In an hour, wind'll be so bad you won't be able to stand up. But that's nothing compared to what's coming. This has been building for *months*. Little storms all across the land from Mega-City Two to Texas City, each one creating the ideal conditions for the next. And they're all gonna converge in this region."

Dredd looked out at the weather-vane across the street. It was starting to rock in the wind.

"You have never seen anything like this," Abraham said. "No one has, not since the atomic wars. The Cursed Earth is fighting back, you see. I'm not saying it's *deliberate*; it ain't sentient, it doesn't know what it's doing... But it *is* fighting. Lot of folks out there have been able to sense it, that's what's been driving them in this direction."

The young man in the cell stood up and approached the bars. "Judge Dredd, your people asked me who I was with, how many people and guns we had. They never asked me *why* we were coming to your town. Sure, some of us came for your supplies and weapons, but that's because we know we're going to need them. That big dust-cloud out there, to the south-west? That's where the groups have been assembling."

"The boy is right," the old man said. "I'm not much of a one for numbers, but there's a lot of people out there now, and more coming every minute. Anyone who can't find shelter elsewhere. They're preparing to head this way all in one swarm."

Montag asked, "How many? Roughly."

Abraham Stinnett shrugged. "Like I said, I'm not good with numbers... Couple of thousand, maybe more."

"That doesn't make sense," Montag said. "If they know the storm will hit here in Ezekiel, why not run the other way?"

Looking at Abraham, Dredd said, "Because it's not the town they're after, is it? The town won't survive the storm. They want to shelter in the mine."

Twelve

O'DONNELL LED THE young woman—still on her horse—to the Brazen Hussy.

As she swung down from the horse, she spoke for the first time. "We have to get to shelter."

"I know, but there's time." He patted the horse's rump. "What's her name?"

"I don't know. I don't speak horse."

"Right... But you could have named her yourself. Daisy, or something." He smiled at the young woman. She was twenty-one, maybe. He thought she was pretty, in a dishevelled and dusty sort of way. Not classically beautiful, but then he wasn't exactly a holo-vid-star himself. "Novena, right? That's a religious thing, isn't it?"

"Prayers for the intervention of a saint."

"Well, we could use some of that around here right now." He tied the horse's reins to the arm of a wooden bench outside the tavern and said, "Come in. We'll get you something to eat and drink."

Novena hesitated at the doorway, and O'Donnell looked

back. "Pa always said never to go into a bar with a stranger."

He extended his hand, and shook hers. "Brian O'Donnell. Some folks here call me Red, because of my hair. Not the most imaginative nickname. I'm the deputy sheriff. There. Now we're not strangers." He tilted his head toward the door. "Come in."

From across the street, Ishmael Stinnett called, "Don't you set one foot in that... that... *cathedral* of debauchery, missy! You mind what I say! Your father is my brother and that makes you kin, even if he *has* been felt-up by the Devil's wandering hands and liked it! You hear me?"

"Ignore him," O'Donnell said.

Novena glanced back at her uncle, then followed O'Donnell into the bar. All of the furniture had been roped together into one enormous pile. Boards had been nailed across the windows, and the shelves behind the bar were empty.

"At least someone is taking the warnings seriously," O'Donnell said. He crossed the room and went behind the bar, then pounded on the cellar trapdoor with his boot. "Open up! It's me, O'Donnell!"

A muffled voice came from below. "What do you want?"

"You hoarding supplies down there, Maddox?"

"They're *my* supplies!"

"I know that. Just pass me up some food and a couple of bottles of water, huh?"

A few seconds later, the trapdoor opened and the tattooed barman peered out. "Here. I'll put them on your tab."

O'Donnell took the packages and passed them to Novena, then said, "I wouldn't bother. When the storm hits and crushes your bar into sawdust, and you die because you didn't evacuate like I *told* you, it won't make any difference how much I owe you."

"Them Judges still pushing your buttons, huh? It's not going to be that bad, Red. Any time there's a storm brewing, there's always some fear-mongering doom-sayer who predicts it'll be the worst ever. They're always wrong."

Novena said, "Not this time. In two hours this whole town will be gone."

"I reckon she's right," O'Donnell said. "Seriously, Maddox... You need to clear out. We're heading for the mines. That's the only chance we have of riding out the storm. That's if the Earthers don't get us first. So get to the mine, and bring all the supplies you can carry because we don't know how long we'll be trapped in there."

"Not gonna happen, Red. I'm happy where I am."

"Then I hate that you're making me do this..." O'Donnell drew his gun and aimed it at the barman's head. "You can stay here if you like, but I'm taking your supplies."

Maddox stared up into the barrel of the gun. "Thought you were my friend."

"I am. But food and water are no good to a dead man. So what's it to be?"

In the Chief Judge's office at the top of Mega-City One's Hall of Justice, Goodman stepped back from his monitors and slowly shook his head. The screens showed a real-time satellite feed centred on the town of Ezekiel. To the east of the town, the rad-storm was beginning to grow. Already, the hyper-charged storm was blocking out all radio communications with the town.

But that one was a wet slap compared to the body-blow that was coming: eight separate storms had been brewing for weeks, slowly drifting north and east, from the Slough of St Louis in the west and the Alabama Morass to the south.

Little more than zephyrs at first, the storms had grown steadily larger and stronger. The Justice Department's weather-control computers had predicted they would all converge just south of Lake Erie.

Instinctively, Goodman turned toward the window, but there was nothing to see from this distance. Most of Mega-City One would be safe. Perhaps a few of the sectors close to the western wall would suffer a little damage, but nothing that couldn't be easily fixed. The city's weather-control technology was the best in the world. It could trigger localised rainfall to an accuracy of twenty-three metres—handy for dampening the spirits of protest marches—or give specific temperatures to individual sectors. Wind-speed, humidity and cloud-cover were all easily adjusted as required.

But the satellites only covered the city itself, not the Cursed Earth. Out there, the weather was unpredictable.

Goodman had occasionally wondered if maybe controlling the weather in Mega-City One only made things worse elsewhere.

He contacted Judge Robertson of Weather Division again. "Give me some good news, Robertson."

The older man's voice came back, "I'm sorry, Chief Judge. We just don't have the time."

"You only need to adjust one satellite, for Grud's sake! How long does it take to reprogram it?"

"Sir, it's not that simple. Right now there are thirty-four active weather control satellites covering the city. They—"

"And I'm just telling you to reassign *one*. The one closest to Ezekiel."

"If we adjust that one, sir, then that leaves a gap over Sectors 195 to 201. We'd be exposing close to thirty million people to the storms. We're not just talking about rain, wind and lightning. The storms carry irradiated dust. That gets into the city's water supplies, and we're looking at a major catastrophe. The only way to do it is to spread out *all* the satellites to continue to provide even coverage, and that'll take the best part of a day."

"Robertson, I know something about satellite control. You don't have to *move* them, just reassign their targets. That should only take a couple of minutes."

"That's true, but unless you want a simple change like an adjustment to the humidity levels, it takes *hours* for each satellite's effects to be felt. To change the weather in a specific location we have to generate precisely-targeted bubbles of adjusted gravity, each one lasting only a few milliseconds. But we'd need to create hundreds of *thousands* of bubbles to have any noticeable effect on even a standard rainstorm, and every change has to be monitored carefully."

"So what are the people in Ezekiel supposed to do?"

"Same as they always do when there's a big storm, sir. Find shelter. And if they can't, then find a pen and start writing their wills."

Goodman glared at the monitors. "You think this is *funny*, Robertson?"

"Uh, no, sir. I just—"

"If we can't stop this storm, then maybe we can prevent the next one. Start looking into ways to extend weather control coverage to the entire continent."

"But that'll cost *trillions* of credits, sir! The weather regions are not isolated from each other. Tweak the weather in one, that has an impact on the neighbouring regions, which in turn impact *their* neighbours. Every time we add a new region, we have to recalculate and adjust the effects on all the others. To do the whole *continent*—"

Goodman sighed. "Just... get your people working on it. We have to do *something*."

Judge Ramini walked away from the town's plaza with her Lawgiver in her hand, clearly visible. With her were Eloise and Travis Crow, also carrying guns.

Behind them, most of the population of Ezekiel had assembled, many of them clutching bags of food or precious belongings. But far too many townsfolk had chosen to barricade themselves in their homes, sure that they would be safe from the coming storm.

Travis glanced back as he walked, then said to Ramini, "They're scared."

"They're not scared *enough*."

"The mercs are going to resist," Eloise said. "They only follow Hanenberger's orders."

"I know," Ramini said. "But the mine is big enough to hold everyone; they *are* going to let us in. You two spread out—don't give them a single target. And hold fire until it's unavoidable."

The burly mercenary, Santiago, stepped out from the entrance as they approached, hands resting on her guns. "What do you want?"

"You know what we want," Ramini called. "I'm Judge Izobel Ramini of Mega-City One, and the people of this town are under my protection. That includes you and your friends. So you're going to let everyone take shelter and you won't have to go searching for a med-kit. Or a coroner."

Santiago shook her head. "Miss Hanenberger gives the orders, and she's already in here with her people. Her orders are that no one else gets in, and as soon as the storm hits, we seal off this entrance."

Ramini took a deep breath, held it for a second, and then exhaled slowly. "Okay... Let's consider what you're doing. There are hundreds of people in this town, and when the Earthers come and the storm starts tearing the place apart, all of those people are going to die unless you allow them into the mine. You want that many deaths on your conscience?"

"I don't *have* a conscience."

"That so? Then maybe you have a sense of self-preservation. If the town dies, so does the mine. Then you're out of a job."

Santiago smiled. "Yeah, good one. But Miss Hanenberger's accountants have done the math. The mine's almost played out, and the town's gonna get blown away anyway. It'll cost more to rebuild than we're gonna earn from what's left in the mine. Plus all those townies would need to be fed and watered." She shrugged. "Miss Hanenberger wishes you well, but she's not under obligation to save anyone."

Ramini stepped closer, and Santiago tightened her grip on her guns. The mercenaries behind her did likewise.

"Look," Ramini said, "We don't have to make this difficult." She looked around. A gust of wind propelled a small dust-cloud along the street. "Wind's picking up, which means that time is running out. Stand aside."

"No."

From somewhere far to the south, Ramini could hear the roar of approaching vehicles.

"They're coming," Eloise Crow said. "The Earthers will be here in minutes."

"Just enough time to say your prayers, then," Santiago said. "See, Judge, there's seven of us here, and one of you. Oh, I know you've got your little pals with you, but look at them. They barely know how to hold a gun. They're not like us. We know what we're doing. You open fire, you might get one shot off—might even *kill* me—before my friends retaliate. And we've got plenty of ammo. You'll end up with so many holes we'll be able to freeze your body and use you as a cheese-grater. So you go ahead, if you've got the guts. Take your one shot before you die."

Slowly, Ramini raised her Lawgiver.

Santiago grinned. "Really? You're going for it? I'm impressed. So which of us are you going to shoot, huh? Me? Seems like the obvious choice because I'm the one talking to you, but... that doesn't mean I'm the leader, does it? *Or* the best shot. Maybe it's one of my friends you should be targeting. Which of us poses the greatest threat? Which shot will give you the best chance of making it out of this alive? And, hey, you might get lucky. Maybe *our* first shot will miss, or only wound you. You might get to shoot two of us. But *which* two?"

"You done?" Ramini asked. "Because I'm going to say one more thing, and then you're going to do as I say."

"And what *is* that one thing, Judge?"

"Hi-ex."

Thirteen

Dredd and O'Donnell—followed closely by Novena—reached the mine entrance as Ramini and the Crows were dragging the mercenaries' body-parts clear.

"Heard an explosion..." O'Donnell said, shielding his eyes against the column of acrid smoke billowing out of the mine.

Ramini turned to Dredd. "Gave them the opportunity to stand down. They didn't feel inclined to take it."

"How many?" Dredd asked. He looked back toward the south. Now, the roar of the Earthers' approaching engines was too loud to ignore.

"Seven," Ramini said. "Means there's still four more inside."

"Deal with them. O'Donnell, go to the plaza, get the people moving this way. They need to be ready to get inside as soon as Ramini gives you the all-clear." Dredd began to scoop up the mercenaries' guns and ammunition.

"Got it," O'Donnell said. To Novena, he added, "Wait here, okay?"

"What about my horse?"

"There might not be room inside... Look, just wait here! I'll do what I can!" He darted away.

Dredd scraped lumps of charred flesh from a shotgun. "You need back-up, Ramini?"

She checked her Lawgiver. "Probably not. As soon as everyone's in, I'll join you on the front line. Dredd, most of those weapons are damaged beyond use."

"Worth checking anyway."

"What about Montag? She still guarding the prisoner?"

"For now. I'm about to set him free."

Ramini hesitated. "I was thinking execution. He did attack the town."

"Considered that. Figure he'll be killed by the storm anyway."

Ramini nodded. "Your call, Dredd. If we don't all make it through this... Just want to say it's been an honour. The Department's lucky to have you."

"Likewise." Dredd gestured toward the mine entrance. "Good luck."

He turned and ran, heading back through the town toward the jail cell.

A sudden gust of wind slammed the door open as he reached it. Inside, Montag was in the process of unlocking the cell's door. The young prisoner was clearly anxious to get out.

The old man, Abraham, asked, "Where's my daughter?"

"At the mine entrance," Dredd said. "Suggest you head there now, too. And you, Montag. Keep the prisoner safe."

"No, you need me at the front line, Dredd." She slid open the barred door and the prisoner darted out.

Dredd grabbed him as he tried to duck past. "What's your name?"

"Bobby!"

"Well, Bobby... You run north, and you *keep* running. You got that, punk?"

"I'll never out-run the storm! I want to go into the mine with everyone else!"

"And how do I know you won't go back to your fellow Earthers and take up arms against us?"

Abraham said, "He won't, Judge. I can *see* that. He's done with them, just wants to lay low."

The entire building creaked, and the windows began to shake.

Dredd pulled Bobby closer: "It's getting bad out there... You get the old man safely to the mine! You screw up, you'll answer to me. Understood?"

Bobby nodded. "Yessir!" He linked his arm with Abraham's and together they made their way outside, shielding their eyes against the stinging dust.

Dredd tossed one of the mercenaries' guns to Montag. "Let's go. You're a weapons specialist: see if you can fix that while we're running."

BRIAN O'DONNELL HAD to shout to be heard over the wind, but it wasn't really necessary: the assembled townsfolk had been watching out for someone to give them the signal to start moving toward the mine.

"C'mon, let's go! Keep it orderly! Slow and steady, that's it!"

Among the crowd he was relieved to see Maddox, the barman from the Brazen Hussy, dragging four twenty-litre bottles of water on a wheeled cart. "Knew you'd change your mind!" He yelled.

Maddox pulled his bandanna away from his mouth, and called back, "Your tab is fifty-nine credits, Red! Not going to let *that* go!"

O'Donnell grinned, and waved the crowd on. "Keep going. Assemble *outside* the mine, got that? Wait for the Judges to give the all-clear before you go in." He stopped the nearest man. "You hear that, Mitch?"

"I heard ya, yeah."

"Make sure *everyone* understands, all right?"

He stepped back and watched them shuffling forward. Over three hundred people, and he knew them all on sight. *How many of them will still be alive tomorrow?* He wondered. *How many of the others hiding in their basements will crawl out in one piece?*

Beyond the crowd, O'Donnell could see Hanenberger's shuttle. He was one of only a handful qualified to fly the craft.

For a moment, he considered taking it. It was fast, it could outrun the storm. And it had a pretty good range, too. It could easily take him north, past Lake Huron and into the Canadian Wastes.

O'Donnell shook his head. It wasn't even an option. You don't abandon your friends to save your own skin.

If the shuttle had been armed, he could have used it to help defend the town, but it wasn't much more than a small cargo vessel, fairly cheaply retrofitted with collapsible passenger seating.

If we had bombs... O'Donnell thought. But then he realised that maybe the shuttle could be used for a different purpose: *I can set it on autopilot,* he thought, *plot a course to take it over the raiders, crash into them. Might take a few of them out.*

Or, better still, keep it buzzing them from a low height. They'll waste their ammo trying to shoot it down.

He was pushing his way through the crowd, heading for the shuttle, when an unexpected sound caught his attention.

JUDGE MONTAG THOUGHT for a second that the storm had come even earlier than the old man had predicted: the southern horizon was a rapidly-growing blur of billowing dust and sand.

No, she told herself, *that's the dust kicked up by the Earthers' vehicles... Grud, there are* hundreds *of them!*

Standing next to her on the roof, Judge Dredd remained impassive. Everyone else assigned to defend the town was hunched over, shielding themselves against the wind, but Dredd just stood there, watching.

"Dredd?" she asked.

"Yeah?"

"There is no *way* we can stop that many."

"True."

"Even if every round was a kill-shot, we'd still be overwhelmed."

Dredd nodded slowly. "Reckon so."

"So... What do we do?"

"We do our job." Dredd turned slightly toward her. "Judge Celia Montag, twenty-four years old... trained as a tech and had no real experience of the streets until a few months ago. And now you're stuck in the Cursed Earth, facing impossible odds."

"Yeah, I don't need a reminder of how dire our situation is."

"Then consider our assets. We're Judges, trained in the toughest academy on the planet." Dredd pointed toward the growing cloud of dust, now seemingly only minutes away. "Out there is a bunch of nomads and misfits and farmers. All of them untrained, each one desperate. And desperate people make mistakes." He walked to the edge of the roof, and shouted down toward the townsfolk guarding the single gap in the barricade. "Drop the drawbridge!"

A pause, then Esteban shouted back, "What?"

"You heard! Drop it—and get clear. Give the Earthers a clear way in!"

"You're drokkin' *insane*, Dredd!"

Montag almost smiled as she realised what Dredd was planning. "He's right!" She called down. "Do it!"

Below, Esteban ordered his people to lower the drawbridge and get clear of the barricade.

"Now, clear out!" Dredd called. "Everyone down off the roofs, make sure you can't be seen from outside!"

Fourteen

RAMINI WISHED SHE'D taken the time to explore the mine. She knew the basic layout from Dredd's description, but seeing it in person was different.

The main entrance tunnel wound its way through the rock, following the course of the first iridium seam that had been discovered, before it reached the central cavern.Hanenberger's mercenaries would be lying in wait for her: there was no way they could have missed the sound of the hi-ex shell that had taken out their colleagues.

Ramini didn't regret the deaths of the mercenaries. She'd given them fair warning, and they should have known better than to threaten a Mega-City Judge.

From somewhere far ahead came a soft, deep *clunk*, then the lights in the tunnel went dark. Ramini immediately dropped to the ground.

A voice drifted out to her. "That you, Dredd?"

She resisted the temptation to mimic Dredd's voice. "No. Ramini."

"Okay. So, I know you Judges are devious little drokkers. Just like I know you've got heat-seeking and ricochet rounds. So just in case you get the idea of firing off a few shots in the hope of hitting us, be warned that we're not alone in here. We've got hostages."

Ramini began to crawl forward, keeping her Lawgiver aimed at the darkness ahead of her. "Oh, yeah?"

"Yeah. Try anything and they're dead."

"And when they're dead, what's to stop me from killing you?" The fingers of Ramini's free hand probed the ground ahead of her. It was smooth—laser-cut—but coated with a layer of dust and small, sharp stones. When the lights had gone out, she'd been able to see four lights ahead of her, each set into the ceiling, about eight metres apart, before the tunnel curved.

"You want to take that chance?"

"Not especially." Something scuffled behind Ramini, and she froze.

"It's me," Eloise Crow whispered.

"Told you to stay at the entrance!" Ramini hissed back.

"I know these tunnels. You don't. On your left, about four metres ahead, there's a secondary junction box for the lights."

"Not a lot of good to me, Eloise—they've shut off the circuit at their end."

More scuffling, and Ramini felt Eloise crawling past her on the left. "I know... But when you get to the cavern, they'll turn on the lights and dazzle you. Shoot you down before you can see where they are. Well, that's what *I'd* do. So we break the circuit here too, and they can't turn the lights back on."

"Good thinking," Ramini said. "You'd have made a good Judge."

"It's in the blood. My grandfather was a New York City cop." A fresh *clunk* ahead, then Eloise said, "Done."

* * *

MONTAG SAW ESTEBAN fire off two rounds at the vehicle closest to the gap in the barricade. A converted camper van bristling with weapons, its windows and much of the bodywork had been replaced with steel sheets, strong enough to resist standard ammunition. Esteban was about to shoot at the camper's tyres when Montag grabbed his arm and pulled him back.

"No! Let it through!" she yelled.

"We can stop it here, block the entrance!"

"Then the others will change direction, find another way in! This way we can pick off at least the first few of them."

The mutant nodded, and fell back with the rest of the townsfolk. They had lined the street on both sides, many of them crouched beneath the raised porches, which kept them hidden from the raiders and provided some shelter from the wind. It also meant that they would be shooting upwards at the vehicles that broke through, which reduced the risk of any of them getting caught in the crossfire.

The camper rumbled over the drawbridge and through the narrow gap in the barricade. Montag waited until it had travelled seventy metres along the street before she gave the signal to open fire.

The camper's tyres and lower half of the body were shredded by gunfire, but even this close, Montag couldn't hear the guns over the roar of the storm.

Already, three more vehicles had passed through the barricade. The first of them—an open-topped convertible with an ancient Gatling-gun mounted on the trunk—swerved when the driver saw what had happened to the camper. Montag's first shot took out the mutant manning the gun, but her second shot missed the driver. He swerved again, gunned the engine toward one of the cross-streets. Montag fired a single heat-seeker in his direction and even before it hit home she had turned her attention to the next vehicle.

A raider on the largest motorbike Montag had ever seen

skirted past a truck just inside the barricade. He was wearing what looked like a medieval suit of armour, and rode with his head down and the throttle full.

Montag's shots ricocheted off his armour, but she'd caught the rider's attention. He steered directly toward her: she dodged to the side at the last moment and he roared past, clipping a wounded Earther who'd jumped out of the camper and sending the man spinning.

Montag glanced up at the watchtower, looking for Dredd. She saw a single muzzle-flash, then the motorbike wavered, toppled onto its side and kept going, with the rider pinned beneath it. It gouged a twenty-metre-long blood-soaked trench in the dirt road before it stopped.

Another flash, from somewhere behind Montag, and she turned back toward the barricade, expecting to see a column of smoke or billowing flames. The townsfolk were still shooting at the raiders as they tried to pass through the barricade, but there was no obvious source for the flash.

She dismissed it; right now, there was enough to worry about.

She darted across the street—stopping long enough to snatch a large pair of goggles from a dying raider—and jumped onto a plastic water-barrel next to the tapered wall of a building. From there, she was able to leap for the edge of the roof and pull herself up. Up there the wind was even stronger: Montag had to grab onto an old radio mast to keep upright. The mast itself was already swaying and creaking far too much for comfort.

Ahead of her, lying face-down on the roof, was one of the townsfolk, armed with a long-range rifle. Montag dropped flat and squirmed forward. The man glanced back as she grabbed his calf, nodded to her and yelled something.

Montag edged forward until she was parallel with him, and handed him the goggles. He nodded thanks, and put them on, then said something else.

With her mouth only a hands-breadth away from his ear, Montag yelled, "What?"

The man pointed ahead, over the barricade, and Montag turned to look.

A few minutes ago, the last time she'd looked, she'd been able to see maybe a hundred vehicles emerging from the dust cloud. Now, she could see fifteen.

For a moment, relief flooded through her. *We're done. We can mop them up and—*

The wind shifted abruptly, and briefly cleared the dust from the air.

A thousand different vehicles were racing over the rough ground.

As they watched, one of the closest vehicles—a wide, flat hoverskimmer carrying perhaps a dozen Earthers—suddenly swayed, hit by a powerful gust of wind. Another gust, even stronger, hit the hoverskimmer from behind; it surged forward, and Montag saw the driver desperately working the controls. Another gust, and the Earther at the rear of the skimmer lost his balance and toppled out.

His colleagues didn't see that: the people around the edges were too busy clinging on, and the three directly behind the driver were shooting at the townsfolk on the rooftops.

Montag took aim with her Lawgiver and fired. Dredd had warned everyone, "Conserve your ammunition. Where possible, aim for the drivers." It made sense: taking out the drivers not only slowed the vehicles down, it caused their passengers to panic.

Montag's shot passed through the driver's throat. He collapsed forward over the controls, and the skimmer veered off to the right.

The fallen Earther scrambled to his feet and left his gun behind as he ran after his colleagues, but he didn't make it more than ten metres before another out-of-control vehicle—a battered, twentieth-century white Toyota with a cracked, blood-spattered windscreen—struck him from behind.

Then the Toyota, too, was hit: an eighteen-wheeled truck ploughed into it sidelong, crushing it instantly.

The truck hit the drawbridge at an angle, and the drawbridge buckled under the massive weight, sending the truck into the pit outside the barricade.

Even before it had ground to a halt, the rear of the truck burst open and a stream of Earthers flooded out.

Swathed in thick, dust-covered rags and carrying handguns and crossbows, the Earthers began to swarm up out of the pit and over the barricade.

Montag set her Lawgiver to hi-ex and fired off three shots, widely spaced. She couldn't hear the explosions over the roar of the storm, but their effect was visible. The high-explosive shells ripped through the swarm of Earthers.

One of them—a middle-aged woman, Montag noted—was blasted straight up into the air, where the wind caught her blood-drenched, charred body and carried her forty metres before slamming her against the side of a house.

Another flash from somewhere to the south, and Montag wondered if the Earthers were using flares. It seemed pointless; in the billowing dust, visibility was down to only a few metres in some areas.

Then a third flash, and this time Montag saw what had caused it: a bolt of lightning from the dense clouds struck one of the trucks and incinerated it.

Montag slapped the arm of the townsman beside her, and yelled, "Fall back! Everyone, fall back!"

He didn't move, so she yelled again, pulling at his arm. His body shifted and she saw that most of his face was gone.

On the building across the debris-strewn street, one of the surviving townsfolk got to his feet and began to run. He almost made it to the edge before another bolt of lightning struck, vaporising him.

Montag swore and squirmed about, desperately trying to

keep low as she headed back the way she had come.

More flashes around her, and she thought she could hear screams.

She reached the edge and pushed herself over it head-first, trusting that her Academy training would kick in; she landed on her feet, in a crouch, and began to run.

They were all running now; defending the town against the Earthers was a lost cause.

Twin bolts of lightning blasted the burning wreckage of a truck ahead of her, showering the street with molten metal.

Then someone crashed into Montag from behind, knocking her to the ground. She had barely enough time to register that it was a panic-stricken Earther before the man turned, wide-eyed, and raised a sawn-off shotgun in his left hand, pointed it at her face. He was shouting something; desperate, terrified, his gun-arm trembling. His right hand was a shredded mass of flesh and fractured bone. Spittle flew from his blood-smeared mouth, tears cutting paths through the dirt on his face.

She pointed in the direction of the mine, unable to think of anything else he might be demanding to know.

The man nodded, turned as though he was about to run, then turned back. He again took aim at Montag with his gun, then toppled forward, hitting the ground face-down in front of her.

Montag looked at the ragged hole in his back, then raised her head. Ahead of her, at the centre of the town, Judge Dredd was still in the watchtower, calmly picking off the Earthers one by one, while the unearthly lightning ripped through the streets, getting closer and closer.

She grabbed the Earther's gun, pushed herself to her feet and started to run.

Fifteen

TIME WAS RUNNING out for Ramini. Even this deep inside the mine, the roar of the storm was almost deafening.

She had already sent Eloise back to the entrance to begin shepherding the townsfolk into the mine, but the entrance tunnel wasn't big enough or safe enough for all of them.

Got to be close to the central cavern by now, she said to herself. Eloise had told her how far it was, and Ramini had been cautiously following the curve of the wall.

She crouched and felt around until she found another small stone, picked it up and tossed it ahead of her. It bounced twice. *Not there yet.*

According to Eloise, the tunnel opened onto a wooden gantry fixed around the upper levels of the cavern. The sound of the stones hitting the gantry should be obvious.

A voice called out from ahead, "You still there, Ramini?"

"We are," she shouted back.

"You're operating blind. Why don't you just quit now? The second we see you, you're dead."

Ramini tossed another stone.

"Testing the ground ahead of you? Smart. It's not going to help, though."

"I want to talk to Hanenberger!"

She heard a frantic, murmured conversation, then Alfonsa Hanenberger's voice drifted back to her. "I'm here."

"Why are you doing this?" Ramini called. Another four steps in total darkness. She resisted the urge to use her Justice Department-issue flashlight: that would instantly tell the mercenaries exactly where she was.

"I don't have to answer to you, Judge. You're trespassing in my mine!"

"Why didn't you take the shuttle and get out of town before the storm hit?"

There was no reply. Ramini threw another stone, which landed with a solid *thunk*. "What is it you're hiding, Hanenberger? Some dark secret?" Ramini dropped to her hands and knees and began to crawl forward. "Maybe you *found* something, is that it? If the mine's running dry, what difference does it make to you if the people of Ezekiel take shelter here?"

Ramini's right hand touched the wooden platform. Still crawling, she edged out onto it. "And those hostages you claim to have... How about some proof, huh?"

Hanenberger shouted back, "You're getting closer, Judge! Stop right there or my people will open fire!"

Ramini took a deep breath. She could hear the muffled footsteps of the townsfolk not too far behind her. *If Eloise was right about the lights...*

Ramini stood up, and one of the mercenaries shouted, "There! Do it!"

There was another metallic *clunk*, then muttered swearing.

Thank you, Eloise Crow, Ramini thought, grinning. She crouched once more and fired an incendiary shell across the cavern, angled upwards: the napalm-filled round struck a stalactite and ignited.

The flare from the burning napalm wasn't as strong as Ramini would have liked, but it was enough: it showed two of the mercenaries waiting for her on the far side of the cavern, and—three levels down—Hanenberger and her advisors hiding behind the two other mercenaries. And no hostages.

Ramini fired two heat-seeking shots at the mercs opposite her as she ran. Even before the shots found their targets, the others below were shooting at her.

Further heat-seekers were not an option: by now, the napalm would be hot enough to draw them away from the mercenaries.

Ramini pounded along the platform, heading for a flimsy-looking ladder ahead. The surviving mercenaries' shots ripped through the platform; one of them was smart enough to shoot ahead of her.

But the Judge had been expecting that; she leaped, landed a little heavily, then threw herself forwards, skidding on her stomach right up to the ladder.

The napalm would burn itself out in seconds: she had to finish this before the darkness swamped her.

She fired again, aiming down past the ladder. Armour-piercing shots, aimed at where her memory told her the mercenaries had been standing.

They could have moved, to get a better angle on her or to defend themselves, but she doubted it. They wanted to protect Hanenberger; she was the one with the money.

The echo of Ramini's shots died at the same time as the incendiary flare above faded out.

All that was left was darkness, and Alfonsa Hanenberger's weak voice begging, "Please don't kill me!"

Ramini stood, and shouted out, "Eloise! All clear—start moving them in!"

* * *

DREDD LOOKED DOWN on the town of Ezekiel. There wasn't much of it left standing. To the south, hundreds of desperate Earthers were scrambling over the barricade, swarming through the houses and stores.

He hadn't fired his Lawgiver for almost a minute.

The lightning strikes were getting closer; it was almost a miracle that the watchtower hadn't yet been hit. It was grounded, and Dredd's boots were heavily insulated, so there was a small chance that the lightning would pass by without hurting him, but Dredd decided he didn't want to take the risk. Besides, the winds were still increasing in strength. The watchtower swayed back and forth; it could be only a matter of minutes before it collapsed. Time to abandon the post.

He jumped for the watchtower's ladder and half-slid, half-climbed down.

Before he reached the ground he saw Montag herding a small group of people out of the basement of their lightning-blasted home. She kept watch as they kicked fragments of burning timber out of their paths. The last of them, an older man, seemed immobilised by rage, staring at the scattered remains of his house.

Montag grabbed the man by his collar, trying to drag him away, but he struggled against her, screaming something inaudible. He balled his fists and took a swing at the Judge. She tried to stop him, but his fury leant him speed: one of his punches collided with her jaw, sent her sprawling back into the red-hot embers.

Dredd paused his descent long enough to shoot the old man in the arm.

Montag quickly rolled free of the embers, glanced up toward Dredd, and nodded. She grabbed hold of the man again, and this time he was more compliant.

Dredd raced to catch up with them, and saw O'Donnell doing the same.

The deputy was limping; crude bandages covered a twenty-centimetre gash in his left leg, and what looked like two bullet-holes in his right forearm. He shouted something to Dredd, pointed toward Montag and the old man, then before Dredd could respond, O'Donnell ran up to Montag, hoisted the old man onto his shoulder, and began to awkwardly run in the direction of the mine.

This close to Montag, Dredd could see her uniform was scorched and torn in a dozen places, blood oozing from deep scratches and cuts, her skin blasted raw by the sand. He pressed his helmet against hers, and yelled, "Go with them! Get to the mine!"

She shook her head, pointed toward the stream of Earthers. "There's too many for you to take on!"

"That's not the plan! Now go!"

He shoved Montag away, and watched for a second as she struggled to follow O'Donnell.

His own rough estimates put the number of Earthers somewhere north of two thousand, though Grud only knew how many of them there really were. Or how many were still alive.

To the south, the wind was now whipping bodies—alive and dead—over the barricade, peeling the roofs off buildings, scattering the town with fist-sized chunks of rock and flaming debris.

There was nothing more he could do, Dredd realised. The storm hadn't yet reached its climax: within minutes, the town would be nothing more than rubble.

And thousands of Earthers, hostile or just terrified, would be dead.

He knew what he had to do.

Dredd ran through the streets, heading for the mine. He caught up with Montag, hoisted her into his arms and kept going.

Montag shouted to him, "Dredd, I can walk!"

"Not as fast as I can run! Keep your Lawgiver ready: shoot anyone who's a direct threat!"

They overtook O'Donnell and the old man. Over the howl of the wind, Dredd heard the deputy yelling something to him, but he figured this wasn't the time to stop for clarification.

They rounded a corner and, ahead of them, saw the last of the townsfolk hurrying into the mine. Travis Crow was standing guard at the entrance.

Dredd skidded to a stop, lowered Montag next to him. "Get inside, Montag!" Dredd yelled. "Travis, change of plan—let the Earthers in!"

Travis stared at him for a second. "*What?* It sounded like you said—"

"Let them in—but take their weapons!"

"Dredd, they came here to kill us!"

"Not all of them. Most are just fleeing the storm." Dredd stepped back, suddenly noticing how the howling wind had fallen. "It's over..."

Travis shook his head. "No, it's not. We're in the eye of the storm now... It's going to pick back up in a few seconds, and it'll be just as bad!" Then Dredd saw the remaining colour drain from the man's face. "Oh, crap. It'll be *worse!*"

Dredd turned to look.

Overhead, to the east, a dark cloud was fast approaching. As they watched, the cloud began to break up, and Dredd realised what he was seeing.

The storm had reached the death-belt, and was pulling the floating debris into its wake.

A boulder the size of a family skimmer was ripped away from the death-belt, and began to plummet toward the town.

Then a second, and a third.

The first boulder slammed into the ground in the path of a swarm of panic-filled Earthers. Those at the head of the pack stopped, but those behind kept coming, rushing past the leaders, swamping them.

The second and third boulders crushed Alfonsa Hanenberger's

house. A fourth crashed into the base of the watchtower.

A pair of Earthers—two desperate, terrified women—reached the mine and slowed to a stop, staring at the Judges and Travis, clearly unsure whether their best option was to try to get inside the mine or keep running.

"Get in!" Dredd shouted. "Now!"

A fresh wind surged along the shattered street as O'Donnell, still carrying the old man, emerged from one of the side-streets. The deputy shielded his eyes from the sand with his free arm, and as Dredd watched, O'Donnell's shirt turned to red-soaked shreds. He slowed, began to stagger.

Montag darted out into the street, ducked at the last second to avoid a flying length of timber thicker than her leg, and caught up with O'Donnell. She pulled the old man from his shoulder, and between them they carried him back across the street to the mine entrance.

As Travis and Dredd took hold of the old man, O'Donnell collapsed to his knees, gasping for breath.

Three of the townsfolk emerged from the tunnel, and Dredd recognised them as the people Montag had rescued from the lightning-blasted house.

The old man looked up at them and muttered, "Left me *behind*..."

"Sorry, Pa. We..."

"Yer all outta the will! I'm leavin' everythin' to the deputy here."

Dredd said, "Carry him inside. Move!" He reached down and grabbed hold of O'Donnell's left arm, and helped him to his feet. "You gonna live?"

The deputy grinned. The left side of his face had been blasted raw, and he spat a mouthful of blood and sand onto the ground. "Right arm's useless. I can barely see, not sure I can walk too far... I've had better days."

"You've done your part, O'Donnell. Go on, get inside."

Dredd turned back to the entrance. On the street, more and more Earthers were approaching. Filthy, caked in sweat-soaked dust, covered with lacerations and bruises, they came stumbling, staggering. Some helping each other, some trampling their colleagues.

The wind began to pick up once more, and Dredd screamed, "Inside! All of you! Into the mine!"

He looked at Travis and Montag. "You too."

Another death-belt boulder, this one larger than a train-carriage, came tumbling out of the sky. It ploughed into the Brazen Hussy and kept rolling, crushing a dozen desperate Earthers.

"Move!" Montag shouted at a hesitant young man. She snatched the crossbow out of his hands and tossed it away. "Get in!"

The ground shook as four more massive rocks crashed down from the death-belt overhead, the powerful winds pulling them free of the gravitational anomaly that had kept them aloft for years.

Dredd shouted to Montag and Travis: "Inside, both of you! You've done enough!" He pushed them into the crowd of Earthers clumsily filing in through the mine entrance.

There were more of them coming, from all directions, across what remained of the town, but most of them weren't going to make it. There was nothing more Dredd could do for them.

As he was about to enter the mine himself, he heard a familiar voice coming from the direction of the plaza. He turned to see Ishmael Stinnett, the preacher, awkwardly running toward him.

And then the preacher stopped, as though he knew what was coming next. Later, Dredd wondered if perhaps the old man had a touch of his brother's psi-abilities.

A boulder the size of a truck slammed into the ground a few metres in front of him. If he hadn't stopped, he'd have been crushed.

The preacher darted around the boulder, and—yelling something about "a miracle from blessed Grud and all his perky little angels!"—raced toward Dredd.

A sudden, powerful gale whipped along the street, picked up a pair of shotgun-wielding Earthers, and bowled them straight into the preacher. All three tumbled in a tangled mass along the street before a cross-wind hit them, lifted them instantly into the air, scattered them across the town.

Dredd looked back toward the south. More Earthers coming, though fewer than before.

Overhead, something other than thunder rumbled, and Dredd looked up to see the death-belt disgorging its entire contents, like giant marbles spilling from an invisible tray, directly above the town.

He grabbed hold of two last Earthers—a woman of about his own age, and a ten-year-old girl—and dragged them in through the tunnel entrance.

"Move!" Dredd yelled at the people ahead of him. "Keep it steady, don't rush... But drokkin' *move!*"

The entire tunnel shook, a string of tremors powerful enough that even Dredd was knocked off his feet, then everything went dark.

Sixteen

DREDD SWITCHED ON his flashlight and looked around. The air was thick with dust, but there was no immediate sign of a cave-in.

There was also a lot of crying and screaming from elsewhere in the mine. He started to move on, but felt resistance and looked down to find the ten-year-old girl clinging onto his leg.

He reached down and lifted her to her feet. He could feel her entire body trembling. "Are you hurt?"

She sniffed. "N-no!"

"Then there's no need to cry, is there? We're safe now." To the woman he'd dragged in with her, he said, "You her mother?"

"Her aunt. I'm the only family she has left. Grud *bless* you, Judge! I didn't think we were—"

"That's okay," Dredd said. He patted the little girl on the head: he'd seen people do that to children to comfort them. He straightened up and shouted, "Everyone! Check the people next to you for major injuries! Call out if you find anything, otherwise shut the hell up!"

For a few seconds, silence filled the tunnel, then one-by-one people started to call out: "Broken leg here!" "This man's not breathing!" "There's a lot of blood!"

Again, Dredd yelled: "Anyone with medical training, make yourself known to the people around you! Treat life-threatening injuries first. Everyone else, stay put. I'm going to make my way along the tunnel. If you're not one of my people and you're carrying a weapon, you'll hand it over to me. Anyone got a problem with that?"

By the time Dredd reached Montag and Travis, his arms were laden with almost too many guns, knives, crossbows and swords to carry. He dumped them into Travis's arms. "You two have a new job. Follow me to the central cavern and gather all the weapons you can. Looks like there's going to be a lot more than this. You'll figure out a way to carry them. Any other townsfolk you recognise, recruit them to help."

Montag looked at the pile of weapons. "If we unload the guns we can leave them behind and just carry the ammo."

"Good thinking," Dredd told her. "Someone here will have a backpack. Anyone doesn't feel like handing their weapons over, threaten to shoot them. If they don't take you seriously, make good on the threat. A leg-shot ought to encourage them to comply. Any word from Ramini?"

"Not yet."

Dredd started to move on. "I'll find her."

A few metres down the line, a sixty-year-old woman grabbed his arm as he passed. "May the blessings of Grud and all his saints be on you, Judge!"

"Thank you," Dredd said.

The woman didn't let go. She pulled a medallion from around her neck and pressed it into his hand. "This will keep you safe!"

He looked down at the obviously home-made medallion and resisted the urge to ask, "How? Is it bullet-proof?" Instead, he passed it back to her. "Judges are forbidden to accept gifts, ma'am, but again, thank you."

The lights overhead flickered on, eliciting a roaring cheer that echoed throughout the mine.

By the time Dredd reached the central cavern, he'd been offered five more sacred relics, had his hand shaken two dozen times, turned down eight offers of marriage, and declined to kiss three babies and one dog.

He found Brian O'Donnell on the wooden platform close to the entrance tunnel.

The deputy was cradling his injured right arm as he leaned over the guard-rail, peering down. He grinned at Dredd, then nodded toward the rest of the cavern. "Take a look."

Dredd looked. Every walkway and gantry was crammed with people, most huddled together.

"Been trying to count them..." O'Donnell said. "Figure there's over a thousand. Could be a lot more in the other tunnels. You made the right call, Dredd. Most of the Earthers were only trying to get to safety."

"You able to keep going a little longer, O'Donnell? We've no idea how long we'll be trapped in here, so we need to start taking stock of food and water, figure out a way to ration it."

The deputy nodded. "I can do that." He pointed down over the rail. "Judge Ramini is down there, with Hanenberger."

"Got it. You need help, let me know."

"Will do. Hey, you got a name other than Dredd?"

"Joe."

O'Donnell tried to offer his wounded right hand and winced. "Have to be the left for now..." He grabbed Dredd's hand and shook it firmly. "Good to know you, Joe."

WHEN THE STORM had finally dissipated, Judge Gillen had ordered her squadron of shuttles and H-Wagons to move in on Ezekiel, and then the first report came back from the advance scouts: "Grud... Nothing but rubble and bodies out here."

"Any sign of Dredd in the town?"

"Judge, there's no sign of the *town*."

She had ordered a complete sweep and scan of the region, and could do nothing else but sit back and wait.

Now, she left her shuttle and walked alone through the devastation.

There was barely one brick still resting on another. Anything that hadn't been destroyed by lightning or sand-blasted out of existence by the storm had been crushed by the rocks from the death-belt, many of which had pulverised on impact.

She'd ordered the Judges to spread out on foot, but held no hopes of finding anyone alive.

Her radio beeped. "Gillen here."

"Judge, we've got an incoming craft. Adrian Hanenberger."

"Remind me?"

"Head of the Hanenberger clan. His daughter was in charge of this town."

"Okay. I'll meet him at the..." She looked around. There were no recognisable landmarks. "Just tell him to set down *somewhere*. I'll make my way to him."

A minute later a sleek shuttle landed on what had once been a rudimentary road. Its hatch was opening as Gillen reached it, and a squat, well-dressed eighty-year-old man tentatively stepped out. He paused for a moment, then looked back at the pilot. "You're *certain* that this is the right place?"

"Yes, sir, Mister Hanenberger."

"Huh. All right, then." He turned to face Gillen. "And you are?"

"Judge Gillen."

"Are you a real Judge? What's with the different uniform?"

Gillen didn't feel like explaining herself. "What's your business here, citizen?"

He glowered at her. "You will address me as Mister Hanenberger, young lady, if you know what's good for you."

Gillen relaxed a little, relieved to be in familiar territory. "Threatening a Judge. Six months."

Hanenberger scoffed. "Nonsense. Where's my daughter?"

"We haven't found anyone alive yet."

"She'll have taken refuge in the mine, I expect." The old man looked around. "Where is it?"

Gillen shrugged. "Not a clue."

Hanenberger sighed, and turned back to the shuttle. "James, get the full survey team out here pronto, and our top three— no, make it top *five*—excavation crews. Order our satellites to scan the area, search for any signs of life. There could be others trapped, too. We'll establish a disaster relief area to the east, full medical teams. Set up a refugee camp next to it. Tents, beds, emergency supplies. Call in the heavy machinery to start clearing a path through to the city." He turned back to Gillen. "Does the Justice Department have any problems with that?"

"No."

"Then let's find our people."

ALFONSA HANENBERGER HAD refused to speak to Dredd—or anyone else—until the first shouts started to come back from the entrance tunnel: "There's something moving outside! I can hear machinery!"

"Looks like our rescue team is here," Dredd told her.

He estimated that they'd been trapped for almost an entire day. During that time, countless wounds had been crudely patched, bones had been splinted, and supplies carefully rationed.

There had been thirteen separate fights, one heart-attack, and seven aborted attempts to start a cheerful sing-along.

Now, Hanenberger looked up at Dredd and spoke, "You have no power over me, you know that? Nothing I've done is illegal." She smiled. "I own this town and I make the rules. Even you can't argue with that."

Dredd nodded. "Agreed."

"So once the rescuers break through, I'm free to go."

"Neither myself, Ramini, nor Montag are legally entitled to stop you."

"Good. *That's* what true power is, Judge. In the city, you Judges think that you're in control, but you're sheepdogs at best. You're able to herd the people because they're scared of you, but you don't truly *own* them."

"We don't want to own them."

"Of course you do. You're fascists. You want all the power, and Grud help anyone who stands up to you."

"Two things, Hanenberger. Everyone here knows that you were willing to let them die. I might not be in a position to prosecute you, but you'll find that the inhabitants of the Cursed Earth are not bound by *any* laws. Even in this blighted land it won't be hard to find a dead tree and a few metres of rope. And, second, we know about the new seams," Dredd said.

The woman froze. "What?"

Dredd glanced down over the platform's guard-rail. "On your most recent survey your geologist discovered a huge, untouched seam of iridium that should yield at least as much ore again as the mine has already given. You've hidden this from everyone, including your own family. You've told them that this mine is played out."

Hanenberger dry-swallowed. "No one knows... How can you possibly know that?"

"An old man came to the town, just ahead of the storm," Dredd said. "Abraham Stinnett. You know his brother Ishmael, the preacher. Abraham is a telepath. Judge Ramini figured you were hiding something, so she asked Stinnett to scan your mind as you slept. You had the geologist killed, along with anyone else who knew about the new seam. You've also bought a plot of worthless land forty kilometres west of here, where you intend to set up a fake mine. You plan to take the ore from here and secretly transport it to the new mine."

Her hand trembling, the woman wiped at her mouth. "This is still my land. Everything on it—and *under* it—belongs to me. Everything!"

"Actually, it's your *family's* land. You intend to steal from them. And since the ore is the object of a planned crime, I'm confiscating all of it."

"You can't!"

Dredd leaned closer. "Stop me."

Seventeen

Two hours passed before the rescue teams were able to break through to the mine, and it was a further hour before Judge Dredd escorted Alfonsa Hanenberger, the last of the survivors, to the surface.

Her father had been waiting for her, and broke into a grin. "Last one out! Of course you are. A true Hanenberger is like a captain, last to desert the sinking ship!"

Dredd said, "Seems self-delusion is hereditary."

The old man turned to him. "Explain yourself."

"Your daughter's arms bear a number of bruises where I had to physically restrain her from scrambling over the others in order to be the first out."

"How *dare* you! I'll have your *badge* for this!"

Dredd took a step closer to him. "Your daughter is a mutant, and therefore by law is denied entry to Mega-City One. The fact that she has apparently somehow circumvented this law on multiple occasions will be the subject of a full investigation. If you are found to have any complicity in that crime, you will be prosecuted."

The man jabbed at Dredd's chest with his index finger. "Don't you threaten *me*, boy! Don't you know who I am?"

Dredd grabbed his hand, twisted it, forced him down onto his knees. "Adrian Hanenberger, you are under arrest for assaulting a Mega-City One Judge. Two years."

A voice from the side called, "Let him go. You no longer have the power to arrest anyone."

Dredd opened his hand, and turned to see Judge Gillen approaching, with three other SJS Judges following close behind. "Gillen. Heard you were on the way."

"Joseph Dredd, I'm in possession of verified witness statements of your attempt to intimidate citizen Stacie Quasarano of Brendan Behan Block. You are hereby dismissed from the Justice Department of Mega-City One. You will be stripped of your weapons and all equipment. Resistance will be considered an act of aggression and will be met with equal or greater force. Do you understand?"

"I understand," Dredd said, "but I'm invoking my right to protest my innocence." He stepped away from Hanenberger, and stood with his arms outstretched at his sides.

"Protestation noted," Gillen said.

Two of the SJS Judges approached him. One unclipped his belt, the other removed his Lawgiver and boot-knife.

"Citizen Dredd, for the crime of unlawful intimidation and abuse of your position as a Judge, you are sentenced to thirteen years in an iso-cube."

As the SJS Judges cuffed Dredd's arms behind his back, someone pushed their way through the gathering crowd shouting, "Let him go!"

Dredd turned to see O'Donnell striding toward Gillen. "He's just saved over a thousand people, and you're arresting him!"

"Correct," Gillen said. "Interference with an arrest is an offence, citizen."

"I'm not a citizen of your damn city, so you can shove *that* attitude where the bees don't buzz. What's he done?"

"None of your concern. Move along or there will be consequences."

O'Donnell grinned. "Oh, really? You and your pals here are going to stop me, are you?" Louder, he said, "You're going to stop *all* of us? We owe this man our lives. If you think you're taking him away, think again."

"The deputy's right," a woman's voice called from the crowd, and Dredd saw that it was Eloise Crow. "You want to take us all on?"

More and more of the townsfolk, and many of the Earthers, joined in with the protest, until Dredd yelled, "Enough! I appreciate the support, but Judge Gillen is operating within the law of Mega-City One and conducting a legal arrest."

O'Donnell said, "Joe, you can't let this happen!"

"You have no idea whether I'm innocent of the charge," Dredd said. "I know Judge Gillen. She has a well-deserved reputation as an efficient and accomplished Judge. If she has reason to believe that I'm guilty, then I agree with her actions."

The old man, Abraham Stinnett, pushed his way through the crowd, clutching the hand of his daughter as he pulled her behind him. "But you *are* innocent, Judge. I can see that."

"Psychic," Dredd explained to Gillen.

"Unless he's registered with the Department," Gillen said, "I can't take his word. Besides, the testimonies of Stacie Quasarano and her family have been verified by our own psychics."

Abraham asked, "What, exactly, do those people say that Dredd has done?"

"We're not under any obligation to explain our actions to you or anyone else," Gillen said.

"Then how about explaining them to *me*?" Judge Ramini asked. "As a courtesy. One Judge to another."

Gillen hesitated for a second, then said, "Joseph Dredd's brother Rico was involved in a physical relationship with

Stacie Quasarano. After the relationship ended, Ms Quasarano apparently refused to accept that and began to pester Rico. Joseph learned of her behaviour, and threatened Ms Quasarano with physical harm if she did not let the matter drop."

"Never happened," Dredd said.

"Four Psi-Division Judges have separately scanned the memories of the Quasarano family and have verified that their recollections of the event are true and consistent." Gillen tried to stare him down. "It *did* happen. And it proves you were aware of Rico's activities and chose not to report or arrest him. That makes you an accomplice to many, if not *most*, of his crimes. Consider yourself lucky that you're only getting an iso-cube and not joining your brother on the shuttle to Titan."

Dredd nodded slowly. "I see. Judge Gillen, I'm not doubting the report of the Psi-Judges, or the recollections of the Quasarano family, but has it occurred to you that Rico and I are physically identical and therefore it could have been him who intimidated the family?"

"Of course it has. But when the incident took place Rico was logged as elsewhere in the sector. Your own whereabouts is uncertain for much of that time."

"And what was Rico allegedly doing at that time?"

"Taking down a tap-gang operating in Dido Westerbeck Block."

"I remember that." Dredd said. "I was the one who initiated the arrest; Rico joined me later to mop-up, and he offered to file the report. Clearly, he switched our names to give himself an alibi. You can have the Psi-Judges scan me if you want proof. If you'd been doing your job, you'd already have scanned Rico to verify it."

Judge Montag said, "The transport to Titan doesn't leave for another twelve days, Judge Gillen. You could order Psi-Division to scan Rico *now.*"

Gillen took a step back. She pulled off her helmet and ran her hand over her hair while she stared at Dredd. "All right... Can't hurt to take that angle. But you remain cuffed and under guard until I hear back from Psi-Div."

"Wouldn't have it any other way," Dredd said.

OVER THE NEXT few hours, every survivor of the storm was examined by Adrian Hanenberger's medical staff, and assigned temporary accommodation in the refugee camp.

Dredd spent this time sitting on the fractured remains of one of the death-belt boulders, constantly watched by the SJS Judges, his arms still cuffed behind his back.

As night fell, O'Donnell approached Dredd again. "Joe... they found Esteban's body."

Dredd nodded. "Figured he didn't make it."

The deputy sat down next to Dredd. "Some of the others were saying he fought like a maniac against the Earthers. Even the Earthers themselves were impressed with him."

"He was a good man. And I know he was your friend. I'm sorry for your loss, O'Donnell."

"Yeah... They found the preacher, too. Guess he's on his way to Grud now. Just hope that Grud has the patience to put up with him."

"Anyone else identified?"

"Conra and Lauren Featherman. They hid out in their basement, along with some of the others. All dead... Joe, what's going to happen to Hanenberger? Alfonsa, I mean, not her old man."

"She can't return to the city, but I'm sure her father will set her up somewhere safe. And far from here."

"He said he's going to rebuild Ezekiel," O'Donnell said. "With much greater security, too. He said everyone who wants to stay on is welcome. I think a lot of them will go for it. Not me, though. I've had enough."

"What will you do?"

"I'll find something. There's always a need for pilots to run supplies between Mega-City One and Mega-City Two. Trouble is, the shipping companies aren't too keen on hiring people who've grown up in the Cursed Earth... Don't suppose you'd put in a good word for me? That'd be against Justice Department policy, right?"

"No, but right now I'm not in any position to make promises. If the charges against me are dropped, I'll look into it."

O'Donnell patted Dredd on the arm, and stood up. "Good man. Appreciate that. Hey, it's just a pity that you only recruit five-year-old kids to be cadets. I reckon I'd have made an awesome Judge."

"Unlikely," Dredd said. "You lack discipline."

O'Donnell smiled, and as he began to walk away, Dredd called to him, "O'Donnell, what was it you were trying to tell me during the storm, when you were carrying that old man?"

"Oh, that. Yeah, I said, 'If I don't make it, tell Novena that her horse is safe.' I heard the horse as I was heading for Hanenberger's shuttle. I couldn't just leave here there to die... So I put her on the shuttle, set it on auto-pilot. One of your H-Wagons has gone after it. All going well, the horse will be fine."

"You used the shuttle to save a *horse?*"

"Yep. I could see that it meant a lot to her. And, you know, she's sweet. I like her."

"I was right. You'd never have made it as a Judge, O'Donnell."

O'Donnell laughed. "Yeah, maybe. See you around, Joe. And... call me Red, okay? All my friends do."

"THE PSI-JUDGES HAVE confirmed that Rico set you up. All charges are dismissed," Judge Gillen said to Dredd, and gestured for her colleagues to unlock his cuffs.

"Glad to hear it," Dredd said. "But not surprised." He stood up and stretched.

It was night, and their breaths misted in the cold air.

"So the investigation is closed?" Dredd asked.

"For now, yes. But... One thing has become very clear from all this. Cloned Judges are more trouble than they're worth if we can't tell them apart."

Dredd looked around at the devastated town. "What'll happen to all these people while the town is rebuilt?"

"Hanenberger has said they'll build temporary accommodation. And the new town will be mostly underground, he said, which should help shield it from the weather." She shrugged. "He's pompous and full of self-importance, but he's not a fool. I think he'll make good on his promises. Especially now that the Department will be watching him a lot more closely." Gillen nodded toward a waiting H-Wagon. "Let's go."

Another SJS Judge was waiting at the H-Wagon's ramp: he handed Dredd back his weapons and utility belt.

As Dredd clipped the belt back into place, Gillen said, "Hurry it up. You, Montag and Ramini are due back in Sector 198. According to Sector Chief Benzon, your next shift starts in four hours. There's no rest for the wicked, huh?"

"None," Dredd said, slipping his Lawgiver into his boot-holster, "and no shelter from the law."

About the Author

Irish Author **Michael Carroll** is a former chairperson of the Irish Science Fiction Association and has previously worked as a postman and a computer programmer/systems analyst. A reader of *2000 AD* right from the very beginning, Michael is the creator of the acclaimed *Quantum Prophecy/Super Human* series of superhero novels for the Young Adult market.

His current comic work includes *Judge Dredd* for *2000 AD* and *Judge Dredd Megazine* (Rebellion), and *Jennifer Blood* (Dynamite Entertainment). *Judge Dredd Year Two: The Righteous Man* is his third book for Abaddon Books.

www.michaelowencarroll.com

DOWN AND OUT

MATTHEW SMITH

MEGA-CITY ONE
2081 A.D.

Joe.

There was a dark kernel at the core of his being into which he could retreat. No; *retreat* was the wrong word. That suggested weakness—that he was running away from the pain. He wasn't yet prepared to admit that he'd been beaten, or that he was even engaged in a struggle. He was consolidating.

He'd always known the calm centre was there. It was what made him so efficient; this ability to compartmentalise. He could shut off external stimuli, zero in on the essence that mattered: The Law. Duty. The badge. That's what drove him, made him what he was. It was his engine, his beating heart, and that which he turned to when he needed... purity, he supposed. A clear line of thought, unsullied or complicated by human concerns.

Joe.

They'd taught him this in the Academy, of course; one of the many training exercises the tutors employed to shape these young children they'd taken charge of and turn them into emotionless guardians. Totems, bound by duty to the people they stood apart from and passed judgement on. They were equally servants and captors, there to protect as well as rule through fear. The dichotomy was why it was so important cadets were taught how to shelve their feelings. Put them in a box deep inside, close the lid, and leave them there. Don't question the system. Justice was required to be delivered by a firm, unwavering, objective hand; it could not run the risk of being impaired by doubt or empathy.

Joe.

The same went for injury. The Academy's extensive Applied Violence module was very thorough in teaching its charges as much how to receive pain as how to dish it out. No cadet graduated without a broken bone somewhere on their body, courtesy of a tutor's daystick; some would be barely into their teens and have already experienced the sensation of a live Lawgiver round passing through muscle. Suffering was the fire that forged you; or rather, how you dealt with that suffering determined the kind of Judge you'd be. Push it down, ride it out, don't let it consume you. Strength of will was everything. The uniform was everything. The Law was everything. It was greater than he was. He had to deal with it, prove that he was in control. He was trying...

Joe.

...he was really trying. He couldn't let it win (no; there was no struggle, remember?). It was just him and his resolve. Any minute now, he was going to force himself up. He was going to put one hand beneath him and lever himself from the ground. Any minute now.

Any—

Joe.

Dredd opened his eyes. Through the fractured visor a silhouette loomed close. His mind scrabbled for his gun even if he knew his hand wouldn't be able to hold it; any messages from his brain were ignored by the rest of his body. He couldn't move. His breath rasped and something rattled in his chest, bringing a fresh wave of pain. He coughed, a coppery taste on his tongue. He must've visibly winced; the figure said, *Stay calm, little brother.*

"Rico?" The name emerged as a croak.

It's okay, I'm here, the figure said, and Dredd felt a hand hold his. *I'll stay with you.*

"Stay...?"

We'll stick together. Like clones. Right to the end.

"What do you mean?" He gripped the hand tighter till the joints creaked.

You're dying, Joe.

One

9.16 am

"How do you feel?"

The question shouldn't have caught him by surprise; after all, the session had been leading up to it. There was a grim inevitability to the counsellor's words. But expectation didn't soften the unease any. While it would've belittled the uniform to have squirmed, the soft plasti-leather couch in which he'd been instructed to recline suddenly felt unaccountably warm and uncomfortable. He was unused to luxury of this nature; it didn't sit well with him. It smacked of indolence, indulgence. No-one made the tough calls—the hard, necessary decisions—from such a chair.

Like sentencing your brother to twenty years. That required backbone, didn't it?

All the same, Perrineau picked up something in Dredd's expression as soon as she'd said it—a muscle twitch, a slight grimace. The young Judge could picture the wheels turning behind the auxiliary's blandly composed face. One hand jotted notes, though her eyes barely left Dredd, as if she was studying an animal behind glass, waiting for it to flinch, to strike, to betray any sign of its mood. She may as well have been poking him with a stick, though he knew her intention wasn't to goad; she just didn't understand him. She'd been chipping away at him—stoney-faced, some said, though he struggled to see the humour others evidently found in the epithet—for over forty-five minutes, and this was the first time she'd seen a crack appear.

Dredd knew she wasn't going to let this go when the pen stopped moving and was set down. Fingers steepled under her chin, head cocked to one side, Perrineau was inviting an answer, one he was struggling to formulate the words for. What did she mean, anyway? How did he feel? Or *how* did he feel? The response to the latter was that he couldn't, not really. He didn't *know* how. He didn't have the apparatus. As a consequence, trying to vocalise what he was experiencing amounted to counter-programming.

He'd queried the decision to send him here, of course. It seemed a supreme waste of resources and a massive impingement on his street time. He'd had a year now under his belt as a full-eagle Judge, and that was enough to whet the appetite, to keep calling him back, to make him aware of how crotchety and impatient he became when he wasn't on the sked. It was where he belonged, and distractions such as this grated, to put it mildly. But he was in no position to disobey a senior command; he was still a rookie in the eyes of many, regardless of his lineage, and was expected to toe the line. When Goodman had told him to go make an appointment with Perrineau, he'd tried to respectfully decline, aware that the Chief Judge had his best interests at heart. The old man was adamant, though, and would brook no argument; he said it was a policy that would reap rewards. Judges should be psychologically fit as well as physically.

He hadn't been slow to pick up the inference about

Rico. Dredd's clone-brother's descent into corruption and criminality—leading to his arrest and indictment to Titan—was cause for concern at every level of the Grand Hall. That the Fargo bloodline should contain such a potential flaw, and for one of the Department's leading lights to have fallen so far, had massive repercussions for their genetics programme; certainly, it shed serious doubt on whether there was any future in further offspring from the Father of Justice's DNA. It had hit them hard, at the very heart of their system, suggested their foundations were built on a faultline. The powers-that-be had done their best to cover up the full extent of Rico's exploits—though they'd been unable to prevent it leaking into the media; the lowlifes his brother employed or did business with were only too happy to sell their stories about the Judge on the take—but they couldn't afford it to happen again. Suddenly, Dredd—even though he'd been the one to pull his sibling in, and sentence him—was under a lot more scrutiny. His passion and devotion to the Law couldn't be questioned, but then again neither could Rico's when they'd both graduated; all it took was a nudge down a road from which there was evidently no return, and all that training was channelled into theft and murder.

Hence the brain-shrinking session Dredd had been press-ganged into this morning. It wasn't enough that they wanted to ensure Rico was the only bad apple; they also wanted to determine how the arrest had affected *him*, whether Dredd's judgement had been compromised, whether there'd be any personal fallout. Dredd found it facile and beneath him, but he'd listened and responded as instructed. Truth was, Rico had broken the Law and brought the uniform into disrepute: there could've been no other possible outcome. He would've been doing a disservice to both himself and all that the badge stood for if he hadn't imposed the maximum sentence. That Rico was his brother—more than his brother—had stung, there was no question of that; all the pair had been through together since

Booth, since the nukes had dropped, had cemented a bond between them that had seen them through the Academy. He'd thought it unshakeable, and thus was cognizant of the tragedy of the situation; that he'd ended the career—and, to all intents and purposes, the life—of the person that had been closest to him. But what he'd done had been right, and that was the moral anchor that he clung to. It had been necessary. Why Rico had chosen to turn his back on all he'd been created to be, they would probably never know; but the important thing was that he was stopped, and he'd been punished for his misdemeanours.

"Well?" Perrineau persisted.

"Justice was done," Dredd replied.

"That's all?"

"That's all that matters."

10.05 am

IT WAS GOOD to be back on the sked, clear away the cobwebs. He'd spent too long in that stultifying room. He didn't think Perrineau got the answers that she'd hoped for—in truth, he got the impression she'd found him vexing—and was no doubt already filing a report to Goodman that Joe Dredd's psychological profile was impossible to catalogue. Whether that would make the old man happy or not, he couldn't say; but if she'd wanted a case study worthy of doctoral thesis she'd been better off interviewing Rico. He loved the sound of his own voice. Indeed, incredible as it seemed, his clone had attained a level of notoriety akin to a folk hero amongst the easily swayed—which was, to be honest, half the city. He did exude a certain charisma that the criminal meatheads fell for, Dredd had to admit, which probably explained how he'd managed to operate for so long unopposed. Already, journalists were submitting applications to travel to Titan and get a face-to-face with the new inmate; they were more than a little amused by the embarrassment that his arrest had brought on Grand Hall, and keen for juicy copy. Dredd found the whole circus nauseating, though he supposed he shouldn't have been surprised. Every psycho and miscreant he'd put away in the cubes had a fan club waiting somewhere in the wings.

He just wanted to be out enforcing the Law, not stymied by bureaucracy or enduring performance reviews; he was already gathering something of a reputation of not doing his fair share of the paperwork. He didn't attempt to deflect the guilt of that charge: he knew full well it wasn't his forte. But practical judgement dispensed on the streets was what he believed should be the priority—leave the pen-pushing to those with an aptitude for it. Anyone on the receiving end of this proclamation would roll their eyes when his back was turned, and then contemplate the steadily-mounting stack of arrest sheets. Many felt he received preferential treatment because of his lineage, though they never said so within earshot, and few could argue with his exceptional record. It was his second year as a full-eagle Judge, and he was putting some veterans to shame.

He accelerated as he hit the Siegel exit-ramp, leaning in to Atwood Throughway as he merged with the traffic, feeling at home surrounded by the Lawmaster's comforting roar. It enveloped him. He flexed his biceps, straightened his back, welcoming the wind whipping past his visor, bringing with it the scent trails of exhaust fumes and factory run-off, burnt rubber and seared hotties, and eased his bike between a pair of hover-trucks. It was moments like this that he felt the most free, furthest from the politics of the Grand Hall. At every opportunity he liked to escape the central sectors and head into the outlying districts; any excuse to experience the metropolis opening up before him. It was what made his job the greatest calling any person could aspire to, this feeling of control.

He cast a glance at the other vehicles racing alongside him, aware that the drivers were conscious of him too, the Judge's mere presence enough to maintain decent behaviour. He could probably find something on any of them if he pulled them over, but for now he was content to ride and exude the authority that kept them in line. In any case, he had his eye on a dark saloon roadster four cars ahead; nothing especially untoward about its appearance, but it was keeping a steady pace that suggested it was trying not to draw attention to itself. He'd already run the registration through the system and come back with switched plates, the name on the purchase docket almost certainly a fake. His instincts were twitching, but he didn't want to intervene just yet; instead, he kept his gaze fixed on its smoked windows and followed at a discreet distance, matching its speed.

It peeled off at the next intersection, heading downtown through a dilapidated area of Sector 9—known locally as the Strickland estate—and Dredd had to hold off some to avoid appearing conspicuously in the driver's rear-view mirror. It was moving particularly carefully, and he got the sense that whoever was inside was looking for an address. It kept pausing at each tenement block, before eventually pulling up on a corner before one of the old pre-war apartment complexes, its façade pockmarked with age and weapons fire, many of the windows shuttered or boarded-up. Dredd couldn't get any closer on his Lawmaster, so instead brought it to a halt a block away and dismounted, watching as the driver and his passenger emerged.

They were a pair of squirrelly looking creeps, visibly stoned on something, which would account for their over-cautiousness. Stepping round to the rear of their car, they wrenched open the back doors and each pulled a container from within, clearly struggling with the weight. They staggered into the building's main entrance, glancing around to check they had no witnesses; the duo might as well have had 'guilty' written in Day-Glo colours on their backs.

The lawman set off at a trot, drawing his sidearm. "Control—

Dredd. Investigating suspicious delivery, Trenmar lux-apts on Strickland. Am engaging."

"*That's a rog,*" his comm answered in his ear.

He paused at the vehicle and cast an eye inside—there were a couple more boxes nestled in the space behind the seats. He looked briefly towards the block, discerned no movement, then yanked a container forward onto the tailgate, feeling the cold even through the insulation of his gloves. He tugged on the lid with his left hand and it cracked open a touch, expelling a blast of dry ice, instantly fogging his visor; he swiped it clear and sighted his Lawgiver on whatever lay within.

The head gazed back at him with a lifeless stare, frost limning its eyebrows and lashes, pupils and lips grey, skin sallow. The freezing process had captured the victim's expression at the point of death—or at the point his neck was severed clean off his shoulders, whichever had come first—and there was a degree of understandable surprise and consternation in the way the mouth had dropped open and the forehead had furrowed. Ice crystals gleamed in his hair. Dredd reached in and pushed it to one side to see what else was in there: a pair of hands neatly stacked like crockery, a wedding ring encrusted around one finger. He let the lid drop and turned back to the block.

He edged through the doors, gun at the ready. 'Lux-apts' was a joke—it had been many years since this had been desirable housing. It stank of rot and neglect, the entire subsector fallen to ruin, where the past hadn't been entirely cemented over. After the nukes had dropped, and once Booth had been run out of town and Justice Department had taken over, the metropolis had grown and developed, pushing north and south to accommodate the swelling population: eight hundred million, at the last count. The gleaming starscrapers that grasped at the heavens and the tangle of meg-ways and zoom-lines that encircled them were just as much a distraction from the forgotten tenements as they were a solution; Old New York may lie beneath their feet, but the Mega-City was still a patchwork of ancient and modern, of destitute, ravaged areas dwarfed by aggressive expansion.

People had to live somewhere, however, especially with much of the country decimated, though the new blocks—Mia Farrow, Ricardo Montalban—were well out of many cits' price range. It grated with Dredd's sense of justice that a lot of the blocks currently being constructed were not intended for the majority of the populace that needed them; the Judges had taken office on the understanding that they would protect its citizens, and if they couldn't house them they were doing them a disservice. But that was the way of things, it seemed: what was right often collided with what was viable, and those caught in the fallout suffered the most, reduced to seeking shelter in borderline-condemned properties such as these. From the sky MC-1 gleamed, but there were those who were forced to exist in its shadows.

Dredd stepped into the entrance foyer, the floor cracked and littered with refuse, the walls rent in places and exposing wiring innards. The lighting looked like it had long stopped working, leaving the interior in gloom, though the infra-red function in his helmet enabled him to penetrate the murk. Moving quietly, he followed two sets of glowing red footprints down a corridor, casting glances to either side at the firmly closed apartment doors, aware that anything could be lurking behind them. One opened a sliver and a curious eye regarded him as he passed, and was quickly shut again when he swung his gun in its direction.

The footprints stopped a few yards later at a doorway which had been hastily fitted with brand-new locks and bolts. He backed against the wall, out of the periphery of the spyhole, and briefly tested the solidity of the wood—he wouldn't be able kick it in without some assistance. He fished in his belt pouch and retrieved a pair of small, circular limpet mines, which he attached near the hinges, thumbing a ten-second fuse on the digital display. Double-checking the ammo selector on his gun, he stood back and waited for the big boom.

The charges shredded the door as they detonated, and Dredd slammed his boot into what remained, knocking the warped wood to the ground. The two creeps he'd seen making the delivery were caught with their dicks in their hands—or rather someone else's dick, in one case; the small organ glittered like a popsicle. Their eyes widened when they found themselves staring down a Lawgiver barrel.

"Hands in the air! Now!" Dredd commanded.

The perps complied instantly, arms shooting above their heads, silvery talisman still gripped in one of their fists.

"Drop that," the Judge muttered, and the guy raised his eyes at it sheepishly before tossing it back into the box, where it landed with a clink.

Dredd moved forward into the apartment, gun trained on the pair. It was barely furnished, little more than a shell, and clearly not used for habitation. What space there was had been given over to stacks of the same containers and a couple of industrial, tomb-like freezer units plugged into the wall, which rumbled quietly in the background. There had to be at least a dozen missing persons cases waiting to be cleared here. It was quite the backstreet operation: too organised and well stocked, Dredd considered, to be the handiwork of a couple of bozos like this. They had to be just the delivery men, which suggested they took their orders from the brains—or at least the less chemically-befuddled leader—of the outfit.

"You," the lawman said to the scraggily-bearded meathead on the right, motioning with his weapon. "Anyone else on the premises?"

The creep rolled his eyes to one side, towards an adjoining room behind a closed door. The forefinger of one upraised hand pointed discreetly in the same direction. Whoever was in there couldn't have failed to be alerted to the Judge's entrance.

"Hey, man, come on," his partner whispered. "I know it looks bad, but we ain't got a choice in this; w-we just do what we're told. We just pick this stomm up—we ain't killers or nothin'."

"Shut up and move over there," Dredd growled, beckoning for them to sidle away from the next room. He quickly patted them down, finding nothing in their overjaks. He fished for his cuffs on his belt, and chucked them towards the duo, the whiny guy catching them. "Put them on, one wrist each. Then sit down with your backs against each other."

"Look—" the perp started, doing as instructed regardless.

"I thought I told you to shut up. Not a sound, understand?"

It was at that point that the third occupant of the apartment came out blasting. The first shot tore through the door and punched a hole in the wall above his prisoners. Plaster, masonry and dust rained down on them; yelling and panicking, they tried to scoot out of the way, pulling uselessly in opposite directions. Dredd booted them onto their sides, where they lay sobbing, then ducked low and circled around the doorway. Another shot blew apart the latch, and the door swung open on one hinge. It listed for a moment, then a figure came barrelling through and tore it down completely. Dredd followed the figure's trajectory and pumped three Standard Execution rounds after it, but it disappeared behind a freezer unit.

"This is the Law," he said, gun trained on where he surmised the perp was hiding. "Drop the weapon and come out with your hands raised. You will get no further warning."

No response. He moved closer, aware that the appliances ruled out a hotshot; there'd be the risk the bullet would boomerang back and strike him as the nearest heat source. He glanced to his left and saw an open container. He reached in carefully and retrieved what appeared to be an expertly removed lung, encased in a vacuum-pak. It shifted beneath his fingers, already starting to defrost. He hefted it once then slung it over the freezer and took a single shot, piercing the pak and spraying brown blood and dark matter in a wide arc. He heard a cry of disgust, and his perp clambered to their feet to avoid the shower, revulsion temporarily overriding safety.

Dredd had a bead on her as soon as she appeared—a wild-haired woman in her fifties, surprisingly light on her feet considering she was more than several pounds into the obese category. She was wearing a kind of smock, covered in what he judged to be human stains, and she was wiping gore streaks off her face, still holding the shotgun.

"Drop it," he barked, knowing even as he said it that she wouldn't cooperate. Half blind, she swung round at the sound of his voice, finger on the trigger, and he fired without hesitation, drilling an SE slug through her skull. She hit the floor with a thump.

He crossed through the shattered door and found a makeshift laboratory-stroke-operating theatre: the shelves were lined with jars and medical equipment, a heart monitor and several oxygen cylinders stood by the wall, and in the centre were two gurneys that had seen better days. Upon one, hooked up to a saline drip, lay an unconscious male eldster, covered up to his neck by a green sheet. As Dredd got closer, he saw that one of the cit's eyes was missing: just a riven, bloodied black hole. On a tray nearby stood a solution-filled beaker in which floated an eyeball, optic nerve trailing after it. Given the freshness of the organ, he guessed it hadn't belonged to the patient. Dredd checked the old guy's pulse and found a weak sign, then headed back into the main apartment, where the two delivery creeps were still whimpering under a film of filth.

"Control, need catch-, meat- and med-wagons to Trenmar," he muttered into his comm. "Uncovered a considerable organ-legging operation. Could do with a forensics team here too—multiple body parts from numerous victims, will require some piecing together."

"Sh-she was just trynna help, man," the whinger said.

"People round here, they can't afford the insurance, can't go to the hospitals. They needed a cheap op, th-they came to her. She was savin' lives best way she knew how, that's all…"

Dredd didn't reply, merely surveyed the damage in the room, Perrineau's words from earlier that morning coming back to him. How *did* he feel?

He looked at the blood splatter. The simple answer was that he couldn't afford to.

Two

10.33 am

HE STUCK AROUND at the scene for the catch-wagon to cart away the two perps and for forensics to do their work. Curiosity made him linger. It didn't take much encouragement for the creeps to talk while they waited, though what they knew was frustratingly sparse: couriers, basically, instructed to pick up body parts from specific collection points. A first-year cadet could tell that these two were not capable of murder, much less dismemberment, and they freely admitted the only way that they could handle the deliveries was to be wrecked on Banana City Brown (both were holding, and Dredd added a few years for possession on top of the organ-legging charges, though neither seemed to care by this point). They'd done more than two dozen of these runs in the past year, and they'd never met the killer, or had any clue to their identity, stating with some vehemence that the dead woman—Mama 'Doc' Carrington— wasn't guilty either. The Judge suspected this was true, though the kills were almost certainly carried out at her behest; she was more than likely contracting a reliable out-of-sector hitman to keep her supplied.

The doltish pair seemed to have no shortage of respect for Carrington, believing that she was only doing what was necessary to come to the aid of those that would otherwise be neglected. Dredd ran the woman's details through his bike computer: she'd been trained as a med-assistant over at St Bart's in Sector 12 but had been made redundant a couple of decades ago. Since then, she'd barely appeared on the system, falling through the cracks like so many in this twilight world. Employment records would be sketchy to the point of non-existent that close to the war, and would probably lead nowhere, but he had a fancy that her hired associate was also connected to the hospital—the victims were too cleanly disassembled for the perp not to know his way around the human anatomy. Dredd made a mental note to chase down KAs and cross-reference them with the targets, once they'd been fully ID'd. Could be that they'd been specifically chosen—rare blood group, low rad-count, healthy genes; info that someone with access to med-records could determine— rather than random snatches off the street.

He watched as the delivery goons were shipped off to incarceration, where they'd be interrogated for locations and details. Surveillance footage would be studied, witnesses canvassed. The old boy, head heavily bandaged, was being similarly hurriedly loaded into the back of a wagon, the attending med-Judge diagnosing him as going into toxic shock, infection running rampant. Given the state of the apartment, Dredd wasn't surprised. He wondered exactly how much good the cherished 'Doc' was actually doing in this stommhole of an operating theatre; for all her laudable intentions, she was surely responsible for many a botched job, killing as much as curing. How many had she seen over the years, the injured and infirm who couldn't afford the health insurance or didn't want to draw the attention of the Judges?

He looked around the rockcrete canyons, at the equally destitute blocks opposite, and pictured Carrington's patients dying alone and in pain, stitches unknitting, limbs blackening, so far from the reaches of the med-services. Ghosts haunting their own apartments, undisturbed in their tombs until the city finally decided to bulldoze the whole sub-sector. These forgotten citizens were no more than shadows on the wall, the war's living dead that may as well have been atomised by one of Booth's missiles for all the mark they made on the metropolis. It was a marginalised existence beyond the reach or control of Justice Department. Dredd felt a restless urge to put it right, but it seemed outside the capabilities of just one Judge.

He shook his head, turning back inside. Forensics were still piecing together the remains that has been gathered from the doc's lab. McCready saw him enter, put down a jar of something old and shrivelled, and wandered over.

"Quite the haul," he said.

"What's the count so far?"

"At least ten different bodies, in variable states of decomposition. Despite the freezers and pickling solutions, she wasn't much good at keeping the parts preserved. Some of them date back a couple of years—no wonder the eldster had septicaemia, she was trying to graft some seriously rank tissue."

"Working with what she had," Dredd mused, watching heads, legs and a string of ears being bagged.

"Yeah, well, Shapiro's Hottie Emporium this ain't. Hell, a beefalo slaughterhouse is more hygienic. I'm amazed *anyone* walked out of here after she'd finished with them."

"You managed to run any DNA traces yet?"

"Still on it. Something of a jigsaw puzzle. I'm fairly sure none of them are local; looks like they were imported from the outlying sectors. We'd be talking about abductions and missing persons logged across city in the last twenty-four months. No easy task."

Dredd grunted in agreement. "How long till you come up with some names?"

"Few hours at least."

"Okay, keep me informed." He cast one last eye around the room, then headed into the welcome fresh air.

Standard operating procedure would be to conduct some door-to-doors, he thought as he swung his bike around, see who else had benefited (or not, as the case may be) from the ministrations of the good doctor, or at least find out how many were aware of what she was up to. The chumps he'd arrested made it sound like she was a local hero—the backstreet shaman where surgery came with complimentary blood poisoning. Chances are the cits from around here wouldn't be too pleased to learn that he'd gunned her down, no matter what she'd infected them with, or how many poor saps had to die to keep her in the organ business. Down here there was a protect-your-own mentality; a not unexpected resentment towards the glittering Mega-City crowding the sky overhead that manifested in a closing of ranks. He'd been taught crowd psychology at the Academy, mastered the ability to read a civilian's body language, but all the same, the cits were alien to him at times: selfish, tribal, gullible. He still found it difficult to gauge their thought processes, understand them. He'd been schooled in the art of pre-empting what their intentions were, but couldn't say *why* they did what they did. That was a part of human nature that escaped him.

Morphy had told him once that flatfooting it amongst the populace was part of being a good Judge—not every case could be solved with a bullet. Sometimes it meant tedious, menial police work that involved engaging with the public, as frustrating and aggravating as that could be. It was meant to build up your people skills, enable you to approach the dangerous on their own terms, defuse potential scenarios with minimum risk. It was typically sage wisdom from an old hand like Morph; perhaps it came from an earlier age, or Dredd was simply too impatient. Whichever, it was an area he struggled with, and looking around him at Strickland's grey tenements he knew it'd be a lost cause attempting to glean anything from here. It was too closed off, too entrenched. Another piece of advice Dredd found useful was not to waste time.

He gunned the engine and peeled away, heading for the ramp that would lead him back to the meg-way. Climbing towards the main thoroughfare, it felt like he was rising out of the past, breaking free of the suffocating, clinging taint of the city's history. He had to admit there was a small, unprofessional sense of relief to be leaving it behind: it made him uncomfortable to see the wreckage the gleaming metropolis had been founded on, and those that had to live amongst it. Of course, he'd been there when the bombs had dropped, him and his brother; he'd seen the destruction that had been wrought, and what needed to be done to save what remained of mankind. He knew Fargo had made the hard decisions—evidently it was to become something of a family trait—but so much had to be sacrificed, and those choices were to inform the future of the city years into the future. To witness the legacy first-hand, down here in Strickland, was to confront the appalling cost they had paid as a species, perhaps even more than the vast wastes of the Cursed Earth—it was what they were prepared to accept on their own doorstep that was the true gut-punch. What they could live with if it was removed far enough from sight.

Dredd threaded back into the traffic and immediately spotted a limo indicating for the junction back down towards the ghetto. He experienced a moment of dismay: the sub-sector hadn't finished with him. There was no question his suspicion was aroused; it was far too expensive a model to be innocently cruising through such a district. Either it was lost, or the driver had business down here, and the latter was unlikely to be legitimate. He sighed; if he'd believed in fate it would feel like it was making a point. Since he didn't, he figured today was simply going to be a challenge.

He accelerated, veering across several lanes, and hit the downslope. The limo had almost disappeared among the warren of blocks already. He called in its registration and it came back as unlisted; that answered that question, at least. It was definitely up to something, though the owner couldn't have chosen a more conspicuous mode of transport if they'd tried. Chances were that it was deliberately sending a message, that some level of intimidation was going on here. Dredd's curiosity was piqued— and, he had to admit, he was pleased at the opportunity. Given the battering his reputation had received recently, a high-profile collar would go some way to returning honour to the name.

The car was stationary when he turned onto a boulevard between Len McCluskey and Russ Meyer blocks, idling. He radioed in his position to Control, then hit the siren, a single whoop that resounded between the buildings, far louder down here than it would be among the hubbub of the city proper: a piercing, mournful wail. He pulled alongside the driver's side and tapped the mirrored window.

It buzzed down, and the meathead behind the wheel looked up at him impassively, a wiry, hollowed-out enforcer that had had cybernetic replacement surgery to his lower jaw, scar tissue stretching up to his right eye. Something had taken a chunk out of him at some point. Dredd felt his trigger finger twitch: he knew a dangerous creep when he saw one, and the guy was eyeing him with little fear. This was a career criminal—unlike the blissed-out organ-couriers, he'd have no compunction about killing. Just those first four seconds before either of them spoke was enough for Dredd to assess and strategise.

"Help you, Judge?" The voice was like gravel in a garbage-grinder.

"Turn the engine off, citizen." Languorously, the creep did so. "Ask you what your business is here?"

"Just dropped off my client. I was asked to wait while he visited his associates." He nodded beyond Dredd's shoulder at Meyer, behind him. The Judge tilted his head, following where the driver had indicated: the block looked as dead and unforgiving as the rest.

"Your client?"

"Mr Gilpig."

The name didn't ring a bell. Dredd hadn't been on the streets long enough to become familiar with all the underworld movers and shakers, though new ones could crop up overnight, especially if there was a power vacuum to fill. Local knowledge would come with experience. The Strickland estate was one area that was particularly hazy.

"And who's he going to meet?"

The punk shrugged and smiled. "I'm just the ferryman." He leant back and rested an elbow on the window frame with studied nonchalance that irritated Dredd as much as it was unquestionably supposed to.

"Out of the vehicle, citizen."

He sighed and clambered from the car as Dredd dismounted his bike. He was bigger than the Judge has assumed; he had a good four or five inches on him, and what Dredd had mistaken for scrawn was lean muscle. He could've injured his face playing aeroball, he had the physique for it.

"Turn around, hands on the roof." The creep slowly complied. Dredd patted him down, pulled a snubnose from a shoulder holster—"I've got a licence for that," the driver said without looking round—and wrenched a wallet from his back pocket, which he flipped open, glancing at the ID within. "Control, what we got on a Buzz Calhoun, 1154/67 Emily Pankhurst?"

"*In and out of the juve cubes: gang rumbles, mainly,*" came the reply on his comm after a moment's pause. "*Did a five-stretch for assault, 2072. Received an extra year for knifing an inmate while inside—Bill Bigley, the Night Glider Murderer. No outstanding warrants, been clean since then.*"

So much for the aeroball theory. Dredd tossed the wallet onto the car roof just beyond Calhoun's reach, tucked the snubnose in his belt. "You know it's illegal for a convicted felon to possess a firearm?"

"That's not what the guy who sold it to me said. Anyway, Mr Gilpig insisted it was a, y'know... requirement o' the job."

"Ignorance of the law is no excuse. Neither is incitement."

"Incitement?" Calhoun shot a look sharply over his shoulder.

"You drive a Foord Optimum down here onto Strickland, you're asking to be jacked. That's incitement to commit a crime, punishable by six months."

"Hey, whaddya think I got the gun for? It's a preventative measure. An' who exactly am I meant to incitin'?"

"You think a set of wheels like this would go unnoticed?" Dredd had no doubt multiple sets of eyes were watching them from many different apartments right now. "I hadn't come along, the natives would've stripped it in five minutes. Let me guess: Gilpig likes to make a statement, right?"

"I s'pose. I only worked for him for the last coupla months." He tried to turn around and Dredd shoved him back against the car. "C'mon, man, gimme a break. I'm just a chauffeur; I drive the boss to where he wants to go. I ain't doin' no harm to no-one."

"Which makes a change, regular cube-bunny like you," the Judge remarked, then unhooked a pair of cuffs and slapped on them on Calhoun's wrists, to which he groaned and swore under his breath. "A year for the possession with intent—let's call it eighteen months, all in." Dredd spun him around, his prisoner glaring at him. "Reckon I'd like to have a word with your employer, too, when he deigns to show his face." The creep didn't reply, just breathed furiously through his nose. "In fact," Dredd added, "I've got grounds to conduct a search of your vehicle right now. You want to save me some time, let me know if there's any more contraband inside?" No answer. "Well, then."

Dredd yanked him to one side so he was standing next to the Lawmaster, hands bound behind his back, and walked around the front of the limo to the passenger door, which he threw open. It was spotless inside, the cream plastex interior buffed until it shone. He pulled out the glove compartment and a couple of drawers hidden beneath the seats, but they were conspicuously empty; it was if the car had just rolled off the factory production line. He remembered when he'd called in its registration it had come back as unlisted, which suggested it may well have been driven straight from a showroom. Untraceable, clean... Dredd didn't like it.

"Keep everything spick and span, huh?" he said to Calhoun, who was watching him run his gauntleted hands along the dashboard and between the sun-visors. Dredd cast a glance at his prisoner then unsheathed his daystick and began to sweep it over the upholstery, poking the end into the soft padding at intervals. Nothing. "Let's try the trunk."

He strode to the rear of the limo and popped the back open. Same story: vacuumed methodically, spare tyre still gleaming. He prodded around, but couldn't feel anything untoward. Except... the polished rubber betrayed a flaw—he caught a glimpse in the reflection, a tiny tear in the lining behind the lip of the trunk that he wouldn't have seen otherwise. He reached in and felt a flap of material had come loose; he pushed deeper with his fingers and a small oblong-shaped object dropped into his palm. Holding it into the light, he saw it was a plain, unmarked zipdrive, the kind you could buy at any mega-mart. He twisted it between thumb and forefinger in front of Calhoun.

"Care to explain this?" The creep shrugged, and the Judge glanced again at the memory stick before placing it in one of his pouches. "The less you talk, the harder it'll go for you. The teks'll soon take it apart, make no mistake about that. Don't think we won't discover its secrets." Calhoun just watched Dredd as he drew nearer. "Control—"

With frightening speed, the perp impossibly brought both bound arms over his head and lunged at the Judge, wrapping the cuffs around his throat and pulling tight. Dredd stumbled back and tried to shake him off, choking as the monofibre restrainers cut deep into his neck, but Calhoun was seemingly equally as strong as he was, capable of maintaining the pressure. Stars danced before his eyes, and raw panic flashbulbed in his head before the training reasserted itself.

Dredd slammed his elbow into his attacker's midriff once, then again and again, until he felt the cuffs slacken slightly, then smashed the back of his helmet against the bridge of Calhoun's nose. He toppled backwards, bringing Dredd with him as both men crashed to the ground. The Judge managed to get his hands under Calhoun's and push upwards, easing his head under the creep's grip, then swung round and delivered a piledriver blow to his jaw, his fist skating off the metal casing. The punk had the temerity to grin before lacing his fingers together and punching Dredd in the side of the skull; his helmet softened much of the blow, but there was still enough force to send him tumbling to the side. His ears rang. He hadn't received a strike like that since his cadet days when a rubber bullet ricocheted off his visor. Then, he'd spent several hours in the infirmary with concussion. Now, he was outside the training arena and fighting for his life with no available back-up.

"Control—" he started again, but Calhoun was up on his feet and brought a boot crashing down on the lawman's head again, snapping his comm mic. All he heard was static, until it was broken by the unmistakeable crack of a rib buckling when Calhoun stomped on him a second time. He rolled, felt the snubnose in his belt, and reached for it, bringing it to bear before the perp punted it from his hand, the weapon skittering across the sked and into the shadows.

Calhoun grabbed hold of his own right hand with his left and twisted, his right arm detaching at the shoulder—it was cybernetic too, the joint popping clean from its metal housing. Gruddammit, Dredd thought, admonishing himself; he should've checked his prisoner more thoroughly. He'd screwed up big-time here. The creep put his foot on his right wrist and pulled, the hand unlocking so it was free of the cuffs. He advanced on the Judge.

Dredd drew his Lawgiver and fired from his sitting position; the SE slug passed though Calhoun's abdomen, but it barely slowed him. He aimed for the head and pulled the trigger again, splintering a section of his metalwork. By that point, the perp was on him, his left hand closing over the gun, and thrusting it towards Dredd's chin. His strength was incredible, like nothing the lawman had encountered before; pain shot through his arm as the bones in his fingers fractured, Calhoun squeezing harder until the Lawgiver was released from his grip. Calhoun flipped it and pistol-whipped the Judge repeatedly: muscles in his cheek tore and cartilage ground. Blood filled his mouth. Dredd's left hand went for his boot-knife and stabbed it into the creep's thigh, which was evidently still fleshy, as a crimson fountain followed when he pulled the blade free. Calhoun grunted, and Dredd drove it up to the hilt again, the rockcrete beneath them now slick with both of their blood.

The punk changed tactic and grabbed Dredd's injured hand and wrapped it around the Lawgiver butt, threading his finger into the trigger guard. He pushed the barrel backwards, aiming it at the lawman, and fired: the first shot ploughed through his shoulderpad. Calhoun pushed further, and Dredd resisted with all his might, but felt his energy sapping. The second shot entered the shoulder just above his clavicle. He grimaced; he'd taken a bullet before, but never at such close range. His skin felt as if was aflame. Fear, very human and very real, rose up in him—these could be his last seconds on Earth. All that had been invested in him, those precious genes that were the building blocks of justice, was about to be rent asunder.

Here.

Now.

The gun barrel was centimetres from his carotid artery. It was game over if he didn't act now. Dredd twisted the knife still sticking out from Calhoun's thigh until his attacker roared, then, using his foot, flicked towards him the perp's detached right hand, lying nearby. He snatched it up in his left fist, and slammed it onto the Lawgiver's grip, relaxing his own as much as could even as he pushed up and squeezed the trigger. It was enough. The palm-reader detected an unauthorised user at the exact same moment that Calhoun realised what Dredd had done.

The bullet seared past his throat and the gun exploded between them, the perp taking the brunt of the blast. Calhoun was blown backwards, his left arm now a smouldering stump, his face shredded. Still, he was attempting to lever himself up. Dredd, vision swimming, barely conscious, crawled the couple of feet between them, retrieved the knife with a hard tug, and without a word drove it into the punk's neck. Calhoun let loose a gasp, and was then silent.

Dredd knelt for a moment, swaying; then he collapsed onto his side and closed his eyes.

Three

11.02 am

Joe.

11.03 am

When they'd heard the explosion, Dax couldn't not check it out. It wasn't, of course, the first time their walls had been rattled—something went off on Strickland, with varying degrees of seriousness, at least every month or so—but a good solid boom like that one had a magnetic attraction to her. Mohawked head would tilt upwards, brow furrowed, you could damn near see her ears twitch—she'd been known to pick up on a fireball blossoming three blocks away. She claimed she wasn't a pyro—she certainly wasn't any more likely to set something alight than the rest of them—but it had special fascination for her, definitely. She'd sit and watch the flames lick the sky until the jays arrived to put it out.

The rest of them had followed her lead as soon as she'd leapt up and crossed to the window; Dax was kind of their leader without anyone ever saying so. She just had the spark, spoke the loudest, probably was the smartest. The others—Bonedog, Sheema and Juice—stopped divvying out the tobacco they'd scored from the Monk and watched her press her face to the glass, before scrambling to their feet themselves.

"Badge down there," she muttered as they joined her at her shoulder. "Looks like his gun blew."

"Jeez," Sheema breathed. "He dead?"

"He ain't standin', that's for sure."

"Bike's still in one piece," Bonedog said, eyes gleaming. "Furies are gonna be all over that in a micro-second."

"C'mon." Dax turned and headed for the door. "I wanna go see."

"Could be it's called in," Sheema protested. "Helmets could be just around the corner."

"Then we gotta be quick," she replied from the other side of the doorway. They could already hear her boots slapping down the corridor toward the els. The three exchanged a glance, shrugged, and went after her, like they had a choice in the matter.

They caught up with her at ground level, spying on the scene from the corner of their block. Smoke rose from a second blackened figure splayed near the Judge, who looked very dead. The bluejay himself was lying in a spreading pool of blood, twisted over on his side, his helmet dented as if someone had taken a crowbar to his skull.

"What do you reckon?" Juice whispered.

"I reckon we strip the wheels fast as we can," Bonedog answered. "Engine parts, ammo—all worth top cred."

"Ain't those things protected?" Sheema murmured. "Y'know... self-defence?"

Bonedog started to respond but Dax was already edging

forward. Sheema grabbed her shoulder to pull her back, but she shrugged it off. She took another few steps, then seemed to stumble over something. She looked down, crouched, and picked up a handgun that had been obscured by the building's shadow. Turning, she showed it to the rest of the gang.

"Holy drokk," Juice exclaimed. "It loaded?"

Dax shrugged, flipped open the chamber, squinted inside then nodded.

"Holy drokk," Juice said again, grinning. "Fun we can have with that."

"Time's wastin'," Bonedog complained, motioning to move. "We wanna take what we can off that bike, we gotta do it now." He started to follow Dax, but she'd turned back towards the Judge, sort of bending slightly to study him, waving one hand at Bonedog to stop him coming any closer. He paused.

Dax took another couple of steps, the snubnose still held her hand, now only half a dozen feet from where the prone jay was curled. She shuffled a little nearer then stopped dead when she saw movement: the Judge was breathing shallowly, the heel of one boot scraping on the rockcrete. She glanced back at her friends, redoubled her grip on the weapon, and just as she peered down once more the lawman rolled suddenly onto his back with a pained sound. Dax visibly jumped but stood her ground.

The Judge arched his back, and appeared to look straight at her; she couldn't tell for sure because his eyes were hidden behind that shattered visor, but his head was now facing her, and in that moment she felt frozen, held within his gaze. His blood-flecked lower face scowled as if he was trying to say something, or he might simply have been struggling for breath. He was about the same age as they were, she realised. Still he regarded her, his left hand clutching a knife and flexing around the handle. Dax retreated slowly, then turned to usher the other three back towards the block entrance.

"What the hell...?" Bonedog enquired testily, casting an eye over his shoulder at the scene, the jay now attempting to rise. All that primo scrap was there for the plucking, and the badge didn't look like he'd put up much of a fight; Resyk fodder, most likely. He chose not to resist, though; he knew well enough not to argue with Dax.

"We wanna be somewhere else," was all she'd say, tucking the gun into the waistband of her pants and pushing him through the door.

11.04 am

CONTROL OPERATIVE OAKLAND called her supervisor over, swivelling in her chair to watch as he threaded his way unsteadily through the banks of monitors. The hubbub was ever-present, rank upon rank of her colleagues on either side stretching from wall to wall of the vast room, all dealing with thousands of street officers' requests for info, pleas for assistance, and detailing perps' sentences before pick-up, so when he stood at her side she had to raise her voice to make sure she heard him. The white-haired Davidson—a contemporary of Fargo's, now frankly showing his age—bent a little, turning his head so she spoke directly into his ear, a sanctimonious affectation that never failed to irritate.

"Had an interrupted communication logged at eleven ayem, sir. Been trying to return hails for the last two minutes, but no response."

"The badge?"

"Joseph Dredd, sir. The system shows he's red-flagged—any unusual circumstances to be reported, Chief Judge's orders."

"I'm aware of policy, Oakland," Davidson replied testily. "What was his situation?"

"Radioed that he was investigating a suspect vehicle on the

Strickland estate, Sector 9, at"—she scrolled down her screen—"ten forty-six. Then thirteen minutes later, a one-second burst of traffic. Fifty-seven seconds after that, another. He called in both times using his unique transponder; since then he hasn't answered."

"Hm."

"I was going to send in a nearby unit to assist, as per. Given the flag, I thought you should be informed."

Davidson straightened and nodded. "I'll direct it up the chain of command. Get a helmet out to his location and keep me updated of his status."

"Sir." Oakland tapped her headset, regarding the old man as he hobbled off slowly down one of the aisles. The name Dredd meant nothing to her; she had no idea why the powers-that-be were so interested in his whereabouts or tracking his communications. But she did hear—surprisingly clearly, given the background chatter—Davidson mutter "Damn clones" before he disappeared from sight, though the significance was lost on her. She shook her head.

"All units in the vicinity of Sector 9, we have a possible Code 99 Red, Strickland estate," she stated into her mic. "Back-up required, please acknowledge…"

11.05 am

THE PAIN BROUGHT him round, the fringes of it gnawing at him until it forced him to surface into consciousness. It took several seconds to orientate himself, vestiges of dream-figures dissipating; he was aware he'd heard voices, that someone had even spoken directly to him, but the details were hazy, and it was now all becoming mixed up in one big ball of hurt. The more his senses returned, the louder his nerve-endings screamed: every second seemed to bring a fresh report from some corner of his body demanding attention. He'd flopped onto his back, but as he tried to galvanise his legs to get him at least halfway upright, his strength deserted him. His head felt woozy, and he heard his heart thrumming in his chest, veins pulsing weakly: he'd lost a lot of blood, he knew that.

Recall dawned in pieces—Calhoun, his Lawgiver. He glanced over at the charred remnants of his attacker, then realised he was still holding his boot knife in his left hand. He studied it, the blade dark and slick, then slotted it, trembling, back into its sheath, put an elbow under himself and manoeuvred into a sitting position. The air rushed out of him, and he thought for a second he was going to black out.

Control, he told himself. *Control the pain. Don't submit to it. It's secondary to my duty. It's just another obstacle to overcome, an enemy to neutralise.*

He took stock: his right hand was unresponsive, the bones evidently fractured; the skin of his torso was scorched from his gun exploding, and the pain in his side told him at least one broken rib; his head pounded and his jaw was swollen, most likely a shattered cheekbone too (an injury from last year that hadn't set properly; he wasn't surprised to find that the bone there had splintered again). He needed med-assistance, and quickly. He tried to speak, and an ache spread across his face, the muscles frozen; he gave up on it, remembering that Calhoun had destroyed his helmet-comm anyway.

He couldn't physically call for help, but he could signal Justice Central from his bike. The Lawmaster was undamaged—he just had to get to it.

Wavering, he planted a foot firmly beneath him and, through force of will, levered himself upright and began to hobble towards his vehicle, his right ankle protesting every time he put weight on it. There didn't seem to be any part of him that wasn't aching, and nausea was starting to claw at his throat. The head injuries he'd sustained interfered with his vision, the bike blurring as he got closer. He began to feel vulnerable, too, a sensation he wasn't at all familiar with. Isolated.

He considered programming the bike computer to take him back to Grand Hall—even if he requested help, he was in no fit shape to fend off any attacks should the locals try their luck in the interim. Better to pass out over the handlebars and be ferried to safety. He crossed the last couple of feet and fell against his Lawmaster, steadying himself by gripping the seat with his one good hand; letting it prop him up, he reached across and pressed the emergency button. Nothing. It had powered down to protect itself from misuse, wouldn't boot up without the correct voice-activation. He tried to speak again, a viscous growl emerging in place of any identifiable words.

"*This unit has been coded only to be operated by its designated user,*" the bike's onboard comp warned. "*Step away or necessary force will be applied.*"

"Bike," he muttered, the effort exhausting. "Respond."

"*Judge Dredd? Please verify identification.*"

"I... need help."

It didn't answer for a second, then said, "*Judge Dredd, this unit has detected a weapons-lock signal within close range.*"

"...What?" He looked up, scanning the buildings.

The missile streaked out of a fifth floor window of Meyer; Dredd just had time to see the stream of its wake twist in the air before it struck the front of the Lawmaster. The bike flipped as it detonated, throwing the lawman back—he grunted in pain, landing on his already lacerated side. It exploded a second time as the fuel tanks caught, and Dredd was forced to roll to escape the heat of the blazing vehicle. His lungs sucked in dry, hot air and he coughed until he vomited, specks of blood visible in the thin gruel that hung from his lips. He spat, clearing his mouth.

Then came the rattle of gunfire; he looked over his shoulder and saw a line of impacts splintering the sked and closing on him. He scrambled to his feet and dived behind the limo just as the shooter found his aim. Bullets rattled against the bodywork and blew out the windows. Keeping low, he tugged open the passenger door and hurled himself across the seats, relieved to see the key still in the ignition where Calhoun had left it; he twisted it and the engine rumbled into life. Twisting himself around, grimacing as shards of glass dug into his flesh, he stomped on the accelerator, thrust the gearstick into drive and the car lurched forward. Shells continued to *spang* off the hood, and the windscreen cobwebbed; he slid down as low as possible in the seat, one hand on the wheel, the limo picking up speed as he drove blind. He knew he wasn't going to make it very far, but at least it could offer some cover as he fled the line of fire.

Inevitably, a round burst a rear tyre and the car lurched, Dredd struggling to keep it steady. The air was filled with the shriek of grinding metal as the wheel rim screeched on the sked, slowing the limo's progress. Another tyre exploded and it started to swerve; the Judge took his foot off the gas to control it, but the shredded rubber snagged on the kerb and it tipped as it fishtailed. Dredd braced himself as best he could as the vehicle rolled onto its roof, spinning once on the spot before coming to a standstill. Pushing aside the dizziness, he scrambled through an open window, shots continuing to pockmark the bodywork and chassis; when he saw one ricochet off the exposed fuel line, he knew he had to make some distance. He steeled himself, then pushed away from the shelter of the limo and limped quickly towards the shadowy entrance of a subterranean car park. Bullets whined over his head and clipped the walls either side of him, one passing through his side, just under the ribcage; he grunted, stumbled and fell, sliding the last few metres down the shallow incline into the underground space.

He was swallowed up by the darkness and oppressive stillness, the rattle of gunfire sounding far away. Eventually, the shooting ceased. Here, in this cool, tenebrous enclosure, Dredd's last, pain-wracked thought was that this was must be how it felt to be buried alive.

11.10 am

"WELL?"

"Nothing. It's gone."

"Jovus drokk. You looked everywhere?"

"We looked where you told us it was. We had a nose round inside, too, but the car's a mess, ain't nothing still in one piece."

"Yeah, and whose fault is that? Your men had carried on shooting, the whole thing would've gone up."

"Wouldn't have made no difference. Data-stick was gone anyway."

"But we didn't *know* that. For all we knew the badge hadn't found it. If the fuel tank had blew and it was still in the trunk, all this would have been for nothing."

"Well. You wanted the bluejay dead."

"Something else, I might add, that you have significantly failed to deliver on. You're telling me there's no sign?"

"Think he made it into the McCluskey car pool. It's a warren down there, all sortsa crawlspaces and hidey-holes he could lose himself in. Dark, too. We found some blood traces, reckon he took a bullet, but didn't lead nowhere. Gonna need a good search, an' plenty of feet on the ground. Plus there's the, y'know, the Murder Corps to contend with."

"Will they play ball?"

"If'n they get a cut, sure. Ain't no fans of us Furies, but throw 'em a percentage an' they'll let us on their turf."

"Jovus... Look, the Judge obviously has the zipdrive. Find him and get it back. Spread the word—first musclehead that gets me my property back is on a bonus. Call it a five-kay finder's fee; that's how important this is to me."

"That'll motivate the troops, certainly."

"It better. Christ, what a drokk-up. I haven't got a ride back now, either. I don't want to be stuck here while you deal with the cop—can one of your boys give me a lift back up-sector?"

"Don't know if that's a good idea right now, Mr Gilpig. We've got company."

"What? What can you see? Rawlings, you there?"

"Yeah, yeah, keep it down. Badge on the approach—probably checking out our buddy's last known whereabouts."

"Oh, stomm. The estate will be crawling in no time—"

"Cool your boots, boss-man. I got an idea that might buy us some time."

"Rawlings?"

"Gotta go. Stay outta sight, we'll handle this. It'll mean double on the advance, though."

"Whatever it takes."

11.25 am

OAKLAND TOOK THE call. "This is Control, go ahead."

"*Collins on Strickland, responding to that possible Code 99 Red. That's, uh, a negative. Made contact with Dredd—he's having comm problems, is all. Kept cutting out on him.*"

"Understood." She checked the transponder signal on her screen; it matched Collins, all right. "Tell him to return to Central—that'll need to be rectified immediately."

"*Wilco. We'll both head back now.*"

She date-stamped the transcript and forwarded it for Davidson's attention, red flag and all. Let them know their prodigal son whatever-the-hell-he-was was alive and well.

*   *   *

11.26 am

Rawlings waved the gun barrel slowly between Collins' eyes as he finished speaking into his mic, then he snatched the Judge's helmet away and tossed it in a corner. The badge eyed him and the others in the room nervously, sweat beading his face. Strapped to the chair, missing one hand—severed to aid co-operation—he looked helpless, stripped of all authority. Take away the uniforms and their daysticks and they were all just scared little runts, Rawlings thought, beatin' on the folk beneath them.

"Bye-bye, Mr Bluejay," he said, putting the gun to Collins' forehead and pulling the trigger. "Fly away home."

He turned to his Furies. "Dispose of *that*. Then find me the other one. *Now*."

Four

THE STREETS OF Eminence were alive with creeps. Joe squeezed his trigger as he advanced, picking his targets carefully, his Academy-trained brain forcing itself to stay calm, controlled. It was all too easy to panic when faced with multiple hostiles, to set the Lawgiver to rapid fire and spray; it was the mark of a badge on top of the situation that every bullet was economically and precisely spent. Buckshot blasts punched holes in the warehouse wall behind him, kicked up the dirt at his feet, but he didn't flinch or falter. He sighted on the nearest mutie that was trying to get a bead on him and drilled an SE round between his eyes—one set, at least—before assessing the next threat.

He glanced over at Rico, several feet ahead of him on the other side of the street, and knew he was guided by the same by-the-book tactical thinking. They were in synch, a well-oiled, two-headed justice-dispensing weapon; few were their match when it came to combat, whether in classroom simulations or real-world exercises like this Hotdog Run. They were in their element: the odds against them, the last twelve years of schooling finally put to the test. Beyond the Academy walls—indeed, beyond the city—their lives were at risk. It was as much a fight for survival as a performance review. But the Judges they'd been shaped to be were now emerging, born in fire. This town was the kiln that would make them.

They'd all heard the rumours, the locker-room scuttlebutt, about the high failure rate of Hot Dog Runs. Deaths were rare, but many cadets were put back a year or put through the process again or—worst-case scenario—dismissed from the Academy entirely. Joe and Rico never believed that would be an option: too much was at stake, there was a bloodline to honour. It was unthinkable that they wouldn't be Judges; it was in their DNA. They'd rather take a fatal bullet than return to the metropolis in disgrace.

But that wasn't going to happen.

Their self-assurance probably rankled amongst their peers, but to the Dredd clones it was immaterial: these kind of personal feelings were an irrelevance, anyway.

Still, clockwork precision was required; they weren't out of the woods yet. Faulder had been taken out, bringing the scam to an end, but the gun runners didn't care about details. Joe watched Rico duck beneath the swing of a homemade mace and jammed his gun barrel under the mutant's chin, his round detonating the creep's skull. It was perfectly fluid, almost effortless, and a move he could've anticipated as if it was happening to him. They were bonded on a cellular level, connected to a far greater degree than any regular sibling; but neither felt fear for the other. He knew that his twin was up to the challenge.

The bodies were piling up, Eminence's main drag turned into a charnel pit. None of them—Joe, Rico, Gibson—were offering their foes much of a chance of surrender. Termination was what was required now, to show the townsfolk that the perps had been judged, that the law was as resolute out here as it was back in the Big Meg. By the time the shooting tailed to a halt, nearly two dozen corpses littered the ground, and hazy smoke drifted across the scene. Joe joined Rico, who had his boot on a struggling mutie's chest and was training his gun on him, snapping off a headshot.

"Made good time," he said.

Rico turned to face him. For a moment, Joe thought he saw something like disdain etched on his twin's face; then he realised he was studying his arm. "You're bleeding," he remarked.

Joe looked down and saw shrapnel had carved through his bicep. In the midst of an adrenaline surge, he hadn't even felt it. Now, the ache was beginning to spread, and the blood was starting to soak the uniform. "Need a med-pack," he muttered, glancing around. Suddenly the town felt very quiet and empty. His brother was turning away from him and walking up the street, cadavers crunching beneath his feet.

His arm was aflame. "Rico, help me," he said. A crimson gauze was curtaining his vision, blurring the sight of his clone.

"It's too late, little brother," Rico said, pausing, turning his head to the side but not looking at him, not moving to assist. "You failed."

11.48 am

DREDD'S EYES SNAPPED open. It took a moment to reorient himself; he adjusted to the gloom and realised he was in a maintenance antechamber, little more than a couple of metres square. It was mostly filled by a large junction box, but had also been used as a walk-in storage cupboard; various items of cleaning equipment were stacked against the wall. He'd used the hose of a deactivated robo-cleaner to tie the door handle shut so it couldn't be opened from the other side. He'd had enough of his wits about him to realise his attackers may well be looking to finish the job.

He must've passed out; for how long, he didn't know. The cold rockcrete floor had numbed his legs, and as he tried to shift himself into a more comfortable position, he had to battle a wave of cramp. He hissed as he sat up, massaging feeling back into his limbs, and with that returned attendant aches from all over his body. He was in a bad way, there was no disguising it: weak, feverish, in constant pain. He'd been suffering enough before he'd taken the slug, but now that compounded matters—although it seemed to have passed through his midriff without striking anything vital, his attempts at patching up the wound using the basic personal med-kit he had on him had been cursory at best. He was no doctor. The sutures would hold, he hoped, but he couldn't help but be reminded of the poor saps under Mama Carrington's care and the half-hearted treatment they'd received. The tissue damage was no doubt playing havoc on his system.

He shook his head to clear it, the dream still vivid. Fever had jumbled some of the details of a firefight on his and Rico's Hot Dog Run, less than three years before they attained the full eagle. He hadn't given it much thought since, and wondered why his sickly mind had dredged up that particular memory. There was something to that connectedness the clones shared, and it made him consider whether Rico was in any way aware of his twin's predicament right now; that out there, across the gulf of space separating the pair, in a prison cell somewhere on Titan, his brother felt a twinge, an intuition, that his blood-family was in trouble. It seemed unlikely, frankly; Dredd wasn't one to indulge such fancies. Yet... there was a reassurance there, in an unbreakable DNA-bond, despite all that had come between them. If Dredd ever saw his brother again, he would have to ask him, though the chances of him returning from the penal colony were admittedly slim.

Rico could do nothing for him now, though; he needed to look closer to home, to Justice Central. His absence would be noted eventually, but the question was whether he'd survive long enough for it to make any difference. Time was clearly of the essence, given his state. He'd heard voices beyond the door while he'd stitched his bullet-hole, but they'd quickly moved off, and all appeared silent now. He had to get moving.

Dredd eased himself to his feet, drawing his boot knife from its sheath and wincing at the tightness in his side. He felt three times his age, as if he should need support from a cane. Gripping the blade in his teeth for a moment, he unknotted the vacuum hose one-handed and gently eased the door open: all was quiet, vehicles—many evidently abandoned—were ranged in rows, just silhouettes in the darkness. Few of the strip lights in the ceiling were working. Knife back in hand, he considered commandeering the nearest roadster and gunning hell for leather for the exit; but a brief recce of the ramp showed that was a no-go. The creeps had parked a couple of cars across the sked and littered the route with debris. There was no way out on two wheels or four.

There were shouts from the top of the ramp, torchlight flickering on the walls, and Dredd turned and headed towards the el. He jabbed the call button, eyeing the emergency stairs— attempting to ascend more than half a dozen flights would wipe him out. The voices grew closer. The green arrow above the el doors pinged and they slid open, bringing the Judge face-to-face with three armed perps. They stared at each other for a shocked, frozen second, before the gunmen recovered their senses and brought their blasters to bear.

Dredd lunged forward through the open doors, skewering the middle meathead in the neck with the blade, then yanking it free and ducking as the guy sprayed the interior of the cab with blood. He immediately shoulder-charged to his left and slammed the second perp against the wall, kicking out his foot at the control panel so the doors slid shut, noting as he did so more figures hurrying towards the el. The lift began to rise. Dredd spun and pushed aside the third man's rifle—biting down on the pain as a stitch popped—just as the perp pulled the trigger, riddling the ceiling with bullets and shattering the overhead fluorescent tube. The Judge headbutted him once, drove the knife deep under his ribs and into his heart, then swung the weapon low and used the still-firing gun to kneecap his friend, who collapsed with a yell to the cab floor. Dredd crossed over quickly and pulled the blaster from his grip before he could think to use it, and levelled it between his eyes. He nudged his forehead with the barrel and told him to stop howling.

Dredd glanced at the level indicator; the el had climbed two floors. He jammed the stop button with the rifle butt, bringing it to a juddering halt. An absolute stillness descended, the cramped lift ripe with the smell of spent ammunition and coppery gore.

Dredd caught his breath, his lungs burning. He could feel blood trickling down his hip and thigh from the ruptured suture, but was determined not to let the creep in front of him pick up on how much pain he was in. He had to maintain his authority. Given the crim was in no little agony himself, trembling with shock as he clutched his ruined legs, Dredd doubted he'd notice, but the image he presented was everything. Let an adversary discern any hint of weakness and they'll use that against you: it was Academy dogma.

"Drokkin' *crippled* me, man," the meathead wailed. He wasn't much older than Dredd. "They tol' me they *tagged* you. Tol' me you was bleeding out…"

"Just makes me more dangerous," Dredd replied, poking the rifle barrel at the gang cut on his jacket. "Furies, huh? Thought you were Meyer boys?"

"We are." He jutted his chin out at the mention of his block, territorial pride momentarily overriding his wounds. These idiots lived and died by their address; it became their whole world, their neighbours rivals to wage war with. "The Murder Corps are givin' us a pass, on account…" He winced, his words tailing away. His eyelids flickered—he was passing out.

Dredd gave him a boot. "On account of what?"

"'Cos they're… they're gettin' a cut," he replied sleepily.

"There a bounty on me?"

"Kinda. More of a reward. Boss wants you found… real quick…" He was slumping over, the blood pooling beneath him. "You gonna… gonna call a doc, or what?" His voice was a whisper as he faded into unconsciousness.

"Fat chance of that," the Judge murmured, glancing around the wrecked interior of the el. He slung one of the rifles over his shoulder, holding on to another and hit the button for the upper levels. The lift rumbled into life. He reasoned if he could make it to a pod park, an H-Wagon would be able to airlift him out, provided he could get word to Control. That not one but two gangs were now hunting for him, however, did nothing for his chances.

He watched the numbers climb, his muscles throbbing from the sudden exertion. Resolve, he told himself. Dig deep. Think of this as another training exercise, his own personal Hot Dog Run. He'd been dropped into a situation, and his superiors were waiting to see him make it out the other side. Well, it wasn't over yet: he was still alive, for one. He was rearmed, he thought, tightening his grip on the rifle. It could, theoretically, be worse.

He needed to sound more convincing, he decided.

The el ground to a halt somewhere in the early hundreds, and no amount of button-jabbing would force it to continue any further. He wrenched the doors open one-handed and had to pull himself up where it had stopped below the floor. Dredd got to his feet: the corridor was gloomy and under-maintained, as he should've expected. The walls were festooned with graffiti. Many of the apartments looked derelict. He stopped at the nearest one that wasn't boarded over or fire-damaged and rapped on the door, but received no reply. Electing not to announce himself, he tried again half a dozen times, moving down the row, meeting with the same response each time.

"You won't get much luck findin' someone who'll answer," a voice called from ahead. Dredd followed it, peering round an entranceway that had lost its door entirely and into a bare room. Curled up in the far corner was a figure shrouded in blankets and encircled by shadow. All Dredd could see was a pair of bright eyes regarding him from beneath a knit cap. "Most no-one there anyways," the shapeless heap added.

"You live here?" the Judge enquired, stepping further into the empty apartment. It felt cold and exposed; several windows were broken, he noticed.

"Well, I *made* it my home," the figure said. Dredd suspected it was a woman; the dirt and darkness around the eyes were impenetrable, but he picked up an inflection in her words that he pegged as female. "Wasn't told that I couldn't, an' I ain't had any complaints." She paused, then asked, "You're not here to move me on, are ya?"

"Don't worry, I'm not here for you. I need a vidphone, anything like that, to call out. You know where I can find one?"

She shifted beneath her bundles, and Dredd caught a waft of damp and sour, unwashed linen. He felt a twinge of sympathy for the woman. "No, nothin' like that down here. Lines ain't worked since I was a juve, far as I remember."

"Down here?"

A grimy finger emerged and pointed upwards. "Topside. Thass' where the block boss lives. Everythin' works up there, or so I heard. It's why the el won't go any higher; they fixed it to stop us trespassin'."

"How do they make it down?"

"Got their own service express on the other side of the block."

"Could you show me?"

"Aw, I just got comfortable." She plumped up her blankets,

then stared at him. "Whass' in it for me?"

Dredd bit down on his instinctive response, which was to suggest a vagrancy charge could be avoided. His patience was wearing thin as exhaustion crept up on him, but he didn't want to antagonise her. "I can make sure you get into a welfare shelt, you help me out. You want to escape Strickland, don't you?"

She looked down. "Dunno. 'Sall I know. Feel weird bein' anywhere else."

"You got a better chance of a future—" Dredd started before being interrupted by the *click-clack* of a round being chambered behind him. He spun, his rifle raised.

"Sorry, Judgey," the lead gangbanger said, brandishing his automatic in the doorway. Three others stood behind him similarly armed. "But you ain't *got* no future to speak of."

Five

12.11 pm

"Drokk, jaybird," the lead meathead drawled as he and the rest of his compatriots filtered into the room. They formed a loose semi-circle around Dredd, rifles trained on him. "What a day you're havin'! Look at you; it's a drokkin' miracle you're still standing."

"Put your weapons down before there's further trouble," the Judge responded, his own gun unwavering.

The creep raised his eyebrows and snorted, looking genuinely taken aback. He looked to the others, laughed and then frowned. "Tell me you're kidding." Receiving no answer, he stepped forward, barrel only inches from the lawman's face. "I'm sure they breed juves like you to think you're robots, but have *some* gruddamn sense. You got four guns pointed at you; you ain't in a position to tell anyone to do shit."

After a further moment's silence, he added in a measured tone, "Lower the killware now 'fore we drop you where you stand, spugwit."

"You can try—but don't say I didn't warn you."

The lead perp smiled again and shook his head. "You're a tenacious son of a bitch, I gotta admit that. But enough is enough. This ends now."

"Just pop him already, Fungal," the creep next to him said.

"Not till he tells us where it is," Fungal snapped. He turned his attention back to Dredd. "How about it? You wanna make it easy on yourself, or we gotta pin you down and take you apart piece by piece?"

"Whaddya want him for, anyhow?" the woman under the blankets piped up.

"Ain't none of your damn business, slitch," the gang member nearest her barked. "Keep your drokkin' mouth shut."

"Figure I've got something they want," Dredd muttered, his sights never leaving the perp sticking his gun in his face. "Something important enough that the Russ Meyer Furies and the Len McCluskey Murder Corps have joined forces to get it back—and someone's paying them to find it."

"Yeah? Colour me intrigued. What is it?" the woman asked.

"I don't know myself," the Judge replied. "But I'm sure as hell not giving it to them."

"All right, enougha this crap," Fungal spat. "Just as easy to drag your corpse outta here and search it—"

"That's if he hasn't stashed it already," she chimed in.

"Drokk it, will someone dispose of this bum—" Fungal called over his shoulder and nodded towards the figure in the corner, just as a single gunshot resounded in the room. Everyone swung their weapons in the direction of the noise, seeing one of the perps stagger back with a gaping chest wound and fall to his knees.

Dredd took his chance and drilled a slug in the side of Fungal's head, then snapped efficient, accurate shots into the remaining two before they had a chance to return fire. All four were on the ground in a few seconds. Dredd glanced over at the woman—a circular smouldering hole had appeared in her bedding. She tossed it aside, revealing the compact blaster she held in her right hand.

"When were you going to tell me you were armed?" Dredd asked.

"It's the kind of thing you don't reveal until you need to," she said, staggering to her feet and stamping some circulation back into them. She was younger than he first thought, now that he could see more of her; no more than ten years older than he was, her thin frame swallowed by the tatty, ancient greatcoat wrapped around her.

"You're aware that you've just committed a felony? I'm assuming that weapon is unlicensed, too."

"Hey, you're welcome," she said, giving a mock curtsey. "Next time the Murder Corps come knocking, I won't save your sorry ass. A little gratitude goes a long way, you know."

"I had the situation under control," Dredd grumbled, though even as he said it he felt a fresh wave of dizziness sweep over him, and had to take a step back so and prop himself against the wall. He needed painkillers, and probably some form of antibiotics too: the sweats were back, a sure sign he was fighting an infection. His skin prickled, his head throbbed. He felt disappointed in himself, that the battle his body was fighting was out of his hands, and it was losing, failing. If he'd even known he'd *had* a physical limit, he'd never imagined he would *reach* it; they'd all thought they were invincible back in the Academy, him and Rico especially. Peak triple-A fitness, mentally agile, sharp reflexes—they were prime Justice Department material. Yet all it took...

All it took...

Joe.

"Brother... I don't know if I'm going to get out of this one... "*You're becoming weak, Joe.*

"I'm losing blood. Bones are broken—can feel a rib pressing on my lung. Makes it hard to breathe..."

Weakness is a crime, Joe. A fundamental betrayal. It's the opposite of everything we are, everything we stand for. Even when I fell, I stayed strong.

"Rico, you gave in to temptation. You brought the badge and the name into disrepute. You were greedy, venal…"

I just chose another path, Joe. I had the conviction to do that, the will. The strength. You stayed a—

"Judge?"

—a poor excuse for the DNA that flows through you. A weak—

"Judge!"

—in the shadow of Fargo—

A hand shaking his shoulder brought him round, the room swimming back into focus. The woman was standing before him, concern etched on her face, her hand resting on his bicep. He studied it uncomprehending for a second; then his gaze travelled the length of her arm until he looked her directly in the eye. It took another few seconds for the present to return to him.

"You still with me?" she asked softly. "You were kinda muttering under your breath about somethin'. Somebody called… Rico?"

"Doesn't matter," he croaked.

"You're in a really bad way, aren't you? You need med-attention. You're burning up…" She reached out and put her palm on Dredd's swollen jaw, but he slung the rifle-strap over his shoulder and grabbed her wrist with his left hand, snatching it away. She wrested it free without much difficulty.

"Inappropriate contact with an officer—" he started, but she was already stepping back.

"Whatever. I'm just tryin' to save your life. You don't look older'n eighteen to me, you've been through the mill—I don't think you're goin' to survive without a doc seein' you in the next few hours. Plus there's *them*." She indicated the bodies at their feet. "I do not wanna be around when more of the Murder Corps come callin'. Figure you don't either."

Dredd paused then asked, "Can you get me to this service el?"

"I can show you where it is, but there's no guarantee Winstanley's gonna give us access."

"Winstanley?"

"Block daddy. He who rules the roost. He ain't no fan of you bluejays."

"If he knows what's good for him—"

"Yeah, look, I hate to break it to you... Dredd, is it?" She leaned close, and tipped up the bottom of his badge with one finger, rolling her eyes. "But you ain't callin' the shots no more. You're on your own, half-dead, with a target on your back— Winstanley's just gonna laugh in your face if you think you can lay down the law."

"While I wear this uniform—"

"And you're in Strickland," she interrupted. "They use Judge helmets as pisspots here. We've been left to fend for ourselves for years; don't go expectin' much in the way of respect."

"I can handle it," he replied, taking a step forward.

"You know what? I reckon the only reason you ain't dead already is that you're too gruddamn stubborn to acknowledge it." She held up her hands. "You wanna let Winstanley finish the job, go ahead. No skin off my shin. You lawboys ain't ever done nothin' for me, anyhow."

Dredd stopped at the doorway, cast an eye over his shoulder. "You want to know what I think the gangs are after?" He reached into one of his belt pouches and retrieved the zipdrive, holding it up. "Figure it's this."

"What's on it?"

"No idea. I pulled it from a suspect vehicle an hour or so ago."

"Just before you became the local bullet-magnet."

"Right. The name Gilpig mean anything to you?"

The woman shook her head. "You're thinking it's pretty important, though, right?"

"Important enough to kill for. Important enough to maybe use as a bargaining chip with the creep upstairs for an airlift out of here."

She thought for a moment, considered the corpses again. She was in deep stomm if the MC traced her involvement in the death of a member. Maybe getting out of McCluskey wasn't such a bad idea after all. "We do this," she said finally, "you better let me do the talkin'. I get the feeling you ain't the negotiating type." She joined him at the threshold, motioned that he should lean on her. "I'm Maze, by the way."

"Maze." He hissed, winced, a grinding in his chest driving the breath from him. "I appreciate it."

"Don't start goin' all gooey on me," she muttered, smirking.

12.43 pm

THEY MADE THEIR way through McCluskey steadily but cautiously, sticking to the secluded areas where possible. Maze said she knew a back route that would keep them under the radar. Both knew speed was essential, but Dredd told her not to risk stumbling upon another gaggle of Murder Corps gangbangers on the prowl. The pain came in waves, but he was determined not to let it overwhelm him, even when he felt on the fringes of a blackout. That was when he told Maze to wait for a second, let him grit his teeth and push through, before continuing. It made progress slow but gave them time to listen for the sound of approaching bodies; they heard shouts occasionally, the pounding of feet on the floor above, and only moved when they were sure the coast was clear. The Judge was becoming increasingly concerned that he wouldn't be able to protect either of them in a firefight; that the shakes and the impaired vision were going to make him a liability. Maze was still armed, of course, but he doubted she'd pulled the trigger before today. If they could avoid any kind of confrontation it would significantly increase their survival prospects.

They met few block residents, and those they did encounter just stared at them in silent curiosity. Any one of the cits could easily raise the alarm and make life a whole lot more difficult, but they seemed cowed, submissive. They had no more love for the gangs than they did Justice Department; there were no sides, no loyalties, just fear and isolation.

"The Murder Corps work for Winstanley?" he asked as they limped on.

"No, he just lets them operate," Maze answered. "They probably kick back a tribute to him outta respect, but they ain't his soldiers. Too damn batshit crazy to be relied upon. They're always squabblin' amongst themselves anyhow, fightin' over who gets to be top dog. That's when they ain't kickin' off with the Furies across the way. Big juves, basically."

"Who does he have, then?"

"He's got his own men. You see 'em comin' down in the el. Scary dudes you know you don't wanna mess with. The MC gives 'em a wide berth; they know whose block it is really."

Dredd grunted in response, plainly unhappy with that last remark. That he should be forced to negotiate with the creep at the top when he should be locking him away in a cube grated, there was no question of that. The order of the universe had been upended: here he was, diminished, trying to skulk off lawless territory while he still had breath in his body. He wondered if his thoughts kept returning to Rico because his clone-brother's fall from grace was no more shameful than Dredd's own failure today—failing the badge, failing as a Judge, letting the perps get the upper hand. His authority had been undermined, his ability called into question; if he was facing a challenge like this in his second year, did he have what it took to last another five? Ten? Few helmets made it to retirement age. All of them, no matter what their lineage, were just one random trigger-pull away from a trip to Resyk. Days like today could always be just around the corner, and how you handled them was the mark of a good officer. Dredd, as far as he was concerned, had come up wanting.

He'd never been assailed by doubts before—he'd been pure in his belief, in his devotion to the law, ever since he'd been pulled from a birthing tank—but street-experience brought with it the hard truth of his limitations, something for which the Academy perhaps hadn't fully prepared him. Was he always going to be striving for that perfection Fargo craved? Was it unrealistic to try to achieve it? He didn't think so; any Judge should have high standards.

Black thoughts circled his head, surfacing no matter how hard he tried to tamp them down. He was starting to ache from the strain of remaining composed.

"Here we go," he heard Maze murmur as they came to a corner. They both peered round and saw the nondescript, unguarded doors of the service el at the end of a short passageway. It took Dredd a moment to discern what was wrong with the picture: the brushed-steel surround was free of graffiti, possibly the only part of McCluskey untouched by neglect, and seemingly in working order. A vid-camera was perched above the threshold—that it hadn't been ripped from its housing was again unusual.

"Remember," she whispered. "I'll do the talking. Pass me your rifles."

She walked ahead, pulling Dredd along with her rather than supporting him. The camera jerked into life before they reached them, and started tracking their progress. She looked up into its unblinking eye and waved, then pressed a button on an intercom set into the wall.

"*What do you want, Maze?*" a male voice crackled.

"Kinda thought that was obvious," she answered, yanking the Judge into the camera's field of vision.

"*If that's the lawboy the MC are looking for, give him to them. We ain't got no use for him.*"

"You don't figure havin' a jaybird as a hostage could be useful? Justice Central protects their own—you'd be lookin' at all sortsa leverage."

"*We'd be lookin' at all sortsa heat, too. The last thing we need is the full weight of the five-oh on our doorstep if we try to dangle a ransom in front of them.*"

"An' what do you think'll happen if the MC kill him? They'll blitz Strickland till there's no-one left outside a cube."

There was silence for a moment. Maze raised an eyebrow at Dredd but said nothing. "*He your prisoner or somethin'?*" the voice asked finally.

"The kid's drokked. Taken a bullet, broke some bones, lost a fair amount of blood. He's barely conscious. He don't get some meds into him, he ain't gonna make it."

"*Then he's shit outta luck. Drop him off at Saint Jude's, you're that concerned about him. We ain't got the facilities—*"

"Don't give me that. I know you got the doc up there. You got antibiotics, splints, bandages. He's worth more alive."

"*What's your angle in this, Maze? Why do you care so much about one bluejay?*"

"'San opportunity. Way I see it, he's fallen in our laps, and it'd be a waste to hand him over to the MC. This way, we can all come outta this smilin'."

"*He cut you a deal, you get him outta here alive?*"

"He's a rookie that's taken a beatin'. He can't offer me shit. But we can sure as hell exploit what we got."

Another pause. "*Nah. It's too risky lettin' a jay up here—*"

"Too bad. Maybe Gilpig can make a better offer."

"*Gilpig?*" It was a different voice this time; older, less wiseguy. Not a Mega-City accent. "*How's he involved?*"

"Who do you think's frontin' the Furies and the MC to track the badge down? He's got somethin' Gilpig wants."

"*What?*"

Maze didn't reply, just shot a laconic look at the camera. It was enough.

"*All right. We're sending the el down. Put the guns on the floor and don't move.*"

She complied, and they stood listening to the rumbling coming down the lift shaft. "We're in," she whispered.

12.59 pm

"CLARENCE? IT'S DAVIDSON. Sorry to pull you out of the meeting… Yeah, I'm sure. No, it's just we might have a situation, and I know you've got a vested interest. Well, it's Dredd—we've lost contact.

"Over an hour now. Last reported trace was on the Strickland estate, Sector Nine. Collins radioed in, said Dredd had comms problems. My operative says both were instructed to return to the Grand Hall—neither has yet done so.

"Could well be… If it were anyone else, maybe, but after what happened with the other clone… Yes, we've got a citywide alert to notify us of any sightings. Indeed. Troubling.

"I spoke to Morgan in Special Tactics. He recommended sending a unit into Strickland. Well, it's high poverty, high crime, strong gang element… bit of a tinderbox at the best of times. But something has to be done… Well, quite, considering the bloodline. Yes, of course, I'll be right over.

"Yes, Chief Judge. I'll tell Morgan you gave the green light."

Six

13.03 pm

"JOVIS, WHAT'S KEEPING him together?"

"Sheer willpower, I think. That, an' an absolute refusal to accept when he's beat. 'Slike one of those dinosaurs that take so long to die 'cause their brain has to catch up with the rest o' the body."

"Yeah, but he's just a kid... Anyway, what do *you* know about dinosaurs, Maze?"

"My mom told me all about the old national park, back before the war. Brontosauruses were her favourite. Used to make me cry when she told me they all escaped."

"You always were a damned weird juve. Don't surprise me that your folks skipped town an' left you behind."

"That's enough, Jeperson."

Dredd could hear them talking through the glasseen case, see them looking his way. There were four of them—Maze; a well-dressed, authoritative figure he took to be Winstanley; the melon-headed lackey Jeperson; and another subordinate, a woman, who'd operated the auto-doc. When he'd been told that they had a doctor up here that could patch him up, he'd assumed it to be a trained medic—he hadn't expected what looked to be a modded speedheal chamber, evidently built from purloined Justice Department tech. Either the boss-man had friends on the force passing him components, or there was a thriving black market in Judicial materiel. Either way, it was old stock: a clanking, wheezing affair that wasn't in much better shape than he was, and wasn't doing a great job of knitting him together: the broken bones in his right hand were setting imperfectly and the scorched skin was refusing to regenerate. His cuts and bruises were diminishing, and he felt the rib snap back into place, but it wasn't the complete overhaul that he would've had in a Grand Hall med-bay. By the time the thing shuddered to a halt, he still felt like he'd gone ten rounds with a demolition droid. The dizziness hadn't left him, either; when the woman opened the glasseen lid, he found himself gasping for air.

"He don't look cured," Maze muttered, watching as Dredd fell to his knees and coughed violently. Nobody went to his aid as he spat blood-flecked phlegm onto the floor; they all stepped back as one, as if his injuries were infectious.

"The machine can't work miracles," Winstanley said. "He needs a full course of treatment if he's to recover, not a quick fix."

"Seems to me the machine don't work at all," she replied. "How long have you had that thing?"

"It's on its last legs," the female attendant said, stepping around the prone Dredd to shut it down. "The electromagnetic coils have corroded. You'll find it's only capable of making the most superficial of repairs over time."

"Time to shop for a new one, then," Winstanley remarked jovially, rocking back on his heels with his hands in his pockets. "I'm sure my man could accommodate me."

"What you're admitting to... is criminal," Dredd snarled, wiping his mouth with the back of his gauntlet. He rose, unsteadily. "You're receiving stolen goods."

The older man remained unfazed, the smile fixed on his face. "And you're now party to *using* said stolen goods, Judge. How are you feeling, by the way. Strength returned? You did look at death's door when Maze brought you up, and I gave you safe harbour."

"He still looks like shit with sprinkles on," Maze said.

Winstanley laughed. "True. I did say it was only the most cursory of treatments. But the odds of him surviving the next twelve hours are, I believe, now significantly better. The blood-loss has at least stopped."

"Don't expect any gratitude," Dredd responded.

"I wouldn't dream of it. My experience of Justice Department is not one of politeness and appreciation."

"Your accent—you're from Brit-Cit."

The older man nodded. "Sought a future across the ocean in 2069. Big-city life appealed."

"In other words, the heat was closing in on you, and you skipped town. What made you end up in this cesspool of a sector?"

"Poor career choices, I'm not ashamed to admit. But what's the saying? 'It's better to rule in hell than serve in heaven'? Some kingdoms just aren't blessed by their looks."

"Something to be said for being at the top of the dungpile," Dredd replied, taking a step forward, his legs still feeling wobbly. Jeperson bristled, preparing to step between the Judge and his boss, but Winstanley didn't seem perturbed in the slightest. They were in a kind of makeshift lab/workroom. Beyond the door, Dredd could see living quarters, where other goons were shifting merch or cleaning guns. "I figure you must've been here long enough to be itching to escape the slums, to take your business up a level. Let me guess: you control the drugs and insurance rackets for at least the four-block area. Too much competition to be solely running crime in Strickland. But you need an edge, an advantage—something that's gonna finally let you break out, if you ever want to progress beyond lord of the dump."

Winstanley raised his eyebrows. "Eloquent *and* perceptive, Judge. You've got quite the serious head on those young shoulders. I rather think it must've been something of a tough call to have given yourself over to me as your one chance of getting out of here alive." He cast an amused eye towards Maze. "I knew Maze here couldn't have been instrumental in apprehending you; she's more than likely helping you in exchange for her own rewards. But still, walking willingly into the lion's den, not knowing what awaited you... you must've felt you had no options left. That your one chance out of here other than in a bodybag was to make a deal with the Devil."

"Don't flatter yourself," Dredd grumbled.

"Oh, yeah? I haven't thought twice about putting a bullet in a bluejay's heart in the past," Jeperson snarled. His bravado did little to challenge Dredd's first impression of him as a small-time oaf. "You're lucky you weren't whacked on the spot."

"Indeed," Winstanley said. "The forces of law and order aren't traditionally very popular around here."

"Whoa, whoa," Maze interjected hurriedly. "Thought it was agreed he was an asset. Justice Central will pay more for a live cop."

"Justice Central won't negotiate at *all*," Winstanley replied. "They'll string us along till they secure our location and set a drone on us. Or drop a nuke on the whole district."

"They'd do that?"

"Any excuse to raze Strickland to the ground."

"They'd sacrifice one of their own?"

"Like I said, they won't give an inch—and *he* knows that." Winstanley jerked a thumb at Dredd. "Juves like him, they're indoctrinated into the Department, brainwashed into giving their lives to the law. They know no single individual is greater than the system, and will walk into the fire to protect it."

"But he's valuable leverage, a bargaining chip. Why put him in the auto-doc if he's that disposable?"

"I didn't say I didn't want him around—at least for the next hour or so. We *do* have an opportunity before us, one we can use to our advantage." Winstanley addressed Dredd. "You're right, Judge. I want out of this..." He cast around, searching for the word. His quarters were comfortable and functional, but Dredd guessed the Brit wanted the trappings associated with status. "...quagmire," he said finally. "And you have brought the means to do so." He slid one hand out of his pocket and held up the flashdrive. Dredd must've been so out of it when he and Maze had arrived that he hadn't even been aware it had been removed from his belt pouch. She must've told them it was there; he guessed it went a long way to stopping Jeperson putting a bullet in him. "Do you know what's on it?"

"Enlighten me."

Winstanley chuckled. "Marcie?"

He tossed it to the engineer, who blithely caught it one-handed, plugged it into a nearby computer terminal and hit a few keys. A string of numbers scrolled past on the black screen. Dredd cast an eye at them: they looked like dates, times and codes.

"Recognise them?" the older man said.

"Some kind of delivery schedule," the Judge murmured, the stream of figures flickering against his visor. One he picked out among the many—today's date, June 16th, alongside the time 13:37.

"That's exactly what it is," Marcie answered, leaning against the monitor, tapping the glass with a finger. "Shipment times. The codes denote the cargo and the transport ID."

"Shipments from where?" Dredd asked.

"The Cursed Earth. Automated container craft bringing in munce stock, treemeat, synthi-derivatives from the outlying farms. There's no crew, just an A.I. pilot taking each ship on a round trip; deliver to the city, then the flight-path is programmed for the next destination. They're in constant motion, arriving every six hours or thereabouts."

"How do you know this?"

"Marcie's my on-staff tek expert," Winstanley said. "I... recruited her from Eastside U. I wrote off her gambling debts in exchange for her coming to work for me. She's digitised my entire client base."

The woman smiled, but looked away when she saw Dredd studying her.

"But we're not just talking solely a delivery schedule, are we?" continued the crime lord.

"No," Marcie replied, tapping a key so the numbers froze. "The memory stick seems to contain a program that allows you to hack into any given transporter and remote-access its directives. You can control it, fly it to wherever you want, even set it to self-detonate, should you wish. Essentially a massive back-door security lapse in the A.I. that whoever wrote the program must've been aware of."

"Does it work?" Dredd asked.

"We haven't yet put it to the test," Winstanley responded. "All in good time. Right now, though, I'm more curious as to how you acquired it. Because I seem to recall the name Bertram Gilpig being mentioned."

"Who is he?"

"I'm surprised you haven't encountered him before. Maybe they don't let you baby Judges rub shoulders with the great and the good. He's a perennial thorn in my side, let me tell you." Winstanley started to pace, hands behind his back. "Gilpig's a councillor; he's on the zoning committee for Meg South West. Planning, construction contracts, he's got his greedy fingers in all of it, as well as the inevitable kickbacks. He's been pushing for regeneration of Strickland and the surrounding areas for years."

Dredd was studiedly ignorant of city politics; he saw it as what those at the top occupied themselves with while he got on with what he did best: breaking heads on the street. Of course, there was no shortage of criminals in the corridors of power either, and they would eventually cross his path when necessary—but that was his sole experience of politicians and their ilk. It tended to colour your opinion somewhat. "What's stopped him?"

"The displacement problem. Too many cits with nowhere to go if they rolled in the demolition droids. As much as I'd imagine Grand Hall would like to see this place sealed in rockcrete and forget it ever existed, they haven't got room for all the poor dinks that make it their home. City's at capacity as it is; it's more convenient to keep them living in squalor, where they don't have to worry about them."

"I thought you were keen to escape this... what did you call it? Quagmire?"

"In my own way and under my own steam. Right now I'm beneath Justice Central's radar, which suits my business, and a regeneration project would bring all sorts of attention that I could do without."

"So you've been instrumental in blocking any motions, presumably."

Winstanley smiled. "Let's say I've been putting my faith in the right people to see sense."

Dredd grimaced. Corruption at the highest level: so many of them could be bought off. The uniform was inviolate, unimpeachable—their code was rigid and morally uncompromising—but put civilians in positions of authority and they buckled under the temptation. "So, Gilpig," he said. "Not a local boy."

"Good Grud, no. He's resident over in Dean Learner, south

of Central—which begs the question, what was he doing down this way?"

"I found the zipdrive hidden in the trunk of his driver's car. Gilpig himself was in Meyer—I would assume he was in the process of delivering it, or talking terms before it was handed over."

"Meyer is Furies turf—Jeb Rawlings' crew. If Gilpig was dealing with anyone, it'd be him."

"Selling on the means to hijack food shipments... for what? A cut of the profits?"

"Plenty here in Strickland going hungry. It'd be a poke in the eye for Grand Hall if the sector gained control of the distribution of imports, however briefly."

Dredd wasn't convinced. "From what I've heard of the councillor, he doesn't strike me as the philanthropic type. Whatever he's doing this for, I seriously doubt he has the good of the people in mind."

"He's certainly concerned about retrieving the memory stick, given the efforts the Furies and the MC are going to. This was no minor street deal. He's put a target on a Judge's head— that could have significant repercussions, if he's not careful." Winstanley nodded at Jeperson, who pulled a handcannon from his waistband and levelled it at Dredd. "His only chance of surviving this, career-wise, and not spending the rest of his life in a cube, is if you're dead—with you as a corpse, no-one knows of his involvement."

Jeperson grabbed Dredd's arm and hauled him towards one of the adjoining rooms.

Winstanley patted Maze on the back. "He *will* be our bargaining chip, my dear," he said, "but not with Justice Department. We let Gilpig know Dredd is alive and in our hands, and we'll have the sneaky little bastard in our pockets."

"What about the hack program?" Marcie asked.

"Oh, we'll be making use of that. Who'd have thought black-market treemeat would be my ticket out of here?" He shook his head, chuckled, then started to follow Jeperson. "Why don't you make a start, Marcie, on bringing our first container online?" he called over his shoulder. "Oh, and Greening?" Another lieutenant appeared from the living area. "Escort young Maze back downstairs."

"Hey, wait," the woman protested as she was manhandled towards the entrance. "I was the one that brought him to you, convinced you that protecting him was a good idea—"

"And I'm grateful, honestly," he replied, as she disappeared through the door, struggling. "But events have overtaken all of us. Best you sit this one out. I wouldn't want you to get hurt."

13.05 pm

Justice Department was rolling.

Cits on the Strickland estate tore themselves from their Tri-D sets, paused their illegal activities, put aside their trashzines, and found a window to watch as the pat-wagon rumbled down the main drag. The wagons were distinctive, with their low roar and the dull, bass-heavy vibrations that rattled the window glass as they passed, and only the most committed career criminals didn't feel a primal fear at the noise. Nothing sounded quite like Judges on the move. It was a sound to make you stop what you're doing to double-check your innocence; if the jays were out in force, then someone was in their sights, and you better make damn sure it wasn't you.

A Judicial presence on Strickland wasn't unknown, but few could remember ever seeing the heavy mob hitting the sked in quite this fashion. There were at least a dozen Special Tactics officers on board, fully armed and armoured, Lawrods slung over their shoulders. A co-pilot swung a high-calibre machine-gun lazily on its pintel, casually sweeping the blocks the vehicle was passing. Retribution, raw and terrible, rolled off the Judges in waves, merciless and brutally efficient. Even those with nothing to hide ducked out of sight and prayed that the patwagon wouldn't stop at their door. All mouthed a brief word of thanks to Grud when it carried on its way.

One thing was certain: Grand Hall didn't mobilise the ST division unless it wanted to drop a whole heap of stomm on an individual. When the eagle struck, it came down hard—few were left standing in the aftermath.

13.06 pm

JEPERSON FORCED DREDD into a wooden chair at gunpoint and bound his hands. The muscles in his arms protested, poorly-knitted bones popped out of joint, and a surge of pain almost brought unconsciousness crashing down on him again.

For a second his mind retreated to another hard chair, in the centre of a bare interrogation cell. It was an Academy exercise, fellow cadets performing the role of the SJS. Rico was one of them, trying to break his clone-brother, force him to confess to an imaginary misdeed. Dredd was resolute, unwavering, his heart rate—his tutors told him later—steady as a rock. Rico had tried to push ever harder; was it hindsight that was colouring his recollection, or did Dredd detect a streak of bitterness in his sibling, an urge in Rico to see his twin crack? It should've been a warning sign, if it was there at all, but the simulation was stopped before Rico could go too far. Dredd could see him now, leant over him, pushing him to breaking point: a mirror image, berating his own reflection.

Then the chair softened and the face became Perrineau's, asking him how he felt about destroying his clone-brother's life. As the therapist spoke, the seat grew softer, becoming liquid, until he felt himself merging with the cushions, unable to move or look away. He was trapped, paralysed.

A sharp sting brought him back to his senses, Winstanley standing over him. He backhanded him across the face again. "Need you conscious, son," he remarked. He motioned to Jeperson, who now held a small vid-camera and was training it on the Judge. "We're going to send a short message to Councillor Gilpig, let him know his future lies in our hands."

Jeperson edged closer with the camera, near enough to Dredd that he clearly saw the shards of plastic embed themselves in the jelly of his eye when the bullet smashed through the casing and out the other side of his skull. Winstanley managed a half-turn before the second shot caught him in the throat and he went down on his knees, hands clamped to his neck, trying to hold back a crimson fountain. A third slug hit him in the chest and put him on the ground for good.

Marcie stepped cautiously into the room, glancing at both corpses to make sure they were dead. She finally met Dredd's enquiring gaze. "Wally Squad," she said flatly. "We need to get the hell out of here right now."

Seven

13.07 pm

"Are you fit to stand?" she asked, slicing through the restraints around his wrists.

"I'll make it," Dredd replied, accepting her hand and letting her help him out of the chair. His legs felt leaden, tightness cramping around his calves and thighs, but he hobbled forward, determined not to let it slow him up. He bent and took Jeperson's gun from his body, trying to hold it in his haphazardly repaired right hand, but he could barely bend his forefinger into the trigger guard without the tendons twitching unhappily, so he resorted once again to his left. It wasn't his strongest, and he missed the support the double-grip gave him, but he'd manage.

"We have to hurry," she said, already heading out the door. Dredd followed, casting an eye back at Winstanley one last time, lying on his back in a spreading pool of blood, mouth set in a rictus of disapproval as if he'd been denied the chance to prove himself. Too late now to escape McCluskey, the lawman thought; now it's your tomb.

In the main living area of the crime boss's apartment, further corpses littered the carpet and furniture. Winstanley's men had been dealt with ruthlessly: single bullet holes to the skull, mainly. The undercover officer had been busy.

She picked her way over the tangle of limbs towards the main entrance. "This isn't anywhere near the total of his workforce," she remarked without turning back to address Dredd. "We'll need to hurry. I don't want to get cornered up here, trying to explain a massacre." She pulled the flashdrive from her pocket and held it up. "There's also the question of this. A closer inspection of the files revealed that they were incomplete."

"Incomplete? Then—"

"Smart money says the Furies already have half the program. Gilpig held back the rest for some reason—maybe to make sure they didn't double-cross him. Either way, that's why they're so keen to get their hands on this."

"Can they do anything with the files they have?"

"Not sure. Possibly. What's on here looked like a lot of failsafe commands. If they bypass those, we could be in trouble."

"Damn."

"I hear that. Talking of the program, I did a practice run on the hack code, and... I don't think this is about hijacking shipments. It couldn't get me into the A.I. core and allow me to take control—but from what I saw, I think once transmitted, you could shut it down from the outside."

"Shut down the A.I. pilot..." Dredd caught up with her and grabbed her arm. She turned to face him.

"Ship comes tumbling down," she replied flatly. "C'mon, we gotta go."

"This tek-knowledge... How sure are you? What's your name, actually? I figure Marcie's part the cover."

"Saunders. Erin Saunders." She brought her right hand up to her forehead in a cursory salute. "Been with Wally Squad nearly five years; computer science a specialty. I'm eighty per cent sure

I'm right—I wish I wasn't, 'cause we're going to be in a world of stomm otherwise." She opened the door to the corridor outside the apartment and poked her head out, beckoning for him to join her once she was sure the coast was clear. She crossed to the el, jabbed the call button. "This is our best shot. Winstanley has made sure the stairs from the upper mid-levels are impassable. If we're lucky, we can ride the express near enough to the ground floor."

"Can't we call in aerial assistance, have an H-Wagon pick us up from this level?"

Saunders shook her head. "Take too long. Like I say, I don't want to be here now my cover's been compromised. I've contacted Control. Special Tactics is heading this way; they can extract us, providing we make it to the sked in one piece."

"They're sending Tac-Div into Strickland? Someone at Grand Hall trying to start a war?"

"Apparently Goodman signed the order. Looks like you're too valuable to write off."

Dredd considered this. Was it *him* they wanted to retrieve, the Judge they'd forged; or was it the DNA, the blood, too precious to end up in the hands of others? Were the two separate at all? He never felt more like a construct, the property of Justice Department, than he did when the-powers-that-be turned their eyes on him. Chief Judge Goodman was taking a personal interest; maybe it was the tragedy of Rico, the desire to avoid further embarrassment, the unwillingness to waste potential. It was both reassuring and concerning: would he ever be allowed to stand on his own two feet? He resented being made a special case on the basis of his genes. He didn't need protecting. His failures should be his own, they would inform his future career—if, that is, he still had one, he thought, noting the patchwork of injuries his body had become.

The el dinged, the doors slid open, and a surprised-looking henchman who'd evidently just been down to the nearest

Shapiro's on a hottie run had a moment to register the two figures standing in front of him before Saunders shot him in the face. She wasted no time, hauling the corpse from the car, ushering Dredd into the lift and hitting the ground-floor button.

"How long you been part of Winstanley's outfit?" Dredd asked once they started to descend.

"Just over a year."

"It true he recruited you from Eastside U?"

"That's where I was placed. The gambling thing was part of the lure. Sector House has been trying to get someone on the inside since the Brit's been making a name for himself in Strickland. My handler created quite the backstory for me—had to be convincing if it was going to work."

"Feel like I ruined your op."

"Wasn't your fault, you weren't to know. Choosing between pulling you out and keeping my cover ain't no choice at all." She looked him up and down. "What the hell *happened* to you, anyway?"

"Just having a bad day. Comes with the territory, I guess."

"You've not long got your full eagle, am I right?"

Dredd nodded. "Second year."

She rolled her eyes. "It's a learning curve."

"And then some."

The el shuddered, then bounced to a stop, creaking on its cables. Saunders instinctively looked up. "Oh, drokk," she whispered. "That doesn't sound good."

"Fault?"

"Or someone's stopped the el. Could be my little bullet party upstairs has been discovered earlier than I hoped." Dredd glanced at her. "Winstanley's men have access to another el on the north side," she explained. "That's why we had to get out of there fast." The car juddered again, tipping slightly. "Think they might be trying to disconnect it, blowing the cables."

"Would they know it was us?"

"The boss-man's quarters were CCTV'd to the hilt. Anyone checking the feed would've seen which way we went. I didn't have time to disable it."

"Give me a boost," Dredd instructed, pointing to the maintenance hatch in the ceiling. Saunders nodded and laced her fingers together, and the uniformed Judge stepped into her hands, reaching up for the hatch. It resisted at first, until he sharply elbowed it free of its hinges and pushed it aside. He got an arm through and pulled himself up; he struggled a little, but gritted his teeth and tried not to vocalise the pain from his midriff.

"You okay?" she enquired.

"Been better," he muttered, holding a hand to his side where the bullet had entered. Felt like something new had ripped. He looked around, saw the doors to a level they'd just passed several feet above him to his right. The el suddenly lurched, and a cable whipped down the shaft. He stepped back quickly, jerking his head out of its way as it struck sparks from the grey metal walls. The car was now tilting sharply; they really didn't have much time before it became a literal express all the way to the bottom. If this was a more modern block, it'd have foam safeguards in place at the base, anti-grav emergency protection ready to kick in. McCluskey was a pre-war wreck, of course, with none of those features. It was unlikely it had graced an inspector's report for the last fifteen years—which meant the standard of repair must've seriously deteriorated all over. Still, there would be *some* safety measure from the original build...

It was pitch black in the shaft, but he scanned the walls with infra-red and saw the panels scored by decades of rust, the scrapes left by the plummeting cable that had gouged out holes in the metal. He sighted his gun just below the bottom corner of the el and pumped the trigger, punching deep impact craters into the side. He then scrambled back to the hatch and put his arm through, indicating Saunders should grab hold. She jumped, and used her feet against the el doors to push herself upwards. Dredd grunted as he pulled the undercover officer onto the lift's roof. His muscles screamed, but she was through.

"This is going to hurt," he breathed as they both stood on the sloping lift.

"More than it already is?" she replied, noting a fresh bloodstain blossoming on his uniform.

"Yeah. Be ready to jump on my mark. The angle the el's at, the moment it drops it's going to collide with the shaft wall."

"Where are we going to be?"

"Heading through the wall. It's going to be split-second, so don't hesitate."

"What's on the other side of the wall?"

"Your guess is as good as mine."

The lift trembled, then jolted downwards just as a tremendous *bang* echoed down the shaft. The bottom edge of the car smashed through the rusted panels Dredd had shot, leaving a gaping rent.

"*Now!*" Dredd ordered and grabbed Saunders' arm, throwing the pair of them off the el and through the tear in the wall as the car continued its fall, pinballing off the walls. The lawman felt the ragged edge of the hole slice his back but he flung out his left hand and found purchase, his fist closing over a rung. For a moment he took the weight of them both and nearly lost his grip

you failed, Joe

but Saunders clung on too, her feet scrambling, finding a lower rung to secure herself. They hung, motionless, panting, listening to the roar of the el as it plunged towards the ground floor. An almighty crunch followed, the whole shaft reverberating.

"How... how did you know this access ladder would be here?" she asked at last.

"I guessed."

She laughed despite herself, a short bark of hysterical relief, but there was a catch in Dredd's voice that was concerning. She could barely see him in the dark, but he clearly hadn't come through it unscathed. He'd warned it was going to hurt. She felt like she'd torn a ligament herself.

"You ready to climb?" she heard Dredd say.

"When you are."

13.13 pm

"JOVIS, DAX, YOU seen this?" Bonedog pointed from the bench in Scott Potasnik plaza. They all turned and stood as one.

"Holy drokk," Sheema breathed.

The pat-wagon rumbled into the thoroughfare between Meyer and McCluskey and came to a halt, the Judges dismounting and spreading out. Even from this distance, the scatterblasters the badges were wielding looked huge, intimidating. The jays meant business.

Bonedog glanced down at the snubnose he'd been twirling on his finger, then hurriedly stuffed it in his pants. They'd been taking potshots at batgliders for the last couple of hours, held up some dinks on the pedway and scored a few creds, which Dax had used to purchase half a dozen grams of sugar off the Candyman. The gun falling into their laps had felt like a stroke of luck, a means to have a little fun. Now it was impossibly heavy, a millstone that he wanted to discard as soon as he could. Dax saw him sweat and fidget nervously.

"Relax," she said, turning her attention back to the helmets. They seemed to be going door to door, rousting the bums from the entrances. "They ain't gonna turn out in force like this for a stolen piece of hardware. Probably don't even know we got it. They must've come for the bluejay."

"But he saw us," Sheema said. "Remember? He saw you take it, Dax. What if he fingers us, reports us for not calling it in?"

"Will you calm down? He'd just had the stuffing kicked out of him, he ain't gonna remember shit." All the same, Dax was worried. She should've known pilfering the weapon would be bad news, but she couldn't help herself. To be honest, she hadn't expected the Judge to have made it; she would've anticipated the Furies or the MC to have taken care of a wounded badge without much trouble. She assumed he was still alive, that that was what this was all about: officer down, back-up required. Kid must have some sand to have survived this far.

"Reckon we should dump it," Juice remarked. "Lose it before the jays track it to us."

"Just don't blow your cool, okay?" Dax was insistent, as much for her own benefit.

"Easy for you to say," Bonedog scoffed.

"I'll take it, you're so scared." Bonedog surreptitiously passed it to her, and she jammed it in her belt, pulling her vest-top over it. "Jays ain't lookin' for us. Long as we stay under the radar, nobody does nothin' stupid, we'll be all right—"

It was at that moment that the first firebomb came arcing out of Meyer and exploded in front of the pat-wagon.

13.15 pm

THEY CLIMBED IN silence and darkness for several long minutes before they reached a service door that Dredd had to shoulder repeatedly until it buckled enough for them to squeeze through. They came out on a middle level, quietly relieved to be back on firm ground. Under the grimy ceiling-mounted fluorescents, Saunders could finally see the damage that Dredd had inflicted upon himself in the jump from the el roof: a deep gouge between the shoulder blades, the uniform soaked in blood. His right arm was also hanging oddly, limp and unmoving against his side.

"Christ, Dredd, what's happened to your arm?"

He glanced at it, brought his left hand round and tested the unresponsive limb. "Took the full weight of both of us on this side. Pulled it from its socket, I think."

"You climbed the ladder with it like that?" she asked incredulously.

"Wasn't easy, admittedly."

"Here, let me," she said, stepping forward and firmly placing one palm on his bicep, the other on his shoulder. "On three." She got as far as 'one' before she slammed his arm back into place. Dredd yelled like she'd never heard him respond before, a primal cry of pain that he must have been desperate to let out. The kid had been through so much, borne so much, that this latest physical trauma needed some release. The sharp, guttural roar was over in a second, and he looked angry with himself for having given voice to his agony, like it was a display of weakness. She got the impression that any emotion should be buried deep down inside, that it was a betrayal of his own personal code to allow it to escape. It couldn't be healthy, she thought—if he kept this up, in a few years he'd be a roiling mess of stifled fear and anger that would see him either retreat within himself completely, or quit.

He pulled away, but nodded nevertheless in gratitude. "Appreciate it."

"You've got a hell of a wound on your back, too."

"I'm aware. It'll have to wait."

"It might not, if you're losing blood."

"Just one more deadline we gotta beat, then." He motioned towards the el doors. "Lift's out of action. Are the stairs going to be viable from this point?"

"Yeah, Winstanley didn't bother controlling access this far south."

"Guess we're walking."

In fact they ran, as much as they were able, half-tumbling down the emergency stairs, Dredd losing his footing occasionally but waving off support and indicating that Saunders should concentrate on her own descent. They'd gone down nine flights when gunfire striated the wall, ricocheting off the metal bannisters, forcing them to retreat and hunker down—a six-man group of Murder Corps members came streaming up in the other direction, stutter-rifles blazing. They had them pinned down. Dredd managed to take out one with a well-aimed shot down the stairwell, but they had the numbers; a sustained barrage kept the Judges from manoeuvring into a better position to return fire. Dredd tried his belt pouches, but came up empty of stumm grenades, or indeed anything else: Winstanley's men had been thorough.

"Any ideas?" Saunders asked.

"They're being paid to get the flashdrive back," Dredd answered. "We could give it to them."

"That's not going to stop them killing us."

"No, but it might make them pause." He ejected the clip from his automatic, and held out his hand for Saunders' blaster, which she passed over reluctantly, eyebrow raised. "Tip from my final-year firearms instructor," he said. Then he shuffled over to the edge of the step they were perched on, waited until there was a lull and called down, "You want the memory stick? It's yours."

There was no response, so Dredd tossed the clip, which clattered down onto the next landing, then drew a bead on it with the blaster. They heard murmuring, and shadows moving up from the level beneath. The lawman waited until he saw the first MC meathead edge within a couple of feet of the landing, then fired, the slug striking the clip dead-centre; the bullets detonated, becoming a bright fireball. Screams and curses echoed up the stairwell, and Dredd took advantage of the chaos, standing to shoot down the stairs. He put one perp down, still beating flames from his clothes, and another two followed, too stunned by the explosion to seek shelter. Saunders used the covering fire to retrieve one of the dead men's stutter-rifles and found a corner to take out the remainder. Once the last body hit the deck, the two Judges regrouped and collected as much ammo as they could carry.

"Remind me to thank your tutor," she said, pocketing a handful of clips.

"Died two months ago," Dredd replied, chambering a round. "Random drive-by." He looked around at the distant thud of explosions outside the block. "Let's keep moving."

Eight

13.21 pm

THE SPECIAL TACTICS unit was coming under fire from both sides, and had fallen back to regroup at the pat-wagon. Pools of liquid flame were scattered around them, courtesy of the improvised weapons thrown from above. It seemed the Russ Meyer Furies and the Len McCluskey Murder Corps had buried the hatchet and joined forces to repel the Judges—the jays hadn't been down on Strickland like this for years, hadn't shown any interest in the cits that scraped a living amongst the half-ruined towers of the old city. If they thought they could move into the estate in force, start throwing their weight around, they had another think coming.

Jeb Rawlings watched from his vantage point as the helmets sought cover behind the wagon, their progress impeded by the automatic gunfire tearing up the rockcrete between the two blocks. He knew why they were here: they'd been sent in to extract the badge that had turned up this morning. Quite why he deserved the overkill treatment, Rawlings didn't know, but the jays sure were keen to pull him out. Rawlings should've had his head by now—he'd promised Gilpig as much—but now things were getting messy, which wasn't going to please the councillor one bit. More witnesses, more loose ends: it was spiralling out of control. Maybe they should've hung back and let the ST-Div conduct their search, not drawn any more heat onto themselves, but it's hard to deny a Fury when his blood is up—and those uniforms weren't popular among his crew. Just the sight of a single bluejay was enough to get them riled; a fully-armoured squad rolling onto Strickland was an automatic target. It wasn't smart, but feelings were running high.

No, Gilpig wasn't going to be happy. He'd bet the farm on this scheme of his, and now it was unravelling, thanks to a random—seemingly indestructible, it had to be said—helmet being in the wrong place at the wrong time. It was mad of the councillor to have come onto Strickland in person to deliver the codes—Rawlings had warned him about keeping a low profile—but it was typical of his paranoid arrogance that he didn't trust anyone else to hand them over. Even then, he'd held back half the files until he was sure the Furies weren't going to stiff him, which, ironically, had been his undoing—if the jay hadn't found the zipdrive in Gilpig's car, then they wouldn't have been put in this position.

To be fair, his mistrust wasn't entirely misplaced; Rawlings had been contemplating selling on the codes to the highest bidder (someone who could've made better use of black-market treemeat cargo), much preferring the immediate creds to the long-term plan Gilpig had in mind. It had sounded impressive, and could've meant serious paydirt in the future, but the gang leader wasn't that patient; it would've been years before they saw a return on the risk they were taking. All very well for the councillor to shut himself away in Learner, far from the scene of the crime, while the Furies did the dirty work. He was the kind of uptown drokkwad who saw the people of Sector 9 as nothing more than variables in a potentially lucrative project. Why should their feelings come into the matter when there was an area that needed gentrifying?

Rawlings had done a five-stretch in the same iso-block as a knucklehead who later became one of the politician's minders; Bertram wasn't picky about where he hired his muscle. Rawlings was serving time for robbery, the goon a manslaughter rap. When Gilpig wanted a contact in Strickland, the chief Fury got the call—and when he'd heard what the councillor had to say, he told him to go to hell. But in the end, greed won out.

Still, all moot now. The jays were going to call for reinforcements if they got beaten here, and more waves of Judges would be on their way: the gangs would be pummelled into submission by the sheer weight of Grand Hall forces, and the trail of evidence would lead back to Gilpig, who would be looking at thirty years. There'd be questions asked about who he had leaked the transporter codes to, and a major internal review—heads would roll, security access would be scrutinised. Ripples cascading outwards, people across the board exposed in a chain of events that originated with that one badge zeroing in on the councillor's car. It didn't really matter now whether they killed the jay or not; there were too many eyes on Strickland now for anyone to get away.

Part of Rawlings felt a little relieved that Gilpig's plan wasn't going to come to fruition. He'd been born in Meyer, and like most of the locals, hadn't come close to escaping it. Glum acceptance led to a perverse sort of pride, an obstinate belief in keeping Strickland the way it was for the people unlucky enough to be stuck here. If he was honest, he didn't want it bulldozed and replaced with something else, he didn't want redevelopment, even though it would've set him and his brothers up for life, if Gilpig had come through on his promises. He shouldn't feel anything for this dump, but... you grew attached.

A sharp *boom* as the cannon mounted on the pat-wagon took out a corner of the block, and the whole building rumbled. The helmets were forcing their way into Meyer, getting under the arc of burning bottles and rubble; the Judges knew their tactics. Within minutes they'd be coming for him—there would be nowhere to run, nowhere to hide. He doubted any quarter would be given.

As much as he wanted to preserve Strickland, he didn't want it to forget him, either. If the jays were going to trample all over the estate, then he wasn't going to make it easy for them. Rawlings turned from the window and woke up the laptop sitting on the table, fishing a zipdrive from his overjak pocket and plugging it in. A wash of data flooded the screen, and he flicked through it quickly, finding the time and code he'd been seeking. He started the hack program running, aware that without the other half of the codes it wasn't going to give him much control—as a final note of payback, it was going to be untargeted and somewhat random. But needs must, he supposed.

As the numbers scrolled by and he got a lock on his particular cargo vessel, Rawlings considered the deal with the Devil that had brought him to this point, and wondered which of them was the innocent party seduced into corruption. He laughed, despite himself. They were *all* going to hell, he thought. Every damn one of them.

13.26 pm

McCLUSKEY WAS DESCENDING into chaos. The regular cits that still called it home were trying desperately not to be caught in the crossfire between the Judges and the Murder Corps, who were lobbing firebombs and using any window available to open fire on the officers on the ground. If Dredd had hoped that he and Saunders could pass through the panicking throng unmolested, he was disappointed—if anything, the MC were more hopped up on destruction than before. Maybe they recognised that they never had any realistic chance of withstanding a Justice Department onslaught, and were determined to go out in a blaze of glory. Perhaps they wanted to set a fire to Strickland and burn it down themselves before the jays could get close. Whichever, the madness was palpable, thick in the air as much as the stink of gasoline and oily smoke. But they evidently hadn't forgotten they were meant to be finding Dredd, and whenever the pair was spotted they had to take cover from guns and blasters, punching chunks out of the plaster walls haphazardly. The uniform was making him a target.

Every delay dealing with these attacks was critical. As far as Saunders could see, her companion was growing paler by the minute, the blood loss becoming more acute. His breath was shallow, and his attempts to cover up his pain were less and less convincing. The MC were becoming increasingly wanton in their violence, and the Wally Squad Judge found that taking them out was not especially difficult; Dredd's aim, however, was deteriorating, his left hand wobbling. She blew holes in the latest two creeps and before they'd hit the dirt pulled Dredd into the corridor to continue their descent. But the young Judge resisted this time, his attention elsewhere, and instead walked through the open door into a vacated apartment. She barked his name a couple of times, and when she received no acknowledgement, she followed him, sighing. A figure was silhouetted against the window on the far wall, watching the insanity outside.

"Maze," Dredd murmured.

The figure didn't turn, but the lawman could see her reflection lit by the orange glow of burning petroleum. It was impassive, mask-like. "This was my home," she said softly. "It was everything I knew."

"We'll get you out of here," Dredd replied. "Come on."

She cast an eye over her shoulder as if only just becoming

aware that there were others in the apartment with her, and shook her head. "I don't want to leave. I belong here."

"I promised I'd get you out. I can't guarantee your safety if you stay. The whole building could come down."

"You don't have to guarantee me anything. You're not beholden to me, Dredd. I'm just another Strickland bum; I should be doing time for vagrancy. I'm a perp, like all the others."

"You're a citizen. I'm sworn to protect you, regardless of your station."

"Really? How's that going?" She turned to face him, jerking her head back at the window as a fresh explosion blew out a balcony across the way in Meyer. "Have you seen yourself lately? You look like you've been dragged through a garbage grinder ass-backwards."

"So everyone keeps telling me. But that's secondary to my duty, as long as this is still intact." He tapped his badge, an echo of a gesture that Maze had made—hours? It seemed like a lifetime—earlier. "Everything else is just flesh and blood."

"Can we have this conversation another time?" Saunders interjected. "Dredd, we need to go before you pass out, or one of us is shot, or McCluskey topples over, whichever comes first. Leave her if she wants to stay."

"Do you want me to arrest you?" Dredd asked Maze, ignoring Saunders. "I haven't forgotten that unlicensed firearm you've got about your person."

Maze laughed, raising her arms. "One prisoner, amongst all this. Feels kind of pointless, don't it?" As if to underline her comment, an MC gunman came crashing into the apartment, drunk on disorder. He had a moment to recognise Dredd before Saunders grabbed him by the throat, slammed him into the door frame, and swung the door repeatedly into his head until he collapsed. She rolled him into the corridor and kicked the door shut behind her.

"Okay," the undercover officer breathed. "*Now* we're getting the drokk out of here."

"This doesn't have to be your life," Dredd said. He remembered hearing Jeperson's passing remark back in Winstanley's quarters. "Your parents abandoned you here, didn't they?"

"No, they just never came back. Drug deal over in Earhart—must've gone sour. Funnily enough, the local jays didn't assign it top priority, and Welfare didn't quite stretch all the way down to Strickland. So I fended for myself, and McCluskey became my family. Became everything. I couldn't leave it."

"It's a trap, that way of thinking. I thought you wanted out."

"So did I, what with…" She waved at the bloodstained door. "But when it came down to it, I couldn't. I *can't.*"

"It could all end up being razed to the ground."

"Then I'll go with it." Maze reached down and picked one of the musty-looking blankets heaped at her feet and tossed it to him. "Wrap yourself in that, cover up the uniform. You're a sittin' duck otherwise." Dredd did so hesitantly, hooding his helmet, and she smiled approvingly. "Now you're one of us. Go on, go."

She turned back to the window as Saunders yanked open the door and impatiently pulled him through, back into the mêlée.

13.33 pm

DREDD DIDN'T CARE for hiding beneath a disguise—the Academy had always taught him that the man and the uniform were indivisible, and it was a tenet that he stood by—but he had to admit it was working. With his Wally Squad companion leading him, the Judge kept his head down and sought to avoid confrontation, and they looked like any other McCluskey tenants fleeing the fighting.

Some Justice Department personnel found plainclothes work a

lot more natural than others. Maybe it was a mindset; certainly it required courage and unshakeable self-belief. Dredd simply felt uncomfortable with any kind of pretence, ungainly. He could intimidate, exaggerate and insinuate, but he couldn't lie. Saunders was clearly very adept at it, to have been embedded within Winstanley's outfit for so long without arousing suspicion, but lengthy periods came with attendant psychological problems. The lack of discipline, the total immersion in the criminal culture, meant some deprogramming was necessary once they were brought back into the fold. For Dredd, that bending of the law was unconscionable.

For the moment, though, he was doing a very realistic impersonation of someone on the edge of unconsciousness. The blood loss was taking its toll: his limbs were growing ever heavier, his vision blurring. His clumsy tumble through the crowds was becoming a nightmarish plunge into a sea of grotesques, faces swimming past. He would catch a fleeting glimpse of a gang member stalking past, spitgun hoisted on their shoulder, and had to actively suppress himself from drawing his blaster from under the blanket. If he was to survive, he had to go below the radar, concentrate on breathing, and allow this lawlessness—for the moment—to go unpunished. It was a wrench, as painful as any he'd sustained over the course of this testing day.

As they neared the ground floor, the mass of bodies grew thicker, a logjam caused by McCluskey residents scurrying for the main entrance to escape the MC's rampage, and those reluctant to venture outside, where gunfire was still rattling. Adding to the obstruction was one of the Special Tactics officers standing at the doors, trying to instil some kind of order while at the same time casting an eye over the faces present. When Saunders caught sight of him, she redoubled their efforts to push through the throng.

"There's our way out," she muttered over her shoulder.

The crowd was solid and panicking, and the Judges met with more than a little resistance and no shortage of anger. A meathead squared up to Saunders as she elbowed her way past, and she punched him hard in the face without hesitation or warning, leaving him on his backside and cupping a broken nose. The sea of citizens parted a touch after that, but still the press separated them. Dredd's breathing devolved into halting rasp—it felt like the oxygen was being sucked from the block—and he stumbled, his head hot and dizzy. Unable to prevent himself, he collided with a figure in front of him, and the blanket was knocked from his shoulders.

Blearily, he looked at who he'd walked into, and she looked vaguely familiar—a young adult with a Mohawk and face tatts. He was sure he'd seen her before, but couldn't place it; she was staring at him with both fear and recognition in her eyes, as were the three juves standing behind her. Sandwiched in the scrum, Dredd and the girl held each other's gaze for a long uncomprehending second before she silently pulled a snubnose from beneath her vest-top and proffered it to him.

The cry went up. "*Gun! Everyone on the floor! Now!*" The Tac-Judge brought his Lawrod to bear, and the crowd scattered. Dredd still had the wherewithal to snatch the weapon from the fem and strongarm her to the ground, while Saunders yelled her Wally Squad I.D., holding up her hands non-threateningly.

"Dredd? Good to see you're still alive," the Tac-Judge called, edging towards him, rifle trained on the woman in the lawman's grip, who wasn't offering any resistance. The name on his badge was Pearce. "We're here to pull you out."

"Yeah. Textbook... operation, from what I've seen," he murmured in reply, wincing and glancing around at the chaos. Saunders smiled thinly.

"C'mon, we need to get you to a med-facility asap," Pearce said, and talked quickly into his comm for back-up. He unhooked a pair of cuffs from his belt and bound the punk girl, who appeared shellshocked.

As they were making for the doors, a low rumble filled the air, which made everyone, cit and Judge alike, look up quizzically. It was coming from beyond the block and slowly growing louder; Dredd saw a shadow passing over the thoroughfare outside. He turned to Saunders.

"What time is it?"

Nine

13.37 pm

THE CARGO VESSEL loomed large above the peaks of the blocks, a black brick-shaped slab filling the world like the flawless blue sky had simply been taken away, leaving only an impenetrable absence. Only the red blinking lights lining its undercarriage broke the illusion. An automated carrier transport had no need of decals or cockpit, or indeed to be especially streamlined—it wasn't much more than a flying crate in both looks and function, programmed with a single flight path, held aloft by the twin anti-grav engines positioned towards its rear. Normally the sky-barges cruised at an altitude that ensured they didn't interfere with Mega-City traffic; it was rare to see one so low and close-up.

At this height—and clearly still descending—the roar of the craft's engines was deafening, making the teeth and bones feel like they were rattling loose. When Dredd and Saunders exited McCluskey and stepped into the dim light, escorted by Pearce, the fighting had all but dribbled to a halt, everyone's eyes drawn to the immense ship.

"Jovus drokk," the Wally Squad Judge whispered. "Is that…?"

"The thirteen-thirty-seven treemunce special," Dredd intoned. "Looks like the Furies decided to upload the hack program."

"But they won't have control without—"

"I don't think they're going for control—"

Any further words were drowned out by the ear-splitting cacophony of the turbines as the vessel bore down on Strickland. It sounded like the end of the world; the blare of trumpets signalling the last day of judgement, if you believed in that sort of thing. The backwash of the anti-grav lifters was sending a squall through the estate, winds whipping around every corner of the rockcrete canyons, smoke plumes twisting and dust and debris spiralling in the air. The Special Tactics officers motioned a retreat towards the pat-wagon, but Dredd didn't believe that there was going to be enough time to pull out of the impact zone. The ship was coming in hot and heavy.

"Get down!" Dredd yelled at Saunders, raising his voice as much as he was able above the din. "Find cover! You try to take your chances in the open, you're not going to make it!"

The plainclothes cop nodded and made to do as Dredd suggested before he stopped her with a hand on her shoulder.

"Wait. The zipdrive."

"Dredd, no. You're not going into Meyer?"

"Not going to stop it otherwise."

"It's suicidal. That thing's going to take out every block in its path."

"If you've got another solution let's hear it."

"I'll come with you. I'll have a better chance of accessing the data anyway."

Against his better judgement, Dredd found himself shaking his head. "No. No point us both taking the risk."

"Don't patronise me. I'm a Judge too. It's my duty—"

"You don't understand. Figure this is a one-way ticket, and there's not much left of me still to break."

"Exactly. You're in no fit state—"

"No point getting yourself killed holding my hand. I can do that well enough on my own."

"What, hold your hand?"

"Get killed."

She sighed. "This isn't heroic, you know."

"Just trying to save lives rather than put them in danger." He held out his palm, his expression grim, implacable. She knew he would not be swayed, and reluctantly passed the memory stick over. "Now go," he shouted.

She backed away, scowling, and dashed for a nearby narrow alley. Dredd turned and saw Pearce push his Mohawk Girl prisoner back towards the entrance of McCluskey, the direction many of the other residents were taking. The panic was almost tangible as bodies collided at the doors. Dredd tried to shout orders, to try to stop the stampeding, but no-one was in the mood to listen; sheer animal instinct had taken over. When the transporter clipped the top of the first building—Arthur Mullard Con-Apts—and brought several hundred tons of masonry crashing down onto the sked below, the chaos intensified. Dredd could do nothing to quell it; he could only watch—for a moment, uncharacteristically paralysed by the enormity of what he was witnessing—as the ship continued its trajectory and carved off half of Sarah Jessica Parker, an explosion of glass and rubble raining down in a wide arc. He hobble-ran as best he could, throwing himself to the side to avoid a plummeting timber beam embedding itself in the ground. He glanced at the rapidly reversing pat-wagon just in time to see a plate of glass the size of a door go somersaulting through the air and smash into the driver, who disappeared in a red mist. The vehicle careened wildly and tipped, the Tac-officers tumbling out in a flurry of limbs. So much for his exit.

Dredd picked himself up and continued to stumble towards the entrance to Meyer, his boots crunching on crystal shards, casting an eye up at the cargo ship falling inexorably towards them. Its shadow spilled over the estate like ink. The front of the block was free of people now, the last combatants having fled, and he had little trouble getting to the building. The foyer was littered with corpses where the heavy-weapons unit had engaged the Furies, and he had to pick his way carefully. He heard a groan rising from a heap at his foot, and stopped to pull aside a couple of cadavers, revealing a semi-conscious creep in gang colours holding his stomach, his face a sweaty grimace. Dredd prised apart the guy's fingers and saw an entry wound too severe to be treated; the entire front of his shirt was dyed crimson.

"Help me," he rasped, blood speckling his lips.

"Where's Rawlings?"

The creep didn't answer, just struggled around a string of sharp sucking breaths that suggested he wasn't long for this world. Dredd put his hand over the Fury's and leant down on the wound, causing a hiss of pain to issue forth. "Keep the pressure on that," the lawman said. "You're going to bleed out otherwise."

"Need a... gruddamn... ambulance," the meathead spat out.

There was an almighty crash from outside, and more rubble came plummeting to earth. Screams could be discerned beneath the throbbing, ever-present whine of the transporter's engines, and it was growing darker, like the onset of a storm. Dredd's nerve-endings had been fried by the day's events, but even he could feel the hairs on his arms and the back of his neck prickling with the electricity building in the air.

"You hear that?" the Judge asked. The Fury's expression suggested that he did. "Right now we're at ground zero—in a few minutes there's going to be nothing left of Russ Meyer, Len McCluskey or much of Strickland itself. All any ambulances are going to do is pick up the remains. You want to be around to see tomorrow, you tell me where I can find Rawlings."

"What's... happening...?"

"Your glorious leader saying goodbye to the neighbourhood, is what. Quickly, tell me—where did he run operations from?"

The crim coughed and closed his eyes tightly as a fresh wave of pain wracked his body. "On third," he croaked finally. "Four-two-seven-seven." He squeezed one eyelid open and fixed Dredd with a bloodshot stare. "You... call in the docs, get me... inta a hospital."

But the Judge was already striding quickly away, deaf to the cries for medical assistance. The el was obliterated, so he began to stumble up the stairs, blaster raised. He reckoned he could make it three floors.

Dredd met minimal resistance. He'd kept the blanket and now had it wrapped around his uniform again, the helmet buried beneath the hood. He passed for any of the Meyer lowlife, some of whom were cowered in the corridors, eyes raised to the heavens as the sound of the descending ship grew louder and louder; they had more pressing concerns than molesting one more down-and-out, who staggered a little as he went on his way. Those that did challenge him—mainly Furies, the closer he got to the third floor—were summarily dispatched with single shots, the retorts easily lost in the roar of destruction outside. He had not much more than a couple of minutes left, he knew, and couldn't afford any delay—the fate of thousands was at stake. Justice, in this case, had to be swift and ruthless.

He hit the third at a run, muscles screaming, lights pulsing behind his eyes, but by now adrenaline was his sole fuel, overriding any physical limitations. Failure was not an option, he would not allow it. Equally, time would grant him no mercy, and he was aware that the two were about to collide.

Was it a symptom of his addled mind that he thought he caught flashes at his peripheral vision? A ghost figure, with him in spirit. The harder he pushed himself, the more it tracked his steps. By now he suspected he couldn't trust his shocked, fatigued brain, and refused to acknowledge it was there, even though he had the unaccountable feeling that it was looking at him as they moved together, smiling grimly, urging him to go further.

Thundering down the corridor, he fired without pause or warning, dropping Furies where they stood before they had a chance to delay him. He threw off the blanket, no longer needing to hide who and what he was; indeed, he wanted the gang to witness the law descending upon them in these final moments, as powerful and unstoppable a force as the cargo vessel heading their way.

He found apartment 4277 and shoulder-charged the door without hesitation, urgency lending him strength, drawing down on the expected occupants. But there was only one man facing him, arms folded, in front of a large picture window in an otherwise Spartan living space. Beside him on a rickety table sat a battered laptop, code streaming across its screen.

"On your knees, Rawlings. Hands behind your head." Dredd edged forward, blaster sighted on the chief Fury. He couldn't have much more than sixty seconds left.

Rawlings snorted. "What's arresting me going to achieve? Huh? You've left it too late, bluejay. None of us are getting out of here."

"On your knees," Dredd repeated, circling round to the laptop. "Now."

"If it's all the same to you, Judge, I'd rather die on my feet. Considering what's coming down on us, you're in no position to order me to do anything."

Dredd crouched by the computer and plugged the zipdrive into one of the available ports, gun still trained on the gang leader. There was a sullen beep, and a new window popped up on the screen. "Get. Down. On. Your. Knees. Do it quickly."

"You deaf, Judge? I ain't movin'."

There'd been worse last words. A fraction of a second later the picture window shattered and the wall around it crumpled like paper as the nose of the container craft came smashing through the block, bisecting Rawlings at the base of the ribcage, carrying away his upper half like a gruesome hood ornament.

"Your choice, creep," Dredd muttered, grabbing the laptop and hugging it to his chest, shielding it from the destruction as part of the ceiling and many of the apartments above came tumbling down in a shower of debris. The noise was intense, like the heart of a hurricane. Dredd remained crouched, feeling the wind tear at him and chunks of plaster patter his body, grey dust silting his skin.

The floor shifted under his booted feet, and he cast a grime-encrusted eye down to see the entire floor tipping beneath him. He started to slip, his heels sliding and failing to find purchase; he threw away the gun, reached out, and the fingers of his left hand hooked around a door frame. Keeping the computer tucked under his right arm, he pulled himself up, away from the new cliff face, pieces of floor splintering and disappearing from sight. The cargo vessel continued on its trajectory with a bone-shaking rumble, and he watched it pass with his breath caught in his throat, so close to it he could see every rivet and bolt on its surface. The deafening racket of grinding rockcrete blended with the awesome drone of the turbines.

Dredd looked around. The ship had taken out a corner of Meyer, leaving him clinging to a half-demolished supporting wall, the remains of the apartment ending just a few feet from where he was curled. Exposed girders creaked ominously, accompanied by fresh splintering sounds. It didn't take a genius to realise that Meyer was unstable, and what was still standing above him could collapse in on itself at any moment. Either that or the floor beneath him would fall; it would be race between the two to see which gave up the ghost first.

He pushed open the lid of the laptop with his elbow. The new directive was asking him if he wanted to talk to the craft's A.I. pilot: the failsafe. His damaged right hand mashed the keypad, linking him in—typing proved impossible, so he activated voice command.

"Mega-City cargo vessel"—he squinted at the filthy screen—"AR370, this is Judge Joseph Dredd. You are ordered to terminate your current flight path and revert to standby. Do you copy?"

"*Your order is noted, Judge Dredd,*" came a metallic reply. "*However, my programming states that I am to follow this terminal route. Unless I—*"

"I'm countermanding that programming," Dredd barked, his voice rising. "You should be receiving new code that overrides all previous instructions. You will now do what I tell you, do you understand?"

There was a pause. "*I... can see that my programming is being rewritten, and I am no longer obliged to execute my current task. May I ask on whose authority you're acting, as this is highly irregular—*"

"I'm all the authority you need," the lawman shouted. "Activate standby mode now."

"*Standby will necessitate the powering down of certain functions—*"

"Just shut down, you stupid drokking machine, before I put a bullet through your core!"

"*Okay, okay. Jeez.*"

The howl of the engines dropped to a low hum so suddenly that Dredd almost overbalanced, disoriented. The wind calmed, too, leaving a rare stillness. For a moment, all he could hear was the steady creaking of the girders as the half-destroyed block twisted on its foundations; then something shifted and the building started to lean precariously, a crack zigzagging through the rockcrete near where he crouched. He braced himself, a vertiginous feeling rising out of his stomach as the skyline swayed above him, and the floor disappeared out from under him. There was nothing left to cling to—what was left of the wrecked apartment was unfolding, dismantling. He was going to fall.

He refused to let his fear get the better of him. He'd known that this was only going to end one way.

Dredd heard turbines firing up again and dropped his head in frustration—the ship's A.I. must've rebooted itself. Dammit, he thought he'd stopped it. When he looked up, he found himself gazing up at a hovering H-Wagon, its gantry lowered and a smiling Saunders leaning out from it, one hand clutching the stanchion, the other reaching for him.

"Come on," she said, the craft inching closer to the block to allow her hand to clasp his. "Let's go."

She pulled him aboard, just before the back of the apartment chose that moment to crumble into the street. He glanced at the auto-container, which was now stationary, hanging quietly in the air. Saunders followed his gaze.

"First time an A.I.'s been threatened into doing what it's told, I bet." She ushered him into the H-Wagon's hold. "Do you scare *everyone?*"

13.40 pm

DAX WATCHED FROM some distance as the Judges' vessel pulled away from Meyer, more of the block's structure sloughing off like an eroding mountain. Great plumes of dust rose as rubble crunched into the sked. Cuffed to the holding post like this, she could do nothing but watch Strickland fall apart.

Bonedog came over, seeing her shake her head. "What's the matter?"

"End of an era," she replied sadly.

The jay that had arrested her had left her here on an HP while he aided with the relief effort. She was small fry, she'd be processed eventually once they'd stopped shovelling 'crete.

The badges would come back for her, and when they did the gang would split; until then, they'd stuck around to offer moral support.

Bonedog studied her. "Why'd you do it, Dax? Why'd you give the bluejay the gun? You said yourself, don't do nothin' stupid."

She was silent for a moment. "I dunno. Compelled to, I guess. It felt like he knew I had it, and hiding it was pointless. Somethin' I saw when he was lyin' there an' I first picked up the gun. I... I got the sense he's pretty mean, that I don't wanna get on the wrong side of him. Like, *ever*."

"Gonna be lookin' at five years, min."

"Yeah."

He whistled. "Helluva time to grow a conscience, girl."

She laughed bitterly. "Couldn't help it." Dax scanned the sky, the H-Wagon just a dot in the distance. "The guilt got the better of me."

Ten

BERTRAM GILPIG WASN'T, he believed, an immoral man. He empathised with the unfortunates in society, understood full well the hardships they faced—Grud knew he had to listen to them often enough in the monthly surgeries he endured as councillor. Life for many in Mega-City wasn't easy: jobs were notoriously hard to come by, drug use was widespread, crime rates were rocketing; no wonder many of them felt angry and helpless, seeing the decades stretching before them with a sense of utter hopelessness. They had nothing to work and strive for, little in the way of creds; years of unemployment beckoned. Offspring could be born in block nurseries, educated in block schools, and spend the rest of their adulthood in front of the Tri-D before they made the final journey to Resyk. Who wouldn't be pissed at the sheer futility of their existences? Gilpig got that, he really did, and he wished he could do more to help—but the metropolis was so vast and the citizens so numerous that resources were stretched to the limit. They were all survivors of a global apocalypse, waking up to a future in which much of the planet was uninhabitable. Things were going to be tough for everyone.

No, he was all too aware of the challenges of the late twenty-first century, and liked to think he was sympathetic. If he was going to admit to any fault, it was that he was an opportunist. He saw chances to change things, improve the quality of life for many, and he took them—seized the fire, so to speak. Grand Hall red tape was legendary, and, yes, perhaps he did cut corners to expedite matters, but the people would appreciate the final result: the ends did indeed justify the means. The Strickland estate was a case in point—Justice Department seemed all too happy to let the district fall into ruin, effectively abandoning its residents, but Gilpig felt that was too short-sighted. It frustrated him, this lack of vision, and so he'd decided to nudge progress a little, take a hand in shaping the city's landscape for the post-atomic age.

The problem was you couldn't build a better tomorrow without demolishing the old.

All these justifications raced through his head as he hurried across the spaceport concourse, suitcase in hand. He'd had to pack light—speed was of the essence—and hadn't even waited for Darlene to come home before fleeing the apartment; he figured he'd drop her a line once he was past Luna-1, explain the situation. Maybe they'd be reunited, but most likely not. He wasn't going to shed any tears over walking out on twenty-four years of loveless, miserable marriage. This was probably the fresh start he needed: another opportunity he wasn't shy in taking advantage of.

More pressing was that he get off-world with the minimum of fuss. Dean Learner was thankfully very far from Strickland, but the reports of the disturbances were filtering back across city, news crews already on the scene and detailing the destruction. It was all going to blow back on him, he knew it. He'd hoped that Rawlings' crew would have been able to quietly eliminate the Judge and retrieve the datastick, but evidently that had gone south quite spectacularly. He should've known better that to entrust a task of that magnitude to others—especially a bunch of dolts like the Russ Meyer Furies—but there was a limit to what a man of his standing could achieve on his own without someone there to handle the dirty work.

'Dirty work' made it sound so seedy. This was damage limitation. Force majeure. Gilpig had been placed in an unacceptable position, and events had spiralled beyond his control in his attempt to right it. He was a victim of circumstance, really; his best laid plans unravelled by misfortune and the actions of a badge who didn't know when to just lie down and *drokking die.*

He felt his grip on his suitcase handle tighten, aware his anger was resurfacing. He had to be careful—he had a tendency to vent when riled, as his staff could well attest. He didn't want to draw attention to himself now when he just wanted to slip anonymously out of the city. All it would take is one rant at a jobsworth luggage-handler, and eyes would be drawn his way.

He slowed his pace, willing himself to calm down, and considered finding a PF—to collect his thoughts, splash some water on his face, relieve his trembling bowels—but he didn't want the delay. Nevertheless, he could feel the sweat on the back of his neck, between his shoulder blades, in the palms of his hands, and became self-conscious of his breathing. He couldn't afford to panic, he had to act normal. Unsurprisingly, there were Judges stationed throughout the terminal, trained to recognise the signs of a man with something to hide; just their presence was enough to make the most innocent cits soil their Us over imaginary infractions. He pulled down low the baseball cap that he'd picked up on the journey over, and kept his gaze on the polished floor, counting the steps to freedom.

Gruddammit, he thought, he didn't deserve this kind of luck. If all had gone like clockwork. The residents of Strickland would've had a complete regeneration of their sector (it was unlikely they would've been able to afford to continue to live there, but still); his construction contacts would've been assured several years' work; Rawlings would've had exclusive territorial rights to all drug distribution amongst those fancy new occupants with their disposable income; and he, Bertram Gilpig, would've been creaming a percentage from all of it. It was beautiful, and all down to a couple of well-targeted treemeat-freighter accidents. Everybody would've won, in the end, and limited casualties, he guessed. He should be *rewarded* for this kind of pioneering risk-taking, not reduced to scurrying away like a fugitive.

He chose to pick up his boarding pass at the automated check-in machine, the better to keep a low profile. As it printed out his details, he glanced left and right at the crowds, envious of those greeting loved ones or embarking on holidays; they knew nothing of what it took to make the hard choices, to gamble everything. He looked forward to a clean slate far from Earth, where he too could appreciate such simple pleasures, and as he plucked the printed card from the slot, he felt it was within his grasp.

Or it was until a gauntleted hand gripped his shoulder, gloved fingers pinning him where he stood, and he knew that future was about to be snatched away.

16.02 pm

JOE.

Voices in the fog. He'd been here before: a warning of his imminent death.

"Joe."

Dredd's heavy lids slowly opened. Rather than the mirror-image he expected to see, an older man leaned close, benevolent eyes searching his face with genuine concern. It took a moment to put a name to the figure, his mind fuzzy, his thoughts struggling to coalesce. "Chief Judge Goodman."

"Welcome back to the land of the living, son. How do you feel?"

Strange that he should be asked that question twice in less than twelve hours—he'd probably never hear it again in the next twenty years—and still he didn't know how to answer it. "Sore," was all he could muster.

Goodman nodded gravely. "Meds say it'll take the rest of the week for you to recover, even with an accelerated healing programme. You did yourself some serious damage."

"I wasn't solely responsible."

The Chief Judge's face broke into a smile. "No, you're right. There may have been one or two factions at play. You did put yourself in the firing line, though."

"Only place a Judge should be, I would've thought, sir. What's the latest on Gilpig?" Dredd tried to sit up in the bed, and for the first time became aware of the state he was in—his torso was encased in bandages, his right hand in a brace. Movement fired hot needles beneath his skin so he eased back down on the pillow. He touched his head and felt a hard dome encircling his crown.

"Skull fracture," Goodman explained. "Quite a bad one. The doc was worried there may have been some pressure on the brain. Could've affected your perception. Did you experience anything like that?"

—*You failed, Joe*—

"Nothing I couldn't handle," Dredd replied. "Gilpig?"

"Local units picked him up a couple of hours ago at the spaceport, trying to flee off-planet. He's in custody now, spilling his guts."

"The hack code...?"

"We're looking into that. SJS are conducting a top-down review of Tek-Div, seeing if they can plug the leak. Gilpig says he dealt with a middle man—it'll be a matter of following the money."

Dredd nodded slowly, looking down at his hands. A killer headache was forming behind his eyes.

"Joseph," Goodman began, breaking the brief silence. "Saunders submitted her report. She's suggesting you broke protocol."

The younger man glanced up. "When?"

"You broke rank, entered Meyer in no fit state to enact judgement."

"I was trying to save lives."

"I understand that, son. But a Judge is more than a mere man or woman—they're a weapon. The damage you sustained made you a potentially malfunctioning weapon. Perhaps you're unaware how dangerous that could be."

"I was in control."

"So you believed." Goodman softened his tone. "But judgement can be impaired. You... you should know that."

Dredd dropped his gaze. "I'm not Rico."

"That's a matter of biological debate," the Chief Judge said with a chuckle, which faded as Dredd stared at him. "But now you've got more to prove than anyone on the force. That the bloodline's secure. That you're street-ready. That you're *not* Rico." He smiled sadly. "You're your own man, Joseph."

Dredd didn't reply.

Goodman turned to leave. "Oh, Control wanted to pass on some info. Apparently there's been a lead in the organ-legging outfit you were investigating—Breyer in Sector 12 found a stash of limbs in a locker off Portman. DNA traces. File's ready for you when you get out of here."

"Thanks."

The older man lingered by the door. He paused then said: "You'll make it, son. You're stronger than your brother."

Wasn't that the truth.

About the Author

Matthew Smith was employed as a desk editor for Pan Macmillan book publishers for three years before joining *2000 AD* as assistant editor in July 2000 to work on a comic he had read religiously since 1985. He became editor of the Galaxy's Greatest in December 2001, and then editor-in-chief of the *2000 AD* titles in January 2006. He lives in Oxford.

ALTERNATIVE FACTS

CAVAN SCOTT

**MEGA-CITY ONE
2081 A.D.**

One
How Glamorous

YOU WEREN'T SUPPOSED to dream using a sleep machine. That's what the manual said. Ben Peck knew differently. Ben Peck knew that every minute in the snooze-tube gave him the freakiest drokking dreams he'd ever experienced. Really weird stomm: twisted, nightmarish images that made the aftermath of the nuclear war look like a teddy bear's picnic. He couldn't be happier when the buzzer sounded in his ears and he was pulled out of his artificially-induced slumber.

Peck yawned, plucking the sensors from his temples, the pads reluctantly yielding their tacky hold on his skin.

He swung his legs out of the sleep machine, the bedroom floor cold beneath his feet. Grud, he ached. These things were supposed to give you the equivalent of a full night's sleep in ten minutes, reinvigorating body and mind. How come his body felt like it had done ten rounds with a cage fighter and his mind was shredded munce?

Peck stood—his spine popping as he stretched—and trudged over to the grubby wash basin on the other side of the poky room. The faucet spluttered as he approached, the proximity sensor recognising his presence and providing a stream of piping hot water. At least that was the idea; Peck couldn't remember the last time the water supply at Ron Burgundy Block had worked properly. Instead of a gush of steaming clear water, he was presented with a trickle of luke-warm liquid the colour of cold tea.

He slapped his palm over the cut off. He could go without a wash tonight. He was going to get filthy anyway. Peck scowled at his reflection in the warped mirror above the basin. He looked even worse than his stomm-hole of a hab. Every now and then, Peck would be expected to tidy himself up for parties, mingling with advertisers and sponsors. When they found out he was an investigative journalist, their eyes would widen, their mouths dropping open.

It must be so exciting.

Do you go undercover?

How glamorous!

Walking back into the bedroom, he looked around for the shirt he'd dumped on the floor before crawling into the sleep machine fifteen minutes before. Oh, his life was glamorous, all right—if your definition of glamour was earning just enough to rent a flea-pit next to a slug rock band who played their 'music' turned up to one-hundred and eleven, twenty-four hours a day. He knew for a fact that the spugwits didn't own a sleep machine, which either meant they went without shut-eye or somehow managed to sleep with that racket blaring out at them.

Of course, if it wasn't for his own sleep machine, he could afford a better place, but most of what *MC-1 Today* laughably called his 'wages' went on maintenance cover for his Somnus 3000. How else could he be expected to hold down three separate jobs, covering three different stories at once, and all so the mindless cits of Mega-City One could gorge themselves on 24-hour rolling news?

It must be so exciting.

Yeah, life was a real thrill.

*   *   *

GRABBING HIMSELF A synthi-caf from the StarYuks concession
at the skyrail station, Peck stood and watched a replay of last
night's Aeroball match between the Perry Tigers and the Swift
Shakers. The long-standing rivals were knocking seven shades
of stomm out of each other when the game was interrupted for
a mayoral campaigning vid. Peck sighed, fishing his podphone
out of his jacket. Chucking the empty StarYuks cup into an
overflowing garbage grinder, he crammed the phone's buds into
his ears and tuned into the local newscast. A tinny voice filled
his ears as the skytrain slid into the station and the carriage
doors whined open. Peck allowed himself to be bustled onto the
train with the crowd as he listened to the broadcast.

"*This is Judge Whistleblower,*" the voice in his ears said,
"*telling you how it is, direct from Justice Central. The law sees
everything; and I see the law.*"

Peck snorted as the train slipped out of Ron Burgundy along
the rickety skyrail. Judge Whistleblower claimed to be a real
jaybird, airing the Grand Hall of Justice's dirty laundry in
public; the computer-modulated voice was supposed to protect
his anonymity. Peck was pretty sure that the spug was just a
Jimp—a Judge impersonator—spouting whatever fantasies he'd
read on anti-Justice forums. There was no way the Jays would
allow one of their own to leak sensitive information. Still, it
made an entertaining diversion on train journeys.

"*It's hot out there in the Big Meg, and getting hotter every
day. Don't blame Weather Council—it's this mayoral election.
Democracy always brings out the crazies. If Chief Judge
Goodman had his way, the office of Mayor would be made
illegal, but the Council of Five likes cits to believe they control
their destiny. Why? Because otherwise the less-dormant would
rise from their torpor and realise that there's enough of them to
make a difference. We're talking wide-spread insurgency, maybe*

even revolution. The plans are already in place to combat a city-wide revolt, and trust me, they're not pretty. Better that we continue to suppress any nutjobs stirred up by the election, so that crosses can be scrawled on ballet papers and Mega-City One's pleb-heads think that their vote makes a difference—the three percent that turn out to vote, that is. What a drokking waste of time."

Peck hung onto the handrail, rocking with the train's juddering motion as the city sped by. Whistleblower was right about that. Elections *did* bring out the nutters, both on and off the campaign trails. It was the only time of the year that he was glad not to be in the newsroom. He could imagine the poor schmucks running around, desperate to scoop the other channels, network executives breathing down their necks and threatening a sudden career move to the obituary desk.

Still, perhaps obits would be preferable to his current assignment. The carriage had thinned out by the time they reached MegWest Terminal, the end of the line. Peck cut off Whistleblower's paranoid blather and pulled the buds from his ears as he trudged down to the pedway. You needed your wits about you in Sector 187, especially this near the West Wall. Distractions around Sector 187 got you killed.

Peck shoved the podphone back into his pocket, his fingers slipping easily into the knuckle-dusters he kept hidden for the final schlep to work. There were no slidewalks this far out. You kept your head down and your weapons concealed, and avoided eye-contact until you were safely at your destination.

Peck's heart was hammering by the time he made it to Dependicorp. A juve had dogged Peck's heels all the way from the terminal, keeping a discreet distance. He was tall and lanky, with a hawk-like nose, pock-marked skin, black leathers and the ridiculous knee-pads that the kids seemed to be wearing these days. Peck had tried to lose the spug, but the juve had stuck to him like glue, matching pace with him when he tried to throw him off. At any minute, Peck expected a sonic-knife between his shoulder blades, or a cosh around the back of his head, but nothing came.

As they approached Dependicorp Haulage Depot, Peck hurried through the sliding doors, only for the juve to slide into the lobby behind him. The reception was empty, Dependicorp's security guard having sloped off for an illicit smoke or sugar-hit. Peck's fingers tightened around his clandestine knuckle-dusters and he whirled around, facing his tail, who took a step back, eyes wide.

"What's your game, kid?"

"Woah, it's okay, man. I was just, er... just a little scared, you know. First time walking through this sector. You looked like you could handle yourself, so I hung near, just in case of trouble. Didn't mean to spook you. I'm new, that's all. Name's Hyke. Hyke Masfield."

Hyke held out a hand, and Peck slipped off a knuckle-duster and gave it a perfunctory shake, identifying himself as Greg Weld, the pseudonym he was using at Dependicorp. "Good to meet you, Hyke."

It wasn't good to meet him. Not today. Today, Peck was meeting with Kell Sanchez, the contact he'd been grooming for the last few weeks. The last thing he needed was a new friend, no matter how much Hyke wanted to fit in with his teammates.

For all Peck knew, Hyke was a plant from the gang using Dependicorp to run a trafficking operation. Were the Valverde Boys onto him? He scratched his chest as the suspicion gnawed away at him. That damned fake tattoo he'd gotten had set off some kind of allergic reaction. His skin was red raw under his shirt.

PECK LEFT HYKE waiting for his security pass at the front desk and got to work, stacking crates—imported from Mega-City

Two—using an eco-lift hydraulic-suit. He didn't see Hyke all morning, or in the cafeteria at lunch where Peck chewed his way through the worst pro-slab chilli he'd ever had the misfortune to shovel into his mouth. Perhaps the kid had been on the level after all. Paranoia was a killer in this business.

The rest of the day went without incident, Peck counting the hours until the end of his shift. His work at Dependicorp done, he clocked off, then doubled backed into the depot instead of starting the walk to the skyrail station. Dodging the CCTV drones hovering above the yard, he crept out to the labyrinth of heavy-duty shipping containers, each larger than his hab. Checking off the serial numbers stencilled onto the sides of the containers, he found where he had agreed to meet Sanchez. A new delivery had shipped in that afternoon, seventy-eight crates of high-tech components that had just made the long haul across the mutant-infested Cursed Earth. He'd received a tip-off that the plasteen containers actually held dozens of muties bound for the workhouses and pleasure palaces of the undercity. If he was right, Sanchez was in on the deal, a middleman for Mega-City One's burgeoning blight-slave trade.

Peck had spent three months working as a doorman to expose a mutie meat-house in Sector 33. The depravity he'd witnessed— the indignities heaped upon the poor saps from the radlands, like they were less than human—still fuelled his nightmares.

Peck glanced at his chronometer. Where was Sanchez? Had he got cold feet? Or had the Valverde Boys got wind of Peck's plan?

It was getting late. Too late. If he was discovered, it would be difficult to explain what he was doing hanging around the depot so long after he'd clocked off. But the news desk wanted the story tonight. Peck needed evidence, and he needed it fast.

He couldn't wait for Sanchez any longer. He would just have to break the story on his own. As a contingency, Peck had stolen a set of override codes from the foreman's office, just in case.

It was riskier than using Sanchez's master key, but needs must.

Glancing around, Peck made for the nearest container and entered his filched code into the keypad. The door opened, the internal lights flickering on to reveal boxes piled high inside the corrugated container. Peck listened, but there was no sound or movement in the crate. Convinced he was alone, he tried one of the boxes, but it was filled with mechanical equipment that matched the customs declaration back in the office: tray after tray of widgets and doohickeys, none of which meant anything to Peck. Everything was as it should be. No illegal immigrants. No muties.

The next container was the same, and the next. The contents of the fourth gave him a start, the crate filled with naked mannequins that stared back at him with blank faces when he yanked open the door. Had his tip-off been wrong? But Sanchez had confirmed the plan. Had he set Peck up?

There was noise from outside. Peck closed the container door, shutting himself inside. The lights died as soon as the lock clicked into place, and Peck felt a stab of panic. He *hated* shop dummies, and had ever since he watched an old British vid-show when he was a kid, where mannequins came to life and turned on humans. What was it called? *Professor What* or something.

Telling himself not to be so drokking stupid, Peck listened. There was a crunch from outside, followed by a mechanical whirr: Finch, the night-watchman, with his cybernetic leg, a trophy of a block war between Hopkins and Schofield three years ago. Robo-limb or not, Finch was a solid wall of muscle. If he was discovered hiding in the crate, Peck wouldn't stand a chance.

The container door rattled as Finch checked the lock. In the darkness, Peck pushed his fingers through the knuckle-dusters and waited for the inevitable. Heard Finch cough... and then go on his way. He didn't dare breathe until the sound of the watchman's mechanical limp faded.

He was running out of time. Peck fumbled with the catch and yanked at the door. It didn't budge. Grud, had Finch deadlocked it from the outside? He tried again, and this time it slid open. Peck spilled out of the container and fought the urge to drokk his deadline and go home. One more container. He'd check one more container, and if he couldn't find anything, he'd give up. He'd send a message to the news desk that the story was a bust, or at least try to get an extension.

Peck moved to the next container on his list, entered the code and pulled open the door to reveal yet more wooden boxes— this time, not so tightly packed together. He sniffed. Sweat hung in the air, the sour stink of the unwashed.

There was a scrape of leather against plasteen in the shadows at the back of the container. Someone was in there. A rat? Not unless it was wearing shoes. Of course, knowing the Cursed Earth, that was a distinct possibility.

"Hello?"

There was no response. Peck squeezed himself through the boxes, pulling out his podphone to activate the flashlight function. Light shone from the back of the handset, illuminating two figures crouched in the corner, a woman and a man, both mutant if the cyclopean eyes in the middle of their domed foreheads was anything to go by. They shrunk back against the plasteen walls, trying to escape the beam of light, the male throwing a malnourished arm over his partner to protect her.

"I don't want to hurt you," Peck told them, raising his free hand in what he hoped would be seen as a friendly gesture. "I just want to tell your story. But we need to get away from here. You're in danger."

They didn't move.

"My name's Peck. Ben Peck. What about you? Can you tell me your names?"

The pair stared at him with wide watery eyes, but didn't answer.

"It doesn't matter, you can tell me later. Let's get you out of—"

Peck froze as both cyclopses suddenly looked past him. There was a *click* from behind, the tell-tale snap of a safety disengaging.

It had to be Finch. *Drokk it!*

Peck turned, putting on his best smile. But there was no guard's uniform, no cybernetic leg; just a tall man in a long coat, a scarf wound around his face and a trilby hat low on his brow. Something was tucked into the hat's band. A ticket? No. It was a press card, like in old movies. But there was nothing old-school about the gun the guy was pointing in their direction.

"Okay, pal," the reporter said, trying to ignore the tremor in his own voice. "I'm sure we can sort this out. There's no need for any—"

The gun twitched to the side and fired twice, the shots muffled by the integrated silencer.

Pfft. pfft.

Peck whirled around to see the mutants slide down the wall, leaving two red smears as their bodies settled on the floor.

By the time Peck turned, the gun was trained on him.

"Now, wai—"

This time, Peck didn't hear the shot at all.

Two
Who Was That Masked Man?

Judge Joseph Dredd shielded his eyes against the glare of the morning sun. A sky-surfer was flitting back and forth above the Dependicorp depot, a familiar logo emblazoned across the bottom of his hoverboard.

Dredd's lips curled as he turned to the Lawmaster parked beside the shipping containers.

"Activate screen. Vid-channel."

"*Which station do you require?*" the bike's telecommunication unit enquired in a prissy voice that didn't quite match the vehicle's sleek powerful lines.

"*Hound News*," Dredd snapped, glaring at the news report that immediately filled the screen between the bike's curved handlebars. The network's logo was tucked discreetly in the corner of the picture, the same stylised letter *H* painted on the board high above his head.

Dredd was looking at footage of himself shot from the air, captioned with the headline: *Haulage Homicide Horror*.

"*This is Seymour McKenzie,*" announced the reporter currently flying above Dredd's head. "*Your eye in the sky, reporting live from the West Wall. As you can see, a Judge has arrived to investigate the body found in a container unit early this morning; a body that has yet to be identified."*

Dredd activated his bike's loudspeakers, linking them directly to his helmet mic.

His voice boomed. "They'll be identifying *your* body if you don't move along," he said, looking up at the sky surfer. "Do I make myself clear?"

The picture on the screen picked out Dredd's hand moving to the Lawgiver gun holstered on his belt.

"And now back to the studio," Seymour McKenzie stammered as the image switched unexpectedly to *Hound News'* resident anchor Bret Barnet, who looked up, shocked, from flirting shamelessly with a make-up girl.

Satisfied, Joe killed the screen as the hoverboard sped away.

Dredd stalked back into the container where the haulage firm's security guard was waiting for him, a bulky man with a thick beard, an even thicker neck and a clunky artificial leg.

A corpse was lying on the floor of the crate, its head circled by a halo of dried blood.

"And you didn't touch the body?"

The security guard raised a pair of shaggy eyebrows. "Why in Grud's name would I do that?"

"You'd be surprised." Dredd stepped over the stiff to examine the blood stains he'd spotted in the far corner. He crouched down beside the red spatter on the plasteen wall, noting the fragments of bone and brain matter lodged in the gore. Whoever had been shot had been sitting on the floor; the gun was angled down. Both bullets had ripped straight through the plasteen. Two bullets, two bodies, both removed before the security guard had discovered the corpse—or so the cyborg claimed.

Dredd reached into a pouch on his belt, drawing out his snuffler, a hand-held DNA scanner usually reserved for Tek-Judges. Dredd had requisitioned one from Justice Department stores in his first month on the skeds. Why wait for forensic examiners to arrive at a crime scene when he could do it himself?

He swept the snuffler over the blood, the unit automatically sending a sample back to the sector house.

"Control," he said into his helmet mic. "Have sent unidentified blood samples for testing. Require full DNA sweep."

"*That's a rog,*" a voice came back immediately. "*Have forwarded to Tek-Division. Stand by.*"

Slipping the snuffler back into its pouch, Dredd returned to the corpse, looking down at the rubber mask covering the stiff's face. The exaggerated features of an old-school clown, complete with ruddy cheeks and red nose, stared back.

"Any idea who it is?" he asked the watchman.

The guard shrugged. "I was gonna check, but thought I should wait for you boys."

"The right choice," Dredd told him, reaching down to prise the mask from the dead man's face. "Otherwise you'd be looking at eight months in the cube for tampering with evidence."

The rubber was stuck fast to the blood caking the sap's face. Dredd peeled it back to reveal a nondescript male in his mid-to-late thirties, nondescript except for the gaping bullet hole in his forehead.

"Greg," the guard gasped as he saw the face. "That's Greg Weld. Works the exo-lifters."

"Knew him well?" Dredd asked.

"No, he was pretty new. Only been here three or four weeks."

"Long enough to make an enemy?"

Dredd looked at the clown mask in his hand. There was no hole in the rubber, meaning that it had been placed on Weld's face *after* he was shot. Some kind of message?

He turned over the mask and something fluttered to the floor, a folded piece of paper, no bigger than a postage stamp. It must have been sandwiched between the rubber and Weld's skin, stuck to the blood on the inside of the mask.

Dredd retrieved it, opening it carefully so as not to rip the gore-soaked paper.

"What does it say?" the guard asked, trying to peer over Dredd's shoulder pad. Joe fixed the watchman with a glare and the creep backed off.

"S-sorry," the bearded man said, retreating out of the container with a clank of his mechanical leg. "I'll leave you to it. I-I'll be back in the office if you need anything else."

Dredd returned his attention to the paper as his comm sounded.

"*Control to Dredd.*"

"Dredd here. You got the results?"

"*Mutants.*"

"Say again?"

"*You got yourself some dead muties, Dredd. No doubt about it. Can't you tell from the bodies? They're kind of easy to spot.*"

"No bodies, just bloodstains. Unless you count Weld."

"*The stiff in the container?*"

"Greg Weld. Mid-30s, exo-lift driver at Dependicorp Haulage company. Got anything on Mac?"

There was a pause while Control checked the Justice Department's central database, the Macro Analysis Computer system.

"*That's a negative.*"

"No criminal record?"

"*No anything. Greg Weld doesn't exist.*"

Then who was the body at his feet? Dredd glanced at the writing on the paper, reading the text again, four words printed in stark black ink on the now scarlet paper:

YOU MET YOUR DEADLINE.

Three
Crowd Control

"HEY, MEATHEAD—EITHER you get behind the cordon, or you feel my boot. Understand?"

Isiah Morphy was no fan of crowd control. A Judge with over thirty years' service under his belt, Morph had seen City Mayors come and go; helped break up hundreds of protests, both peaceful and otherwise; and been given security detail at music concerts, employment lines and binge-eating conventions. He knew that getting thousands of cits together in one place was just asking for trouble, especially at political rallies like the one he was covering today. Worse, he couldn't give his full attention to the hundreds of punks crammed into Boris Johnson Plaza, not while he was assessing his latest rookie, Zidane Lint.

The kid was standing a little way along the cordon, scanning the throng of mayoral supporters for any signs of trouble. He'd done well so far. Since they'd arrived, Lint had busted six dunkers, broken up three fights and spotted a juve using the rally to shift illegal comic books. The criminal scum of Mega-City One never missed an opportunity for lawbreaking, that was for sure.

Still, Morphy had a good feeling about Lint. The rookie had aced his tests, and handled himself with distinction in a recent armed robbery at Racy's department store. It wouldn't be long until he was awarded his full eagle. Still looked about twelve, though. Morphy couldn't remember ever being that young.

The Senior Judge ran gloved fingers through his moustache as he watched Lint give a punk six months for back-chat. Grinning, he turned towards the floating stage that hovered at the far end of the plaza, the platform where mayoral candidate Jocelyn Piper would soon address her followers.

Giant banners displaying Piper's face wafted in the breeze on either side of the podium. She was a good-looking woman, that was for sure, in her early fifties with a fine head of golden hair and piercing green eyes, but her stomm-eating smile was getting old, real quick. Morphy had never seen anyone with that many *teeth*. He dreaded to think how much the woman had shelled out on dental treatments. Enough to feed three blocks in MegSouth, no doubt. But money wasn't a problem for the likes of Jocelyn Piper. An overexcited supporter had insisted on telling the Senior Judge Piper's life story when he and Lint had first arrived, giving him chapter and verse about how the trillionaire had built her tech-empire from scratch, selling second-hand back-scratchers from a stall in Alan Sugar Block. The star-struck teen had related how many businesses Piper had to her name, how many penthouses she owned, how many shoes, dresses, private hover-yachts, dogs, cats, robots and diamonds were in the woman's various collections. The list went on and on, the drokker only shutting up when Morphy threatened her with a year for wasting Judge time.

Morphy didn't care how many millions Piper held in her bank account, how many times she'd been married, or any of the other trivia spewing from the Meg's news outlets. All he cared about was making sure that the afternoon went without public disaster, gang warfare, zombie outbreak, or any of the other scenarios a Mega-City Judge had to be prepared for at any given moment.

"Judge Morphy."

Morphy turned to see a familiar face walking towards him.

"Dredd!" Morphy said as his former rookie approached him, stopping only to knock an e-cigarette out of a cit's mouth and give the vaper a month in the cubes. "It's good to see you."

"You too, sir," Dredd said with a polite nod.

Morphy raised a hand. "That's enough of that, Joey Boy. I've told you before; it's Morph to my pals."

Dredd's jaw clenched beneath his helmet and Morphy had to stop himself from laughing. Two years since Morphy had passed Dredd for full service, and Joe was still as uptight as ever. When the lad had been assigned to him for final assessment, Morph had been told that his tutors at the Academy still had their doubts, and not just because of the controversy surrounding the cloning programme. Dredd was considered too inflexible, too tied to the letter of the law, to cope with life on the street. Morphy had liked the kid from the minute they'd swung their Lawmasters onto the sked outside the Grand Hall of Justice. Dredd had guts, that much was clear. He'd made his first arrest within two minutes of leaving the Hall. The first of many, it turned out. Since getting his shield, Dredd had had it tough, what with Rico and everything, but who said being a Judge was an easy ride? As far as Morphy could tell, Joe was doing fine. He was pleased to see him. His presence would make the afternoon go quicker, and having a Judge of Dredd's calibre on hand would be no bad thing either.

Dread greeted Lint with his usual professional detachment, and the three lawmen swept the crowd for more signs of trouble, discussing recent cases as they did.

Soon, the conversation turned to a homicide Dredd had responded to two days earlier, a stiff found in a haulage depot.

"And there's no evidence of who popped him?" Lint asked.

"Nothing firm," Dredd confirmed. "No DNA, no vid-footage. Turns out he had plenty of enemies, though."

"How so?" asked Morphy.

"Control was right. Greg Weld didn't exist."

"A spook?"

"A reporter, working undercover. Lived a dozen lives under different identities in the last year alone. Real name Ben Peck, currently working for *MC-1 Today*. According to their records, Peck used a face-changer to alter his appearance before securing the job at Dependicorp, even going so far as having a gangland tattoo inked on his chest."

"Permanent?"

"No. Looked real enough, but wasn't sub-dermal. Would wipe clean away with a laser scrubber."

"Which gang?"

"Valverde."

Morphy whistled. "Tough bunch. Think they found out he was faking?"

"And took him down?" Dredd plucked a can of soda from the hand of a nearby cit to check its sugar content. "It's possible, although no one's claimed the hit." Satisfied the drink was within regulations, Dredd returned the can and sent the supporter on her way. "I made enquiries in known Valverde hangouts."

"Cracked some heads?"

"No one had even heard of Peck, by either name."

"Going by the note, someone must have known he was a newsman," Lint said. "That crack about the deadline."

Dredd nodded. "The note's interesting. The letters were typed, not printed."

"As in a typewriter?"

"Affirmative."

Morphy crossed his arms in front of his chest. "I haven't seen a typewriter in... well, I don't know how many years. Not outside a museum anyway."

Lint clicked his fingers. "There's a typewriter museum in Jessica Fletcher Block."

"Already checked it out," Dredd told him. "All the exhibits are present and correct, and none of the keys match the letters on the note."

"Any idea what Peck was investigating?" Morphy asked.

"Not conclusively, although the mutie blood suggests wall-hoppers."

Every day mutants from the radlands tried to gain entrance to Mega-City One. Judges were permanently posted on sentry duty, but refugees still flooded through, some peaceful, some with extreme violence. However they came in, their fate was sealed. Mutation was illegal within city limits. Muties were either deported back to the Cursed Earth or executed on sight.

Morphy nodded. "Could Peck have discovered them?"

"Maybe, but who shot the muties? We found three bullet holes in the container."

"Same gun?"

"Tek-Division's not found the bullets, so we can't be certain, but—"

Dredd's sentence was lost as music blared from the floating platform's loudspeakers. Dredd pulled a sensor from his belt to check the decibels, grunting when they appeared just below the legal limit. The needle on his device bucked as a roar went up from the crowd, but Morphy was sure even Dredd would think twice about arresting every supporter in the plaza.

Probably.

Morph looked up, watching through his visor as Jocelyn Piper strode confidently across the platform, waving at the crowd, her self-assured image splashed across holo-screens on either side of the stage.

He looked around the assembled throng and shook his head. The woman standing behind the podium was as rich as they were poor, and yet they worshipped her as if she was Jovus reborn. To the right of Lint, a cit in threadbare clothes babbled excitedly to her partner: "Ain't she wonderful, Clive? She cares about us, you can see it in her face. She cares about the people, Clive. The people!"

Yeah, Morphy thought. *As long as you keep buying her crud, she'll care about you come what may.*

Four
Making Mega-City Work

BEHIND THE PODIUM, Jocelyn Piper raised her hands to quieten the crowd.

"Thank you, my friends," Piper drawled, her smile broadening. "Thank you for such a warm welcome today."

"That accent..." Dredd said.

"She was born in Texas City," Lint told him. "Moved to the Meg when she was a teen." The rookie glanced at Morphy. "A good Judge does his homework before any public event, sir."

"You telling me how to do my job, rookie?" Dredd growled.

Lint look flustered. "No. I was just pointing out—"

Morphy shut both of them down. "You were trying to impress, I get it. But *I'm* trying to listen."

"Sorry, sir," Lint said, although Dredd still glared at the cadet.

Wasn't long since you were quoting the law book at me, Joe, Morph thought to himself. *You're not all that different, you and Lint.*

On the stage, Piper continued her speech.

"For too long, the poor and needy of this great city have been left behind. Is it any wonder we have crime? Is it any wonder our young people are disillusioned? Is it any wonder that we live in terror? Why, only yesterday, Sector 39 suffered that terrible tragedy in the Redwater shopping mall. One hundred and forty-nine dead after a sales-bot decided to rupture its power core."

Morphy's eye twitched at the comment. He hadn't attended the explosion at Redwater himself, but from what he'd heard, there was no evidence that the detonation had been deliberate. There had been numerous incidents linked to robots in recent weeks, and the press had been quick to suggest it was some kind of mechanical protest, android activists fighting for robo-rights. Morphy wasn't so sure, and the last thing the city needed was mechanoid lynchings. The Big Meg was a tinderbox: half the population were just waiting for the right cause.

Even here, he could hear the murmurings. The atmosphere in the plaza was charged, like the air before a storm. Piper had to be careful. She was whipping her people into a frenzy, every sentence punctuated by rapturous cheering.

"What does the City give you?" she bellowed, pointing a finger at the crowd. "Nothing! What does it take? *Everything!* Mayor Amalfi talks about you as if you were cattle. No, worse than that: as if you were *sheep*."

Morphy doubted if many people in the plaza even knew what a sheep looked like.

"Dumb animals to corral and control. That must stop. Mega-City One is not what it should be, what you *deserve* it to be. Mega-City One is broken, but that can change. It *will* change. Together, we will make Mega-City work again."

The crowd picked up her words, chanting them over and over again.

"*WORK A-GAIN! WORK A-GAIN! WORK A-GAIN!*"

Beside him, Lint shifted uncomfortably.

"Steady," Morphy said quietly. "Don't show them you're rattled."

"I'm not, sir," the rookie insisted.

"You should be," Dredd snapped. "A Judge never gets comfortable. Never relaxes."

The muscles of Lint's jaw tensed. "Yes, sir. Sorry, sir."

On the holo-screens, Piper continued to rabble rouse.

"Do you want it to work?"

"*Yeah!*"

"Do you want it to work?"

"*Yeah!*"

"Do you *want* to work?"

"*YEAH!*"

"And that's how we'll rebuild. That how we'll *Make the City Mega Again*!"

The crowd was reaching fever-pitch, Piper yelling over their roar as she brought her message home.

"Ninety-nine percent unemployment. That's what we're faced with today. What *you're* faced with. Ninety-nine percent. And why? Because our factories, our stores, our restaurants, even our hospitals, are run by robots. By machines.

"Now, I'm no luddite. You know that, I know that. And Mayor Amalfi knows that, no matter what he says on the news-vids. I love technology. Hell, technology is my business. But technology should never, *ever* replace human beings. It should *assist* human beings, *help* human beings, but take our jobs? That—is—*wrong*.

"If you vote for me, I will prohibit robots from working jobs that you could do. You want to work, don't you? You want to earn creds?"

The crowd responded with a deafening, unified, "*YES!*"

"I *want* you to earn creds. I want you to earn an honest wage that you can spend in any way you want. And I know what some of you are thinking. You're thinking, 'Jocelyn, even if I earn money, I'd be too tired to enjoy it. I'll come home and flop in front of the Tri-D, too exhausted to move.' But why should you? If you've earned your money, you should be able to *enjoy* your money."

On the holo-screens, Piper's gigantic face was replaced with promotional videos of cigar-shaped pods the size of coffins, gleaming white on a bright yellow background.

"Sleep machines," Dredd muttered, recognising the devices; sleeker, more sophisticated versions of the snooze-tubes that all Judges were required to use at the end of every shift.

A ripple of confusion went through the crowd.

"And yes," Piper said, "I know what you're thinking once again, my friends, because we're alike, you and I, like peas in a pod. 'Why is she showing us sleep machines? How can *I* afford a sleep machine?' Well, I tell you this: elect me as Mayor, and you won't *need* to afford them. Elect me as Mayor, and Mega-City One will supply *every* citizen with a sleep machine of their own. Men, women, boys and girls. Hell, we'll even buy one for your dog. Why? Because we want to give you the most precious thing of all. We want to give you *time*. Time to go to work, to feel the satisfaction of contributing to society, and then, when you get home, time to enjoy what you've earned. Ten minutes in your new, state-funded sleep machine and you'll be ready to party, party, party!"

The crowd cheered louder than ever.

"Unemployment will fall! You, my friends, will have a new sense of purpose—of pride—and Mega-City One's economy will soar as you spend all your money!"

The noise in the plaza had swelled with every word, the crowd becoming frantic as they imagined the credits. Now, the chants returned in force.

"*MAKE THE CITY WORK!*"

"*MAKE THE CITY WORK!*"

"*MAKE THE CITY WORK!*"

On the platform Jocelyn Piper exuberantly flashed the victory sign. Anyone would have thought she'd already won.

Beside Morphy, Dredd's stance had shifted. His shoulders were hunkered down, his hand resting on his Lawgiver. Morph felt it too.

"Something wrong," Dredd said.

"Yeah," Lint agreed. "The citizens want to work. When did *that* happen?"

"Not all of them," said Morph, pointing out a couple of placards among the sea of *VOTE PIPER* banners and flags

They were held by a pair of morbidly obese men, with multiple chins rolling into flabby chests, and guts so large that they needed a belliwheel™ to prop up the bulging blubber.

Fatties. Yet another suicidal craze gripping the Big Meg; citizens who gorged themselves silly, their bodies bloated out of all proportion. Morph remembered the mess that had gone down at the Herc last year. This pair were the biggest he'd seen so far. One had a scrappy brown beard, the other clean shaven, although the resemblance between the two was startling. They had to be related, maybe even twins. Scrappy Beard was wearing a black vest over his titanic tummy, whereas his porky sibling had decided to throw caution—and decency—to the wind and go topless, rolls of unsightly flesh basting in the sun. They were chanting, stubby arms so weighed down they could barely hold the placards above their neckless heads.

"*NO JOBS!*"

"*NO WORK!*"

The slogans weren't complaints, but demands.

Other placards appeared among the crowd. Near Lint, a juve so pale he was almost albino had unfurled a banner.

Dredd spotted it too, three letters scrawled in green paint on the fabric. "It's the CPF Grud!"

The spud was shouting a chant of his own now, his weedy voice joining that of his fellow protestors, who, by the look of things, had been hiding in the crowd all the time.

"No—to—jobs! No—to—jobs!"

Dredd's Lawgiver was in his hand, the CPF chants challenging even Piper's ecstatic supporters.

"*No—to—jobs! No—to—jobs!*"

"*Down—with—work! Down—with—work!*"

"*What do we want? Apathy! When do we want it? Whenever!*"

"Who the drokk are the CPF?" Lint asked, looking around the crowd.

"Couch-Potato Front," Dredd said, striking the nearest protestor with the butt of his Lawgiver. "Anti-work activists. They *want* robots taking their jobs."

Another protestor had found himself on the wrong side of Dredd's fist, but it was too late. The mood in the plaza had changed, discontent rippling through the crowd, swelling by the second. In less time that it took to say, 'work-shy dross,' punches were thrown and some of Piper's supporters trampled.

The Judges went to work, busting skulls and delivering sentences, but it was clear the rally had descended into a full-scale riot.

On the stage, Piper struggled to make herself heard above the rabble: "Please, my friends, there is no need for this! Please, settle down. Remain calm."

She might as well have tried to convince the Earth to stop spinning. Piper's bodyguard—a mountain of muscle in dark glasses and a sharp suit—rushed to the podium to get his employee to safety.

"Morph! Four o'clock!"

Morphy turned at Dredd's warning to see a protestor lifting a long cylindrical weapon onto his shoulder. Drokk! Was that a rocket launcher?

Dredd brought up his gun, but the perp had already pulled his trigger.

A shell streaked out, slamming into the floating platform with a bone-rattling *FOOM*. The explosion set off a chain reaction, the stage's hoverpads exploding in succession.

"It's going down," Dredd yelled as the platform ploughed into the crowd, screams of terror replacing the rival chants.

Five
Riot-Foam

THE CROWD SURGED forwards, baying for Jocelyn Piper's blood. The would-be Mayor was going to be ripped limb from limb by the very citizens she'd just pledged to help.

Dredd charged through the mob, immediately taking a punch to the jaw.

"Assaulting a Judge," he barked, knocking the perp onto his back. "Five years."

He didn't stop to check if the punk gave himself up. Justice Department hover-wagons had descended on the plaza, capturing the riot on camera, every misdemeanour logged, citizens marked for arrest. Dredd need to focus on Piper. He had no loyalty to the woman, only the City, but wasn't about to let a mayoral candidate be slaughtered in front of him.

Above him, the H-Wagons were getting into position, ready to deploy riot-foam, a quick-hardening polymer that would immobilise the crowd until they could be cut free for processing.

"Hold the foam," Dredd yelled into his helmet mic. "Piper may be injured."

He didn't want to give the Justice Department's political enemies any more ammunition to spread discontent.

"*Standing by, Dredd, but you haven't got long.*"

"Understood."

The shirtless Fattie with the CPF placard rammed into Dredd, propelled by the wheel supporting his obscene belly. Was that thing *motorised?*

Dredd went down, the gutlord's bulging breadbasket blocking out the sun.

"Attempting to smother a Judge, six years," Dredd shouted, bringing his boot up hard to connect with privates the perp probably hadn't seen in years.

His foot just sank into whalemeat, the chubster's crotch protected by mounds of flabby padding. There was nothing else for it. Dredd pressed his Lawgiver into the belly threatening to smother him and yelled a muffled, "Armour piercing!"

The bullet sliced through the Fattie's gargantuan body, exiting through the top of the creep's head. The walking blimp toppled forward, Dredd rolling clear before he was flattened by the prestigious paunch.

"Out of my way," Dredd yelled, jumping to his feet and shoving protestors from his path. Piper was on the floor in front of the wrecked stage, her bodyguard stretched over her body.

"She hurt?" Dredd yelled.

"I'm looking after her," the bodyguard replied.

Dredd grabbed the muscleman's jacket and hauled him from Piper. "That's not what I asked."

Piper looked up at Dredd, her eyes fearful despite her usual bravado. "I'm all right, Judge..."

"Dredd, ma'am."

"Thank you, Judge Dredd. Hendry has everything under control."

Dredd couldn't agree with her assessment of the situation. The crowd was pressing in, and Piper herself was in a terrible state. Blood was pouring from a gash above her right eye, and at least three of her teeth were missing, knocked out by either the crash or a well-aimed boot.

Dredd offered the woman his hand, his Lawgiver raised in the other. "Let's get you out of here."

"These poor people," she said as she allowed herself to be manhandled through the crowd, Dredd and Piper's bodyguard—Hendry—forming a protective shield around her. "They don't know what they're doing."

"Wouldn't bet on it," Dredd growled as Hendry stopped and scooped up a discarded *Make Mega-City Work* sign and batted a protestor across the head with a sharp thwack.

Dredd snatched the placard from his hand. "Leave the violence to me, or your boss will be looking for new muscle."

They were almost at the edge of the plaza, Lint joining Dredd to clear a path.

And then there was someone in front of them, a small, weasel-faced woman brandishing a microphone as if it was a sword.

"Loreen Peston, *Hound News*. Judge Dredd, what could the Justice Department have done to prevent this incident?"

"Out of my way." Dredd tried to barge past her, but the reporter stepped back in front of him.

"Not until I have an answer. Were the Judges watching the CPF before the tragic events of this morning?"

All the time, Control was yelling in his ear: *"Dredd, we can't wait any longer. We need to deploy the foam."*

"What do you say to critics who claim the Chief Judge has lost control over the City?"

"*Dredd?*"

"Judge Dredd, I'm going to have to press you for an answer."

"*Dredd!*"

"Do it," he roared into the comm. "Press the button!"

A sound like thunder rumbled above their heads, and a thick, milky substance smothered protestor and Judge alike. Dredd held his breath; the last thing he wanted was to swallow any of the stuff. It looked innocuous enough, but that would change the moment it started to solidify. He'd seen perps suffocate as the foam expanded in their mouths, or suffer heart attacks as they found themselves encased. There were fatalities with every deployment, but the numbers had been crunched at the Grand Hall, and acceptable losses calculated. Dredd didn't let such things concern him. All he cared about was restoring the peace.

He forced himself to relax, the spume having hardened around his limbs within seconds, gripping like rockcrete.

Dredd couldn't move, Loreen Peston couldn't move, Jocelyn Piper and her tank of a bodyguard couldn't move, and—more importantly—the crowd couldn't move.

Dredd glared at Peston, who was standing like a statue, her microphone still held out towards him.

"Any final comment?" she mumbled through the unyielding gunk.

Dread grimaced. "Sure. Three years for obstructing justice. How's that for a headline?"

Six
Back to the Studio

IN THE HOUND News studio, anchor Bret Barnet raised a sculpted eyebrow and smouldered into the camera-drone hovering in front of his heavily made-up face.

His voice was like honey running from a spoon. "Shocking scenes today at Boris Johnson Plaza. As you've just witnessed, political correspondent Loreen Peston has been arrested for asking questions by"—Bret glanced at the monitor, still showing scenes of the riot—"by Judge Dredd, a new lawman who has certainly made a name for himself in the last year." Bret turned to camera two and unleashed a devastating wink, designed to make the city's housewives and -husbands go weak at the knees. "One to watch, although with *that* chin, he'll be kind of hard to miss."

On the monitor, Loreen was already being chipped out of the riot-foam. Bret wondered who he'd have to bribe to keep her stuck in the stuff. He was no fan of the network's up-and-coming political correspondent. He still couldn't believe the little madam had spurned his advances at the *Hound News* Summer Hottie-Fest. Didn't she know who he *was?* Newsflash: Bret

Barnet was the bee's knees. In fact, he was the bee's *everything*. The camera loved him, the viewers loved him, and all eighteen of his mistresses loved him. The gall of the girl! Well, now she had three years in an iso-block to rue her decision.

Bret turned back to camera one, reading from the autocue he'd had grafted to his optic nerves back when he was a cub reporter. "Official reports suggest that at least 878 people have been confined in the riot-foam, including mayoral hopeful Jocelyn Piper herself. Let's go to everyone's favourite eye in the sky, Seymour McKenzie, who's on the scene. Seymour, what can you tell us about the incident at Boris Johnson?"

Bret paused, waiting for Seymour's response. He frowned. That was odd. All they could hear was the sound of somebody sobbing.

He checked his earpiece to make sure it wasn't malfunctioning. "Seymour? Are you there?"

Was there something wrong with the feed? He glanced at the monitor, seeing the footage streaming from McKenzie's hoverboard. What was the fool playing at? This is what you got when you employed a skysurfing stoner as a roving reporter. Bret had told the network it was a bad idea, especially after he found out that McKenzie had somehow hooked up with Loreen after she'd turned him down. Those two deserved each other.

But something was awry. The images were great, a dramatic shot of the foam-encased rabble, but the only commentary was the sound of snivelling.

Bret flashed an apologetic smile at the cam-bot. "Sorry about this, folks, but we seem to be having trouble with Seymour's report. I'm not really sure what's happening, but as you can see—"

A voice whined over the studio speakers. "*I'm sorry...*"

Again, Bret's hand went to his earpiece. It didn't help him hear any better, but always looked good on camera, ramping up the drama and—with it—the ratings. "Seymour, is that you?"

"*I did it. I... I did it.*"

Bret laughed nervously for the camera, although inside he was punching the air in glee. McKenzie was obviously as high as a kite, in more ways than one. The kid was finished, and once again it was down to Bret Barnet to steady the ship.

"Done what, Seymour?" Bret mugged to the camera, wagging an accusatory finger. "You haven't raided my stash of newsroom biscuits again, have you?"

"*I shot him.*"

Bret's smile dropped away. "I'm sorry. What was that?"

"*I killed him,*" McKenzie wailed, his disembodied voice thick with emotion. "*I didn't mean to. I didn't want to. I... I just pulled the trigger.*"

This was... *brilliant.* Tri-D gold. An unexpected confession live on air. If Bret handled this right, he'd probably be able to ask for a bonus... not to mention find lucky Miss Nineteen. He'd had his eye on the network's celebrity reporter for a while, a cheeky little minx if ever he saw one. Sure, she was engaged, but hey, he was married—twice. What did it matter?

"Okay, slow down Seymour. Who exactly did you shoot?

"*Ben Peck,*" came the strangled reply. "*I killed Ben. Shot him right between the eyes.*"

Seven
Chasing the Story

"YOU BETTER SEE this, Joe."

Dredd tried to look up, but the riot-foam still held him tight. A Tek-Judge was attempting to slice him free, but progress was painfully slow.

Morphy appeared in front of him, brandishing a datapad, Bret Barnet's unctuous voice emanating from the unit's tiny speakers.

"*That's right, folks, you heard it first on* Hound News. *Our very own Seymour McKenzie has confessed to the murder of MC-1 News reporter Ben Peck.*"

"What?" Dredd spat. "Where is he?"

Morphy pointed into the sky. "Looking down on us."

Dredd followed Morphy's gaze, spotting a sky-surfer high above the plaza, the same punk he'd seen flying over Dependicorp.

"Grud. Get me out of here," he barked at the Tek-Judge.

The woman continued chipping away at the hardened foam with her laser-cutter. "It'll take as long as it takes. The last thing you want is for me to slip and accidently disembowel you."

The Judge had already freed one of Dredd's arms. He used it to snatch the cutter from her grasp. "Give me that."

Before she could stop him, Dredd ignited the torch, sweeping its beam across his body to carve a line through the congealed lather. The foam's grip on him loosened and Dredd forced himself out, bursting from the cocoon like a particularly bad-tempered moth.

He shoved the cutter back into the Tek-Judge's hands, ignoring her sudden gasp, echoed by Morphy.

"Dredd, your chest."

Joe looked down, seeing the blistered line across his torso. Grunting, he peered at Morphy's screen. "Nothing that can't be patched up. Let me see."

McKenzie was continuing his on-air confession: "*I did it. I killed him. And now the Jays will be after me. Oh, Grud. They're going to lock me away!*"

"Damn right we are," Morphy said grimly, as above them the hoverboard streaked away from the plaza. "Creep's running!"

So was Dredd. Leaping over the foam-covered bodies of the rioters, he raced for his Lawmaster, ignoring the pain in his chest and threw himself in to the seat. He gunned the engine, tires squealing as he accelerated away, eyes locked on the fleeing skysurfer. "Dredd to Control. Am in pursuit."

The punk was heading north, followed by an army of rocket-powered drones and hoverbikes. Dredd guessed they belonged to McKenzie's fellow ambulance-chasers, desperate to get the scoop on their colleague's unexpected confession. Dredd ordered his bike to tune into *Hound News*, Barnet's oily commentary filling Dredd's helmet as the Lawmaster swerved onto the sked.

"I TOLD YOU Dredd was one to watch," Bret Barnet told his audience as he watched the young Judge weave in and out of traffic. "Joe Dredd, class of '79, and cloned from none other than Chief Judge Fargo himself. That's some legacy resting on those shoulder pads."

On the monitor, McKenzie threw his board around Bruce Forsyth Block, screaming through the narrow gap between Jimmy Tarbuck and Ronnie Barker, all luxury retirement homes for eldster-entertainers. Dredd didn't miss a trick. He zipped up a pipeway, disappearing from view, before roaring out onto the Jenson Button Megaway. The kid was good. *Really* good.

"If you've just joined us, Judge Joseph Dredd is in pursuit of fugitive from the law Seymour McKenzie. I've never seen anything like it. A lone Judge on the ground pursuing a hover-boarder high in the sky; and a champion hover-boarder at that. As you're no doubt aware, McKenzie was a Mega-City skyboard champion three years in a row."

For all that Bret despised the sky-punk, McKenzie's skill with a board was obvious. He was sweeping past antigrav flyers with ease, pushing his board higher and higher, although Dredd wasn't far behind, zooming along the Megaway, his mastery of the thundering Lawmaster matching—if not surpassing—McKenzie's dexterity in the air.

"Dredd really is a wonder, although, from what we can tell, his standing in the Justice Department isn't what you'd expect. According to our sources, he's already been forced to prove his innocence on at least one occasion. Recently, Judge Whistleblower provided a damning indictment of Dredd, describing the young Judge as, and I quote, 'a humourless freak no different to the muties on the wrong side of the Wall. He's a flawed experiment, just like his no-good brother, a miscarriage of Justice made flesh...'"

"...*TOUGH WORDS THERE from our Judge on the inside, referring of course to Dredd's wayward brother, Rico, who—despite graduating at the top of his class—was arrested by Dredd himself—*"

"Channel off." Dredd needed to concentrate on the perp, who had now entered a stream of heavy traffic, dodging hoverpods and juggers with ease. It was just a shame that the other pilots didn't share McKenzie's skill. There had already been one collision, a flyer slamming into an airbus, the drivers only just managing to maintain altitude. McKenzie had to be taken down, and fast.

"Control, where's air-support?" Dredd yelled as his Lawmaster streaked between two lumbering mo-pads, the gap between them only inches wider than the bike's handlebars.

"*Right on top of you, Dredd. Look up.*"

Dredd looked up to see two H-Wagons swing around a monumental construction site to his right—a partially-built Palais-de-Boing destined to house another of the Meg's emerging crazes. McKenzie responded with preternatural speed, banking left even before the wagons had cleared the scaffolding and disappearing behind a stream of low-slung hover bikes, a convoy of heavily-muscled Air's Angels patrolling the skies.

The punk's reactions were incredible. Unless...

"McKenzie's using a Justice Department scanner."

"*What's that, Dredd?*"

"Standard journo-tech. He's tapping into transmissions. That's how he knew the H-Wagons were coming, how he knows *I'm* coming."

He didn't wait for a response. "Bike, disconnect from Justice-Net. No comms in or out."

The Lawmaster's computer chimed and the Justice Department chatter in Dredd's helmet silenced. Control would still be able to monitor him on surveillance cams, but would hopefully have the sense to keep their mouths shut about his position.

McKenzie was ahead of him again, heading for the West Wall. Was he going to take his chances in the Cursed Earth? The sentries on the wall would take him down before he escaped the City limits, but the way the spug was flying that thing, there was every chance he could dodge their guns.

Dredd drew his Lawgiver. McKenzie was too high. There was no way he could draw a bead on him.

Unless he got higher.

The ramp leading up to the West Mutieland Turnpike was ahead. Dredd accelerated, civilian vehicles swerving to get out of his way. He picked up speed, hitting the ramp at a solid one hundred and fifty. Racing up towards the turnpike, he triggered his bike's turbo boost and shot into the air like an anti-aircraft missile.

He aimed, waiting until he felt himself start to fall, then fired twice; Standard Execution rounds. His shots slammed through the back of McKenzie's hoverboard, taking out the rear stabilisers. The surfer screamed as he dropped into a dive, his board corkscrewing out of control.

Dredd's bike crashed back onto the sked; the sudden jolt aggravated the already angry wound across his chest.

McKenzie came off worse, bouncing once off a covered pedway, his safety line breaking along with both his legs. He hit the ground with a sickening crump and lay still.

Dredd's Lawmaster screeched to a halt beside the downed sky-boarder. The creep was barely conscious, his blood soaking into the sked as his eyes fluttered in a fractured skull. He glared down at the punk.

"Seymour McKenzie, you're under arrest."

Eight
Two Places at Once

MORPHY AND LINT found Dredd being treated near to where McKenzie had come down, a Med-Judge spraying plasti-skin over the burns Dredd had inflicted on himself.

"Dredd always gets his man," Morphy told Lint, as they jumped from their bikes. "If you can make half the arrests, you'll be doing well, rookie."

"Yes, sir," Lint acknowledged.

Dredd waved the Med-Judge away. "That's enough. See to McKenzie. We need to make sure he's well enough to survive forty-six years in the cube."

Lint squinted as he made the calculations. "Eighteen for murder, another three for leaving the scene of the crime, fifteen for fleeing for justice..."

"Plus ten for dangerous flying."

Morphy looked over to the remains of the hoverboard, scattered across the sked. "Looks like he took a tumble."

"More than I d-deserve..." McKenzie whimpered, before dissolving into fresh lamentation. "I did it. I killed Ben. I can... I can still see his body."

"But why?" Lint asked the perp. "Why do it?"

"Doesn't matter," Dredd told him. "Creep confessed. Sentence has been passed."

Morphy raised a hand. "Rookie's got a point, Joe." The Senior Judge turned to McKenzie. "What was it, kid? Professional jealousy? Peck get the scoop on you once too often?"

"Or was he 'going undercover' with your better half?" Lint added, a sneer on his young face that vanished at a sharp glance from his instructor.

"He certainly was not," said a voice from behind. The Judges turned to see a black man in his late twenties running up to them.

Dredd rose from the med-wagon to block the newcomer's path. "Move along, citizen. There's nothing to see."

"There certainly is," the cit replied, pointing at McKenzie. "That's my husband. And he didn't do it."

"Your husband has confessed," Morphy told him.

"To the murder of Ben Peck, yes. I saw it on the news. But it's impossible."

"What's your name?" Dredd asked, pulling a datapad from his belt.

"Rufus. Rufus McKenzie. We live in apartment 1890, Johnny Utah Block, Sector 58. How is Seymour? Is he okay?"

Dredd ignored the question, checking the screen of his pad. "Story checks out. Seymour and Rufus McKenzie, married four years ago."

"I know this is hard to accept, McKenzie," Morphy said, putting himself between the worried spouse and their prisoner. "But your husband *has* confessed to the crime. It's a done deal."

"A crime he didn't commit. I don't know what's going through his head, but there's no way he killed Ben Peck. When did the murder take place?"

"Two nights ago," Dredd told him.

"On Tuesday, yes, that's what they said on the news, but

Seymour was at home with me on Tuesday night."

"Anyone else with you?"

"Only a family bucket of chicken wings and the *Game of Groans* season three box set."

Dredd's hand went to his belt and he pulled a lie-detector from a pouch. "Testify to it?"

"Gladly."

Dredd thrust the birdie in Rufus McKenzie's face. "Tell us again—where were you on Tuesday night around 8pm?"

"Watching Tri-D with Seymour, at home."

"And he never went out?"

"Not once. We watched five episodes back to back."

Dredd checked the readout, his lips thinning into a single line.

"Birdie says he's telling the truth."

He stalked back to the injured sky-surfer, this time placing the birdie beneath the perp's split lips.

"Seymour McKenzie, were you at home with your husband on Tuesday night?"

McKenzie nodded.

"All night?"

"Y-yes. We… we watched *Game of Groans*."

"Then why say you killed Peck?"

"B-because I *did*. It was me. Why don't you believe me?"

"Because you can't have done it, babe," Rufus cut in. "You were with me all evening."

"I know. But I did it all the same. I shot Ben with my own hands, before putting on the mask."

"You wore a mask?" Lint asked the boarder.

"N-no, I put it on Ben's corpse, after he died."

"No-one knows about the mask outside the Justice Department," Dredd said. "I kept it from the public record."

"Thought it was f-funny. One last face-change."

"He's delirious," Rufus insisted. "Doesn't know what he's saying."

Dredd's lie detector bleeped conclusively. "Birdie says the creep's telling the truth."

"About what?" Morph asked. "The murder, or a night watching holo-vids?"

Dredd double-checked the readout. "Both."

"It must be malfunctioning." Morphy produced his own lie detector and repeated the interrogations. Again, his birdie reported that they were telling the truth. The alibi checked out, as did McKenzie's confession.

"Doesn't make sense." Dredd indicated for the Med-Judge to get McKenzie on a stretcher. "Take him in. We'll continue this at the Sector House."

"But he didn't do it," Rufus maintained. "Your own machine proved it."

"It proved nothing; machines can be fooled. But there's more than one way to get to the truth..."

Nine
Judge Ruan

ONE HOUR LATER, Seymour McKenzie lay in a Sector House infirmary, his arms, legs and neck already knitting together in a speedheal force-bubble.

Dredd had changed into a fresh uniform and finally conceded to a dose of painkillers, if only to shut up the prattling robo-doc scuttling around the ward like an overprotective mother hen.

McKenzie himself was sedated. Dredd glowered at the perp as he slept. Whether McKenzie had shot Peck or not, he was still going away, for reckless endangerment and resisting arrest. If it turned out the creep *was* innocent of Peck's murder, Dredd would charge him with false confession and wasting Justice Department time.

One way or another, *Hound News'* eye in the sky had been permanently grounded.

What Dredd couldn't understand was how McKenzie had fooled not one, but two birdies? He *had* to be lying, one way or another. He was either innocent or guilty. It wasn't possible to be both.

The infirmary's doors swept open and a female Judge walked

in. She was around Dredd's age, of Chinese descent, with close cropped hair and keen green eyes. Instead of a name, the badge on her chest displayed the letters PSI.

Dredd's experiences with Psi-Division had been limited to a breakout of psychic phenomena twelve months ago. Dredd and a Psi-Judge by the name of Riorden had found the source of the disturbance and eliminated it, but not before Riorden had sacrificed himself, his body and mind burnt out.

Riorden had been a good man, but Dredd still felt uncomfortable dealing with Psi-Div. He understood their benefit, but that didn't stop his jaw from clenching. Back at the Academy, Dredd been classed a double-zero: not a telepathic bone in his body. To him, psykers were as alien as the extra-terrestrial refugees flooding from the Meg's deep space colonies. The rational part of his mind told him that to distrust something just because it was different was wrong—foolish, even. But weren't psychic abilities just another form of mutation?

"Judge Dredd, my name is Ruan Keiko." The Psi's voice was softer than he'd expect for a Judge. She nodded at McKenzie. "This is the victim?"

Dredd's brow furrowed. "This is the *perp*."

"Apologies." She rubbed her gloved fingers against her forehead as if trying to push away a headache. "I'm getting *waves* of anguish and grief."

Dredd grunted. "I'm not surprised. I shot him out of the sky. You're an empath?"

"Empath, telepath and precog," she confirmed. "Your basic overachiever. The other cadets hated me in the academy."

She smiled; Dredd didn't. But if his demeanour made her awkward, she didn't show it. She carried on, all business.

Good. That's the way Dredd liked it.

"I've already scanned the husband, Rufus."

"And?"

"And his memories match his story." She nodded at the

dozing sky-boarder. "He was watching *Game of Groans* on Tuesday night."

"With Seymour?"

"Yup. Although I wish I hadn't caught got a glimpse of the season finale in his mind. Talk about spoilers. You watch the show?"

Dredd ignored the question. "And Seymour didn't leave the hab?"

"Not that I could see."

Not that she could see... from someone else's memories. He'd witnessed a scan during the psi-kids incident, Riorden rifling through a juve's mind as if reading a paper. It didn't seem right. Some called it an invasion of privacy, and Dredd didn't agree with that—perps waived their rights the moment they committed a crime—but plucking memories from another's head felt to him like catching water in your fingers. Dredd liked his evidence to be solid, incontrovertible. Thoughts were ambiguous, inconclusive. Let Psi-Division deal with vagaries. He dealt with facts.

He indicated the prisoner. "You know what to do."

Ruan nodded. She took off her regulation gloves, placing them beside McKenzie's medi-bed, and moved around to stand at his head. "It would be better if he was conscious."

"That can be arranged." Dredd turned to the robo-doc. "Wake him up."

"*We should let him rest,*" the android argued as it wheeled across to the two Judges.

"Creep can sleep in the cube. We need him awake, now."

Grumbling, the robo-doc checked its patient's stats before the tip of its right index finger flipped back to reveal a slender needle. McKenzie groaned as the hypodermic was pressed into his neck.

"W-where am I?" he slurred, heavy eye-lids opening. "What happened to me?"

"Sector House 9. I'm sure it'll come back to you." At the sound of Dredd's voice, McKenzie tried to sit up, crying out in pain as the restraints around his arms and legs held him in place.

"You need to remain calm," Ruan told him. "I'm going to read your mind."

"My m-mind?"

"We need to find out which version of the truth is real."

"I k-killed him. I killed Ben."

"Let me check."

"W-will it hurt?"

"No. Not at all. Everything's going to be all right."

Ruan was talking to the perp as if he was a frightened puppy. She was trying to put him at ease, Dredd understood that, but didn't approve. By its very nature, the Law was uncomfortable. Pandering to a prisoner was a waste of time and resources.

"O-okay," McKenzie agreed. "That's fine."

This was what Dredd was talking about. They were Judges. They didn't need McKenzie's co-operation, or his consent. You committed a crime, you paid the price—cause and effect.

Closing her eyes, Ruan placed her hands on McKenzie's head. The perp let out a whimper, and Ruan's eyes snapped open. The Psi-Judge's eyes were completely blank. No colour, no pupils. Just orbs of eerie, unnatural white.

"Ruan?"

"I'm in," she whispered. "Taking him back."

McKenzie was echoing Ruan's words, his lips moving silently with hers.

"Back where?"

"To his confession."

"Forget the confession, take him back to the crime."

"These things take time, Dredd. It's... it's a mess in here."

"A mess how?"

"His memories are fragmented. Uneven. He's at home, with Rufus. On the sofa, the vid-screen on."

"Is there a clock? Anything to prove he was there around 8pm?"

She paused for a moment, frowning. "They're talking. *Do you want to watch another?* Seymour's looking at his watch. It's 10:23. *I need to be in work early tomorrow.*

"*Just one more episode. Come on, babe, don't you want to see what happens?*"

It was weird, hearing Ruan relating both sides of the conversation, McKenzie murmuring in unison. Still, 10:23 was too late. Peck had been dead for two hours by then. "Anything earlier?"

"They were there all evening, on the sofa."

"Didn't go out for food?"

"Had it delivered." She licked her lips. "Chicken wings with spicy 'slaw, Seymour's favourite."

Her brow creased.

"What is it?"

"Something's wrong."

Dredd hated this. Relying on someone else. Being shut out of his own investigation.

"All night. On the sofa. Chicken wings. 'Slaw. One more episode. Need to know what happens."

She was rambling now, stumbling over her words.

"But?"

"Chicken wing. 'Slaw. Need to know. Need to know."

She was going down the rabbit hole. Dredd had read about this in class. Psi-Judges lost in a past that didn't belong to them, unable to break free.

"*Judge Ruan's heartbeat is racing,*" the robo-doc reported. "*We must break the connection.*"

"No," Dredd told it. "Not yet. Ruan, what do you see?"

"'Slaw. Vid. One more episode. Blood. Blood on the wall."

"Blood?"

"On the wall. Gun in his hand... in my hand. *Okay, pal... we can sort this out. No need...*'"

She had adopted a rough accent. South Meg. Unlike either of the McKenzies.

"No need for what?"

"No *need for any*—" She gasped. "Muties... muties sliding down the wall. Dead. Just one more episode. Okay, pal. Aiming. firing. Need to see what happens. We can sort this out. Just one more episode. One more. Sort this out. Sort this..."

McKenzie shook violently on his bed, his body going taut, veins popping on his neck and arms.

Ruan cried out, snatching her hands away, her eyes returning to normal as she stumbled back against the wall. Dredd ignored her, his eyes on the prisoner.

"What's happening?"

"*Blood pressure 240 over 120,*" the robo-doc replied, activating its finger syringe. "*Brain activity spiking. We're losing him.*"

The android slammed the needle into McKenzie's neck and the perp relaxed, his body going slack.

Dredd turned to Ruan. "What *was* that?"

She held a hand up to Dredd, still catching her breath. Patience wasn't one of Dredd's gifts, but he had no choice but to wait for the psi to regain her composure.

"The images... were disjointed, overlapping." She forced herself to stand without the support of the wall. "Peck died in a shipping container, yeah?"

Dredd nodded. "Near the West Wall."

"I saw. McKenzie with a gun in hand, Peck in front of him."

"So he *did* shoot him."

She wiped sweat from her forehead with the back of her hand. "Yes and no."

"Explain."

"McKenzie was right; he killed Peck, or at least he *remembers* killing him, pulling the trigger, the back of Peck's head blowing out. But he also remembers being at home with Rufus at *the same* time. One moment, two memories, in two very different locations."

"That's not possible."

"But it happened."

Dredd stared at the unconscious prisoner. The robo-doc was checking McKenzie's limbs for signs of any further damage sustained during the seizure.

"Can you try again?"

"Go back in there?"

"*No,*" the robodoc interrupted. "*The prisoner is too weak. The chance of permanent brain damage is too great.*"

"Besides, it wouldn't do any good," Ruan said.

Dredd narrowed his eyes. "How so?"

Ruan looked like she needed medical attention herself; her face was pale, her once steady hands shaking. "The more I tried to focus, the worse things got in there. Both sets of memories were slipping away, becoming unstable."

Like catching water in your fingers.

Dredd fists clenched by his side. "Then what do we have? A killer that can be in two places at the same time?"

Ten
Evidence

Judge Morphy leant back on his chair, staring at the image on the Sector House monitor. He flexed his toes, his feet aching inside his regulation boots. Morphy's feet ached every day; he purposely wore boots one size too small. They hurt like hell, but the discomfort kept his mind from wandering. It was an old trick, passed from one Judge to another, and it worked like a charm. There would come a day when he would pass the advice onto the next generation, to Dredd and maybe even Lint, when the job started to get to them, when they started to brood. Better to walk with pain than to take the Long Walk before your time.

Morphy heard a creak at the door and turned to see Lint enter the evidence room.

"Judge Morphy?"

"Pull up a chair, son."

"I prefer to stand."

"Of course you do. You and Dredd; so alike."

Lint hesitated. "Yes, sir."

Morphy took off his helmet and laid it by the monitor,

regarding the rookie with renewed interest. "Got something to say, Lint?"

The rookie shook his head, but his expression made him a liar. "No. It's just..."

"Spit it out, boy."

"It's just the stories we heard back in the Academy. About Dredd and his brother."

"The best cadets we ever saw."

"Until they hit the skeds. Rico—"

"Rico was a troubled soul, and paid the price. Don't judge Joe on the actions of his brother."

"His *clone* brother. Isn't that the point? Aren't they *exactly* the same?"

"Obviously not, because Rico is serving time on Titan while Joe's serving the City."

Lint wasn't letting this go. "But... they're not natural. Neither of them."

"I've had folks say that about me. They probably say the same about you."

That stopped Lint in his tracks. "Sir?"

"The way we're trained, taken from our families as children..."

Lint removed his helmet, revealing cropped blond hair and a pair of startling blue eyes. He set it down beside Morphy's, white against black.

"At least most cadets *have* family to begin with."

"So did Dredd."

"He was born in a lab. It's not the same." Lint pulled up the chair next to Morphy and sat down. "They say he was artificially aged, his brain..." He seemed to struggle for the right words. "It was electronically stimulated—"

"And they're right." Morphy leaned forward, mirroring the rookie's posture. "Lint, there's no secret here. All of this in the public record. Both Joe and Rico had the letter of the Law surgically imprinted on their brains, yes. Try it out next time you speak to Dredd. He can quote the rulebook chapter and verse."

"Like a machine."

Morphy smiled. "Joe Dredd is a lot of things, and while he likes people to *think* he's a machine, he's not. I've seen him in action. I know what he can do. He's loyal and he cares, more than he likes to admit. Whoever you've been talking to, I suggest you stop listening. Making an enemy of Dredd won't help you."

Morphy regretted his choice of words as soon as he saw Lint's blue eyes widen.

"Why? What will he do?"

"His job, to the best of his considerable ability. And you'll look a fool."

Lint's face flushed. "I was just saying—"

Morphy sat back. He'd had enough, now. "I know what you're saying, and *I'm* saying you should drop it. Mark my words, Joe Dredd will be a Judge long after I'm gone—and a damned good one, to boot. Look beyond your prejudice and you'll see for yourself."

Lint shifted uncomfortable in his chair. The kid's jaw had clenched so tight, Morph thought his teeth might crack.

"Have I made myself clear?"

"Perfectly, sir."

"Good." Morphy turned back to the terminal. "What do you make of this?"

He didn't have to be psychic to feel the relief from Lint. They were back on common ground, inspecting evidence.

The rookie studied the vid-screen. "The crowd at the rally."

"Just before things went south, starting with these two."

He pointed at the Fatties who had first raised the CPF placards—straggly-beard and his shirtless sibling.

"I should have noticed it at the time, sir."

"We *all* should have, but it's left me wondering."

"Sir?"

"Couch Potatoes. What do they do?"

Lint was quick to answer. "As little as possible."

"Exactly. Work is abhorrent to them, to be avoided at all costs."

"Then why protest?"

"Exactly. They never have in the past. The CPF aren't activists. They rage from their sofas, or their beds, ranting on online forums, picking fights on Mega-City Radio call-ins." He waved a hand at the screen. "All this? Making banners, organising demonstrations...?"

"Takes effort."

"And firing a rocket launcher? It's all these spugheads can do to shove chips in their fat mouths."

Morphy hit the keyboard in front of the terminal. The image on the display froze.

"Here's our shooter." The screen zoomed into the bearer of the rocket launcher. The man was tall, the muscles on his thick arms defined, a single star tattooed onto a powerful shoulder. "You don't get a body like that watching *Name That Loon* on Crackpot TV."

"Do we get a clear shot of his face?"

"Barely. And when we do, the image is blurred, like he's wearing a scrambler."

"So we can't run it through Comp-Ident. Facial scramblers, they're expensive. Most members of the CPF can barely scrape two credits together."

Morphy scrolled back to the Fatties, the computer instantly providing names and addresses. "Jamie and Oliver Truss, Frederick Fudge Block, Sector 14."

"That's a long way to come to disrupt a political rally," Lint commented.

"Especially when you're that size." Morphy checked the arrest log. "Oliver Truss—the creep who forgot to pack a shirt—was executed by Dredd on site."

"And his brother?"

Morphy shook his head. "His name's not on the log."

"He wasn't picked up?"

"Must have absconded before the riot-foam was deployed."

Lint turned to address the computer. "Track movements of surviving Truss brother." The image shifted to CCTV footage of the Fattie wheeling into a waiting hover-car, the computer picking up the registration plate—*FLAB4EVA*.

"Private number?"

"Part of a sponsorship deal. Turns out Truss and his brother were competitive binge eaters."

"Figures."

Traffic cams next picked up the car in the fast lane of the throughway, heading in the direction of Sector 14.

"And this little piggy went wee, wee, wee all the way home," Lint said.

"Apparently not." The spy-in-the-sky footage was replaced with CCTV pictures of Truss squeezing his bulk through the doors of a floating diner. Morphy pulled up the address. "Url's Place, on the corner of Fannie and Cradock. Looks like someone got peckish. Fancy a munce-burger, son?"

Lint grinned. "Thought you'd never ask."

Eleven
Award-Winning

Loreen Peston couldn't sleep. It wasn't surprising. She'd been using sleep machines every day for the last three years. The recommended ratio was six nights of the snooze-tube, one night of regular slumber, but Loreen had never been one for following rules. Who needed sleep anyway? Did sleep get you to the top of your game at twenty-three? No, it did not.

Of course, it had side effects. After a while, the brain became dependent on the machines, unable to drift off without their assistance. Users literally forgot how to sleep. There was also supposed to be a risk of psychosis and/or death, but Peston was all about risk. Wasn't she the woman who'd climbed the Statue of Justice to interview the exiled Duke of Milton Keynes before he'd jumped to his death? Hadn't she smuggled herself to the Moon to expose a land-grabbing conspiracy in direct contravention of the International Lunar Treaty of '61?

She never gave up until she got her story—as Judge Dredd was about to find out. Shifting on her bunk, Loreen turned her back on the holding cube that would be her home until she was transferred to an iso-block. All she'd wanted from Dredd was a comment, a pithy soundbite that could be played every hour on the hour, and what had she got instead? Imprisonment? Humiliation?

No. She'd got the scoop of the year. Loreen was going to write the story to end all stories. A courageous journalist falsely imprisoned, her future snatched away. If she had to spend three years in a stinking iso-block, she would document each and every indignity. The harassment, the brutality, the disgusting food rations. The people of the Meg would be so moved by her words, so outraged by her treatment that they would batter down the gates of the Grand Hall itself.

She could almost hear them chanting outside the Chief Judge's chambers:

"*Free the* Hound News *One! Free the* Hound News *One!*"

There would be book deals, maybe even a holo-movie. Her harrowing experiences would win her the Howard Stern, the highest accolade for any serious journalist. No, this wasn't the end; it was just the beginning.

Imagining herself marching up onto a rostrum, the world watching as she collected her award, Loreen started to finally fall asleep, her body relaxing as her adoring public called for Dredd's head...

Just the beginning...

Just the—

Behind her, the door unlocked. Loreen twisted sleepily to see who had entered the cube, the bunk creaking beneath her.

The first blow took her by surprise, and she tumbled to the floor. Her hand went to her head and came back bloody, her fingers trembling as she went into shock.

She tried to lift her head, but it felt ridiculously heavy, like her neck couldn't take the weight.

There were boots beside her. Green boots, with a thick tread.

The blows kept coming. Once, twice...

"Please... don't..."

Blood splattered across the floor, across the boots... Another hit. And another. Pain... pain like she'd never felt before, white hot one minute, numb the next. She could hear something cracking. She couldn't work out what.

The world was fading away, the colours dimming.

She didn't care. She could barely remember her own name, but could hear applause. *Her* applause. She was on the rostrum, the world watching as received her award.

This was the beginning...

Just the beginning...

Just—

Twelve
Jamie Truss

Jamie Truss ate when he was stressed. To be fair, Jamie Truss ate when he was relaxed, but not in the same quantities.

Yesterday, for example, he'd only chomped his way through 42 stodge-burgers. Today, he was already way past that, not to mention all the fries, onion rings and hotties. He knew he should go home—should be hiding out—but in many ways Url's Place *was* home. He easily spent more time here than anywhere else. He even had his own booth, the table removed to make room for his belly. Who needed a table when you could balance your tray on your own gut?

Belching like a sealion, Jamie threw his latest carton in the direction of the garbage grinder. It fell short, tumbling to the floor to be swept up by Cher-L, the diner's friendly robo-waitress.

"*Had enough, hun?*" the mechanoid asked, swivelling on her chrome wheel to face her favourite customer.

"Perhaps one more for the road," Jamie wheezed. There was no point heading back while still peckish. He'd only end up flagging down a mega-kebab wagon.

Cher-L pulled a notebook out of a compartment in her waist.

"*Same again? Triple-stacked beef-o-lard with double bacon and salad?*"

"Maybe leave out the salad," he told her, patting his engorged stomach. "I'm trying to be good."

"*I could swap the green stuff for a rack of ribs?*"

"Sounds great. Thanks."

"*Want the entire thing deep-fried this time?*"

"Sure, why not?"

"*You got it, hun.*"

Cher-L turned and whirled back to the kitchen.

"And tell Url not to skimp on the sauce, okay?" he called after her as she bustled through the swing doors.

Jamie gazed out of the diner window while he waited. He could sit for hours, watching people scurry like ants on the pedway below. He felt safe here, floating above the scum of the city. It was his own personal oasis, where old-skool rock 'n' roll played on the digi-juke and the food kept coming. Grud bless 24-hour service. Grud bless the sponsorship that paid his tab. Up here, his troubles melted away like cheese on a griddle. Up here, he was left alone.

"Mr Truss?"

Jamie jumped, nearly regurgitating his last five burgers in shock. A kid was standing beside his booth, holding out a notebook and pencil, expectation plastered all over his freckled face. Jamie looked up at the lean woman who stood with a protective hand on the boy's shoulder, and tried to keep the disgust from his face. She was all skin and bones, not an ounce of flesh on her. Disgusting.

"I'm sorry, sir," she said, her voice a nasal whine, "but little Johnny's a big fan."

"A big fan of a big man," the kid piped up, grinning a gap-tooth smile. "Can I have your autograph?"

"He watches the Flab-League all the time. You and your brother are his favourites."

The mention of Oliver was like a punch to Jamie's ample stomach.

"Yeah, where is Oliver?" the kid asked. "I have all your action figures, even the Battle of the Bloaters exclusives. They're super-rare."

Jamie glanced at the empty seat on the other side of the booth, where his twin brother would usually be wolfing down gallons of fried chicken ice-cream, their guts pressed comfortably against each other.

The specially reinforced bench was empty now.

"He... he couldn't make it today," Jamie managed to say, his voice thicker than one of Url's megashakes. He went to reach for the kid's autograph book, eager for the brat and his stick of a mother to leave him the drokk alone. His arms still ached from holding that snagging placard. At least the mother showed a modicum of consideration, grabbing her son's book and depositing it into Jamie's blubbery fingers. He scrawled an approximation of his signature on the paper, already having forgotten the kid's name. It didn't matter. Little drokker would be dining out on this for a month anyway. His pound of flesh given, Jamie shoved the notepad back into the boy's hands and hoped they'd leave.

Fortunately, Cher-L reappeared from the kitchen, shooing the pair away and depositing the burger in front of Jamie, the bun encased in two inches of deep-fried batter.

She wheeled back and forth beside him, waiting. He peered at her, getting more than a little annoyed.

"Can I eat my meal in peace?"

"*Awww, go on, hun,*" the robot replied in a sing song voice. "*Do the thing. You know I like it when you do the thing.*"

"What am I, a performing walrus?"

Cher-L crossed her metallic arms. "*You want me to tell Url you were mean to me? After he sponsored you and your brother for so long?*"

Tears stung Jamie's little piggy eyes. Why was everyone mentioning Oliver?

He saw his brother charging forward, ramming that Judge, the jay going down beneath his championship gut—and then the bullet bursting out of the back of Oliver's skull. That's when Jamie had run. Okay, 'run' was a stretch; he'd *tottered* to the car waiting to whisk the Truss Brothers to safety. Only Jamie had made it, and all because Oliver had got greedy.

Well, *greedier*.

"*Hul-lo, Earth to fatso*," Cher-L trilled. "*Come on, hun. Just one more time. For me.*"

Jamie sighed, picked up the deep-fried burger and clacked his teeth together twice, activating the implant. His artificial jaw, installed at considerable expense by Url, stretched open, the hydraulics extending Jamie's gob until he could swallow the entire stodge-burger in one gigantic gulp.

Cher-L's tin-plated palms clattered together as she applauded. "*So gross. It's* won-*derful. Another?*"

Jamie nodded, screwing his eyes tight so her optical-sensors wouldn't register his tears. He listened to her wheel squeaking across the floor, remembering the day he and Oliver had checked into the Burger-Emperor's Private Hospital for the Purposely Obese to have the implants fitted. Jamie hadn't wanted to do it at first, but Oliver soon talked him round.

Oliver always talked him round.

"Jamie Truss?"

More Flab-Fans. What was wrong with these people? Why couldn't they leave him—

Jamie's hardened arteries almost burst as he opened his eyes. Two Judges stood in front of him; one older, with a greying moustache, and the other younger, wearing the white helmet and badge of a rookie.

"C-can I help you..." Jamie looked at the senior officer's badge to find his name. "Judge Morphy?"

"You were at the Piper Rally this morning," Morphy said. It wasn't a question.

"No. I... I don't think I was."

"False testimony," said the rookie. "Two years in the cube."

Morphy barely acknowledged the sentence. "We saw you, and have vid-footage. You were there with the CPF."

Jamie's stomach gurgled.

"That was my brother," Jamie admitted, guessing that lying would only make things worse. Wasn't as though he could make a run for it. "He... persuaded me to come alone. I didn't want to, but..."

The gurgle turned into a growl.

"But what?" the Judge pressed.

It was time to come clean. "We were paid to be there. To protest. We've never been members of the CPF"

"Conspiracy to incite violence," the rookie said. "You just added another five years to your sentence, punk."

Morphy raised his hand to silence the young firebrand. "Who paid you?"

Jamie shrugged—or he would have, if his shoulders could have taken the weight. "I don't know. Honestly, I don't. Jamie dealt with that kind of thing. We've... we've been overextending ourselves recently."

The rookie looked down at Jamie's gut. "That's an understatement."

"No, I mean financially. It's these motorised belliwheels. They cost a fortune, and Url's money only goes so far..."

The growl of Jamie's stomach turned into a roar.

"You still hungry, son?" Morphy asked, as Jamie clutched his belly.

"No... I don't feel too good, actually."

The rookie sneered. "Guilt will do that to you."

Jamie felt as though his insides were churning. Something was wrong. And there was a beeping somewhere nearby, like a muffled alarm.

"That your communicator, citizen?" Murphy asked.

Jamie burped. "No, I haven't got one. Oliver always handled our calls."

The beep was getting more insistent, as was the rumble from his tummy.

Judge Morphy pulled out a scanner, sweeping it over Jamie's paunch.

"Explosive device!"

"Where?" the rookie said, pulling out his gun as if he could somehow shoot the bomb dead.

"In his belly!"

Jamie looked down at the rolls of fat that jutted out in front of him. "What?"

The Judges were already running for the exit, yelling for the other customers to clear the diner. Jamie tried to move, but his belly wheel jammed. So much for new technology.

The kitchen doors burst open and Cher-L whizzed out, holding his latest order on a tray. "*What's all the kerfuffle?*"

"They say I've got a bomb in my belly!" Jamie told her.

Cher-L giggled, a high-pitched mechanical trill. "*Oh, that. Url slipped the bomb inside your last burger. Think of it as a secret ingredient. Enjoy your mea—*"

MORPHY AND LINT made it out of Url's Diner with seconds to spare. The explosion ripped through the floating restaurant, throwing them into the air and shattering the anti-grav chutes still shuttling Url's terrified patrons to the ped below.

Morphy grunted as he hit the ground, burning debris tumbling all around.

"You okay, kid?" he asked Lint, who was already on his feet.

The trainee offered Morphy his hand, but the Senior Judge swatted it away, trying not to wince as he pushed himself up.

With a sudden bleat of a siren, a Lawmaster drew up beside them, a helmet Morphy didn't recognise in the saddle.

"Judge Morphy," the new arrival said, glancing at Morph's badge. "What happened?"

Morphy gritted his teeth as he turned to look at the carnage around him, pain shooting up his leg. "Creep ate until he burst…"

Lint kicked the charred remains of Cher-L's head in frustration. "And before we could get him to spill his guts, too…"

Thirteen
Dereliction of Duty

"Dredd, we have a 793."

Dredd's head snapped up as Control's message came over the comm. A 793—violent death in the cubes.

"Which prisoner?"

"One of yours. Loreen Peston."

Dredd took off at a run, bolting out of the infirmary. He was only half aware of Ruan behind him, keeping pace.

Even in his relatively short career, he'd lost cubed perps before, suicides mostly. And there were the punks who simply gave up, wasting away in the cubes. But a violent attack? That was new, at least for him. By their very definition, cubes were the most secure places in Mega-City One. No one could get out, and no one could get in. It shouldn't be possible for prisoners to be attacked, especially by their neighbours, unless...

The thought turned his stomach.

Unless the attacker was a Judge.

Dredd saw the green shoulder pads of Med-Judges outside Peston's open cell and skidded to a halt beside her door, a grisly sight greeting him the moment he entered the cube.

Behind him, Ruan gasped.

Loreen Peston lay on her back beside her bunk. Her face was barely recognisable, a mass of bruises. Her blood was everywhere, up the walls, on the floor, but that wasn't the worst of it.

A daystick had been crammed into the dead reporter's mouth, shoved so deep that, even from here, Dredd could see her jaw had cracked in two.

Dredd stalked into the confined space, Shepherd—the stocky Judge currently in charge of the Sector House's holding cubes—looked up from his datapad. "You Dredd?"

"That's what it says on the badge. When was she found?"

"Ten minutes ago," Shepherd said, sounding bored. From the way his tunic strained against his bulk, it was clear he was a desk jockey who hadn't pounded the skeds in many a year. "Spot inspection. The door was unlocked."

"Shouldn't that have set off an alarm?" Ruan asked from the doorway.

Shepherd shrugged, looking down at his screen. "Some kind of computer error. Tek are looking into it."

"Doesn't sound like you care one way or another."

For the first time since they'd enter the cube, Dredd saw something like steel in Shepherd's dull eyes. They fixed on Dredd, his wet lips thinning. "I'm not sure I like your tone."

"File a complaint. I'll be doing the same."

"About what?"

"About your conduct."

Shepherd's face flushed. "Now look here..."

Dredd cut him off. "Vid-log?"

"What?"

"Regulations state that on discovering a 793, the first course of action is to check the vid-log. You have done that?"

"Of course I have. What's your problem, kid?"

"My *problem* is someone murdered a perp in your custody. What does the log show?"

The duty Judge hesitated.

"Shepherd, who came into this cube?"

"He doesn't know," Ruan said, staring intently at Shepherd's flustered face. "He's embarrassed. Ashamed."

"So he should be."

Shepherd raised a finger to warn them off. "It's not my fault. The vid skips."

Dredd held out his hand. "Show me."

"I'm filing the paperwork."

Dredd stood firm. "Show. Me."

Shepherd handed him the datapad, taking a step towards Dredd and lowering his voice. "Look, Dredd. I need to keep a lid on this. I'm..." Shepherd glanced up at the Med-Judges in the corridor outside. "I'm on report. There have been... misunderstandings recently, cube-heads not getting their rations on time, issues with sanitation." He laughed, sounding forced. "Sanitation! Can you believe it? These people are the dregs of society, and some bleeding heart in the Grand Hall is concerned about *plumbing?* You end up in the cubes, you should expect some stomm, am I right?"

"Should you expect to end up dead?" Dredd asked, swiping through the footage on the screen.

"Of course not, but look..." He glanced down at the body. "You must have seen the Tri-D reports. This bitch has been trying to put the boot into the Justice Department for years. Way I look at it, someone finally shut her up. In my book, they deserve a medal."

"Twenty years."

Shepherd looked sharply at Dredd.. "What?"

"In *my* book, dereliction of duty gets you twenty years on Titan. Don't make it worse for yourself. Hand yourself over to the Special Judicial Squad."

"The skull heads? Just wait a minute—"

Dredd took a step closer, his helmet almost touching Shepherd's nose. "You refusing to comply?"

"No, but—"

"*Thirty* years. Questioning the judgement of an arresting officer. Wanna make it forty?"

Shepherd looked to Ruan for support; Dredd could see the Psi-Judge's reflection in Shepherd's eyes. She had her hands clasped behind her back, her face neutral. She was staying out of this.

Clever girl.

Shepherd's shoulders sagged. His stubble-strewn chin resting on his chest, the disgraced Judge trudged out of the cube a broken man.

"That was harsh, Dredd," Ruan told him when Shepherd had gone.

"That was the Law. If Peston deserved to die, I would have pulled the trigger myself. She committed a crime, but she should have walked after serving her time. That's justice. That's who we are." He pushed the datapad into her hands. "Here."

She took the device. "What am I looking at?"

"Shepherd was incompetent, but he's right. Footage jumps. One minute Peston's on the bunk, the next her brains are munce."

"What about the cameras in the corridors?"

Dredd crouched down beside the corpse. "Same deal. Someone's covering their tracks."

Ruan threw Shepherd's datapad onto the bunk. "So where does that leave us?"

He pointed at the gore-smothered floor.

"What do you see?"

"Boot prints."

"Correct. One size nine, one size eight, that's maybe an eleven."

"It's not surprising. The place will have been swarming with helmets."

Dredd tapped the floor, picking out a set of treads. "Not that one. That's our killer."

"How can you tell?"

He scraped his finger against the footprint and checked his glove. "Blood's already dry. Prints are older; they were made when Peston bought it."

"And the chances of a blood-stained boot being found in the vicinity are..."

"Miniscule. Doesn't mean we shouldn't look." He turned to the Med-Judges still waiting outside. "You two. What are your names?"

The medics looked at each other in confusion. The elder of the two, a dark-skinned Judge with white hair, answered, "I'm Cooke. This is Wilmot."

Dredd acknowledged the answer with a nod. "We need to search the Sector House."

"Search for what?"

"Regulation boots, size 10, Loreen Peston's blood in the tread."

"You want us to do it?" Wilmot asked.

"You and anyone else you can find."

"But we're medical staff," Cooke told him. "We need to take the body to Resyk."

"You're Judges. You need to do your duty. Look for the boot." When they didn't move, he added, "Now."

Shaking their heads, the medics turned and left.

Ruan blew out. "Wow! Remind me to stay on your side when you make Chief Judge."

"I have no interest in promotion," he told her, turning back to the body. "Only justice."

Bending down, Dredd gripped the daystick and yanked it from Peston's mouth. Dislodged teeth clattered across the floor as he turned the stick over in his hands.

"It's seen a lot of service," he said, examining the dents along the shaft, before checking the handle. "Serial number's indistinguishable. No way of tracing it. Unless..."

He turned to Ruan.

"Unless what?" the Psi-Judge asked.

He held the bloodied stick out to her. "Unless you scan it."

She held up a hand to stop him. "Sorry, not my discipline. I could put a call through, have Williams sent over. He's good."

Dredd wasn't listening. He'd noticed something.

Handing Ruan the daystick, he crouched down, peering into Peston's ruined jaw. Carefully, he reached inside her mouth with two fingers, drawing out a small plastic bag.

"What's that?"

Dredd ignored Ruan's question for now, ripping open the bag and opening the note stashed within, his gloves leaving bloody marks on the paper as he read.

```
YOU MET YOUR DEADLINE.
```

Fourteen
Down Among the Dead

"WE LOOKING AT a serial killer, Dredd?"

He slipped the note into an evidence tube. "Two journalists, two bodies. Same message found on each. What do you reckon?"

Ruan looked down at the corpse.

"Think Shepherd was in on it?"

"You're the empath. What did you sense?"

She sighed. "Boredom, mostly. Shepherd was ambivalent to Peston's murder. Sure, he panicked when you questioned him, but there was nothing to suggest he was trying to conceal anything."

"Other than ineptitude."

"Correct. I get the feeling Judge Shepherd isn't a man of hidden depths."

"What else?"

"About Shepherd?"

"About the cube."

She narrowed her eyes. "What about it?"

"Do you get anything from the room? Any... I don't know... lingering emotions?"

"It doesn't work like that, Dredd. I told you, I can't read inanimate objects."

"What about bodies?"

"I'm sorry?"

"Look, I've had some experience with you people..."

Her eyebrows shot up at his words. "*Us people?*"

"...but I'm no expert. I need to know what you can do. You scanned McKenzie..."

Realisation dawned on Ruan's face, her mouth dropping open.

"McKenzie was *alive*."

"So was Peston, not that long ago. Can you do it, or not? Can you read her mind?"

"The mind of a dead woman..."

"Yes or no, Ruan?"

"Yes, but..."

Dredd stepped aside, indicating the corpse. "Proceed."

"It's not that easy, Dredd. A living brain is one thing, but necrotic tissue, that's something else"

"You've done it before?"

"Yes, but I don't like to."

"There's a lot of things about this job that I don't like, but I do my duty. I expect you to do the same."

Her eyes like boot knives, Ruan turned to shut the cube door.

"Is that necessary?"

"If we're going to do this, I need total silence. No distractions."

There was no *we* about this. Dredd knew he was pushing Ruan, but didn't care. He watched as she circled the body, kneeling at Peston's head. Again, her gloves came off, but this time the Psi-Judge hesitated before touching the journalist's waxy skin. Dredd was about to clear his throat to hurry her up, when Ruan's fingers made contact.

At first there was nothing. The psi knelt, her head bowed, face impassive. Then she flinched, her lips parting. Dredd crossed his arms, forcing himself to remain silent. He couldn't imagine what she was experiencing, nor did he want to. A vein throbbed blue on Ruan's temple, sweat breaking across her brow.

She muttered something under her breath, too quiet for him to make out.

"What was that?"

"Stern," she repeated, her voice wavering.

"Who was Stern? Peston's attacker."

"Not a person. Something that meant a lot to her."

"What do you see?"

"Shadows. She's been gone too long. She..." Ruan's voice trailed off. She'd hunched forward, inches from Peston's mangled features. A bead of sweat splashed onto the dead woman face to run down her cold cheek like a tear. "She was angry... angry at you..."

"At me?"

"You arrested her... and then..."

Another pause. Longer this time.

"And then what, Ruan?"

"Then... triumph. She thought she was going to win... to come out on top. Optimism. Ambition and... fear. Sudden, sharp, terrible fear. A door opening, the scrape of a boot..."

Ruan cried out, as if struck. Dredd took a step forward.

"Pain," Ruan gasped. "Repeated, over and over. One blow after another. Helpless... unable to fight back..."

"Against who? Who did this?"

"Green boots. Blood. Blood everywhere. My blood. Stop hitting me. Why won't they stop hitting me? Hurts so much."

Ruan cried out in agony. Dredd took a step forward.

"Okay, Ruan. Break it off."

"Can't stop them hitting me."

"Ruan!"

"Can't stop them—"

Without warning, the Psi-Judge pitched forward, slumping over Peston's body.

"Ruan!"

Dredd knelt beside her, rolling her off the corpse. Her eyes were closed, her mouth slack, Peston's blood smeared all over her tunic. Dredd felt for a pulse.

Nothing.

He jumped to his feet and threw open the door.

"Code 99 Red," he bellowed down the corridor. "Judge down."

Returning to her body, Dredd started CPR, pumping her chest with interlocked fingers. Behind him, Med-Judge Cooke barrelled into the cube.

"What happened?"

"She's not breathing"

The medic shoved Dredd out of the way. He got to his feet, stepping back to give Cooke space to work.

"Cardiac arrest," Cooke reported as Wilmot ran into the cell. Dredd watched as the pair worked in unison, Cooke unzipping Ruan's jacket, Wilmot attaching circular sensor-pads onto the psychic's bare skin.

Cooke touched a smart-device he wore around his wrist like a cuff, the sensor pads emitting a low-pitched whine that rose in intensity at the Med-Judge's command.

"Charging... and clear!"

Cooke jabbed at his cuff, and Ruan's body bucked. When she made no other movements, Wilmot resumed compressions.

"Anything?" asked Dredd.

Cooke shook his head.

"Again," Wilmot barked, kneeling back.

"Clear."

The pads delivered another charge, but again Ruan didn't respond.

"She's gone," Dredd concluded.

"Not yet," Cooke insisted, grabbing a hyospray from a pouch on his belt. Priming the device, he slammed it onto

Ruan's chest, directly above her heart. The injector hissed, and Ruan's eyes snapped open. She gasped for air as Cooke swept a scanner no bigger than Dredd's thumb over her body, checking her stats on his cuff.

"Is she okay?" Dredd asked.

"Do I *sound* okay?" Ruan wheezed.

"What happened?"

She looked up at him through sweat drenched air. "Now do you see why I don't like reading the dead?"

Fifteen
Strength and Weakness

"What in Grud's name did you think you were doing?"

Chief Judge Clarence Goodman's eyes bored into them, furious and fiery. Dredd kept his own gaze on a point just above the Chief Judge's greying hair, not out of defiance, but respect.

Ruan stood to attention beside him, her back ramrod straight. The Psi-Judge had looked like death after they'd been summoned to the Grand Hall, her pallor as leaden as her eyes were pained. But her transformation as they'd entered Goodman's presence had been remarkable; all signs of weakness were banished in an instant.

Dredd liked that. Perhaps there was more to this woman than he'd first thought.

"A prisoner had been murdered—" Dredd began.

"I know she was murdered," Goodman snapped. "I've read the report, and agree with your assessment of Judge Shepherd. However, to coerce Psi-Judge Ruan into performing a mindscan post-mortem—"

"With all due respect, sir," Ruan cut in, "there was no

coercion. I acceded to Judge Dredd's request. It is as much my responsibly as his, if not more."

Goodman sat back in his imposing chair, the light gleaming on his chain of office. "Is that so?"

Another surprise. Not many people dared interrupt Clarence Goodman.

"I understood the risks involved. Judge Dredd did not."

"And yet you proceeded anyway."

"It was my duty... sir."

Goodman steepled his long fingers, considering them both in turn.

"Do you understand why you are here, Dredd?"

"I... *we* did not follow correct procedure, sir."

"You did not. Reading a corpse requires special dispensation from Psi-Division. Do you know why?"

Dredd shook his head, annoyed at the gap in his training.

Goodman turned to the Psi-Judge. "Care to complete Dredd's education, Judge Ruan?"

There was no pleasure in Ruan's voice when she spoke: "When connecting to dead brain tissue, there is a risk that the Judge's own cerebellum will mistakenly conclude that it too has died."

"Thereby shutting down the Judge's vital organs. Lungs, heart, central nervous system, all gone, like *that*." Goodman snapped his fingers.

"I was not aware of that possibility," Dredd admitted.

"Furthermore," the Chief Judge continued, "it opens the practitioner to forces *from outside our plain of existence*."

"Sir?"

"According to Psi-Division, the world we experience is only the tip of a particularly perplexing iceberg. There are realities beyond our comprehension, populated by entities beyond our nightmares. These beings would do anything to gain a foothold on our territory. All it takes is one mistake, one error of judgement, and the floodgates could open."

Again, Ruan chose to chip in. "With all due respect, sir, I am trained to—"

Goodman slammed his hand on the desk in front of him, rattling the golden pens that had signed every executive order since he had deposed President Booth.

"Was I *talking* to you, Judge Ruan?"

"No, sir. I just thought—"

"You are not here to think, but to *listen*."

Ruan fell quiet, a sensible precaution if she didn't want her career to end standing in front of this desk. Goodman let the silence reinforce his authority before speaking again, his voice abruptly calm again.

"Well, Dredd?"

Joe didn't flinch. "I take full responsibility, sir. I insisted that Judge Ruan conduct the scan without fully understanding the implications. I accept any punishment that you see fit."

Goodman didn't respond, but instead let his grey eyes linger on Dredd before switching his attention back to Ruan.

"Judge Ruan, you are to report to Psi-Div, where you will be assessed for any lasting damage to your abilities or psyche. Until cleared for duty, you are hereby removed from active service. Do you understand?"

"Yes, sir," came the clipped reply, although Dredd heard a catch in Ruan's voice.

Goodman nodded. "Dismissed."

The Psi-Judge didn't look at Dredd as she turned on her heels and marched out of Goodman's chambers.

The gilded doors slid shut behind her and Goodman sighed, his hands resting on his desk, fingers interlocked.

"Dredd—" he began, but Joe didn't give him chance to finish.

"Sir, I believe taking me off the case would be a mistake."

"Is that right? And do I *often* make mistakes, in your opinion?"

"No, sir. However—"

"However, you presume to tell me my business. A Judge

who—while he has the unique advantage of breeding—has only served for, what? Eighteen months? Twenty?"

Goodman's words stung. *Breeding*. A reminder that Dredd was an experiment, from the man who had—until now—championed him all the way.

"Twenty-two, sir."

"Would you like to sit in this seat, or wear this chain around your neck?"

"No, sir."

"No?"

"I do not possess the required experience, sir."

"Exactly. So remember your place, Joe. You're a good Judge. You could be one of the best, if you wound in that neck of yours. You rub people up the wrong way, even people on your side."

"With respect, sir, I'm not—"

"Dredd, if you're about to tell me that you're not here to make friends, then I suggest you shut up before I bust you back to rookie."

Dredd bit his tongue. "Yes, sir."

"No one's asking you to make friends, but you need to play the game. I know you think that you're the embodiment of the Law, and not without justification, but the Law is more than one man. Different departments, working together. Hand in hand. That isn't weakness; it's strength. I don't need lone guns. I need people who can play their part. Can you do that, Dredd?"

"Yes, sir. I..." he paused, articulating a word that did not come naturally. "I apologise."

Goodman held up a hand. "Then, let this be the end of it. Look, I'm not expecting you to become the life and soul of the party, but I need you to learn respect, not just for the Law, but the people around you. I commend you for taking responsibility, and I understand exactly why you did what you did, but you need to consider the consequences next time."

"Understood."

"And, for the record, I agree with your assessment. Taking you off the case would be a mistake. A prisoner has been murdered in their cube. It's bad enough that we're having to cope with this 'Judge Whistleblower' madness, but now this? I want you to find what links the deaths of these two journalists. Find out who did it, but for Grud's sake, be careful. The press will be all over us like a rash. The last thing I need is for them to pick up on dissension in the ranks. Have I made myself clear?"

"Yes, sir."

"Glad to hear it. I look forward to your report."

Goodman turned to the computer on his desk, activating the screen to signal that the meeting was at an end. Keeping his head high, Dredd strode from the Chief Judge's office without looking back.

He had work to do.

Sixteen
Double-Zero

Isiah Morphy was frustrated. He was frustrated with the investigation, frustrated that Jamie Truss had been blown up before they could get to the bottom of who'd paid him to protest at Piper's rally, frustrated that, with both Truss brothers now dead, the case had grown cold. The Teks were swarming over the wreckage of Url's Diner, searching for evidence, but Morphy wasn't holding out hope. He'd already had Lint check the makes and models of the robo-chef and waitress, but, other than the fact that they worked at the diner, there was nothing to link the explosion to them, or to the other acts of robo-terrorism rocking the Meg. They had no reason to kill Truss, especially as he had publicly stood up *against* Piper's anti-robotic policies.

Above all Morphy was frustrated that his body ached as much as it did. Yeah, so he'd jumped eighteen feet from a floating burger joint, but in the past, he would have picked himself up, dusted himself down and got on with the job. Today, it was all he could do to put one foot in front of the other. The Meds had given him a clean bill of health, save for a few cuts and scrapes, but he felt every bruise across his tired body. He'd seen the way the Med-Judge had looked at him when he'd pushed himself from the medi-bed. How they *all* looked at him. Morphy was being assessed even as he assessed his rookies. How long would it be before he was offered a cushy desk job—or took the Long Walk, the last hurrah for Judges too long in the tooth to handle the rigours of Mega-City One?

"You sure you're okay, Judge Morphy?" Lint said, as if he could read his thoughts. Perhaps he should recommend that the rookie be transferred to Psi-Division.

Morphy picked up his pace, forcing himself to stand just a little taller. "Nothing a few minutes in the sleep machine won't cure."

Lint snorted. "Good luck with that. The number of glitches those things have suffered recently... The Department needs to invest in new equipment rather than just patching up the old models. Have you seen how many workmen we've had trooping through the Sector House this last week? If they put more money into judicial support rather than supporting pointless elections..."

"We'd have more problems on our hands. As long as the electorate are distracted by politicians, they're not waging Block Wars. Politics has its place, son. Never forget that."

Lint argued his point, but Morphy stopped listening. He was looking ahead, where a young Psi-Judge was waiting in the corridor; waiting for someone they all knew.

"Dredd," the woman said, as Joe stomped in her direction.

"We've nothing to say, Ruan."

She stepped in front of Morphy's former rookie. The kid had guts. Joe was like a cyber-mastiff; once he'd picked up on a scent, no-one got in his way. Right now, though, he was forced to stop.

"I think we do. Thank you."

"For what?"

"For taking responsibility. You didn't have to do that."

"I ordered you to make the scan."

"Ordered? Dredd, you *asked* me, and I said yes." The girl's voice had shifted from grateful to piqued in one sentence; impressive even by Dredd's standards. "You may get off by ordering around medics, but you've no authority over me."

"Is everything alright here?" Morphy asked, approaching the pair.

"Judge Morphy," Dredd acknowledged, taking in the damage to both Morphy's and Lint's uniforms. "What happened?"

"We had an argument with a bomb."

"Robo-agitators killed a suspect," Lint cut in. "Blew up a floating diner."

"*Suspected* agitators," Morphy corrected. "But we're fine." He turned to introduce himself to the Psi-Judge. "Judge Morphy, and this know-it-all is Lint."

Morphy couldn't help but notice the way Lint's eyes swept up and down the woman's uniform. "Never met a psi before," the Rookie said, flashing a lop-sided smile.

Ruan's eyes turned to ice. "Think of me that way again, and I'll remind you of your oath of celibacy... with extreme prejudice."

Lint's face flushed. "I-I didn't... I mean, I wouldn't..."

"Consider yourself warned," Morphy said, filing the encounter for his report. A wandering eye or, in this case, mind, wasn't enough to fail a rookie—Grud knows enough Senior Judges still struggled with abstinence—but it would have to be noted. "Apologies, Judge...?"

Dredd answered for her. "This is Judge Ruan. We worked together earlier today."

"And I'm guessing it didn't go well."

What Morphy could see of Dredd's face was an impassive mask. "What's done is done. Now, if you'd excuse me..."

"Not heading towards the sleep machines, Dredd?" Morphy asked. "You must be at the end of your shift."

"No time," Dredd called over his shoulder as he took his leave. "I've a killer to catch."

"Should we report him?" Lint asked, as they watched Dredd stalk away.

"For what?"

"Not complying with the required sleep machine rotation. Regulations state—"

"That in pursuit of a case," Ruan interrupted, "a Judge may forgo a sleep cycle if necessary."

"Unless by doing so they put themselves or others at risk," Lint pointed out, irritably.

"You think Dredd's a risk, Ruan?" Morphy asked.

The dark-haired woman shook her head. "I don't know *what* to think about him," she admitted. "Most people are an open book to me..."

She glanced at Lint.

"But not Joe?"

"I've never met anyone so shut down. Usually, there's a glimmer of emotion, but Dredd..."

"He's a double-zero. You might as well try to read the Statue of Judgement. But don't worry, he's stable. Trust me, it would take a lot to get under that boy's skin."

Seventeen
Grilled

"Miss Piper, thank you for joining us here on *Hound News*."

"*Always a pleasure, Bret. Always a pleasure.*"

Not so much of a pleasure that you could be bothered to come to the studio, Bret Barnet thought as Jocelyn Piper's holo-presence buzzed in front of him. The mayoral candidate had been booked to appear live, but 'due to security concerns' following the rally disaster had rescheduled as a holo-interview. More likely the trillionaire was squeezing in half a dozen more interviews with Hound's rivals. Still, this would be the one everyone would be talking about, Bret promised himself.

"And how are you; after your ordeal, I mean?" he began, a softball, sure, but one designed to lull the woman into thinking this was going to be an easy ride.

"*Oh, bless you for asking, Bret,*" Piper replied, turning on the home-spun charm. "*But I'm fine. Absolutely peachy.*" She looked it too. Even through the holo-field, Bret could see she'd been patched up. Photos of the trillionaire covered in blood and missing several teeth had circulated online following the crash this morning. Bret had forwarded them himself at least half a dozen times. Now, her smile was perfect again, new pearly-whites plugging the gaps, the scar on her forehead barely noticeable, buried deep beneath lashings of hyper-heal make-up.

"*There are those*," she continued, "*who will stop at nothing to derail our political process, but I'm not about to let that happen. We're back on the campaign trail, more determined than ever.*"

"And I see that you've also offered to pay the medical bills of your supporters injured in the incident."

Piper spread her hands in an expansive gesture, diamond rings glistening on at least six of her fingers. "*Those people turned out to support me. The least I can do is support them.*"

Bret smiled, giving the candidate her moment. "A kind gesture, and one you can obviously afford."

"*I've been blessed, yes. It's important to give something back, to contribute. If anything, that's the core of my campaign.*"

"To contribute. To 'Make Mega-City Work.'" He made sure to add the inverted commas with his fingers.

Piper's expression hardened. "*Precisely.*"

Bret let his smile drop. It was time to twist the knife. "It seems to me, Ms Piper, that blessings will continue to flow if you win this election."

"*That's kind of you to say. But, yes, the City will prosper...*"

"I'm not talking about the City. I'm talking about you."

"*I'm sorry. I don't follow...*"

"At your rally, you pledged that Mega-City One would supply every citizen with a sleep machine of their own. Another kind gesture, and an expensive one."

"*I've looked at the City's budgets, Bret, and—through diligence and smart accounting—we can more than afford it. Besides, it'll be an investment in our future.*"

Now he had her. "And an investment in *you*, Ms Piper. Or should I say in your business empire?" He didn't give her time to respond. "Does PiperTech not own a controlling share in

Somnus Industries, Mega-City One's foremost producer of sleep machines?"

"*Yes, but—*"

"Is there not a conflict of interest in a Mayor committing millions of credits of City funds to purchase items from her own company?" He let that one sink in for a moment. "Or are you considering purchasing sleep machines from your competitors? Sleep machines that you yourself said at last year's Morpheus Expo are, and I quote, 'inferior in every possible way'?"

"*Well, obviously, we would have to find the best deal for our citizens—*"

"By buying inferior products? '*Dangerous* products,' you called them."

Piper's holographic smile faltered. "*Look—*" she began, a sure sign that a politician was on the back foot. "*Somnus Sleep Machines* are *the best—*"

"So, if elected, you will directly profit from your policy?"

"*I didn't say that—*"

"Will you be selling your interest in Somnus?"

"*No decision has been made—*"

"And have you actually asked any of your potential voters if they *want* sleep machines of their own? As we saw at your rally, there is considerable resistance to your policies, not to mention the continued unrest cause by your anti-robot platform."

"*Bret, I am* not *anti-robot.*"

"You don't want them to work..."

"*I don't want them taking honest citizen's jobs.*"

"Just a few hours ago there was an incident in Sector 14. A diner, destroyed by robot activists. Were you aware of that, Ms Piper?"

"*I was not, however—*"

"You weren't? A political candidate unaware of the deaths of at least five citizens as a direct consequence of her policies?"

"*What I'm aware is that, once again, we're seeing the corruption of the Mega-City One press.*"

Bret allowed himself to scoff at the allegation.

"This is hardly *our* fault, Ms Piper."

"*Isn't it?* Hound News' *owner holds a sixty-eight percent share of the Geppetto Robot Company, does he not? Wouldn't a ban on robo-workers cause financial inconvenience for* him? *How much would he be set to lose?*"

"*Shut this down*," Bret's producer warned in his ear-piece.

"Now, I'm not sure—"

But the woman wouldn't let up. She was like a dog with a synthi-bone: "*And while we're at it, let's consider the integrity of your news service. Didn't one of your own reporters confess to homicide earlier today?*"

"We're not talking about *Hound News*, Ms Piper—"

"*Then perhaps we should. You forget, I was there. I saw Loreen Peston obstructing the work of our brave Judges; Judges who were attempting to quell a riot you say was caused by robo-sympathisers.*"

"I've said nothing of the sort—"

"*Bret,*" his producer hissed. "*The network executives are watching...*"

"*I'd like to thank you, Bret, for once again, highlighting the bias of Mega-City One's press. Perhaps instead of spreading lies about my campaign, you should turn the spotlight on yourself. Something to consider for your speech tonight, maybe?*"

Now what was the woman talking about? "M-my speech?"

"*At the News Anchor of the Year award. You* are *up against Ken Wallaby of* MC-1 Today, *aren't you?*"

Bret's heart sank. He *was* up for the award tonight, and expected to win, but for once, he hoped the judging panel weren't watching his broadcast. This car crash of an interview was the last thing he needed them to see.

"Ms Piper," he said, keen to wrap things up. "Thank you again for joining us."

She grinned like the cat that had got the alt-cream. "*Always a pleasure, Bret. I'm keeping my fingers crossed for you tonight, really I am. I've seen the billboards promoting your show, of course. Who hasn't? We all know how you like to have that face of yours plastered over the City."*

Eighteen
Limo-A-Go-Go

ON THE OTHER side of the sector, Judge Dredd strode into the gallery of *MC-1 Today*. In the studio, presenter Tommy Shuffleknackers was reeling off the forecast from Atmosphere Control, the high-altitude meteorological station that governed the Big Meg's weather systems.

Producer Helen Vince took one look at Dredd's uniform and stood up so fast that she nearly garrotted herself with her own headphones.

"J-Judge," she said, extricating herself from the cable. "Is there a problem?"

"Ben Peck. I need to know what he was working on."

"Which story?"

"He had more than one?"

She shrugged. "Sure. Before he... well, before he died, he was working undercover at the haulage firm in the day, an oldster care home at night, and the Mega-Force power plant at weekends."

"When did he sleep?"

"He didn't. Most of the time he used a sleep machine. Pretty much everyone does. Take Ken there..."

Dredd followed her gaze to the *MC-1 Today* anchor, who was signing off in the studio, telling his viewers to "Stay Mega" before winking cheekily at the cam-bot.

"What about him?"

"He's been on the air for eighteen hours. Would never manage it without the snooze-tube. Excuse me."

She bent over her control, opening a channel to the studio. "Great show, Ken. One in a million. After you've had your shut-eye, check out Bret Barnet getting roasted by Jocelyn Piper. Poor spug didn't know what hit him. Trust me, you've got that award in the bag, Kenny-boy. In. The. Bag."

Ken gave her a thumbs-up and she killed the channel again. "Sorry about that. News anchors are like kids. You need to keep their egos regularly massaged. But in all honestly, Ken should romp home tonight. After today's performance, Bret Barnet is dead and buried."

"If that woman thinks I'm finished, she's got another think coming!"

Bret Barnet ranted into his watchphone as he stomped across the roof of the towering *Hound News* building towards the waiting hover-limo. He was wearing a maroon-coloured tuxedo only slightly darker than the flush on his cheeks.

"Coming on *my* show, trying to show *me* up. She doesn't know who she's dealing with."

As he approached, the limo's rear door swung open to reveal sumptuous luxury seats—and none of your cheap rubbish either; Bret always demanded genuine mock leather, especially on a night like tonight.

"You just wait and see. First, I'll win this award, and then I'll run a comment piece and tell the world *exactly* what they should think of Ms High-and-Mighty Piper."

He slid onto the back seat, surveying the limo's comprehensive drinks cabinet. Some of the liquors on offer were legal, most weren't. By Grud, Bret needed a drink, but he didn't like drinking alone.

He raised his watchphone to his mouth, a quizzical look on his face. "Hilary, where's Susan? She was supposed to meet me in the limo."

His PA sounded nervous as she gave him the bad news.

"Not coming?" he repeated in disbelief. "What? Has she had a better offer?"

Like that would happen. What could be better than going to the event of the year on the arm of Bret Barnet?

Hilary dropped another bombshell.

"She's going with *Ken Wallaby?*" This was *unbelievable*. "But she was *my* date. I even tipped off the photographers at the *Mega-City Gazette*. They're waiting for us on the red carpet."

What a day. Bret couldn't go to the award ceremony by himself. "What about Cindy? Or Miranda?"

He listened to the long litany of excuses from his PA. At this rate, he'd be forced to take one of his wives.

"Okay, that new girl with the travel show, what's her name? Wendy? Wanda, that's it. She needs the publicity. Have her get ready and we'll pick her up on the way. Just give the driver her address, will you?"

Hilary's next comment had him staring at the front of the limo, and the empty seat in the cab. "What do you mean I haven't got a driver? I *always* have a driver."

The assistant burbled something about the network's new contract with a fleet of driverless hover-cars, but Bret cut her off.

"Whatever. Just make sure Wendy's ready." He went to shut off the call, before adding, "And tell her to look good!"

With a cry of frustration, he yanked the watchphone from his wrist and threw it the length of the car.

With a whine of its stabilisers, the hover-limo rose into the early evening air. "No date," Bret grumbled. "No driver. Heads are going to roll for this, mark my words."

The disgruntled news anchor leaned forward and poured himself at least four fingers of musk. He slugged it back, grimacing as the coarse liquid burned the back of his throat. *Ugh!* Drokking stuff tasted like window cleaner.

He finished it anyway.

Bret was pouring another glass when the hover-limo lurched to the right. Bret slipped from the shiny seat, landing on the limo floor, the open bottle of musk dropping into his lap.

"Stomm!" He wiped at the dark stain spreading across this crotch as the spilt hooch soaked into his trousers. "Stupid, drokking..."

Slamming the bottle back into the cabinet, he clambered back onto the seat. Now he was going to have to go home to change.

"Driver—I mean, *computer*—take me home. And make it snappy."

The limo's course didn't waver.

"Hello? I said take me home. I need to change, okay?"

Still the driverless hover-car flew on.

"Grud on a greenie." Bret pushed himself forward, throwing out his hands to steady himself on the windows as he tottered towards the computer-controlled cab. The limo banked to the left, clipping a hover-bus. Bret tumbled forward to the floor, whacking his head on a door.

"What the drokk?" He grabbed the partition between the back of the limo and its non-existent driver and hauled himself up. "Computer, what do you think you're doing?"

As Bret looked through the front windscreen, he realised something was wrong. They weren't heading towards his home, or the awards ceremony.

"We're going the wrong way. Computer, do you hear me?" There was no reply. This was the last straw. Uttering at least a dozen illegal curses, Bret scrambled to find his discarded watchphone and dialled his assistant's number.

The watch beeped. No signal. How could there be no signal? *Everywhere* had a signal.

The limo lurched again, ramming into the side of a flying fuel tanker. The driver blared a horn, but that didn't stop the computer scraping along the full length of the tank with a noise slightly worse than rusty nails on glass.

"What are you *doing?* That tanker's full of—*aargh!*"

Bret was thrown into the bar as the limo swerved carelessly across at least three air-lanes, narrowly missing a rocket-bike. Bottles and glasses smashed to the floor as the car veered back and forth, the computer's proximity sensors seemingly not registering any other vehicles.

Bret thumbed the control panel mounted on the door to his left. It didn't respond. Neither did the one on his right. Stupid lump of stomm!

As the limo bucked and weaved, he stumbled towards the cab, leaning across the partition to reach the main computer console.

"Must be some kind of emergency communicator," he said, randomly jabbing at buttons. He'd just hit a red switch when the limo performed a perfect loop-the-loop that threw Bret around the interior like ice in a cocktail shaker. Shards of broken glass shredded his already tattered tuxedo.

He landed with a yelp on his back, on the ceiling. The limo was flying upside down.

"*Hello?*"

Bret's dazed head snapped up. A tinny voice was echoing around the car's interior as it narrowly avoided a head-on collision with a mobile library.

"*This is the Limo-A-Go-Go customer helpline. My name is Sheila. How can I help you?*"

"Yes!" Bret cried, scrambling up to look imploringly at the dashboard computer. The inverted features of a girl wearing far too much make-up stared back at him from the screen. "Your limo's gone crazy."

Sheila's mouth dropped open, a chewed globule of bubble gum tumbling from her lips in amazement. "*Okay. Hey, you're Bret Baker!*"

"Barnet. Yes, yes, I am."

"*My mom loves you!*"

"Get this limo under control and I'll take her to an award ceremony."

"*Really?*"

The hover-car shunted into the back of an airbus, the bonnet crumpling with the impact. Bret rolled forward along the ceiling at the exact point that the limo decided to right itself, dropping him into what would have been the driver's seat.

"*Mr Baker?*"

"It's *Barnet*. Bret *Barnet!*" the anchorman yelled. "Now, get me out of here!"

Nineteen
No Cause for Concern

BACK AT THE *MC-1 Today* studio, Dredd's conversation with the producer was interrupted by a call from a researcher in the newsroom.

"There's trouble on the Eastern Air-way. Hover-limo out of control."

"Sorry, I need to see this," the producer told Dredd, instructing the researcher to send the footage to the gallery's main monitor.

"This is important."

"So is the news," the woman replied, as the image of a battered limo appeared on the screen. The car's bonnet was a twisted concertina of crushed metal, once-gleaming paintwork largely scraped away.

Dredd activated his comm. "Control, are you seeing this? Hover-limo flying against the flow of traffic on the Upper Eastern."

As he watched, the car ploughed into a citizen wearing a wing-suit, knocking him out of the sky.

Beside him, the producer snapped at her assistant, a spotty kid with the chunkiest glasses Dredd had ever seen. "Do we know who's in that thing?"

The assistant thumbed a control and the image zoomed into the limo's cracked windows, the newsroom computer enhancing the grainy image to bring the limo's occupant's features into sharp relief.

Dredd recognised the face. So did the producer.

"Oh, my Grud. It's Bret Barnet."

"*MR BARNET? MR Barnet, can you hear me?*"

Grateful that Sheila had at last grasped his name, Bret steadied himself against the dashboard. The hover-limo was skidding from left to right, bouncing off vehicles as if he were in a vast pinball machine.

"I'm here. For now, at least."

"*Limo-A-Go-Go would like to apologise for your experience today.*"

"Apologise after you get me out of this death-trap!"

"*Not a problem, sir. I'm pleased to say that your limo is not malfunctioning.*"

The car threw itself around a shoplex, turning so sharply that Bret smashed his elbow through an already weakened window. Air rushed in through the broken glasseen, forcing Bret to shout to be heard.

"You sure about that?"

"*Absolutely, sir. We're afraid your flight systems have been hijacked, remote-controlled from an unknown location.*"

"What?"

"*But there's no cause for concern.*"

"That's easy for you to say!"

"*I will simply restart your vehicle from here.*"

"Restart?"

"*Please be aware that you may experience some plummeting as the systems are rebooted.*"

"Plummeting? Wait, what do you mean, plumm—*"*

The hover-limo's engine stopped, the internal lights flicked off and the screen went dark.

Bret screamed as the flyer went into a nosedive, the solid, bone-crushing, spine-snapping ground rushing up to meet him. He was just adding to the stains on his tuxedo trousers as the dashboard lights flashed back on. The stabilisers reactivated, the hover-limo pulled up and Bret started to cry, his nerves as shredded as his dinner jacket.

Sheila's face reappeared on the monitor, smiling broadly. "*I'm pleased to say that your limo has just restarted.*" The smile dropped. "*Oh.*"

Bret looked at her through his tears. "What do you mean, 'oh'?"

The helpdesk engineer had the decency to look apologetic. "*I'm sorry to say that it hasn't worked. The limo is still under external control.*"

The car smacked into the side of a speeding hover-truck, the back door ripping from its hinges, the shattered contents of the bar streaming out of the limo behind him.

"I'm going to die, aren't I?"

A new sense of purpose seemed to come over Sheila. Popping a new stick of gum in her mouth, she picked up a hefty operator's manual. "*No, you're not. I'm gonna talk you through the manual override.*"

Bret didn't respond.

"*Sir, can you hear me?*"

He was looking through the cracked windscreen. A large screen rose ahead of him, mounted on the side of a rapidly approaching mega-block. It showed someone he recognised, albeit dishevelled, their face covered in oozing cuts, hair a sweaty, tangled mop. It took a moment to realise the face was his own, stretched across a screen the size of a soccer pitch.

In a daze, he looked around, spotting camera-drones weaving through traffic, the lenses trained on his careering hover-limo. He wondered if *Hound News* was covering the car's erratic flight. At least it wasn't swerving now. The limo seemed locked on a single course, heading straight towards the screen.

"*Mr Barnet!*"

Sheila's voice snapped him out of his reverie. He sniffed loudly and ran a hand through his tangled hair.

"Yes, yes, I'm here." If his public was watching, they wouldn't see Bret Barnet sobbing like a sports reporter who's just taken a rogue hyperball to the happy-sacks. No, they'd see Bret Barnet making headlines. They'd see him save the day. "What do you need me to do?"

"*Do you see a control panel in front of you?*"

The dashboard was awash with computer terminals and dials. "Which one?"

"*A numeric pad beneath a matrix display?*"

Bret wiped a gritty cocktail of snot and blood from his nose. "Yes. I see it."

"*I need you to enter a code.*"

Bret glanced up to check his appearance on the colossal screen ahead. It was better; not by much, but it would do.

"*Mr Barnet? Can you do that? Can you enter a code?*"

He looked back down at the keypad.

"Yes. What's the number?"

"*9-7-8-1-7-8—*"

The computer beeped as he keyed in the digits.

"*1-0-8-5-9-6-7—*"

"How long *is* this number?"

"*Security is important to us, sir!*"

He snorted. "Could have fooled me!"

"*1-7-8-1-0—*"

The limo increased its speed.

"*8-2-7-4-X.*"

"X?" Bret looked at the keypad, not knowing what to do. "There's no X!"

From her desk in the call-centre, Sheila checked the manual

with her manager. "*Sorry, that's a typo. You don't need to enter the last letter.*"

The screen on the side of the block was bigger than ever.

"Now what?"

"*Now press the green button underneath the numbers.*"

He did what he was told. The control panel buzzed.

"And?"

He could hear his voice repeated from the floating news screens around the City, every channel now broadcasting a live stream of the helpdesk call.

"*Can you read what's on the matrix display please?*"

The display was blank.

"Nothing. There's nothing there."

"*Perhaps we should try inputting the override again.*"

The giant screen was all Bret could see out the front of the limo now. "You're kidding me!"

There was another bleep, and words started scrolling across the display.

"It's working!"

"*What does it say?*"

"'You'…"

"Is that it?"

"No, there's something else. Grud, why is this thing so slow?"

"*Try to remain calm, sir.*"

The words continued to crawl across the display.

"'Met'… 'Your'…"

The last word died in his throat.

Sheila flipped through pages of her manual. "*Sir? Can you please repeat? That doesn't sound right.*"

"Deadline," Bret whimpered. "You met your deadline."

THE HOVER-LIMO SMASHED slap-bang into centre of the screen, exploding into a ball of flame that could be seen for blocks around.

Twenty
To the Scene of the Crime

THE NEWS OF the hover-limo crash came over Dredd's helmet. He'd abandoned the studio, as the newscaster's producer had all but ignored him to cover the breaking news. For once, there was little the Law could do. She'd answered Dredd's questions to the best of her ability, but it was clear that she knew nothing. Naturally paranoid, Ben Peck had played his cards exceptionally close to his chest until the moment he submitted his reports. He kept no records on the network's computer system, and no one other than Peck knew his sources. He'd always been a loner, with few friends.

Dredd was wasting his time; he needed to move on. He was racing back to the haulage company. While there was a chance that Peck's homicide was linked to the stories he was covering, it was more likely that he was killed for sticking his nose into what didn't concern him at the depot.

Dredd switched his bike to auto and brought up *Hound News* on the Lawmaster's terminal. An image of the now-late Bret Barnet's face filled the screen, not how it had been in the seconds before the crash—bloodied, bruised and borderline deranged—but airbrushed within an inch of his life, the perfect Tri-D host.

The picture was replaced by a report from the crash-site, a *Hound News* correspondent talking solemnly to camera.

"Bret's last words bring a chilling message to Mega-City One. 'You met your deadline.' This is, of course, the same message that was found on the body of MC-1 Today *reporter, Ben Peck, and—as* Hound News *has learned—in the mouth of political commentator, Loreen Peston, who has been found dead in her holding cube at Sector House 9."*

Grud! How had they found out about Peston's death? Goodman had wanted the 793 kept under wraps. Was there a leak in the Grand Hall?

Dredd flicked channels, bringing up *MC-1 Today*, a female anchor addressing viewers in urgent tones.

"The Deadliner strikes again. Who is waging war against the Mega-City press? Hound News' Seymour McKenzie had previously confessed to Ben Peck's murder, but according to our sources, his testimony has been questioned by Judges working on the case—"

Dredd killed the screen and resumed control of the Lawmaster. The Deadliner. The press had even given the nutjob a name. Dredd wasn't even sure it was one person. If McKenzie *did* kill Peck, the sky-boarder was already in custody when Peston was bludgeoned to death. And then there was this limo-crash. Justice Department reports said the hijacked flyer had been remote controlled. Until his injuries were treated, McKenzie was being kept in an induced coma, standard practice for convicted perps. It couldn't be him.

Were they looking at a copycat? A series of gang hits? But why target journalists? They were annoying, sure, but there were plenty of annoying people in this city. You might as well take out estate agents, or PR executives.

Nothing about this made sense.

* * *

THE FOREMAN AT the Dependicorp depot looked as though he would rather clean stomm from his boots than talk to Dredd.

"I need to take another look at the container," the lawman told the haulage worker, a gruff Scot by the name of Campbell.

The foreman made a show of checking through the lists on his datapad. "You could be too late, laddie. The thing may have already been cleaned and reused."

Dredd's scowl intensified. "I told you it's off-limits until the investigation is closed."

Campbell shrugged. "But the fella on the surfboard confessed. I saw it on the news."

Dredd took a step towards the man. "You wanna confess to anything, punk? We've already found mutie blood in one of your containers."

The man's face blanched. "That was nothing to do with us. The damned muties sneak in when the convoys stop for refuelling en route. There's nothing we can do about it."

"Sounds like you don't want us looking in your other containers. Afraid of what we might find?"

"We're clean, I tell you. 100 percent legit."

Dredd activating his comm. "Control, request a tek-squad for immediate—"

"It's here," Campbell said quickly, checking the pad again. "Still on site and completely off-limits, just like you said."

"And you couldn't find it a minute ago?"

The man shrugged. "We've got a lot of containers."

"And we've got a lot of cubes. Doubt you'll like yours. Eight months for wasting Justice Department time. Oh, and tell your replacement, this place is getting audited..."

DREDD CUFFED CAMPBELL and made his way across the depot to container 146175.

The scene inside was exactly how Dredd remembered: the

bloodstains, the bullet holes. The teks had already crawled over every inch of the place, but Dredd needed to make sure they hadn't missed anything. Starting at the back, he began opening the boxes to examine the cargo stashed inside. They were all filled with identical mechanical components he barely recognised. He checked for contraband hidden within the freight, false bottoms that could be used for smuggling drugs or moonshine. Nothing. Everything was as it should be.

Until he heard the noise behind him.

Dredd whirled around, Lawgiver in hand, pointing at the newcomer.

Psi-Judge Ruan raised her hands. "Hey, it's just me, Dredd."

He dropped the weapon to his side. "Ruan. What you are doing here?"

"Same as you. Trying to get to the bottom of the case."

He holstered the Lawgiver. "You been cleared for duty?"

"Not exactly."

"Then you should be at Psi-Div."

"I can help, cleared or not."

"How'd you find me?"

"Pulled in a favour with Control. Thought you might like a hand."

He turned away from her, returning to the half-examined boxes. "I don't need assistance."

Behind him, Ruan hissed. Dredd turned to see the Psi-Judge doubled over, a hand on the side of the container to steady herself. He rushed toward her, grabbing her arms before she could sink to the floor.

"Ruan? Ruan, what's wrong?"

When she looked up, her pupils had dilated so much that her eyes were black discs rimmed with a narrow band of green, her breath coming in ragged gasps.

She clutched his arm, the fingers of her hand digging deep into his bicep. "Fear. Such... fear."

Twenty-One
The Path of Fear

"RUAN. WHAT ARE you talking about? What are you afraid of?"

The Psi-Judge shook her head, sweat dripping from her hair. "No, not me. Someone close... someone *terrified*."

She pushed away from him, stumbling out of the crate and into the cool night air. She paused, looking around, as if trying to listen. Dredd couldn't hear anything other than the clank and whirr of heavy machinery as cargo was loaded onto nearby hover-trucks.

"There..." she said, stumbling as she ran to her left. Dredd followed as she darted between containers. She was tracking something—or someone—but not by sound. She was *feeling* her quarry, following a trail of emotions, a trail that finished up in a dead end against the West Wall itself, containers stacked three high to either side of them to form an alley.

"There's no one here, Ruan."

She held up a hand to silence him. The furthest container wasn't completely flush to the wall, leaving a narrow gap between the corrugated plasteen and rockcrete.

Ruan crept closer to peer into the gap and then gasped,

slumping against the wall, briefly overcome.

"No," she said as Dredd moved to assist her. "Stay where you are."

She crouched down beside the container, holding her gloved hand towards the gap.

"It's okay," she said, softly. "I know you're scared, but we're here to help. You're safe."

Dredd didn't like not knowing who Ruan was talking to, but held back. He was rewarded by a small, delicate hand reaching out from the shadows to take Ruan's own.

"That's it," the Psi-Judge encouraged. "Nothing to worry about."

It was a girl, dressed in dirty rags that hung from a fragile, malnourished frame. Her age was hard to guess, but she couldn't have been more than eight years old. Her head was a hairless dome, a single yellow eye in the middle of a broad forehead. The rest of her features were shrunken, a small, lipless mouth little more than a slit.

"A mutant," Dredd growled.

Ruan ignored the comment, keeping her attention focused on the child who looked at Dredd with something approaching sheer terror.

"No, no, it's fine. He's with me. My name's Ruan. What's yours?"

The mutant girl looked back at Ruan, but didn't answer.

"Can you tell me?"

Still the child didn't respond.

"Reckon she doesn't speak English?"

"Oh, she understands. She just can't speak. Maybe because of her mutation, maybe out of fear." Ruan brushed her hand gently against the child's face and the mutant flinched, ready to bolt back into the gap behind the container.

"I'm sorry. I didn't mean to scare you any more than you already are. Because you are very, very scared, aren't you?"

"She knows she shouldn't be here," Dredd said.

"No, that's not it. She's not scared for herself—well, no more than any child would be in this situation—but for someone else. Someone she loves." Ruan's eyes widened. "It's your mom, isn't it? You're scared she might die."

The child nodded, a tear rolling down her tiny nose.

"Can you show us where she is? We can help you."

The child nodded and, keeping hold of Ruan's hand, timidly led her past Dredd.

Stopping frequently to look for haulage workers, the child dragged Ruan towards a large building at the back of the yard. The door was shut, but not locked. Inside, Ruan and Dredd found themselves in a storage area, rows of shelves piled high with boxes and files that looked like they hadn't been disturbed for months, maybe years.

She led them to a pile of blankets up against the far wall—a pile that moved.

Dredd brought up his Lawgiver, but Ruan waved him back, shaking her head frantically, as she inched towards the heap of linen. Gently, she pulled aside a blanket to reveal a woman with the same mutation as the girl. She was lying on her side, face pale in the weak light of a lantern.

"The mother?"

Ruan nodded, checking the mutant's pulse. Her large eye fluttered open at the touch, but the woman didn't start or cry out. She was too weak, blood-stained rags wound around her shoulder.

"She's been hit. Lost a lot of blood."

"The mutants in the container."

"Maybe." Ruan turned back to the daughter. "I'm going to help your mom, okay? There's nothing to be scared about. I can read people's minds. Do you understand? Do you have telepaths where you come from?"

The child nodded, clutching her frail hands together.

"I won't hurt her, I promise. Here, Joe will stand with you."

"I will?"

Ruan shot him a look. "Yes, you will."

She leant into the child and smiled conspiratorially. "I need you to hold Joe's hand. He gets nervous sometimes."

She winked and the child's little mouth almost twitched into a smile. Dredd scowled as the girl held up a shaking hand, before giving in and walking over to join them. The mutie's thin fingers slipped into his and his frown softened. She barely had any flesh on her bones at all. He thought he'd feel revulsion, but as she squeezed weakly against his gloves, Dredd found himself kneeling on one knee beside her. He told himself he wanted to observe Ruan, although he didn't push the child away when she nestled into him.

Ruan removed her gloves and raised her hands, resting her fingers on the mutant woman's hairless head.

"That's it. Let me in. Let me help."

The woman barely stirred.

"I was right," Ruan said, her voice husky as she made contact. "They don't have vocal cords. They can't speak. Can't cry out, even—"

She gasped, a sudden intake of pain.

"Ruan?"

"Shot," the Psi-Judge breathed. "Hiding in the container. Shot in the shoulder. Beside her... Grud, he's dead. They killed him."

"Who's dead?"

"Her partner. The girl's father."

Dredd looked down at the girl still clutching his hand as Ruan continued.

"They thought... they thought if they could get into the city... they could get a better life."

Morphy had been right. "Wall-hoppers."

"And then... they were found. By a man—no, two men. One with a gun." She gasped again, screwing up her face. "He shot them. Pain. Fear. They... they shielded their daughter... hiding behind them... the mother... willing her daughter to play dead... so she could get away. So she could escape."

Ruan flinched.

"What is it?"

"Another shot. The other man. He said he wanted to tell their story, and now he's dead."

"Can you see the shooter's face?"

"No... it's dark and..." Ruan was crying now, weeping the tears of another soul. "There's so much pain. She's slipping away..."

"Look closer."

"I can't see his face. He's wearing a hat. And he's doing something... to the body..."

"To Peck?"

"Bending over him, pulling something out of his pocket... He's... doing something to Peck's face. I can't see what."

Had to be the mask. Ruan went quiet, swaying slightly. The mutant girl pressed herself closer to Dredd.

Ruan recoiled, but didn't break contact. "He's coming towards us... the man with the gun... Oh, Grud, he'll see our daughter." Ruan was speaking for the woman now. "Please, try not to breathe, baby. Try not to react. He'll kill you, like he killed your pa. Don't—"

Ruan gasped and pulled away, the mutant woman sighing as the telepathic link was broken.

Dredd placed a hand on Ruan's should. "What was it? What did you see?"

The Psi-Judge looked at the girl, her eyes brimming with tears. "She bolted, ran out of the container. The perp went after her, leaving the mom for dead."

She wiped her cheeks. "I saw—I felt—the woman crawl out of the container, leaving her partner behind." Her bottom lip was quivering, her voice thick. "Every inch was agony, Joe, but she had to find her daughter."

"And they've been hiding out here ever since." Dredd reappraised the girl. This little thing had evaded a vicious murderer and helped her wounded mother set up a shelter. She must have been terrified. Unable to communicate, to ask for help. And even if she could, who would help a dying mutie anyway?

Ruan blew out her cheeks, visibly exhausted. "There's something else. Something you need to see."

"Me? What do you mean? I can't do what you do."

"But I can help you. Take off your helmet."

Dredd shook his head. "It won't work on me, Ruan. I'm a double-zero. No telepathic ability. Just tell me."

"No, you need to experience it."

Before Dredd could stop her, Ruan touched his face and, in the blink of an eye, Dredd was no longer holding the hand of a scared mutant in a Mega-City One haulage company; he was somewhere else.

No, that wasn't right—he was some*one* else.

Twenty-Two
Through the Eye of Another

THIS JUST WASN'T possible. Dredd couldn't be here. It was like standing in a dream... in *someone else's* dream. He looked down at his hands, expecting to see his gloves, but the hands were not his own. They were calloused, trembling; the thin arms were bruised and scarred.

His head spun. The walls around him were shifting, their perspective skewed. It was like being drugged.

Dredd tried to speak, but couldn't. He gripped his throat—lean and emaciated—but no sound came.

Dredd... relax.

Ruan?

It's fine. I'm here with you. I'm in your head, as you're in hers.

No, he wanted to yell. I can't be. I'm a double-zero. I'm immune to telepathy.

No-one is totally immune, Dredd. You just need to know what buttons to press... and I've had a lot of practice.

He whirled around, as if he could escape from Ruan's touch. Instead he fell, tumbling forward, landing hard against wooden floorboards.

Except... suddenly, he wasn't alone. He was in a room, filled with people. Filled with...

Mutants.

Mutants everywhere, laying on the floor, huddled in groups. Snoring and grunting in their sleep. Mutants with too many hands, too many heads. And the stink: oh, Grud, the stink. Ripe bodies that hadn't seen water for months, wallowing in their own filth.

He gagged, turning over, realising that his thin arms were draped over someone. The girl from the depot. She was snuggled into him, fast asleep. His daughter... No, the *woman's* daughter. This wasn't real. This wasn't happening to him.

No Dredd, but it happened to them. This is how they lived before they came to Mega-City One, if you can call it a life.

He was standing now, in some kind of workhouse... a factory. He couldn't remember moving, and yet here he was, in front of a conveyor belt. Mechanical components jangled as they passed, the woman's hands checking the ever-moving supply for flaws. It was so hot. Dredd's mouth was dry and his body ached from standing for hours. It was hard to focus, hard to see the component numbers he was supposed to check off from the list beside the conveyor belt. But he needed to check them, that much he knew, otherwise the girl wouldn't eat tonight.

The same number, over and over. Unit 74141/KS. The digits blurred as sweat dripped into his eye. The noise was unbearable, machines roaring like monsters all around. He wasn't wearing ear protectors, none of the mutants were: standing shoulder-to-shoulder, checking, processing, discarding faulty units and packing the rest in wooden boxes. No respite, no breaks, no water.

This is how they spent their days. Like slaves.

The girl wasn't with him. He didn't know where she was. He looked around, searching for the woman's daughter among the mutants. Someone shouted behind him: a man, much bigger than the woman Dredd was inhabiting. He was a norm, with broad shoulders, a snarl on his lips and a long, tapered crop in his hand.

"Get back to work, scum."

The crop came down hard, lashing across Dredd's back.

He couldn't cry out.

When he opened his eyes again, he was trudging through the factory, carrying a box that was far too heavy. No antigrav trollies to help the mutants, just weary muscles and empty bellies.

The girl was in front of him now, walking in line, similarly laden. At least she was safe. How could they expect a child to carry this much? It wasn't right.

Dredd stumbled and fell forward, hitting the floor, the contents of the box spilling across the floor.

More shouts. More pain.

It was like being in a dream, flickering and jumping from one place to another. Never anywhere better. One minute he was at the conveyor belts, the next passing his hard-earned rations to the girl, a meagre helping of gruel mixed with sawdust to bulk it out. Then he was trying to sleep in the crowded, overpopulated rooms. Holding the crying daughter tight, looking into the eye of the woman's partner, wondering how much more of this they could take.

He blinked, and he was shoving his way through a crowd of fellow mutants, his heart hammering in his narrow chest.

That's it, Dredd. Keep going.

Why wouldn't the others let him pass? What were they looking at?

You need to see why they did it.

The crowd parted and Dredd saw another mutie woman lying in the dirt ahead. He dropped to his knees by the body. By the *still* body.

You need to see why they came to the Meg.

The woman was dead, her solitary eye gazing sightlessly up to the factory roof. Dredd had never seen her before, but knew immediately who she was.

The mutant mother's sister, her body exhausted, her heart giving out. There was a shout from behind, the sound of running feet. Dredd turned, to see the mutie girl pushing through the crowd. No. He couldn't let her see her aunt, not like this. Dredd tried to stop her, but the girl fought past him, sinking to the floor as she saw the body, tears streaming from her eye, her heart breaking.

Dredd heard the mutant's thoughts. He understood, then, why they had smuggled themselves in the container, making the long and perilous journey to the Big Meg.

We can't live like this. We can't *die* like this.

We have to get away...

DREDD SWATTED RUAN'S hand from his face and stumbled back, backing into the shelves behind him, knocking a pile of plastic folders to the floor. He was back at Dependicorp, in the storage shed, Ruan kneeling beside the woman whose memories he'd shared, her daughter huddled into them both, looking up at Dredd with a single wide eye.

"That was... unacceptable." He swallowed, willing himself not to vomit.

Ruan didn't apologise. "I needed you to see why they came here. What they escaped. These are the people we shut out, Dredd. The people we shoot down as they try to slip over the Wall."

"We do as we're ordered," he grunted, trying not to show it as he clung to the shelves.

He never wanted to experience anything like that ever again.

"She needs our help, Joe. They both do."

Dredd's head eventually stopped spinning. He stood, activating his comms.

"Dredd to Control. Two mutants located for deportation." He could feel Ruan's eyes on him, condemning him even as he spoke. "One requires medical attention. Recommend they be assigned to Harborville."

"That's a rog. Wagon dispatched to your location. Stand by."

Then there was no way to avoid Ruan's gaze; she was standing right in front of him, staring him down. "How could you? After you've been in her head. Don't they deserve better? Don't they deserve our help?"

Shoving past her, he strode from the building, his stomach still churning.

"We'll help them out, Ruan. Out of the city, back to where they belong."

Twenty-Three
Friends in Low Places

WITH CAMPBELL ARRESTED, the foreman's assistant—a bright girl with purple hair and a face full of piercings—found herself in charge of the depot. Her name was Samira, and she'd never wanted to be boss, especially now. At least Campbell's chair was more comfortable than her usual seat, although she didn't have much time to relax. No sooner had she sat down than jumped up again, as Judges Dredd and Ruan marched into the depot office.

"The boss ain't going like this," she told them, nodding out the window. The entire depot was awash with Judges, checking each and every container. Once one mutant refugee had been found, the Department wouldn't rest until they were sure there weren't any more wall-hoppers trying to sneak into the Meg.

"She'll like it even less when we fine her for allowing mutants to enter the city," Dredd told her. "I need to see your records."

"What records?"

"All of them. A complete list of every company that uses your firm, in both Mega-Cities."

"At both ends of the line? You're kidding me."

Dredd pointed at his chin. "Does this look like a face that kids?"

"I'd do what he says," Ruan said, backing him up, although Dredd hadn't even looked at her since they'd left the mutie and her mother with the clean-up team. He couldn't, not after what she'd put him through.

Samira threw her hands in the air. "Fine. I don't get paid enough for this stomm, anyway. Computer, give the Judges anything they want."

"Your co-operation is appreciated, citizen." Dredd leant over the screen embedded in Campbell's desk. "Before you go, tell me everything you know about Ben Peck."

Samira shrugged, popping a tab of chewing gum into her mouth. "Not much to tell, other than the fact *we* knew the lying toe rag as Greg. Greg Weld."

"That was his cover."

"If you say so. He kept himself to himself."

All the time Dredd was opening and shutting files on the screen, checking and dismissing potential evidence.

"No friends."

"Not especially. As I said, he was a bit of a loner. Except for Kell, I guess."

Dredd looked up. "Kell?"

"Kell Sanchez, one of the other exo-lift operators. I saw them a few times in the canteen, heads down, as thick as thieves."

"Like they were conspiring?"

"That's a strong word. I reckon they were planning to meet, though. They kept checking their watches. I thought at the time that Weld—I mean, Peck—should watch himself."

"Why?"

"Let's just say Kell has friends in low places."

"Is he working tonight?"

She shook her head, popping her chewing gum. "No-one's seen him for days. Not since Tuesday."

"The day Peck was killed."

"I guess so, yeah."

Dredd nodded once and returned to the screen.

"Am I done?" Samira asked.

"You can leave. And dispense of that gum in a responsible manner, or you'll be looking at a hundred days in a cube."

"Jovus," the woman muttered under her breath as she turned to leave. Dredd let the expletive slide. He was too busy scrolling through the customer list.

"You never let up, do you, Dredd?" Ruan commented, checking employment records on another monitor.

"The Law never rests. You know that. It's good to remind citizens that we're watching them."

He reached the bottom of the list.

"Anything that looks familiar?"

"Not to me," he said. He encrypted a copy of the directory, then spoke into his comms. "Control, I'm sending you Dependicorp's customer index, every transaction for the past five years. I need them checked against the registry for anything suspicious."

"*Roger that.*"

"What do you expect to find?" asked Ruan.

"No idea. That's why we're looking. There's every chance the place is clean, but if muties are using it as an entry point..."

"'I don't want to hurt you.'"

"What?"

"That's what Peck said to the mutants."

"In the woman's memories..." The thought still made Dredd's skin crawl.

Ruan nodded. "'I just want to tell your story...' Do you reckon that's what he was investigating? Mutant refugees?"

"Perhaps Kell Sanchez knows something about that. You got his address?"

Ruan brought up Sanchez's profile.

"Got it. Edwyn Warwick Block."

"We should pay him a visit. The teks can finish up here."

She rose to join him as he marched towards the door. "Still want me with you?"

"We can talk about what you did later. In the meantime, as long as you're useful, you're by my side."

Twenty-Four
Crash Site

OUT ON THE street, Morphy and Lint were monitoring the clean-up of Bret Barnet's crash site. The press was out in force, and Morph had already arrested three camera crews for pointing their holo-lenses where they shouldn't.

Not that there was much to see. Like Url's Diner, there was precious little left of the hover-limo, and as for *Hound News*' top anchorman... well, he'd read his last bulletin. What wasn't smeared on the side of busted screen 1,000 metres above their heads was a charred husk, barely enough for the tek boys to identify through DNA records.

His time in the sleep machine had done wonders for Morphy's aching muscles, but the failure to get enough evidence from Truss still rankled. He'd had an idea when he'd emerged from the snooze-tube. Like most places in this city, most eateries had CCTV. Url's would be no different, and if they subscribed to a remote security service, the footage would be backed-up off site. From what he gathered, the Truss brothers spent most of their time in the diner. If Jamie had met with a conspirator, it would have been there. He'd asked Control to trace any security vid backups from Url's Place. The chances of finding something significant was slim, but it was worth a shot.

Lint walked over to him. The Tek-Judges were already starting to pack up. "We're almost done here. Shall we get back on patrol?"

Morphy didn't answer. He'd spotted a juve, no more than eleven years old, sneaking behind the cordon to grab a shard of twisted limo bumper from the floor.

"Hey! Stop, you little punk." The kid was already running, twisted metal still in hand, destined to be sold at online auction or some such. The Meg's celebrity-obsessed populace would buy anything, especially grisly mementos of a famous fatality.

Morphy had barely drawn his Lawgiver when Lint scooped up a buckled anti-grav hub and flung it after the little ghoul. It soared through the air like a frisbee, striking the kid on the back of the head. The juve went down hard, Lint already looming over him to carry out sentence.

The boy turned over onto his back, scuttling away like a crab. "P-please... don't..."

Lint stopped suddenly, and swayed on his feet. The juve took the opportunity to run.

Morph checked on his rookie. "Lint? You okay?"

The trainee pushed him away, his face like chalk. "Yeah, I'm fine."

"You don't sound it. Do we need to get you checked out?"

Lint shook his head. "It'll be those damn sleep machines. I just had a... dizzy spell, that's all."

"*Control to Morphy.*"

Still concerned over his young charge, Morphy accepted the call.

"Morphy here. You got something for me?"

"*We've found that diner's security footage. Your dead Fattie sure was there a lot. It's like the spug never went home.*"

"But did he meet anyone?"

"*Only his brother.*"

Morphy's heart sank. He thought he had been onto something. "Stomm."

"*Sorry, Morph.*"

"Wait up," said Lint. "Jamie said that his *brother* arranged the protest, not him. It would be Oliver Truss who made contact."

Morphy slapped Lint on the arm.

"Good thinking, kid. Control, check for footage of Oliver Truss in the diner, *without* his brother. See if he meets anyone."

"*Roger that.*"

There was an agonising wait as Control sped through the footage. The computers at the Grand Hall could check a thousand times quicker than a human, but it still felt like an age.

"*We've got something. Oliver Truss met with the same individual on three separate occasions.*"

"Recently?"

"*The last meeting was two days ago. The contact brought with him a large parcel.*"

"Big enough for two placards?" Lint asked.

It sounded promising. "Do we have facial recog, Control? Can you get me a name?"

"*Coming up, Morph. Stand by.*"

Twenty-Five
Can't Trust a Word

DREDD'S BOOT MADE quick work of the door to Kell Sanchez's apartment. The cramped hab had been turned over, furniture in pieces, drawers emptied out across the stained carpet. The place reeked of human waste and rotten food; flies buzzed over the wreckage of an overturned garbage bin.

"Control, suspected break-in at Edwyn Warwick," Dredd reported. "Residence of Kell Sanchez."

A Tri-D set played to the ransacked room, volume turned painfully high. Ruan found the remote and, when the mute button didn't work, turned the set down to a tolerable level.

More flies buzzed through a door from the main living area, the cloying stink intensifying as Dredd approached.

Ruan fell in behind as he nudged the door open with his foot.

A body lay on the bed, arms outstretched. You could be forgiven for thinking that the man was asleep, if it wasn't for the blood splattered up the wall behind him.

There was no mistaking the face, with or without the jagged hole in his forehead: Kell Sanchez. Although the handlebar moustache was longer than in his employee picture, and the punk had had a gold tooth fitted.

Sanchez's body was half under the covers, having seemingly been killed in his sleep. Dredd's eyes fell to the many tattoos scrawled across Sanchez's bare chest.

"The Valverde Gang."

"What's that?"

Dredd pointed at a tattoo of a laughing skull.

"Crime syndicate operating throughout Sector 187. Known traffickers, specialising in muties and freaks."

"So the mother and daughter..."

"Were better off in the sweatshop."

"Reckon Peck was investigating the gang?"

"Make sense. Peck had a fake gangland tattoo in the same place. If Sanchez found out he wasn't genuine Valverde..."

"He killed him?"

"Maybe. Although it doesn't explain the mask, or the typed message. Also, why shoot the merchandise?"

"The merchandise?"

"The muties. You saw the shooter in your vision. Look like Sanchez?"

Ruan regarded the corpse, looking the body up and down. "I'm not sure. The perp was taller—wider, too—but that could be down to the woman's fear. She was hurt, feeling threatened..."

Dredd pulled his snuffler from his belt and held it up to the stiff's skin. The scanner beeped obediently and he showed the results to Ruan. "I'm no tek, but going by the tissue degradation, creep's been dead for three days. We know he didn't show up for work the day Peck was killed."

"Because he was already dead?"

Dredd slipped the snuffler back into its pouch. "Looks that way."

In the living quarters, a familiar voice played from the Tri-D. Dredd walked to the door to see *MC-1 Today* anchor Ken

Wallaby collecting Bret Barnet's award posthumously. Wallaby was in floods of what Dredd assumed were crocodile tears, until he realised what the reporter was saying.

"*I didn't plan to do it. I just wanted Bret to die. I piloted the hover-limo right into that block. Bret always did like having his face plastered over the city.*"

On the screen, a pair of Judges rushed onto the stage and grabbed the weeping news anchor.

"Those words..." Dredd said. "I've heard them before."

Ruan joined him in front of the Tri-D set. "Another confession?"

"But I was with Wallaby when Barnet's flyer went haywire. At least at first. He was heading for his sleep machine."

"Could have been a cover."

"Maybe, but—"

Dredd was interrupted by a call from Control.

"*Dredd, we've found something in the haulage company's records.*"

"Go on."

"*The container where Peck was found: it was registered to Microvost, a subsidiary of Somnus Industries.*"

"Which in turn is owned by Jocelyn Piper," Dredd said, as the woman herself appeared on screen. She was being grilled about her links to Limo-A-Go-Go, manufacturer of Bret Barnet's ill-fated transport. "Stand by, Control."

Dredd grabbed the remote and turned up the volume. "*I've told you before, I have no stake in Limo-A-Go-Go, one way or another.*"

"No," agreed the reporter. "*But their navigation computers do use the FlightMax software produced by one of PiperTech's companies; software that experts are now claiming is simple to hack, as seen in the case of the Bret Barnet hijacking.*"

"*This is complete and utter nonsense, and yet another example of our corrupt media's crusade to blacken my name. All these accusations prove is that you can't trust a word journalists say...*"

"Or politicians," Dredd said, indicating to Ruan that they were leaving. "Control, send a meat wagon to Edwyn Warwick. One stiff, Kell Sanchez. Bullet wound to the head, unknown weapon."

"*You staying at the scene, Dredd?*"

"That's a negative. We're heading for Somnus Industries, following a lead on the Peck case."

"*Helmets already on route to Somnus, Dredd.*"

Dredd shot a puzzled look at Ruan. "Already? At whose request?"

Twenty-Six
The Net Tightens

"THIS IS A raid, everyone stay where you are!"

The workers on the Somnus factory floor obeyed Judge Morphy's order without question, largely due to his and Lint's raised Lawgivers.

"Brandon Kronecker. Where is he?" Lint barked. The workers stared at him, too terrified to answer.

The communicator in his helmet buzzed.

"*Dredd to Morphy, come in.*"

"I'm a little busy right now, Joe."

"*You're at Somnus, right?*"

"Right."

"*I need you to check a component number for me.*"

"A what?"

"*Just do it, Morph. I'm following a hunch. Unit 74141/ KS.*"

Morphy could hardly refuse. He'd always told Dredd to follow his gut. He stalked over to a Somnus employee standing by a computer terminal, a chubby man who looked so scared Morphy thought he might blub.

"I need to check a component in your machines. Unit 74141/ KS."

The chubster looked at him in bewilderment.

"Look it up."

"N-no need," the worker stammered. "It's a torpidity convertor. Used in the hibernation matrix. A small, but vital—"

Something clanged on the gantry above their head. Morphy looked up to see rubber-soled shoes racing along the metal grill.

"It's Kronecker!" Lint shouted.

Morphy's gun was up, tracking the fleeing shoes. "Brandon Kronecker, stay where you are."

The perp didn't stop. Morphy couldn't reliably shoot through the gantry.

"Ricochet," he said, subtly adjusting his aim and pulling the trigger.

The bullet bounced off a ceiling strut to hit Kronecker in the chest. He was thrown back over the railings, landing with a crunch in front of the two Judges.

"You're under arrest for rabble-rousing," Morphy informed him. "We have footage of you paying Oliver Truss to protest at Jocelyn Piper's event." His eyes went to a familiar star tattoo on Kronecker's shoulder. "And by the looks of that ink, you're the punk who brought a rocket launcher to the rally. Why do it? Why try to kill your own boss?"

"I wasn't t-trying to kill her," Kronecker stammered. "Sh-she paid me to do it. It was all her idea. Please... it hurts."

Lint ignored the pained plea. "Piper paid you to disrupt her own rally? That doesn't make sense."

Dredd voice came over the comm. "*Does to me. Somnus uses cheap mutie labour to make the components of their sleep machines, shipping the parts into the Meg via Dependicorp.*"

Morphy shook his head. "So much for Making Mega-City Work."

"*The attack on the rally was designed to make Piper look*

a victim. Plus, there was a journalist snooping around the consignments from her mutie sweatshops. It looks like the Valverde gang are running a trafficking ring from the depot, picking up mutants trying to escape Piper's inhuman working conditions. If the truth got out, her political career would have been shot to hell. She needed the story buried. Next thing you know, Peck is dead, the first in a murder spree aimed at discrediting the press."

"But how is she doing it?"

"Implanted memories. What if McKenzie and Wallaby were seeing other people's memories?"

"How?"

"I don't know," Dredd admitted.

"Dreams?" Lint suggested. "Could they be implanted in their sleep, while using Somnus sleep machines? They were both journalists."

"It would explain McKenzie's contradictory memories. You got any proof for any of this, Joe?"

"Just a working theory, Morph. Let's just say I've been forced to walk in someone else's shoes recently. It opened my eyes to how disorientating it can be."

"You're not kidding," Lint said beneath his breath.

"What's that, rookie?"

Lint ignored Dredd, pulling his Lawgiver on Kronecker. "Somnus has the contract to maintain Justice Department sleep machines, right?"

At first, Kronecker didn't answer, lost in his pain, so Lint repeated the question, this time with his foot on the man's chest.

"Yes!" Kronecker screamed. "Yeah, we do!"

"Who do you send in to make repairs?"

A meek voice sounded from across the factory floor.

"Er... that'll be me."

Lint whirled around, his aim settling on a dark-skinned woman with a mane of frizzy hair.

"Were you at Sector House 9 in the last 24-hours?"

The woman shook her head, never taking her eyes from the barrel of Lint's gun.

"N-no. I was due to go, but..."

She trailed off, as if realising she was about to incriminate herself. Lint took a step forward, the factory's fluorescent lighting reflecting off his white helmet.

"But?"

The woman looked uncertain. "But I was told to stay at home. Someone else went in my place."

"Who?"

"I'm not supposed to say. I was given a bonus to keep quiet."

"Who?" Lint's finger tightened around his trigger.

"Please, don't shoot," she begged. "It was Acton. Acton Hendry."

"Never heard of him."

"*I have*," Dredd growled over the comm. "*Jocelyn Piper's bodyguard.*"

In Kell Sanchez's hab, Dredd pulled a datapad from his belt. "Control, I need access to Edwyn Warwick Block security footage."

"*All of it?*"

"Just show me Tuesday's. Patch it through to my pad."

An icon flashed in the corner of the screen, indicating incoming data.

"Computer, run footage through Comp-Ident, cross referencing PiperTech employee, Acton Hendry."

Stills from the block's security footage flashed across the screen, too fast for any eye to follow, even Dredd's. Then the pad gave a beep, pausing on a grainy shot of the Edwyn Warwick concourse. The computer picked out one figure, striding through the entrance, words flashing across the display:

+++ MATCH FOUND. HENDRY, ACTON.
DATE STAMP: TUESDAY SEPTEMBER 16, 2081 +++

"The day Sanchez was shot and killed," Dredd said.

Ruan ordered the computer to enhance the image.

"Recognise something?" Dredd asked.

"Only the coat, although last time I saw it, I was looking through the eye of a critically injured mutant."

"In the container?"

Ruan nodded. "I'd bet my badge that the bullet that killed Kell Sanchez will match the gun that killed Ben Peck."

Dredd deactivated the datapad. "Stop the press. We've found our Deadliner."

Twenty-Seven
The Piper Palace Massacre

JOCELYN PIPER SAT back in her chair and let out a deep sigh. That had been the fourteenth interview since the crash. This was exhausting. She rubbed her tired eyes, looking forward to the day when she could retire to actual bed, rather than use her own sleep machines to stay on schedule.

A light flashed on her comms unit. Surely not another interview. She wasn't scheduled to talk to *Shout Out Mega-Cit* for another half hour.

Massaging the bridge of her nose, she answered her PA's call. "Yes, Maddie. What is it?"

"Sorry to disturb you, Ms Piper, but there appears to be a gunfight in reception."

Jocelyn stared at the comms unit in belief. "There's *what?*"

BULLETS BLAZED THROUGH the lobby of Piper Palace, Jocelyn Piper's personal stratoscraper. The reception had been decorated as ostentatiously as possible, every piece of furniture a gaudy testament to Piper's wealth. The carpet alone cost more than the City's annual budget deficit. Rather less, now it was soaking up blood, the furniture smashed into equally showy shrapnel.

Judge Dredd was pinned behind a statue of Jocelyn Piper as Venus, rounds pinging off her artistically amplified assets, while Ruan was sheltering behind a rapidly diminishing chaise longue. Piper's security detail was hunkered down across the lobby, next to sets of elevator doors that looked suspiciously like they were made from solid gold. Acton Hendry was calling the shots—literally—his men armed with Widowmaker 1887s.

Dredd had wanted the bodyguard alive, but that was looking less likely by the second. Backup was arriving out on the sked in the form of Morphy and Lint, but the pair would be cut down the moment they approached the front door.

A bullet slammed through the statue of Venus, embedding itself in Dredd's shoulder. He couldn't help but cry out.

"You got winged, lawman," Hendry called across the lobby. "You're dead meat, whatever happens. Why don't you save us all a lot of trouble and shoot yourself through the head?"

Enough was enough. Dredd had wanted Hendry alive, but there would be plenty of other conspirators to confess.

Dredd threw his gun arm around the statue and yelled, "Hi-Ex!"

The Lawgiver bucked as the explosive shell streaked across the lobby, not at Hendry's gunmen, but the gold-plated ceiling above their heads.

KA-BOOM!

The cloud of dust engulfed both Dredd and Ruan, but the rain of bullets had stopped. The front doors were yanked open and Morphy and Lint ran in.

"Dredd, you're hit," Morphy said, noticing the blood trickling down Dredd's tunic.

"It's nothing," Dredd grunted.

They ran into the billowing dust. Piper's minions were half-buried beneath the contents of what had once been the first floor.

He kicked at slabs of masonry until he found Hendry hacking up blood beneath a slab of rockcrete the size of Dredd's Lawmaster.

"Acton Hendry, you are charged with the suspected murder of Ben Peck, Loreen Peston and Bret Barnet."

"You've got no evidence," Hendry spat. "You've got nothing."

"Only a matter of time."

"Shame you won't be around to see it!"

With extreme effort, Hendry swung up his arm, a stub-nosed revolver in his hand.

Dredd's execution round obliterated Hendry's brain before the bodyguard could squeeze his trigger. He fell lifeless to the rubble-strewn floor.

"Threatening a Judge," Dredd told his corpse. "Sentence is death."

CONTROL CHOSE THAT moment to report that the Judges raiding Hendry's residence in Kevin Costner Block had found a trilby hat, complete with press card, a fake Judge's uniform and a computer showing recent access to a FlightMax navigation system, namely the hover-limo of Bret Barnet.

"Missed the evening edition, Control, but better late than never."

Morphy stepped up beside Dredd, calling in Pat Wagons to transport the living to the Sector House and the departed to Resyk. Behind them, Ruan looked around the devastation of the lobby, her brow creasing into a frown.

"Morphy, where's your rookie?"

Twenty-Eight
Guilty as Charged

JOCELYN PIPER WATCHED the carnage on her screen and knew it was over. There was no way even her army of spin doctors could salvage this.

"Maddie, have my flyer ready," she called over to the comms unit on her desk, grunting as she tried to cram the vintage typewriter her father had given her into the waste-disposal unit.

There was no reply from her PA; the little spugwit had probably fled. This was the trouble with young people today. No commitment. From now on, she'd only employ robots.

With a final shove, the typewriter disappeared into the chute, tumbling to the iron teeth that would grind it into dust.

She turned, finding a Judge standing facing her, his mouth a grim line. His Lawgiver was raised, his aim sure and steady.

No, wait. Not a Judge, not yet. The kid wore a white helmet and his badge displayed the word *Rookie* rather than his name.

But she knew it anyway.

"Jocelyn Piper, you have been found guilty of numerous crimes," the youth said. "You ordered Acton Hendry to kill Ben Peck to cover his investigation into your mutant workforce."

"Did I now?"

"You then planted Hendry's memory of the murder—and that of Bret Barnet—into the minds of others using your own sleep machines. You paid protestors to disrupt your own rally, and endangered the lives of innocent citizens by having your floating platform crash into your supporters."

Piper clasped her hands in front of her to stop them shaking. She needed to appear calm. She'd done it before, facing political opponents, journalists, and angry investors. She was a force of nature, everyone said it. Ask the board of SmartyBot, the robot brain manufacturer Jocelyn had bought out, not three weeks ago. She hadn't done it under her own name, of course, not with her anti-robot platform gaining traction, but she'd needed a way to transmit a software patch to any mechanoid fitted with a SmartyBot brain, just a few lines of code that would urge the poor things to commit random acts of terror that would turn the voting public against robots.

"Do you have anything to say?"

Jocelyn's smile widened. "What can I say? We all have our secrets, don't we Lint?"

THE SHOT RANG out as Dredd and Morphy approached Piper's office, Ruan a few steps ahead, her gun in hand.

"Drokk."

Dredd broke into a run, ignoring the throb from his shoulder as he followed the Psi-Judge. They crashed through the door to find smoke curling from the barrel of Lint's Lawgiver.

Jocelyn Piper was slumped in her chair, blood trickling from the ragged hole between her eyes.

"She reached under her desk," Lint told them. "I thought she was going for a weapon."

Dredd crossed to Piper, checking her desk drawers. There were no guns or knives, only papers, files and pens.

"Nothing here."

"Guilt," Ruan muttered, standing by the door.

"What's that?" asked Morphy.

"As soon as I came in," the Psi-Judge replied. "Guilt. Strong."

Lint holstered his Lawgiver. "From Piper."

Dredd shook his head. "Take off your helmet."

Lint turned to face him.

"What?"

Dredd raised his lawgiver, aiming at Lint.

"Either you take off your helmet, or I will."

Morphy stepped forward, stopping short of putting himself between Dredd and the Rookie. "What's this about, Joe?"

"Ruan says she sensed guilt, but an empath can't feel anything from the dead, only the living. Lint was the only other person in the room when she came in."

"This is ridiculous." Lint turned to Morphy. "Sir, Dredd is unstable."

Morphy's voice was quiet. "Take off your helmet, son."

Dredd's bead remained trained on Lint's head.

Setting his jaw, the rookie raised his hands to his helmet. He lifted it slowly, revealing his cold blue eyes.

Without a word Ruan walked up behind Lint, removed her gloves and pressed her fingers against the rookie's temples. Lint gritted his teeth, cords standing out on his neck.

"No point resisting," Dredd told him. "It won't do you any good."

Lint's face slackened as Ruan's eyes went white.

"Blood," she whispered. "Blood everywhere in the cube. On the floor, on the walls, on his boots."

"Loreen Peston?" asked Dredd.

Ruan's mouth twisted into a sneer. "Taking the daystick. Ramming it down her throat."

"I didn't kill her," Lint murmured, but Ruan didn't stop.

"Please... don't..." It was Peston, speaking through the psychic.

"The juve at the crash site," Morphy remembered. "He said exactly the same thing. The words triggered something in you, Lint."

The thread of drool hanging from the rookie's bottom lip broke as he spoke, his words slurred. "New memories. New memories that weren't mine. Must have been the sleep machine. Hendry was in the Sector House, repairing the snooze-tubes..."

"Killing Peston in her cube," Ruan confirmed.

"Dressed as a Judge."

Morphy turned to Dredd. "But why target Lint? He's not a journo."

"We all have our secrets..." Ruan said.

"No..." Lint whined. "You can't."

Ruan's voice had shifted again, taking on a southern accent. Jocelyn Piper's voice. "It's amazing what you can find out when someone slides into a sleep machine. All the things they try to hide. I've compiled quite the little dossier on you and your Judge buddies. It was going to come in handy when I was Mayor, Lint—or should I say Judge Whistleblower?"

Dredd's finger tightened on the trigger.

"Leaking Justice Department secrets to the press for money. Who's a naughty boy? Now, the question is whether you're going to arrest me, or let me escape? If it's money you want, I've got money. Mountains of the stuff. All you need do is look the other wa—"

Ruan's fingers came away from Lint's head, the colour swimming back into her eyes. "That's when he killed her."

Dredd looked at Morphy. "You decided on Lint's assessment, Morph?"

Morphy was still glaring at Lint as he spoke. "I'll leave that honour to you, Joe."

Dredd let his weapon drop. "News just in, rookie: you failed, on every level. But don't worry, you'll spend the rest of your days with Judges just like you. You're hereby sentenced to Titan: life imprisonment."

Lint sank to his knees as Dredd holstered his Lawgiver.

"Make sure you say hi to my brother. What did you call him? A humourless freak? Or was that just me?"

JOE DREDD SAT at the back of the med-wagon, trying not to wince as Med-Judge Cooke dug the slug out of his shoulder. It could've waited until they got back to the Sector House, but Morphy had insisted. His old mentor, still looking out for him.

Cooke's work done, the medic offered Dredd painkillers.

"No, thanks," he said, standing up to recover his tunic. Pulling the zip up to his neck, Dredd turned to find Ruan standing in front of him.

"I'm to report back to Psi-Division."

He nodded. "It was pleasant working with you, Ruan."

She smiled. "Lying to a fellow Judge? Isn't that a felony?"

He had nothing else to say. With a nod, he turned to walk to his Lawmaster.

Ruan called after him. "Dredd. I'm sorry."

He paused, but didn't look back. "No need to apologise. You did your duty."

"I crossed the line. I should never have done that to you without your consent."

Still he kept his back to her.

"You wanted me to understand. You're a powerful telepath, Ruan. Not many psykers can do that to a double-zero."

"And you're a good man. I checked on Harborville. It's a mission for mutants who've been mistreated. You needn't have sent them there."

"Guess I was doing my duty, too."

Adjusting his badge, Dredd left Ruan by the med-wagon. As soon as they saw him, the throng of journalists gathered in front of Piper Palace rushed forward to barrage him with questions.

"Judge Dredd, is it true that Jocelyn Piper was behind the Deadliner murders—?"

"What does this mean for the mayoral election—?"

"Is there any truth in the rumours that Chief Judge Goodman has banned the use of sleep machines by citizens—?"

"—seized Somnus Industries' assets?"

"—Judge Dredd?"

Dredd swung his leg over the Lawmaster and gunned the engine. Before he roared away, he turned to face the expectant cameras.

"No comment."

About the Author

UK number-one bestselling author **Cavan Scott** is currently trying to work on everything he loved when he was ten. He has written for *Star Wars*, *Doctor Who*, *Warhammer 40,000*, *Vikings*, *Blake's 7*, *Highlander*, *Danger Mouse* and the *Beano*. His new Sherlock Holmes novel, *Cry of the Innocents*, is out now from Titan Books. He lives in Bristol with his wife, daughters and an inflatable Dalek called Desmond.

Announcing Abaddon Books'
incredible new series for 2018:

JUDGES

UNITED STATES OF AMERICA
2033 A.D.

In a time of widespread poverty,
inequality and political unrest,
Eustace Fargo's controversial new
justice laws have come into effect.

Protests and violence meet the
first Judges as they hit the street
to enforce the Law; the cure, it's clear,
is far worse than the disease.

Is this a sign of things to come?

Read on for a sample of the
explosive first novella,
Michael Carroll's *The Avalanche*...

THE UNIFORMED OFFICER was busy transcribing a hand-written statement and didn't look up from his keyboard. "With you in a second."

Charlotte-Jane Leandros looked around the open-plan office. Aside from the now-limp Christmas tree in the corner, the top half of a paper Santa Claus pinned to the wall, and an Elf-on-a-Shelf that had what was very clearly a bullet-hole in the middle of its forehead, the police station of St. Christopher, Connecticut, didn't appear to have changed in the two years since she'd last visited. The officer behind the desk, however, had changed quite a lot. He'd put on weight, and his hair was now very grey, as was the thick moustache he sported.

She reached across the officer's desk and poked a pencil at his Schnauzer-a-day calendar. "So... Happy birthday, Benny."

His typing paused for the briefest moment as he said, "Knew it was you, CJ."

"No, you didn't."

He still hadn't looked up from the screen, but he was suppressing a smile. "Sure I did. You're still wearing the same deodorant, and you cleared your throat on the way in. You think I don't know my own baby sister's voice, even if she's just clearing her throat? I'm a cop. I've been *trained* to notice stuff like that." Benny Leandros finally stopped typing and glanced up at his sister. "So, does Mom know you're back or is this a surprise vis—"

He jumped to his feet, and his chair skidded back across the room. "CJ, what are you *wearing?*"

CJ Leandros placed her dark-visored helmet onto her brother's desk and took a step back, giving him a better view of her uniform. Matt-black Kevlar-and-titanium-fibre tunic and pants, dark grey gloves and boots, reinforced grey pads protecting her shoulders, elbows and knees. She turned in a slow circle, ignoring the officers who had been staring at her from the moment she'd entered the station. "So what do you think?"

Benny walked around to the front of his desk, stopped in front of his sister and stared down at her. "I think Mom's gonna have an *aneurysm*. You... You told us you'd quit the police academy, not that you'd signed up to be a Judge! What was all that about working in a hardware store?"

"Cover story. We're not encouraged to talk about it, even with family." She shrugged. "Lot of people are still very hostile to the idea of Judges."

"Can you *blame* them?" He shook his head slowly as he looked her up and down. "Body-armour. It's a bad sign when cops need body armour. And you don't have a body-camera!"

"What would I need one for? I don't answer to anyone. Look, Benny, more than everyone else—even more than *Dad*—you were always telling me that I should go into law-enforcement."

"Yeah, but I meant be a *cop*. That was before there were Judges! I mean, Judges like you. I thought you and me and Stav could be like a team, working the same beat, watch each other's backs. That's what Dad always wanted for us. Not... *this*." He took a step back and again looked her up and down. "Not this, CJ. He'd have *hated* Fargo's Footsoldiers and everything they represent."

A voice behind CJ said, "He's not alone in that."

She'd known that he was there. Unlike Benny, Charlotte-Jane actually *had* been trained to be aware of what was around her at all times, and she was good at it. It was one of the reasons Judge Deacon had selected her for his team.

Her oldest brother, Sergeant Stavros Leandros, had entered the room right after Benny had walked around to the front of his desk. Stav had been watching her from the doorway, and CJ had in turn been watching his reflection in her helmet's visor. On her way into the police station, she'd seen his car parked in the lot outside, and as sergeant he would have already been informed that a Judge had been seen riding through town.

He shook his head slowly. "If I'd known you were going to do this, I'd have stopped it."

"How? It's my life, my decision."

Stavros nodded toward his office. "Let's talk. Right now." To Benny he said, "Not you. Get that report done and go home. You're back on at oh-nine-hundred."

As Stavros stomped away Benny said, "Better do what he says, CJ. You know what he's like when he's under pressure. Until yesterday we had half the town without power because the Settlers knocked out the grid again, and we've got like ten guys down with the flu. So..." Benny shrugged. "I figure the last thing he needs is a bunch of Judges showing up and throwing their weight around."

He paused in the middle of dragging his chair back to his desk. "That's *not* what's happening, is it? Tell me that you're here on your own and you just came back 'cos it's my birthday and you wanted to surprise me."

"I came *early* because it's your birthday. There are six of us, working under Senior Judge Francesco Deacon. The others will be arriving tomorrow."

Benny dropped into his chair. "Oh, Stav is not going to like that. And the *captain* is gonna have a *fit*."

CJ Leandros smiled and shrugged at the same time. "Happy birthday, Benny. I'll see you tomorrow back at Mom's, yeah? And don't tell her I'm here—I want to surprise her."

"I won't say a word... You know, I can't decide whether she's gonna be madder that you became a Judge or that you cut your hair. You always had great hair. Everyone said so."

She was already backing away from his desk. "Judges can't have long hair. Regs."

She recognised some of the other officers and staff—there were a few she'd known her entire life—but right now they were pulling off that awkward trick of staring at her without looking her in the eye.

From the day she'd been hand-picked from the police academy, she'd known that this was going to happen. Ordinary cops didn't like the new Department of Justice, and not just because it signalled the end of their careers.

As she passed the open doorway to Stavros's office, he yelled, "CJ! Get in here!"

She stopped, and looked in through the doorway to see her brother standing next to Captain Virginia Witcombe, a cold-looking fifty-year-old woman with grey hair so tightly pulled back that CJ was surprised she could still blink.

"So," Captain Witcombe said. "Welcome home, Charlotte-Jane." CJ had the impression the Captain was just barely keeping a lid on her emotions.

"Thank you, Captain. It's nice to be back. I honestly never expected to be posted here."

Stavros said, "Yeah, *about* that. So out of the blue this afternoon we get an official e-mail telling us six Judges have been assigned to St. Christopher. We've got forty-three beat cops to manage twenty-eight thousand people, and now we're babysitting half a dozen Judges too? And my own *sister* turns out to be one of them? Hell with that."

"Yeah... I don't like this either," Captain Witcombe said. "Not one bit. You people want to make a difference, you should set up station in one of those towns in the Midwest that're being overrun by gangs. Not here. It's bad enough that I've got to put up with Judges at home in Colton, but I've worked too long and too damn hard to get where I am to throw it all away now. St. Christopher might not be the picture-postcard small town, but it's a damn sight better than most, and I'm not going to stand by and watch while you Judges clear the path for the handcart this country is going to Hell in. You get what I'm saying?"

"You think that the Judges are a symptom of the problems, not the cure. I understand that, Captain, but I don't agree."

Stavros nodded. "Well, *I* agree with the captain. You remember what Dad always said, CJ. I remember Pappous saying it too, before you were even born. The single most important right any American citizen has is due process. The right to unbiased judgement when accused. You Judges have taken that right and flushed it down the crapper." Stavros looked away from her, shaking his head. "It's unconstitutional."

Captain Witcombe said, "No, it's not, Sergeant Leandros. Not since Eustace Fargo got the constitution *changed*."

CJ said, "Captain, when you spoke at my dad's funeral, you said that we need tougher laws to clamp down on drunk-drivers so that sort of thing would never happen again. Afterwards, at the reception, I found you crying in the corridor, and your husband... Harvey, right? He was trying to console you. But you didn't want that. You didn't want to be consoled, and you were furious with him because you said he was trying to pretend it had never happened. Then you saw me, and you took my hands and told me that it wasn't fair, that my dad was a great man, and to have his life snatched away by some drunken loser was the worst possible crime. You remember that, don't you?"

"Yes, I do. And that's not all I remember." The captain stepped closer to CJ, arms folded. "I remember an incident about a year earlier. You were fifteen years old, and I caught you and Tenna LeFevour stealing beer from the One-Stop."

Stavros said, "What?" but both CJ and Witcombe ignored him.

The captain continued, "And now you're a Judge. I heard you all had to be squeaky-clean. Can't see how that's possible if you were a shoplifter."

"I wasn't charged," CJ said. "Remember? Dad asked you to take care of it."

Witcombe pursed her lips. "Hmm. So if I hadn't done that, maybe we wouldn't be having this conversation now."

"Possibly not. But you broke the law when you persuaded the store's owner to drop the charges. That's a bad mark on *your* record sheet, Captain, not mine."

Captain Virginia Witcombe remained perfectly still, and her voice was almost a whisper as she said, "You don't talk to me like that. I don't care who your father was or what happened to him. You *never* talk to me like that. Sergeant? Throw this smart-ass little *punk* out of my station in the next ten seconds or someone will have to arrest me for assaulting a Judge."

Stavros took a step towards CJ. "Captain's right. Get out, CJ. You and your new friends are not welcome in this town. The system we've got might not be perfect, but it's fair and it *works*."

CJ stood her ground. "Recorded crime in St. Christopher is up one hundred and sixty per cent from five years ago. In the same period, conviction rates have dropped twenty-nine per cent." She sighed. "Stav, I drove by Mom's place on the way into town. You know what I saw? Bars on the windows. They weren't there when I left two years ago. Four houses down the street, the Johnstone place? Used to be a nice house. Now it's just a pile of rubble and burnt timber."

Stavros began, "That's not—"

"I'm not done. Six weeks ago Cain Bluett stabbed Kirby Decosta twice in the chest on Main Street. Three sober, reliable eyewitnesses, plus CCTV footage from two angles. Where's Cain Bluett right now? Drinking in Whelan's bar. Why? Because he's rich enough to hire the slickest law firm in the county, and his family has the political strength to bury the case. Dad might not have approved of Judges, but you *know* the drunk that ran him over was awaiting trial for DUI at the time, and wasn't in jail because of overcrowding.

"You want me to go on? No, you don't, because you both know that the system is *not* fair, and that it *doesn't* work." CJ turned from her brother to Captain Witcombe. "Judge Deacon and the others will be here early tomorrow morning. During this period of transition, we will work alongside you and your officers, but Judge Deacon has seniority. His word is final."

Stavros looked away in disgust. "Jesus, CJ! Don't—"

"Judge Leandros."

"What?"

"Judge Leandros. Or just 'Judge,' if that's simpler. That's how you'll address me, Sergeant."

"Right. And does that apply when you're off-duty? Because I can think of a few other names that might apply."

CJ took a step back towards the door. "We're never off-duty. Remember that."

Captain Witcombe glanced at Stavros. "Looks like your baby sister outranks you, Sergeant."

"Matter of fact, I outrank *both* of you," CJ said.

*　*　*

JUDGE FRANCESCO DEACON slowed his Lawranger and pulled in towards the sidewalk on Main Street. The four Judges following pulled in behind him.

Deacon climbed off the bulky motorcycle and trudged back through the refrozen slush, glad of his helmet's auto-tint visor that cut off most of the glare from the morning sun. As he passed his fellow Judges he held out his left hand, palm-down.

Judge Lela Rowain asked, "Sir...?"

"Stay put, Rowain. They're cops."

Judge Kurzweil said, "Cop *car*. Doesn't mean there's real cops inside it, sir."

Deacon ignored that. In the academy, Kurzweil had always been a touch paranoid about police officers and lawyers. She'd always believed that they were going to cause the Judges more trouble than the citizens would.

The police car had signalled them to pull over when they'd turned onto Main Street. Ordinarily, Deacon would have ignored it, but this was their first day in St. Christopher. Ruffled feathers weren't conducive to a smooth transition.

As Deacon passed Hayden Santana, the last Judge in line, the police car's door opened and a fifty-year-old woman climbed out. She stepped towards him, breath misting as she shrugged herself into a padded jacket and zipped it up. "Cold one. Again."

"We were on the way to see you, Captain Witcombe."

"You know who I am?"

"I've been briefed." Deacon extended his hand to her. "Francesco Deacon."

As she shook his hand she asked, "So is that Frank, or Fran? Or...?"

"'Judge Deacon' is fine." He glanced around.

A couple of locals had stopped to stare at the Judges. They were passed by a teenaged boy dragging a large gasoline canister on a battered sled. The teenager glanced at the locals, then looked across the street to see what had snagged their attention.

He said, "Oh, great. Judges." Then spotted Deacon glaring at him, forced a smile and added, "I mean, 'Oh, great! Judges!'" before turning away and increasing his pace.

On the street, an old red pick-up truck was crawling past, its white-bearded driver pointedly staring straight ahead and very definitely not looking at either the police captain or the Judges.

"Suspicious," Deacon said, nodding towards the pick-up. "You want to pull him over, Captain, or should I?"

Captain Witcombe stepped closer to Deacon. "Leave him be. That's not guilt on his face. He's in shock. His name's Henderson Rotzler, seventy-one, lives on the west edge of town. Loud-mouth when he's drunk, but aside from that he's all right. And he's the reason I've stopped you...

"Rotzler's just brought his dogs to his brother's place, now he's heading back home. I'm going to meet him there, and I expect you'll want to, too."

Deacon turned back to face the captain. "So what's happened?"

Witcombe hesitated. "Way I understand things, you're here to work *with* us, yeah? You Judges are gonna replace the entire judicial system, but that can't happen overnight, because there just aren't enough of you. So for now, you work alongside us ordinary cops and lawyers. Tell me I'm right."

Deacon nodded. "That's right." Before the team had left Boston, Judge Fargo had called him in. *"Go easy on them,"* he'd said. *"Let them have their last moments in the sun before the Justice Department takes everything away from them."* Deacon had fully intended to comply with that suggestion, but now, with the captain looking haggard and more than a little worried, diplomacy seemed like a luxury. He told her, "Do us both a favour and skip to the end."

Captain Witcombe slowly shook her head. "It's not that simple, Judge. I spent a few hours last night reading through the new directives. I was hoping to find something that tells me you're not allowed to do anything until I sign you in, something like that."

"We're Judges," Deacon said. "We're *already* signed in. Doesn't matter where we are—we've already got all the authority and approval we need. So get to the point, Captain."

She glanced behind her, towards the back of the red pick-up truck, then said, "Rotzler's dogs woke him up last night. He said they went crazy, barking like there was an intruder. He went out to check it out... There was a body in the back yard of his home. Someone had dumped her over the wall. Female, mid-twenties. Stripped naked. Shot at least once, in the head. According to Rotzler, she was still warm when he found her."

Deacon stared at the captain for a moment, unmoving, and suppressed a shiver that he knew wasn't down to the cold.

Witcombe continued, "Judge Deacon, we haven't formally identified the deceased, but we have every reason to believe that she is Charlotte-Jane Leandros."

Judges: The Avalanche will be available
from May 2018.

Printed in the USA
CPSIA information can be obtained
at www.ICGtesting.com
JSHW021657170624
64967JS00001B/44

AIMEE LaBRIE

Rage & Other Cages

LEAPFROG GLOBAL FICTION PRIZE

Past Winners of the Leapfrog Global Fiction Prize

2023: *Istanbul Crossing* by Timothy Jay Smith
2023: *The Aves* by Ryane Nicole Granados*
2022: *Rage & Other Cages* by Aimee LaBrie
2022: *Jellyfish Dreaming* by D. K. McCutchen*
2021: *But First You Need a Plan* by K L Anderson
2021: *Lost River, 1918* by Faith Shearin*
       My Sister Lives in the Sea by Faith Shearin*
2020: *Amphibians* by Lara Tupper
2019: *Vanishing: Five Stories* by Cai Emmons
2018: *Why No Goodbye?* by Pamela L. Laskin*
2017: *Trip Wire: Stories* by Sandra Hunter
2016: *The Quality of Mercy* by Katayoun Medhat
2015: *Report from a Burning Place* by George Looney
2015: *The Solace of Monsters* by Laurie Blauner
2014: *The Lonesome Trials of Johnny Riles* by Gregory Hill
2013: *Going Anywhere* by David Armstrong
2012: *Being Dead in South Carolina* by Jacob White
2012: *Lone Wolves* by John Smelcer*
2011: *Dancing at the Gold Monkey* by Allen Learst
2010: *How to Stop Loving Someone* by Joan Connor
2010: *Riding on Duke's Train* by Mick Carlon*
2009: *Billie Girl* by Vickie Weaver

* Young Adult | Middle Grade Fiction

These titles can be bought at: https://bookshop.org/shop/leapfrog

AIMEE LaBRIE

Rage & Other Cages

Leapfrog Press
New York and London

To my husband, Dan, who is a way better human than any of the characters in this book.

Table of Contents

The Double Negative Boyfriend

All of this isn't not true.

My last boyfriend had a certain flair, a certain anti-style. That is to say, he might have been fashionable if one were to embrace his lack of variation, his uniform of white T-shirts and thrift store khakis.

On our first date, he brought his own colander in a brown grocery bag. He made me spaghetti with special sauce and taught me how to tell when the pasta was done by throwing a wet noodle at the wall. It stuck there in the shape of an "S." For sentimental reasons, I left it where it landed.

He kept his hair shaved close to his head. The hair looked ashy blond in the sun, gray as an old man's when we were inside watching his collection of Hitchcock movies on VHS. He once told me he had survived childhood cancer, though another time he said his scars came from an emergency appendectomy.

I'd say the sex was good, because then you would understand why I stayed for so long, but I don't recall it being bad or good, just that before he could kiss me, he made me lay down with my hands at my sides like a dead person while he hovered over

me, preparing the perfect way to land the kiss. Or to slice my throat. I decided it was sweet.

He took baths instead of showers. He kept his fingernails long and sharp. He had a husky voice as if he'd been screaming in the night. He had a slightly off-putting smell, like plastic. I didn't not like all of those things about him.

He told me he was in law school because he wanted to save the world. "From feminism," he added, unsmiling.

I could never tell if he was faking the weirdness or if he couldn't help it. Around his law professor, Dr. Downey, he carried on rational conversations about tort law. Later that same night, he confessed to me that he had been molested as a child. By another child. So, did that really count?

The bisexuality was a given, because he'd been in a long-term relationship with his fellow choir member in church (an alto), and I was the first woman he'd penetrated. That's how he described it. *Penetrated*, as though he were in court, presenting evidence, *Your honor, she was penetrated 15 times before my client released his seed*. He would say things like that too, "my seed," as though testing my reaction. I learned to hold my face in check, a blank slate on which he could leave his seed, if he chose to do so.

The drug problem was more of a hobby. You can get high without the needles, and only a junkie would stick it in without at least sterilizing it first with alcohol, which he assured me he did, every time he used, which was constantly but only on certain occasions.

To say he was abusive would not not be false. He never hit me, that *is* true. It was just that at times, he looked as though he wanted to do me bodily harm. If, for instance, I disagreed with his take on the historical double homicide that led to the Baker Act, he might stop in mid-task. Say he was clipping his toenails. He might scissor off the baby toenail and then glance

at me with his head cocked like a German shepherd hearing a distant whistle. I would see the thought ripple across his mind: he could take those heavy toenails clippers and hurl them at the space between my eyes.

I watched him weigh the decision, still still.

Instead, he opened his mouth and poured out a list of my physical shortcomings, ticking them off one by one with the sharp accuracy of a prosecutorial attorney. To my discredit, I stayed to listen, nodding with each criticism. Crossed front teeth, one breast a handful-size bigger than the other, freakishly small feet. Check, check, check.

When I was lying in bed next to him, I felt like one should with another person – a deep, gnawing loneliness.

We dated for about six to eight weeks or months. One night in early spring, he took me to the top of a skyscraper with an outdoor patio at the top level. He asked me to lean over the balcony wall as far as I could without falling. I did as I was told, feeling dizzy with the possibilities.

"I could push you," he said, smiling. He had a dimple in his cheek. It was charming, like something from a story book about Johnny Appleseed. "But I won't, because I love you." He opened his arms, Jesus-on-the-cross-style, and I knew I was supposed to rush into them.

Instead, I backed away. "Oh," I said. "I think of you fondly."

When I finally broke up with him, he mailed me a tape he'd made. I put it in my tape record and pressed play. Symphony-style music welled up from its slippery heart, the theme from *The Omen*, then the theme from *The Exorcist* and part of the soundtrack from *Rosemary's Baby*.

I installed a new lock on the door, one with double bolts. I begged the landlord for a peephole.

"You're not one of them women, are you?" Jack asked. He had a tattoo on his arm from when he was in the Army, a faded green mermaid whose tail disappeared into his armpit.

"I am one of those women," I replied, flexing my own bare bicep in solidarity.

I heard he died on the evening news the day after he died. He'd set fire to his apartment building but it might have been an accident. The cats all escaped; the people did not. You could smell the charring wood from blocks away, mixed in with the chocolate from a nearby factory.

His body was never recovered, but he'd sent a suicide letter to his mother, the words cut out from *The Philadelphia Inquirer* police blotter pages. He used to love the headlines: "Man Arrested for Stealing Child's Woodchuck." It was one of my most least favorite things about him.

I met his mother at the funeral. She wore an old-timey maroon hat with matching dotted netting that covered her face, making her look as if she had smallpox. When she caught sight of me, she gushed and grabbed my hand, "Oh, you must be Laura. He wanted to marry you!"

If it please the court: Laura is not my name.

He had prepared his own montage video, set to music by The Clash. The congregation watched in hiccupped silence, ready to weep, but the rotation of photos was so brisk as to be almost comical – a black and white photo of a boy on a pony, wearing a straw cowboy hat. Another black and white photo of kid at a soda shop, mugging for the camera in baggy overalls. It took a few photos until we all realized that he had used images of Paul Newman's life and times. Paul Newman grew up before our eyes, and the last photo was him with his wife, Joanne, just

before his death at age 83. It was sad to see him age, but he did it so well. Blue eyes sparkling.

Nick's eyes were blue.

They served popcorn at the reception. I ate it by the handfuls, drinking all of the wine. I waited to feel something.

"He didn't want us to cry. He wanted us to forget," said his best friend, an acquaintance from Mergers and Acquiescence whose tie kept falling into the salsa. I brought him home with me and we mourned together by watching *The Verdict* on TMC.

In the last scene, Paul Newman's character sits in the dark, drinking a glass of whiskey while his phone rings and rings. He never picks it up. We see that he has moved on.

The funeral guy turned to me. I forget his name. It was Mark Dimino. He said, "Were you close?"

"Yes," I said. "I'll miss him."

That didn't sound right. I cleared my throat as though about to sing an aria. "I won't forget him," I amended.

If nothing else, that was the truth.

Pygmalion, Before and After: A Weight Loss Journey®

Some days, all I can think about is before. Before I went on the show, before I lost the weight. Who was that person? Late at night, I watch my show: *Liza's Giant Journey*. It's taped, one of the things you get for free after you send in your audition tape, after you're chosen, after you've filled out all of the forms. Forms in case you die on the show. Forms in case you change your mind (you can't change your mind). Forms that say you will allow a camera in your car, your bedroom, your bathroom, and especially your refrigerator. Forms that say you will follow the shows directions to "maximize viewer interest."

First, I visited Dr. Now. He told me to read the pamphlet, exercise, eat right.

I was on board right away, but they told me that I needed to struggle more. "You're addicted to food," they reminded me. "It's your replacement for love." I was given a pair of unflattering, white-lady-flesh-colored leggings to wear and a tight sweatshirt to emphasize the rolls of fat on my arms and legs.

They told not to wash my hair, not to wear makeup. They gave me a pair of glasses, though my vision was fine. I heard them conferring while I sat in the La-Z-Boy recliner they brought in for me. *Like, if she succeeds, there can be that moment where we take off the glasses and the audience realizes she's actually not so ugly after all.*

The weight came off so quickly – "too fast!" they said. *Remember: We need you to go through with the surgery.*

They brought Dr. Now in again. He said, "She's too thin for bariatric surgery. She needs to weigh more or we can't operate." The contract was signed. They told me increase the food intake by 25 percent, because I had to have my epiphany moment where I got serious about losing weight. That meant choking down three milkshakes, two helpings of mashed potatoes, and half of a cheesecake in front of the camera, pretending to like it.

"Stop exercising so much," they told me. "We only want you to lose 20 pounds." They made me stay home and brought me gallons of birthday cake-flavored ice cream and heaping tablespoons of hot fudge.

"We need a good before and after," the producer explained, sidling closer, offering me a hazelnut chocolate bar.

I ate peanut butter from a jar with a spoon, ordered giant pizzas and consumed them on the bed, which they removed from the bed frame and put on the living room floor. *It's more dramatic if the audience sees you struggle to get out of bed.* I physically couldn't do it from the floor, not from lying down; remember, I was 400 pounds at that time, so it was hard for me to get in and out of a chair, let alone to go from lying flat to standing up. I rolled onto my side, burning with shame, legs tangled in the giant blue mumu they had me in. I knew what I looked like: a pupae, wriggling around on the floor, helpless, glasses askew.

"Good, good!" the producer said. "Kick your legs out like that again."

After the surgery, they let me follow the diet and exercise plan. *We've hired a trainer named Dennis. Put on these shoes, eat this chicken, no trips to McDonald's (unless you want to sneak off to McDonald's. Should she go to McDonald's? Wouldn't that be more interesting if she, like, ate three double cheeseburgers?).* While they argued, I gnawed on my thumbnail and jogged in place.

It worked. I lost the weight. I had to pretend to be tempted to eat, even though a valve in me had shut off like a spigot. I looked at macaroni and cheese and saw yellow maggots. Chicken wings and I saw dead baby chicks. Gravy – a pond of liquid fat.

Now, I sit in the dark with the mattress still on the floor, watching Big Me on tape, my stomach slivered down to one-third of its original size, 19 neat stitches and a feathery scar that snakes around my stomach to the middle of my back where they put in a tube and suctioned out the fat. That part is on the tape too, me on a table, cut open with my insides showing, body turned inside out. They give you a warning at the start of the show: "Graphic material. Not suitable for all viewers."

It is not suitable for me, but I can't stop watching. I see me, after surgery when the anesthesia is fading, still huge, wearing a white papery hospital gown, size 4XL, groggy, eyes seeming to go in two directions. "Did I make it?" I ask looking toward the camera. "Did they get it out of me?"

You wouldn't recognize me now, at least not with my clothes on. With my clothes off, you can see the stretched skin where the fat used to be, like I'm wearing an extra suit of flesh. I live on air and ice cubes. I don't need food anymore. They took that part of me out and put it on film, and I can't go back. I miss food. I miss her. She's gone.

Feral

At a recent cocktail party, I asked a circle of women faculty to share their abortion stories. This was after a deadly two-hour poetry reading given by six men with different types of facial hair. I was three martinis, six olives in, but truly curious. Didn't any of them have a funny story about an abortion? Or abortions? They looked away from me or into their drinks, wearing pained expressions. I did not tell them my story, but rather a knock-knock joke with the punch line "Your biggest mistake."

No one laughed but me.

In graduate school, I fell in love with a visiting (and married) professor. What a cliché! Worse yet, I got pregnant. Cue the after school special music! Who could I blame but the father, an Irish poet who disdained birth control – something about the commandments. "*Thou shalt pull out,*" he joked, and mostly, he did. Mostly.

The pregnancy test seemed like a joke. I survived a high school boyfriend, three English majors in college, five broken condoms, and dozens of one night stands. When I saw the positive sign appear, I shook it again, trying to get a different read.

Instead of telling the poet about the pregnancy, I quit going to class and spent most of my time reading true crime books. The nastier the story, the better I liked it. I especially loved the ones where the victim escaped at the last second. She gnawed through the rope with her teeth, threw a vial of perfume in her captors' eyes, and then ran naked, wearing only flip flops, to safety. *Take that!* I thought, giddy with hormones.

Hours evaporated while I hunched in the window seat of my apartment, turning the pages and devouring stale marshmallow bunny Peeps by the packetful. The books had titles like *The Killer in Me* and *Dead before Dawn*, worlds away from the crap I was supposed to be reading for my master's degree in women's studies. These were not literary works; they were grisly tell-alls with dime-sized drops of blood splattered on the covers – stories about twin girls discovered in pieces in car trunks, a severed finger wedged in the "W" pages of a dictionary, a woman's decapitated head peering white-eyed from a fish tank full of guppies. They were mostly Midwestern tragedies that ended with descriptions of weeping mothers and jaw-clenched fathers; true tales where no one was saved and the bodies often stayed missing.

I ate them up and went back for more.

I lived in South Philly at the time, on a street littered with Pabst beer cans and used condoms. The main sound effects at nights were cars gunning and men yelling "Fuck you, puta!" But the rent was just about affordable on my stipend, so I ignored the groaning plumbing, the brown stains on the ceiling, and the moldy basement, where parts of the wall pulled away when I brushed by, leaving dust on my sleeves.

The feral cats multiplied in the backyards of that neighborhood. I saw two of them often – a huge orange tom and a small,

teenage-looking cat, also orange with white spots; a cat a child would name Patches or Ginger. I gave her smelly cans of tuna fish, knowing it was a mistake, because then she would never leave.

One morning while I was staring at the pile of dirty dishes in my sink, I glanced into the backyard and saw her move across the patio wall with something dangling from her mouth. I thought at first it was a mouse or a baby squirrel she'd killed. Squinting, I realized it was a newborn kitten. The mama cat went by with three more of them, hurrying as though late for an important meeting.

Later that week, during a rainstorm, I skipped my evening class, "Women's Bodies: The Skeletal Remains of Gender," to build a makeshift shelter out of a discarded piece of plywood that had turned up in the basement and two wooden crates stuffed with an ugly brown and orange afghan made by my now dead grandmother. I set it up on the back patio with no real hope that the cat would use it. After it got dark, I tiptoed outside and leaned down to look into the shelter. Yellow eyes glowed back at me. She hissed. I counted four small wiggling bodies, all nursing, and left her alone.

The next night, after missing class again and failing to present my paper on Le Fanu's *In a Glass Darkly*, I drank an entire bottle of silty red wine and called the married man on his secret cell phone – this semi-famous writer known for constructing poems having to do with the human anatomy. In bed, he liked to move his hands carefully over my skin, saying things like *This is your patella, your clavicle, your cranium.*

"Something is wrong with me," I said to him when he finally answered, only slightly slurring.

The line buzzed. In the background, I heard a roar of laughter, and then what sounded like a cork popping in the distance.

I recalled his wife, a thin, anemic violinist who couldn't have children of her own.

I pictured him hulking around the lobby of the Walnut Street Theater, waiting for his wife to finish with the orchestra. He was a giant of a man with broad shoulders, a sloping nose, and dark hair that fell across his forehead in a boyish cowlick. He didn't like being tall, and so he was often hunched over, as though perpetually ducking through doorways. In my bed, his feet dangled over the edge of the frame.

After a moment, he said, "Are you ill or are you just feeling down?" He sounded authoritative, fatherly, just as he had in the lecture he presented once, "Crime and Horror in Elizabethan Poetry."

I heard a woman in the background, her voice going up at the end of her sentence. It was likely his wife, the one who could never give him children. I hung up and ran to the bathroom to get sick in the toilet, observing myself from a distance as a pulp fiction author might: *The woman realized that she had made a mistake. Maybe a big one ….*

My favorite story from that fall involved a woman held captive in a man's basement for three days without food or water. She knew that when he returned, the man would cut her into tiny pieces and feed her to his python. I forget how she knew this; perhaps there were remains of other bodies in the basement. When she heard him leave the house, she found a rusty saw and began working on her foot, which was chained to the wall. She kept fainting because of all the blood, but finally, she cut off three of her toes, and that was enough to break free and to hobble up the stairs to escape. It reminded me of the stories I'd heard from my grandpa about how you couldn't keep a fox in a trap because it would eat off its own leg. Sometimes, all that was left in the morning was a fluffy tail or the foot, and sometimes, nothing at all.

Feral

One scene I remember clearly – the one where I could have told him and I didn't. A Tuesday night. He brought a bottle of expensive wine to my apartment. I started to undress when he opened the door, but he said he didn't want to fuck, he wanted to talk. "I want to know who you are," he said, or something along those lines. Likely, it was more poetic. We sat on the sofa. I poured the wine into mismatched juice glasses. I reached for his cock, and he stopped my hand, saying, "There could be more than this."

I took a gulp of wine and told him a story from one of the books I'd been reading, about a man who murdered his wife on their honeymoon in Germany. He told authorities that she had slipped in the shower, just before consummating their wedding, but it turned out that he had held her face in the water of the sink until she drowned. The book was called *True Love Killers*. He listened, his foot jiggling up and down, the shoe hanging from the tip of his socks. He always wore these thick oatmeal-colored socks, even with shorts. "You like to tell stories," he said, and gave a sigh of exasperation, the same one he gave in class when the wrong answer was offered.

When he left, I shut the door behind him and turned the lock, knowing he would hear it. I hovered at the window, out of sight. He walked a few paces away and then stopped dead, now a shadow under the streetlight. I could just make out his profile, the jutting of his Adam's apple, his whiskery cheeks. Then, he looked at his watch and hurried his step, rushing around the corner without a backward glance. For that, I never forgave him.

The feral kittens grew. I imagined my future – them getting bigger and bigger and becoming runny-eyed versions of the mother, my backyard overrun with cats on top of cats on top of cats.

The mother cat kept moving the kittens. Some instinct told her to switch locations often, perhaps to keep them from potential predators like me. I longed to snatch their furry bodies and hold them in my hands. Late at night, I considered their fate. Were they frozen? Would the tattered-ear tomcat slaughter them? The mama cat was so small, barely out of kittenhood herself. Did she know what she was doing?

He liked me to scratch him in bed. He liked me to use my nails to leave long lines in his skin. He liked to quote poetry to me while I scratched. "'Tyger, Tyger, burning bright.' That's not me. I did not make up those words for you, though I wish I had," he said, his eyebrows lifting.

I wondered what his wife would think, how he could talk his way out of those marks, and just imagined that they never slept together anymore. That's what I wanted to believe at the time.

I called my friend JoAnne, a former Texas beauty queen with not one sentimental bone in her body. She gave up pageants because she grew weary of the constant critique. "I know my ass is flat," she said in her sweet, Southern drawl. "I don't need for a panel of men to tell me that on a regular basis." JoAnne showed up at my house the next day with thick garden gloves and a wire cage.

The kittens hissed and spat when I picked them up, wild, electric things. Above me, the mama cat paced back and forth across the top of the wall in distress. I imagined her leaping off and landing, claws first, onto my face. I could lose an eye, be made to wear a patch. She crouched low, meowing. The kittens responded with high-pitched, hysterical noises.

Once we had them all in the cage, I leaned against the patio wall and sobbed. JoAnne patted my back with hard thwacks. She was the only one I had told about the pregnancy. "There,

there," she said briskly. She reminded me that I didn't have to drink or smoke or overdose on cold medicine to change things.

I explained to her that though I supported women's rights and even wore a pro-choice button on my denim jacket all through high school, I didn't want to be a person who had done it. JoAnne touched my hand, uncharacteristically gentle. "Not all life is precious, honey," she said. "Think of Eva Braun."

We farmed the kittens out to other graduate English students who gave them names like Yorick and Dante. I thought of keeping one, but then told myself no, I was not meant to be a nurturing thing. The mama cat kept showing up, howling, searching for them until I took the garden hose to her.

The next week, I made the appointment.

The procedure took no time at all. One minute, I was flirting with the physician's assistant while lying flat on my back on a gurney, and the next, I woke up with a sheet over my legs. For one second, I worried that there had been a horrible mistake. I would whisk back the covers and find my legs bloody stumps – a crazy hospital mix-up! Somewhere, someone else had accidentally been given an abortion!

JoAnne appeared at my side. "You did awesome," she said, as if I had leaped over flames to rescue a family of three.

"Oh, it was nothing," I said, trying and failing to stand up.

My mother called. She told me about the plumber who came to fix the kitchen sink and somehow managed to mess up the pipes so that a dark sludge now bubbled up into the tub. "Where is it coming from?" her voiced sounded frail, like that of an elderly shut-in. After my father died, she became an old lady overnight. He had been a bully of a husband, but without him, she steered rudderless, bumping blindly from one minor

household problem to another. "I can't take baths anymore," she bleated. "You wouldn't believe the mess."

I told her it would be okay. I watched the mama cat run across the wall in an orange streak as if her tail were on fire. I hung up the phone before my mother could ask me to visit.

I borrowed a raccoon trap from an elderly lady who made animal rescues her life's work. She lived in a row house filled with cats. The sharp ammonia smell of pee emanated from under her door. I worried that I might become her, a woman consumed with saving wild creatures.

She said, "Did you know that a female cat can have five litters per year? Multiply that by the average age of an outdoor cat, which is about 10 years, and that's 500 kittens."

"I'm no math whiz," I told her, "but that seems like a lot of goddamn cats."

I thanked her for her time and hurried for the door, trampling on toys shaped like flattened rats.

I caught the mama cat and had her fixed by a local vet for $20. When I let her go, she sprang from the cage and disappeared over the wall into the night. The next morning, she was back on my patio, as if nothing had happened. When I tried to pet her, she scratched my hand. Her claw snagged my skin, drawing blood.

A few years later, I read in the *Inquirer* that the poet would be giving a reading at a local bookstore. I put on my best black dress and high heels. I sat in the back of the room. I waited until he finished signing books and, when the line died down, I approached him with my copy. Not a copy of the poetry he'd written, but one of my favorite books from that fall – a pulpy paperback called *The Killer Inside*.

"I'm sorry about before," he said, moving his shoulder in such a way that suggested that "before" was something that happened just back there, in the other room – some small indiscretion, as if he'd accidentally stepped on my foot.

"I had your baby, you know," I said. He froze his pen in mid-air. "He's called Duncan, after your father. A boy with black curls. He has your eyes, my nose. Some mild allergies, but nothing too serious." I kept talking, watching his face go from open-mouthed surprise to beet red, though I couldn't tell if it was embarrassment he felt, or anger.

If the scene had been one of the books I'd read that summer, he would have throttled me in the parking lot and hidden my body in a dumpster behind the Acme. I continued lying and told him that our boy thought he was dead. "I said you were hit by a bus," I explained. "I made it a life lesson for him. 'Don't be like your father. Always look both ways before you cross the street.'"

He stared at me, his face going slack. I leaned in, as if to kiss him, "Just kidding," I said.

I turned and walked slowly from the room. A tickle went up my neck, as if I could feel him right behind me, his hands reaching for my neck in hot pursuit.

The only other time I saw him was later that same summer on a subway platform. At least, I think it was him – those broad shoulders and that dark wing of hair seemed unmistakable. I hid behind a large woman in a beige raincoat and made sure we stepped on separate cars. I could feel my heart beating in my ribcage like a wild animal. When I looked around the car, I was relieved to see that he had vanished in the crowd of bodies, his once familiar shape indistinct from everyone else's.

I did not tell this story to the faculty women who were inching away from me, one with a pregnant belly the size of watermelon. "Oh, by the way," I might have added. "I thought there would be others." Ha-ha. The joke was on me. There were none.

At the time I got rid of the thing, it was the size of a lentil, a fingernail, and it's not like it could have survived on its own. I never even think about it.

When I really can't sleep, I run it around in my mind. The baby emerges with a shocking mop of black hair, sky blue eyes, an Irish lilt to his cry. Or the baby is born with my eyes, or my mother's eyes, or, worse still, the yellow eyes of a wild creature.

When I dream about it, it's the mama cat I see, pacing back and forth along the back wall, a part of her ear missing, chewed off by some tom. She's looking for her kittens, and it's not as though I can explain to her that they are all perfectly fine, living safe and warm in row homes instead of stuck outside in the cold like her.

She makes a horrible sound, the screech of someone stuck in the ribs by a sewing needle.

Stop it, I want to tell her. *It's over. They are never coming back.*

Dirty

It starts early, before you even have breasts. It starts with a man at a vending machine. You are seven years old. Your parents drink martinis in the hotel bar nearby. The man leans over you, touches your hair. "So pretty," he says. He tells you that he's going to get quarters, and you can buy anything you want. When he leaves to get change, you go into the bar and tell your mom you're not feeling well. She puts a hand to your forehead and says, *You are a little warm.* She orders you a Shirley Temple. You hear the clunk of the Coke can falling in the machine outside and feel bad in a distant way that you were afraid of this man, who probably was just being nice.

Then it's the old man at the bus stop, grinning with his hands down his pants. Then the pock-marked man on the bench outside of Sears, his hand a furious blur, his face a study in concentration, as if he's in pain. You look away, telling yourself that you're fine, you didn't see anything. Then it's the man who follows closely behind you in his car after band practice, saying, *You lost, honey? You need a ride?*

In middle school, it's the boys. The boys will do anything to get you to touch them. They contort themselves in the bleachers at JV football games, pressing your hand against their zippers under a blanket. They suggest sitting in the back of the movie theater and unzip their jeans during the swell of the opening music. They beg, they plead. Once your hand is there, they grow as still and focused as hunting dogs. They watch you like you are the most important thing in the world. You begin to understand a concept you've only read about in novels: eyes devouring, eyes being hungry. Or else it is as if they're injured, and you are the Red Cross rescue nurse. *Help me, I'm dying*, they gasp, out of breath, faces red and distressed. *You did this to me*, they say. *It's your fault.*

This is not what you thought desire looked like. Not after reading books like *Little Women,* where romance took the form of men on bended knees, or movies like *Gone with the Wind*, with Rhett Butler pressing Scarlett O'Hara to him while Atlanta burned to ashes in the background. *Kiss me. Kiss me once.* You thought there would be long sunset walks down winding roads, or afternoons in a rowboat on a clear blue lake, or perhaps a cotillion dance with gentlemen in vests, lining up to kiss your hand while you demurred behind a fan.

Pleasure is a vague thought, like an unreachable scratch on your back. Masturbation. Guys joke about it. *You gonna rub one out?* They have contests, who can do it the most in 24 hours. The guy who wins, David Silver, says, *On the last one, it was like there was nothing left. Just dust.* The guys high five.

You're sick, man, Scott Roach says with admiration.

Girls say nothing.

You spend the night at Diane Dunn's house. You are side by side in sleeping bags on the living room floor. She thinks you're

asleep, and her hand moves quickly under the blanket, just like the man in the park. You smell her body in the way that you have smelled your own body. Is that a good smell?

The next morning, you go home, lock yourself in the bathroom, and press yourself against the hand of your Raggedy Anne doll, moving the doll's hand back and forth. Is this what you're supposed to do? You imagine your teacher's face, Mr. Benson, married, his ring around his finger, his jaw, his chest hair, just a little bit of it showing at the top of his T-shirt. In gym class one day, he had dark sweat stains under his T-shirt. It made your face turn red. Perspiration. Secretions. Ordinary words seem dirty now.

You feel a distant wave of pleasure, but it's muted, not at all like it happens in romance novels where the women have orgasms so strong their heads practically explode. You're not even sure if that's what it was – it was like a tickle, only better, but not by much.

Your mother comes into the bathroom later while you are curling your eyelashes. She frowns, sniffing the air. *It smells funny in here*, she says.

You want to die.

You have to balance so many things. Too much, and you are a slut like Suzy Santana who wears black eyeliner and cutoff shorts so small she gets sent home. Guys say things about her. *She likes to get pounded. She'll take it in any hole.* Too little and you are a prude, like Lynn Anne Thompson, with her khaki shorts pressed into creases and her shirts from Talbots catalogue. She has a perfect bobbed haircut and walks with her head high, nose tilted in the air.

She's too uptight. I'd like to bust that up. Naw, she'd crack your dick in half. Sometimes, you catch a guy talking like that, and

then he'll shout at you full of apologies, like, *Sorry, I can't help it.*

The girls tell stories about Rhonda Gibbons, saying she got a cucumber stuck up her vagina. You go home that night and open the salad drawer, stare at the carrots and rutabaga rolling around, all innocent. There are rumors that you could lose your virginity with a tampon. All of this before seventh grade.

The boys think you want a cucumber up there. It's all they see, it's all they know from video after video after video after video after video after video after video after video after video after video. Women impaled, and liking it. And so, you wonder, what is wrong with you? Why do you not have some primitive urge to stick something inside of you? Why does the thought of a penis, which you have only seen in glimpses of videos, make you worried, maybe excited, but mostly concerned? It's the pummeling, which doesn't actually seem like fun.

In a future life, there will be many different pensises, and they will all be different. There will be a very, very small one, this from someone named Jake, a sweet man who warned you ahead of time, *Size isn't everything.* It's not. It's not everything. But it is something. There is really no way to guess what it will look like, or if it will be thick or pointy or long like a banana. You don't talk about penises with other girls either. Not at all. There is exactly no one in the girls' locker room hooting about how she jerked off Jimmy Deputy at the Cinnabun and his cum shot straight into his own eye. This conversation does not happen.

After you give a passionate speech about abortion in debate class (con: you're still religious at this point), Scott Roach says, *She doesn't need to worry about it. My dick got soft listening to all that blather.* Adam Zimmerman (pro: his dad's a divorce lawyer) says afterward, *You made some good points.* He's talking to

you but looking at your breasts, which have appeared so quickly on your body, your mom has not had time to get you the
next bra size. This inability to look above your breast line to
make eye contact will happen another 879,087 times in your
life (minimum).

Your mother has a hose-like apparatus she keeps under her
bathroom sink, in the way back, near the Kotex and tampons.
Also, a box labeled Summer's Eve with a woman on the cover
wearing a paisley dress like someone from *Little House on the
Prairie*. After you get your period, she tries to explain to you
what the mechanism is for. She sits you down on the living
room couch, itself covered with a clean plastic cloth – kept
pristine until company could visit. "You do it once in a while,
so we won't offend anyone," she says. "Sometimes, women have
a certain smell." The plastic on the couch crinkles and sticks to
our legs.

We are studying symbolism then in Mrs. Bytheway's English class and so the parallels are clear. Your private parts do
not belong to you alone; they are to be preserved for others. For
company, maybe.

In high school, the pressure to go further increases, becomes
a series of battles in the back of borrowed cars as you fight to
keep their sweaty hands from delving too far down your pants.
A part of you still hopes that instead of pushing themselves on
you, they will want to walk down the path and say something
poetic about shooting stars in the sky.

Seventh period health class with Mrs. Hinkle doesn't even
begin to cover it. Young Mrs. Hinkle, who coaches cheerlead-
ing and wears big bows in her hair on Fridays like the other cheerleaders, so young that she looks like a student. Mrs.

Hinkle, who the boys can't stop talking about, staring at, who is so far away from attainable that they don't even joke about her.

Except Scott Roach, who says, *I'd hit that.*

He has said that about lots of girls, but so far, not about you.

Mrs. Hinkle spends 13 weeks on the dangers of cigarette smoking and dropping acid, and teaches mouth-to-mouth on a waxy female dummy with lips that have been bleached away from frequent student practice. She rushes through a mere two days on the importance of abstinence and the risks of STDs, showing full color photos of women with open sores the size of quarters dotting their lips.

The articles in *Seventeen* magazine aren't much more informative. They give advice like "How to Tell If He Really Likes You" and "16 Ways to Wear a Bow." What you really need are articles like "What To Do When No Means Yes."

Make up for your resistance by touching them instead. That is easy. All you have to do is pretend you are someone else, a woman in the USO perhaps, and that he is a soldier on leave. They are polite boys, careful to warn you before they finish, and you are courteous too, offering up a corner of your shirt, a Kleenex, the bare canvas of your skin.

You like to watch their faces turn slack as you unbutton your shirt, three buttons and your bra is showing. Their mouths open wide, as if seeing God for the first time. The bras are white Maidenforms, held up by thick straps and with a tiny flower in the center. It doesn't matter to them. What matters is that they are getting closer to what they want.

This pressure to go further is a slow and constant war, an erosion, a wearing down of your resolve. You kiss in stairwells during a student conference, grind together on the beach, touch the neighbor boy in the garage with the sharp lawn tools

hanging from the ceiling and the smell of gasoline making you so light-headed, you are tempted to let down your guard.

It almost happens with Robbie Hunt in your darkened bedroom while an action movie plays in the background, gunfire and loud explosions. Your mother is in the next room, talking on the phone long distance to your grandmother. *Well, I wish I did still have that snickerdoodle recipe.*

You clutch at his hair, let him kiss your neck. You become shameless, greedy, someone you don't recognize, but when he tries to put his hand down the waistband of your jeans, you push it away. You ruin the moment by saying that you really have to pee. When you return, he has gathered himself together and has his history book arranged in front of his crotch.

"I have to go," he says.

You return home from dates with your mouth raw from kissing, your skin shivery with goosebumps, feeling as if you have been smothered under the weight of something bigger than you. In fact, you have literally been crushed by John Dobosz while kissing on the beach at night during low tide. He hasn't learned how to support himself on his arms while lying on top of you. His entire weight rests on your torso, leaving you breathless. You both pretend not to notice when a droplet of his sweat falls onto your forehead. Afterward, as you're walking away, you look back to see a deep indentation pressed way down in the sand, a distorted blob of your body.

For a short while, in 11th grade, you consider giving your virginity to Sean Riley, a senior and a starting player on the varsity tennis team. He wears white wristbands and gives you a bracelet. *It's made of white gold,* he says. You realize you are supposed to find this impressive.

The first time you see his erect penis while wrestling in the back of his blue VW bug, you are shocked – it's gigantic, unreal, like something from a Saturday afternoon creature feature. The only other male genitalia you've seen in daylight belonged to an eight-month-old baby you used to watch in the church nursery, and his was like a sweet little mushroom.

To cover your shock, you blurt out. "Aw! How cute!"

You both watch as it curls up on itself like a little snail. Now, you have to work harder to make it grow again. That is your job. You learn to watch what you say, so you won't hurt his feelings. You tell him it's okay if he does it on your breasts.

You say no to Sean, Jimmy, David, Danny, Franklin, the exchange student who whispers, *I want to taste your piss.* He says it with a French accent, so it sounds almost romantic.

You might have said yes to the brown-haired boy who believes in Jesus. He wears blue Converse sneakers and plays in a Christian rock band. He is too, too good. You will never know what it feels like to have his eyes on you, to find out how he kisses, to see if you can get him to take the Lord's name in vain.

You overhear him talking about you after the church trip to the beach. "It's too much," he says to his best friend, Mark, the drummer. "She's too much for me."

Charlie has the best eyes, dark green with long lashes. And a deep voice. He drives an old Volvo, his mom's cast-off car, and cassette tapes his ex-girlfriend made him spill all over the front seat. Echo and the Bunnymen, Depeche Mode, other bands you've never heard of and can't find on your AM/FM clock radio. He is clean-cut, a soccer player. One hundred million times cooler than you. At the beginning of your shift at McDonald's, he makes a bet with you. If it's a full moon, he gets to put ice

down your pants. If it isn't, you … you can no longer remember what you would get.

The whole night, you are filling orders for hamburgers and wondering what Charlie meant. You smile at customers, offering them extra ketchup packets, and your manager looks at you as if he thinks he should give you a drug test. He should. You feel high.

At the end of the shift, you and Charlie step outside. The moon is a glowing sugar cookie in the sky. He chases you back into the restaurant, dark now, since the two of you are closing together. He grabs a handful of ice, you rush to get away, sliding on the linoleum, afraid you will fall on the floors he's just mopped. He catches you in the girls' bathroom, pulls the waistband of your pants, and drops the ice on the floor, kissing you hard on the mouth. You both smell like French fries. He says, *I've waited all night to do that to you.*

Later, you will remember, of course he knew it was a full moon. Of course.

When Charlie offers to drive you home that night, you tell him you are cat sitting and you have keys to your friend's house. He drums his fingers on the steering wheel. "Yeah?" he says, still staring out into the parking lot.

You say yes to Charlie Duggan because he has a deep, husky voice and dark green eyes and because he plays soccer, and he has such great thigh muscles and because he knows what he's doing with your body. He is the first boy to touch you between your legs, pressing there, staying there, not in a hurry. He is the first boy to whisper in your ear in the dark of the car, *Do you like that?* You say yes because when you ask him what his favorite part of you is, he brushes your hair away from your face and says, "The way you think."

But mostly, you say yes because you want him to like you. And because you are tired of saying no.

Before you know it, you are on your back in your friend's bedroom. Charlie is on top of you, one of his hands up your shirt, and the other fumbling at his zipper. You can't remember what kind of underwear you wore—oh, my God, is it the huge white hurchie underwear?

He rips something open with his teeth. You say, "What's that?" like an idiot.

He seems surprised you've never seen a condom before. You've heard about them, but had a different picture in mind. You imagined them like already-inflated balloons. You also worried what would happen if it popped inside of you, like, would helium get into your blood system and kill you? This is not something Mrs. Hinkle covered in your two-week express course on the human reproductive system, which ended with you having to carry an egg around for a week without cracking it.

While it happens, the Siamese cat, locked out of the room, scratches at the door and howls as if she is being maimed. Though you keep your mouth shut, you hear a distant echo, the word "no" repeating in your head.

This is not what you thought it would be like. It hurts, it hurts.

When he's finished, he rolls off and says, "Oh, thank you."

You offer to take the condom for him, like you are tidying up.

He gives you a funny look. "You don't have to do that."

You don't have to do that. You didn't have to do that.

When you get home and your mom asks you how work went: *Not good. The drive-thru window got stuck.*

You wait for her to look at you and notice a difference, to grab you by the arm and haul you into the kitchen. She says nothing.

You lock the door to your bedroom and run to look at yourself in the full-length mirror. You look the same, except that your hair has grown frizzy and unkempt, as if you've just had a great shock.

Your experience and his experience were not the same. You will turn this story over in your head again and again. You cannot think that he would be telling this story later, that he has thought of this moment more than two or three times over the last few years, if ever.

In the beginning, there is a kiss. In a hallway, on a porch, in a car. Then, there is a touch, then there is more than a touch, then there is your body and his body. Then it happens and you don't stop it, because at some point, it seems, you have to give it up.

Then, you wait. You wait to see if he returns. Never once do you question whether you want him or not – that seems beside the point.

If you cry about any of them, your mother says, "That's the way men are." She looks at your stepdad, sitting in the den in his chair, the one that reclines, smoking a pipe and watching reruns of *Benny Hill*. The tobacco has a sweet smell to it, like red licorice. You and your mother watch as the smoke floats up to the ceiling. It hangs there a moment and then vanishes.

Jane Err

Reader, I married him in a chapel on a hill with violins playing and swans making heart-shaped figures together on the rolling green lawns while cooing doves were released along with blue-winged butterflies but it turned out that was one too many creatures and the swans ate the butterflies with fierce snaps of their bills. No one slept well that night.

Reader, I married him in a castle with lit candles flaming in the corners of the room and a nun in a starched white wimple singing "Ave Maria" in a high, warbling voice that cracked a little during the super high notes. My gown was a marvel. The train measured 25 feet long and as I swept up the aisle, it followed behind me, gathering lint and gum wrappers. Reader, my veil was handmade by blind, arthritic ladies in Burma. I had never worn a veil before and was surprised at how it gave everything a white, fuzzy glow so that my husband-to-be was a glob-like blur, a destination I moved toward with increasingly confident steps. His features swam into sharper focus the closer I got, and I thought, oh, yes, that's him, I recognize his Adam's apple, that's his eyebrow. But when I finally stood next to him, he seemed like someone I did not know at all.

Reader, I married him on a beach in Key West. The island had a name, I forget now what it was, but sand kept blowing in our mouths, leaving a crunchy taste that later blended into the cordon bleu. Further down the beach, a dead whale had beached itself in some last desperate act. Every once in a while, when the wind changed direction, we'd be knocked flat by its fishy stench.

Reader, I married him in a Holiday Inn reception hall in front of 300 of our closest acquaintances, even though he smelled like mothballs and his mouth held a darting lizard tongue, But you know what? He let me pick the flowers. I wore white. He wore something similar. His aunt Lydia, who lost half her tongue to cancer, drank too much chardonnay at the reception and kept repeating, in an extra slurred voice, "I said to him, I said, 'Either shit or get off the pot. Shit or get off the pot.' He shit."

Reader, I married him. The ceremony was held in Our Lady of Perpetual Heartache Catholic Church, in Langhorne, PA, home of the dairy cow. The church had high ceilings, stone walls, and my heels echoed as I made my way down the aisle toward my beloved, who had shaved his scruffy, rash-inducing beard as a testament of his love for me. I kept my gaze on him, my arm firmly hooked into that of my tottering great-uncle Frank, who had once squeezed my ass at a family reunion and told me I had grown into a fine, fine filly. What can you do? The rest of the men in my family were dead. When my uncle released me to my love, I turned to him and saw how, with me in heels, we measured exactly the same height.

Reader, I married him impulsively on a cruise ship called Bertha Sails, somewhere between Aruba and the Gulf of Mexico. I was drunk, he was high, we had known each other for two fuck-filled months, but what of that? *The soul knows what the*

soul knows, I used to think. The captain gave us our vows in a monotone voice, as if he would rather not be steering this particular ship. My husband dipped me, unsuccessfully, and I fell flat on my back. The gathered strangers laughed and cheered, most of them in white shorts and other leisurewear. He helped me up and I pretended to be okay, but I had trouble dancing after that.

Reader, I married him and we vowed to never stray, to have and to hold. We also made a promise prior to the reception that we would not smash cake in each other's faces. And we kept that promise, though we knew this tiny act of violence was expected of us. Instead, he gave me a forkful of sweet, toothache-inducing wedding cake, pushing it in too fast, so that that the tines stabbed the roof of my mouth. Reader, I smiled, mouth closed, and swallowed the frosting mixed with the coppery taste of blood.

How to Act

First, accept that you are only better than average, talent-wise. As far as looks go, you have understudy potential, but not star power. Your mother warns that you shouldn't get your hopes too high, what with your orthodontia issues. Your father says your mother is just jealous. Your real role in life will be to serve as a captive audience member for their arguments.

(Use it! Use it for scene study class!)

Your mom, a former actress turned secretary for Bloomer's Plumbing Company, isn't one of those people who believes she could have made it if she had only spent more time in New York. Hell, no! She did live in Manhattan for 10 years, scuttling from one audition to another. The closest she came was as a model for Maidenform bras. Photos of her torso hung on department store bra tags across the country for years and years. "Those were some of the best years of my life," she likes to say, after a few gin and tonics. "And then I met your father and had you." She scans the living room, looking for something to reveal character. She catches your eye. "And those were some great years too," she adds with a 50 watt smile.

You will never give up like your mother did. You will also be nicer, have a more stylish haircut, and hire a house cleaner. You will not slam the dishwasher, kick it, and go, "This goddamn piece of shit is the best he could do?"

The "he" is your father, a sad and quiet man with hunched shoulders who likes mystery novels and thinks you are the greatest thing that ever happened. You will later discover that his bar for excellent is pretty low.

You are followed around by an invisible little audience, not a chummy one. They scrutinize every move: *well, that wasn't very believable, was it?* You are always trying to impress them, your cagey onlookers, judging your every move, even when you are merely sitting in a hot car in the parking lot of Piggly Wiggly waiting for your mother to finish talking to the boy who takes away the carts: *The girl sits in the car, sweating. She squints, narrowing her eyes, wondering if her mother knows she's throwing herself at the bag boy.* Even when you are alone, you have to remind yourself to act natural. The audience cheers when you execute a perfect last line aimed at your mother before exiting stage left into the bathroom. They scowl when you flub your lines at dinner, causing your father to drink more. They are particularly raucous at night when you're trying to fall asleep. They sit in their cushioned theater seats, rocking back to replay your performance for the day – oh, look at how she embarrassed herself by attempting to talk to the gym teacher to get out of kickball. How hilarious was that??

Remind yourself that it just takes practice. Practice acting normal, as if everything were okay, and eventually, people will believe you. *Believe in you!*

After you choose theater as a college minor, develop terrible crushes on the actors, or rather on the characters they play

(like the psychopath in *The Zoo Story*). These boys are wounded, vulnerable. They tend to wear James Cagney-type hats and women's cardigans.

The one who stops you cold is Michael Chick – seriously, he is the best actor in the whole program – and when you're near him, even in close proximity, the same building, the same classroom, the same party – your body feels altered, as if you have landed on a different planet and don't know how to breathe. You're weightless, like nothing. You've lost all sense of your own wonderfulness. All those years of tap lessons and vocal instruction, all the training in becoming someone else, and you are rendered only your worst self in his aura. Scarecrow awkward, clumsy, tongue too thick for banter.

George Judy, your scene study acting teacher, also does not believe your grief in Anne Frank's monologue. "You're faking it," he says, arms crossed. Most days, he is a nice man with a calming voice – a grizzly bear with an Abraham Lincoln beard and tousled, thinning hair. Once, years ago, he had the minor lead in a major long-running Broadway show.

He's right. You are faking it all the time – in class, on stage, in bed with your high school boyfriend whose face you used to daydream about and who now, when he visits, makes you feel slightly ill, as if you've swallowed curdled milk. You imagine how sad it will be to break up with him. You feel nothing.

You conjure up the saddest images you can – those starving kids in the Sally Struthers UNICEF commercials, or the commercial that shows pit bulls left in cages with patches of their fur missing, or that time your grandma almost died from high blood pressure but didn't. Remember: she will die, one day. This thought helps you squeeze out one or two tears and George Judy applauds. The praise goes straight to your brain like a cold bite of an ice cream sandwich, making you dizzy.

Later, your friend Wallis Payne (voice major) asks you how you managed to cry on cue. You tell her you thought about your grandma dying. She stares back at you, head cocked. "Why didn't you just think about how Anne Frank's entire family was, like, doomed and being sent to a concentration camp?"

It didn't even occur to you to consider connecting to what was actually happening in the scene.

In your two years as a theater major, you will practice scenes that include: a woman terrorized by a rapist (*Extremities*), a spouse whose husband murders her (*Othello*), a Southern belle driven mad by rejection (*A Streetcar Named Desire*), and a daughter who will shoot herself in the last scene (*'night, Mother*).

In stage craft, practice falling again and again, in a convincing way without twisting your ankle, bonking your head, getting a black eye. Learning to fall is easy, you just have to not think about it, you have to let go of the fear of pain, and go down with grace, with a sudden thud. You practice this again and again in your living room while your roommates watch a marathon of *Law and Order, Special Victims Unit*.

For the spring Mainstage productions, they post the cast lists on the theater bulletin board. Students crowd around in packs, one wave after another. You search for your name, anywhere, on anything. You don't see it. Around you, girls and boys are screaming and jumping up and down, trilling songs.

Tad, a guy next to you who is wearing a turban for seemingly no reason, says, "Hey, congratulations."

You say, "What?"

He says, "Nice job."

You look again at the list, scanning more slowly this time. You check the cast list again, and realize you've been looking for your mom's name, not your own – she is Donna Martelli.

You have a role in *Cat on a Hot Tin Roof.* Not the lead – you're the bitchy neighbor lady. You feel a spike of joy, followed almost immediately by doubt.

Nice try, but you are a minor character.

Then, the counterargument: *It's mainstage! That's a big deal, honey.*

Realize in that moment that these voices are your parents, and they will stay with you, arguing over your value, for the rest of your life.

As a consolation, you are Maggie's understudy. If this were a movie, you would find a way to poison Kiera Reilly so you could be Maggie on opening night. Michael Chick plays Brick, the wounded gay husband who is in love with his best friend, Skip.

During one rehearsal and one rehearsal only, you rehearse as Maggie with Michael Chick. You fan at the sweat under your armpits. You seem to be speaking in a slightly British accent, God knows why. It's Tennessee Williams, for Christ's sake. But you don't have to act, not a bit. You are Maggie – you have her longing for something. Not for something – for *someone.* For Brick. For him.

After rehearsal, you imagine the director going, "I made a huge mistake! We must switch roles!"

He does not say that. Life is not like the movies. Plays are not even like the movies.

But he does say, "I knew I could count on you. You're a good watcher."

Only once does Michael Chick approach you, after a long rehearsal that ends with drinks at the director's house. You stand rooted in the corner, stuck by a sticky table filled with bottles of alcohol and red plastic cups. You will need several of those drinks before the dusty worm of your tongue can

form sentences, and what would those sentences even be? *How was your acting class today? Do you believe in God? Where are you from? What were you like as a kid?* The more you drink, the odder your questions will be, so it's a delicate balance of intoxication. Too much and you will sound blurry and unhinged; too little, and your voice stalls.

He comes over to you. "I like your broach." His finger hovers near your throat.

Your hand flies to the pin. You have forgotten what you're wearing – can't think how it happens to be on your body. "Thank you. I stole if off my grandmother's corpse," you say, trying to joke around.

He smiles and frowns at the same time. He's in advanced acting class. He has learned to convey complicated, mixed emotions in a single handsome glance. And then he leaves. He always seems to be leaving.

Opening night for *Cat on a Hot Tin Roof*. You are onstage with Brick for a total of one, five-minute scene. You have 22 lines.

You know your dad is in the audience. Your mom is unable to attend. You cannot look out to find him, but you feel a wave of love for him, knowing he is there.

Curtain falls. You all embrace, a sweaty group hug where everyone gets pancake makeup on each other. *Great job! We did it!* All but Michael Chick, who has left behind only a smudged handkerchief with his makeup on it.

Your dad, who has temporarily moved out of the house, shows up at the cast party. He presents you with a dozen wilted daises. "Honey, you were the only one I could watch," he says. When he hugs you, he seems smaller than you remember.

Your theater friends squeal and exclaim over your dad. One of the boys sits in his lap, draped across his shoulders like a

stole. "Darling, your father is a doll!" Your father's face is lit up like a flame, but he doesn't move away.

Watching your dad, you decide that you don't have the stamina for that type of ongoing performance, the constant parade of big expressions made so that the people in the back row can see them. Something is wrong with you, because you cannot toss your head, you cannot laugh a laugh from the bottom of your belly, you cannot grow suddenly still and distant eyed and spill out a line of Shakespearean dialogue: "Parting is such sweet sorrow/That I should like to stay again 'til it be morrow."

Later in the party, you and your dad both watch Michael Chick walk in, wearing a butterscotch suede jacket.

"He was phenomenal," your dad whispers.

"I know."

"Is he straight?"

You say, "I have no clue." If your dad tries to talk to Michael Chick, you will combust on the spot. Your dad, weaving slightly, makes his way over to him. You close your eyes; you cannot watch.

A few seconds later, a hand touches your arm. It's him. Michael Chick. "Hey," he says. "Your dad says he's not okay to drive you home. I can give you a lift."

You nod. You now know what true love is.

Michael Chick has brought along a bottle of red wine with a hand-drawn goat on the label. You sit on the front porch of your rented house, drinking the wine as fast as possible, worrying about the color of your teeth.

He tells you a long, involved story about a book he's reading that describes some guys driving motorcycles across country.

"I read that," you say. Your teeth clink on the glass as you take another long sip.

"What?"

"I read that one. The motorcycle maintenance book." You go on to wonder why it is that guys think that's such a great book or how they think it's so subversive to fight the system by riding a motorcycle. Like, if you want to make a difference, how about going to India to save some starving kids? You realize that your real self is starting to poke its head out, like a groundhog. You dig your fingers into your thighs, trying to squash that voice.

He doesn't seem to care, because he's standing now, pulling you up next to him as if the two of you might waltz.

When Michael Chick kisses you, it is exactly like a scene from a love story. Moonlight scatters across the blank sidewalk. He pulls your hair away from your face and leans toward you. Up close, his pupils are huge black circles. He smells like suede and wood smoke. His jacket is as soft as a deer. His kiss is not a disappointment, and when he pulls away, he says, "I've wanted to do that for a long time," which rings familiar, like a line from a play.

You stumble inside the house, relieved your roommates are away for the weekend, and take him to your twin bed, scattering the stuffed animals. He lays down next to you, and says, "Why have you been so hard to catch?"

This makes no sense. Of all the people in all the world, he is the one you most wanted to notice you. You say nothing. You lie in the dark, heart sputtering with fear. You don't know how to move, but he does, and you follow his lead. He is, after all, a leading man.

And when it's over and he sighs asleep next to you, you can't figure out why you feel a sudden sadness, a shooting pain located in the center of your palm. Why are you suddenly thinking about your grandma when there is no one there to see you cry? Even as you feel real tears sliding down into your hair, another part of you is telling yourself to remember this.

Remember this feeling in case you ever need to use it to play a scene of grief.

The next morning, his fingers fluttering through his curls, his eyes on the peeling white ceiling, he says, "I don't know who I'm going to be today."

You pull the sheet up. "I don't know what you mean. Like, you might be a fireman? A farmer?" He continues to stare, like a man who is used to being observed. You say your favorite line from the play: "Why don't you ask if he makes *me* happy in bed?" He looks at you now, just one emotion on his face now – confusion.

He doesn't know who you are. You stare back. You don't know him either. Maybe what you liked about him wasn't him at all – it was Dionysus and Hamlet and Brick.

And he smokes a little pot from a bong he made from a toilet paper roll. You have nothing to say to one another. He doesn't kiss you goodbye. He gets on his moped and he leaves.

Curtain falls.

You watch him go, standing in your underwear and bra on the front porch.

The truth is, you're not good enough. You might make it if you can envision the next 10 years in New York, juggling poverty, waitressing, auditioning, and receiving rejection after rejection after rejection after rejection after rejection. Well, all life has rejection, but not that particular form of rejection where you're told exactly what's wrong with you by a blur of faceless men sitting in a darkened theater after you audition with a piece from *The Vagina Monologues*. You'd like to skip that whole part and be discovered, like Judy Garland at a malt shop.

There are no malt shops where you live, only gas stations and consignment shops and places that promise happy hour for undergraduates.

Plot twist: you discover you are more like your dad than your mom.

Switch your major to English. You call your dad to tell him. He says, "You're an amazing actress, but you also have a sharp mind. You'll be brilliant." When he asks you if you would like to speak to your mother, realize that you can say no. Say no.

In English classes, you will analyze the misogyny of Tennessee Williams instead of embodying it. Discover a whole new genre of longing – Daisy Buchanan, Jane Eyre, Hester Prynne – like you and your dad, aren't we all just waiting for the right guy to show up? Or the wrong guy to leave?

English majors drink black coffee and talk about books. They do not break into songs from *Music Man* in the middle of a Victorian poetry seminar. They lean forward, and earnestly (and quietly) discuss the Western Canon. They are incredibly boring and have their own form of auditioning by using words like "deconstructive narrative" and "neocolonial narcissism." But you already know how to fake it, nod at the right time, pretend to understand.

Though you don't know it then, the theater experience has prepared you for certain future life events, such as presenting a PowerPoint at a board meeting.

"You don't even seem to get nervous," Rhonda, a temp-to-permanent hire from the business office, will say.

"Thanks," you will answer with a shrug, playing modesty.

Animal Shelters

I walk the dogs at 8 a.m. and 6 p.m. Each morning before work, and each evening after, I take SEPTA to Jodie's apartment, and trudge up the three flights to unlock the door. Her apartment is that of an adult — full of things like Kitchen Aid appliances, small bowls nestled inside of other bowls, and expensive, unopened (!) wine bottles resting sideways on a wooden wine rack from Crate & Barrel. Items and furniture from somewhere other than IKEA, and two embroidered dog beds that look more expensive than my futon.

"Take anything you want," she urged me toward the end. But her clothes were too small and her feet too big. *Take the couch. Steal the silverware.* Every action of forward motion requires more energy than I can currently expend. A rental truck. Organization. Friends I don't have.

Today, as always, the dogs are glad to see me. I make my entrance three times in a row, just to be greeted again and again by their wagging tails. Junie, the black Lab, follows me from room to room, certain I'm about to do something interesting. Agnes, the Welsh corgi, eyes me with suspicion, like I might abscond with her pewter water dish. To please her, I do

a little impromptu dance, my winter boots clunking against the hardwood floor. "Ta-da!" I always finish with a flourish of jazz hands.

The dogs don't know what to make of me. They have not been taught how to howl their applause.

We move along the path beside the Schuylkill River, the gray and choppy water unwinding in front of us, unwelcoming and vast. They pull me along, tugging, industrious, sniffing every garbage can and fence post they can find.

When we arrive at the gate of the dog park, they barely allow me to take off their leashes before they bound around with their doggie pals. Even Agnes, the cautious one, gets caught up in the excitement and barks out of sheer joy.

The other dog owners stand around in their windbreakers and sneakers. We say hi and talk about the weather. I can never recall the names of the owners, but I know the dogs: Bogart, Keegan, Oliver, and Blackie.

An impossibly thin woman in a threadbare coat gestures at her skittish greyhound, Bones. She needs tips for how to keep her dog from howling when she leaves the house. "I mean, the neighbors are threatening to call the cops!" They tell her to leave the radio on NPR, to buy him a cat friend, to purchase tiny dog ear plugs. They have many ideas for how to work it out.

Junie has what seems to be an ongoing conflict with an aggressive German shepherd named Snowflake. Snowflake is an oversized pup – big paws – galloping about, trying to bite Junie's tail while the owner, oblivious, talks in Russian on her phone and balances a giant Starbucks coffee. "Can you please control your dog?" I yell to her, suddenly furious at this ditzy blonde in pink sweatpants with the word "Lucky" written across her ass.

She clucks her tongue at the dog, who immediately drops into a sitting posture. "He very bad dog," she says, shaking her finger at him.

Maybe we will become friends. Maybe not.

From the people at the dog park, I learn what dogs remember. Smells and being punished. Their noses imprint with people and locations. These owners can tell countless stories about dogs lost at rest stops who, somehow, though covered with ticks and brambles, found their way home three weeks and 500 miles later. They once heard about a standard poodle reunited with his owner after a 10-year separation. The dog still remembered that with this guy he learned how to rear up on his hind legs to beg for a piece of chicken.

"Aren't there some really dense cocker spaniels out there who can't find their way back from the mailbox? How about the dogs who bite their owners in the face when they return from Iraq?" I demand to know. "Or the dogs who eat the new baby out of jealousy?"

They stare back at me, mouths open, and eyebrows up. "That's an urban legend about eating the baby," says the owner of Frankie, a rambunctious terrier. "And I bet they blamed a pit bull." I expect the rest of them to turn on me, but they don't. Instead, they reassure me: there are many bad dogs. But really, who wants to talk about them?

I bring the dogs back to her apartment, feed them, wish them well, and skip toward the door. They follow me, confused that I'm leaving. Where on earth can I be going? Junie licks my ankle.

I lock the door. "See ya later!" I trill. "Have a good dream!" I sprint down the hallway now, guilty and gleeful to be free.

What do the dogs do all day alone in my friend's apartment? one might wonder, if one were given to such musings. Stare out the window at the waves of the river, a strip of which you can see if you turn your head just so – the view Jodie told me is what sold her on the place? "It's prime real estate," she explained to me over the phone. "Come see for yourself."

And so I did.

The move gave me an excuse to break up with the Married Boyfriend, the one whose wife had stopped having sex with him five years back. His favorite game in the world was to pretend that he and I were married. Whenever he let himself into my apartment with the key I made for him, he'd call, "Hi, honey, I'm home!" The trick to infidelity, I found, is to not get too attached. When we first slept together, he was so very grateful for my body and so relieved to be touched, that I kept seeing him and then it became a habit, so that we were barely sneaking around. He started talking about moving in some day. He began lingering too long in department stores, fingering the sheets, imagining what color paint would look good on a bedroom wall. There was even talk of children.

I left. I left behind the small town in Florida where Jodie and I grew up to have a Philadelphia adventure, only to discover that she was having her own whirlwind romance with Death, and Death waltzed her off, before I even had a chance to get settled.

We didn't have time to prepare for the sudden turn of events. That's the thing with cancer; you know, she looked a little peaked and then maybe fatigued and then there was blood in unexpected places, but neither of us thought it was cancer, but then it was the bad kind of cancer, not the good kind where they just lop off your breasts.

Animal Shelters

The dogs and I are old friends, of course, but it's the difference between seeing your friend's baby once a month and having that baby come live with you. I didn't sign up for this. I didn't sign up for the old dog, Junie, with her flaky nose and threadbare tail or the high-strung Agnes, who fears everything from tree shadows to a man wearing a pom-pom winter cap. They're a lot of work, and I have things to do. I have my own apartment to unpack and letters to write and cupboards to arrange in this new city, this new apartment, this new life. I need time to get used to the creaks and groans of the place, the fear that it might be haunted, the sounds of the neighbors upstairs who seem like they spend most of the night rolling a marble back and forth across the floor.

How long has she been gone now? I can pretend that I'm not counting down the days, but I am, because her lease expires at the end of the month. Her elderly parents will come to pick up the pieces any day now, but I know (because she has told me, on many occasions) that they live in a small retirement community, no dogs allowed. Hey, that's not my problem, you know. Look at what she left me with.

The dogs and I reach an agreement. They are not to expect too much from me. I pat their heads hello, three taps, four at the most, and then they get fed. I sit at the edge of the sofa while they eat, sloppily, crazily, the older dog continuing to come into the room between wolfing bites to make sure I haven't left him. I perch on the cushion because the sofa is covered in dog hair. These dogs, they ran the place when Jodie was alive; they covered the place in their fur. When they're done, we get the leashes. She has taught them to sit when the leashes come out, but as soon as the door is unlocked, both of them

bound out of the door like we're on a sudden police mission to catch the criminals, to catch the bad guys.

The next time I arrive, I find Agnes in the laundry basket. She can't seem to be cajoled out of it, even when I offer her a tasty piece of only slightly hard cheese. I tip the basket over, and she falls with it, sideways, but stays inside. I grab at her collar and pull, pull. She resists, but in this polite way. She's not an aggressive dog, just stubborn. Finally, I pull her free, and set the basket upright again. As soon as I walk toward the door, she jumps back in. We go through this dance a few more times. "Why?" I ask her. "Why do you need to be in the basket with Jodie's dirty laundry?" Then it hits me that maybe she likes to be there because it still smells like Jodie. You can't explain to a dog that she won't be coming back, and even if you could, would it hurt so much to let her keep a piece of Jodie around – an athletic sock, a pair of gym shorts?

I leave Agnes and go into the living room to have a nice long sob on the sofa. The Lab, distressed by the weepy sounds I'm making, tries to distract me with her favorite rope toy, bringing it up and shaking it against my knees like, "Look at me! I'm fun!"

She, the organized one, has thought of everything. This maker of eternal to-do lists, my friend, has arranged for others to come and pick up her things – this one gets the blender, this one gets the measuring cups. I sat with her at her bed while she made the lists, so I know. She wants nothing to go to waste.

Now, whenever I unlock the apartment, I find that things are missing. The coat rack, who used to greet me like a friend with one hand extended, has disappeared, along with the bookshelf and the collection of blue bottles along her windowsills. I imagine the endless stream of friends of hers I never got a

chance to meet coming in and out, Jack, her landlord, letting them in to take what she's left for them and go their merry way.

She asked me what I wanted, and I said her Hummel doll collection, but those are still there, so perhaps she has left them for me after all. This erosion of her things gives me an eerie, tickling sensation along the back of my neck, like a ghost is trailing its finger there, saying, *How are you?* I don't like the unexpectedness of it, and now, when I open the door, I do it with one eye closed to prepare myself for whatever else might be gone.

Not the dogs. The dogs are always there, waiting.

Once the sofa vanishes, they seem to enjoy the extra space to run around, to chase each other. Even Agnes gets into it.

What has she left me? Not a lock of her hair, not a braid, not a piece of her bone, or a toenail, but the most important things to her, these dogs. That's my legacy. These creatures that, like her, will leave me at some point too.

The married ex-boyfriend wants me to return to Florida. "Don't you miss the sunshine?" he asks in his deep, radio announcer's voice. "Don't you miss the salty air and swooping seagulls?"

"I don't miss the cockroaches," I say. "I don't miss the tourists and senior citizens who clog up the roadways." He would like for me to imagine the past without these unpleasant things, in the same way that he would like me to forget about the pesky wife. If you listen to him, it's as if she's just a detail to be ironed out. "Come home," he begs. "Come home and I will build you a sandcastle to live in."

"Not by the sea," I warn. "If you build it by the sea, it will surely be demolished."

Dogs must be washed in the bathtub, at least once a month, in order to keep them from smelling like something that has just washed ashore. They do everything sloppy. Junie, when she drinks, goes at it with a gusto that causes the water to ripple out of the sides of the dish and sprinkle the floor. When they scratch, they scratch hard. They pant hard; they have no decency when it comes to using the bathroom. Everywhere they go, they leave pieces of themselves, so that when I get back to my apartment, I find my sweater covered in their hair.

I worry that the nasty wet dog smell has begun to emanate from my clothes on the subway. I scoot away from the man next to me, noticing all the white hairs on my coat, dotting it here and there and everywhere like something from a Dr. Seuss book. There is a certain etiquette to the subway – we must not make eye contact, and, even if we are pressed up against each other so that my nose is nearly in the crook of your neck, we will agree not to acknowledge it, please, to pretend that it is completely normal for me to be physically closer to you than anyone in my life in a long time.

Jodie was always ahead of me – the first one to lose her virginity in 11th grade, the first to drop acid in college, to get married and then divorced, to move away, to get a deadly disease. I cannot forgive her for always having to be first in everything.

It's not fair, one might say. You might shake your fists at her ceiling, at the glow in the dark stars she's pasted above her bed. You might even take to having a nap in her bed, or putting on her fuzzy blue robe, the one that still smells like Poison, her signature scent. You might wonder when the landlord will knock on the door with two perfectly respectable tenants who would like to assume the lease. Like sands through the hourglass, like Erica Kane in a soap opera, time is running out in these, the

58

Animal Shelters

Days of Our Lives – the show we watched after school each afternoon, while devouring everything we could get our hands on in the cupboard. Her mom was the stay-at-home kind, constantly trying to win us over in our cruel years of adolescence by baking us chocolate chip cookies from scratch and wavering in the den to say things like, "That Erica Kane, like, can't she get a life?" Jodie would tell her to please, if she didn't mind, stop trying to sound cool, and go back to scrubbing a pot or a pan.

I have found work at a lovely nonprofit specializing in helping the wrongfully accused get out of prison. The people are nice, but they are also very earnest about saving lives, so you can see that there's not a lot of joking around. Still, I wish that they could lighten up on occasion. In the few months I've been there to help with marketing, I've learned more than you ever want to know about the death penalty. Lethal injection, death by firing squad, hanging. You wouldn't believe the many ways people can be put to death. I learn that most states have lethal injection, which might, at first, sound like the easiest way to go. Actually, it's not. Actually, they have to shave off the hair on your arm first and they still strap you in with leather bands so that you have no way of escaping. They secure your head too, so that you can't see the shot going into your body, won't know the exact moment of your death.

It's like how they put down dogs. One quick shot to knock you out, and then the real bad stuff goes in your veins and stops your heart in an instant, like magic.

On lunch break, I call the SPCA. A haggard-sounding woman answers. In the background, you can hear the frantic echo of dogs barking – all different registers of panic. I ask her how hard it is to drop off a dog. "We recommend you wait 48 hours after an inciting incident before bringing the dog in."

Her drone tells me she's said this sentence close to one thousand times. "What is your inciting incident?"

I scour my brain. "You mean, like, was there a riot?"

"No, did the dog act out, bite someone, or has the dog been behaving aggressively?"

"No, not any of that," I say. "These are very nice dogs. They would be excellent additions to a family with a home and a backyard."

"Miss," she says. "We get something like two dozen dogs surrendered per week. Most of them don't end up going to good homes. If Lassie was brought in here tomorrow, she'd have about a 20 percent chance of ending up with Timmy."

"Oh, gee," I say. "Thank you for your candor."

After work, I take them to the park. I'm barely paying attention, and Junie suddenly lurches forward. I drop my coffee, trying to pull her back, but the leash slips out of my grasp and she goes bounding down the sidewalk after something – a gray squirrel. I yell after her, but her doggie instincts are too strong, she must, must, must chase the squirrel, it's written into her DNA, and even as I see the squirrel running toward the busy street, I think, "No way would the universe let this happen." Junie leaps after the squirrel, toward oncoming traffic and then I see her snap back. A man walking his own dog, a prim Lhasa apso, has stepped on her leash in the nick of time, saving us all from a terrible accident. The squirrel too has made a valiant escape under a parked car.

I thank the man. He says, "Hey, it happens," and continues on, his Lhasa apso the picture of excellent doggie behavior.

"Bad!" I say to Junie. My hands shake in the after-jangle of adrenalin. "Bad dog!" Both she and Agnes shrink into themselves, tails tucked, Junie trying to both become invisible and to comfort me by licking my face.

For a while, Jodie and I pretended like she would be coming home any day. We talked about how excited the dogs would be. She worried they wouldn't recognize her, that she smelled different, like Lysol and disinfectant and illness – that the cancer would make her a stranger to them. She did smell funny – odd, like plastic. We joked about it and then moved onto other topics involving reality TV shows like *The Dog Whisperer.*

The married ex has opinions about dogs. He's fond of them actually, he tells me in a whispering voice that suggests the wife is lurking nearby. Usually, he waits until she's in bed to call, but even then, he can't shake the idea that she might have the phone bugged. He waxes on about the dogs of his youth. "Didn't you ever have any pets?"

"We didn't have time for pets," I tell him. "My mother was a single mom. I was the pet. She took me outside to go to the bathroom, put food in my bowl when I needed to be fed, occasionally brushed me." He laughs. He always thinks I'm joking when I feel like I'm revealing something very personal and poignant about myself.

Yes, he continues, he's fond of dogs, but he doesn't see himself being the owner of one, let alone two. They're so needy with their sad eyes and their ticks and fleas. "I need something that doesn't require a lot of care."

"Like a mistress," I suggest.

"Don't be silly," he says. "You're not taking those dogs in. You're not a dog person."

"I'm not?"

"No, you've never been a fan, not since I've known you." He states this with such confidence that I know he's wrong.

I am a dog person. I just didn't know it until now.

The second to last time I visited, I remember staring at the blue liquid dripping into the IV above her bed. I couldn't think of what to say, so I made up some nonsense involving my co-starring role as the funny friend. "Remember that poem Mrs. Bytheway taught us in high school? 'Death, where is thy stink,' I think it was." And rage, rage against the dying of the light. Do not go gently into that good night. Jodie did not intend to. That day, she was ragged and pissed off, her eyes filled with the same kind of brimming anger I recalled from the protests against animal cruelty she dragged me to in college.

"What state of Elizabeth Kubler-Ross's am I in?" she asked, throwing a dinner tray.

"I'll guess anger," I said.

She made a list for me. Vet's name and address, type of food they will eat or not eat, what to do if one of them vomited up the squeaky part of a toy. And even though she was clearly exhausted, she went meticulously through each item. I maintained eye contact to show that yes, I understood. I was on the same page. We would get this done. Count on me.

While she went through the list, I thought of all the things she had done for me. She broke up with my college boyfriend, pretending to be me over the phone while I paced in the background, my hand clasped over my mouth, to keep from bursting out into hysterical laughter. When he fought back, I heard her say, "I would never in a million years stay. Oh, one good reason why not? Because you're an asshole." She returned clothes for me when I lost the receipts. She picked up the tab when we went out. She laughed at my stupid jokes. In turn, I wrote her final paper on Andrew Marvell's "To His Coy Mistress." I cooked us dinner. I helped her apply to graduate school. I gave it to her straight when something she wore looked bad. I gave

her ideas for the dogs' names when she rescued them. Up until then, it seemed like a pretty fair trade.

"I have set up a fund," she said.

"Fund?"

"A dog fund. You know, so you don't have to spend your money while I'm gone."

She explained how it would work, this thing I started to think of as the "I Don't Trust You" trust fund.

"Ohhh …." I nodded. "You think I will let them starve. You think I will leave them tied up outside of Starbucks and skip town."

She said, "This is not about you." Her voice suddenly brittle, her jaw clenched. "Okay? Please don't make this about you. This is for my peace of mind, okay?"

I told her I had to go, making up a story about how I was in the middle of a really big case at work, this guy has only hours to go before he might be wrongfully put to death. I promised that the next time I visited, I'd try to bring her something from the dogs, a chunk of fur or an unnecessary molar. She pretended to laugh, but her eyes were shiny and very brown, almost as if she might cry. I left before that could happen.

Here's a story I know I have told her. For my eighth birthday, my mom bought me an aquarium with two black Mollies in it. I named them Bob and Shirley, put the tank on the bookshelf in my bedroom, and was enamored with them for about two days. Then, it got to be a drag to have to feed them every day and to clean the tank. So I started dumping extra food into the water, taking giant finger pinches of flaky food and coating the top of the water. Soon, the fish were swimming in a murky tank with green algae growing up the sides.

And then, for a brief period of time of after-school band practice and sleepovers at a friend's house, I forgot about them entirely. I only remembered when, one morning, I stepped on the petrified body of Bob, who had thrown himself out of the tank in desperation. Shirley, I learned soon after that, bobbed belly up at the top of the tank, one of her gills eaten clean off. I told this story to her once, and she said, "What about your goddamn mom? Who lets a kid take care of anything? That's just bad parenting!" That is why I loved her.

I didn't tell her that in times of stress in my life, I still dream about the dead fish, of being stuck in traffic or stuck in a hot air balloon or behind a wall of slow-moving zombies, unable to get to them in time. Over the years, the fish die again and again in my dreams before I can save them.

One of the dogs has shit in the middle of the daisy-covered rug. My guess is that it's Junie, though both slink underneath the coffee table, ashamed, neither able to betray the other. I don't clean it up right away, even though I can see that it makes them both nervous for it to remain sitting there, like an accusation. I feel something in my chest turn mean and hard as a walnut.

I put both dogs in my car. *I am being decisive. I am putting my foot down*, I think, as I head down the highway. I feel wild, feral with disobedience.

Junie stands with her nose rubbing against the backseat window, panting, with her tail thumping on the seat. She is just excited to be going somewhere. The angst-ridden Agnes lays pressed flat on the floor behind the driver's seat – trying to get under it. Unlike the Lab, she seems to sense that something is amiss.

The SPCA building is surrounded by large oak trees. It looks peaceful enough. No smokestack chimney with black

incinerator smoke snaking into the blue sky. We sit in the car and the engine ticks.

Junie, still excited, licks at the windows as if they're made of peppermint. Agnes groans a long, mournful sound full of dread.

The dogs, they're docile, not biters, possibly even good with children. Someone else may want them. I will have to lie about their ages, especially Junie. She's eight years old, walks as if her back legs are made of wood, and then there is the issue of the lost fur around her nose. The corgi may have better luck, except that she's on the skittish side. When we're on a walk, she tends to stay close to me, as if she needs the contact of her fur on my ankle to make sure I have not fled.

I start to hear another sound, one I cannot place it at first. It sounds like wind across the prairie. I shut off the ignition. It's the sound of dogs in the shelter. It's muted, but if you stay still and listen, you can hear dozens of dogs howling into the night. All different pitches – high, low, frantic, questioning – they present a chorus of barks and yips and howls.

I look back at Junie, this ancient dog with the bald patch on her snout. She tries very hard to jump into the front seat to get a better look at what's going on. I nudge her away with my elbow and she licks it.

I start up the car, put it in reverse, and head back into the city.

On what later turned out to be the last visit, we went over the things she wouldn't miss. The armpit smell of the subway cars in summer. How some Philly summers are so hot, you feel like you're melting and you can do nothing but lay down panting on the kitchen floor. Shaving your legs. Worrying about crow's feet. Watching someone throw a crumpled McDonald's bag out of the car window. "And you know what?" She dropped her

voice to dramatic whispers. "I am so, so, so sick of the home-less." That gets us laughing for a good 10 minutes.

"I miss my hair the most," she said, reaching up, and not quite touching the back of her head. She had baby chick fuzz all over her perfectly shaped skull. On her, it looked glamorous, like she's purposefully punked herself out, become a lead singer in an indie band that yells obscenities into a microphone – "Fuck the government!"

We didn't talk about all of the other things she'll miss. Those were a given.

And when I said goodbye, I did it in the same breezy way as before. I waved and did a little dance. I didn't touch her arm or give her a hug. We just didn't do those things, not in real life. It's not like I didn't have things to say. It's just that the words lodged in my throat like dust.

I can't sleep. All night long, the marble rolls back and forth, back and forth. I put my head under my pillow. I try to listen to music on my iPod. I count dog breeds, starting with the letter "A." Afghan, bichon, collie, dachshund.

The marble continues to roll.

I go upstairs and knock on the door. Almost immediately, it's opened, as if the person were waiting for me to arrive. It's the Russian lady from the dog park by Jodie's house. Why she goes to the park so far away is another mystery of the city. Perhaps she too has just lost someone.

"Yes?" she says. Her goofy dog pants behind her, trying to push past her knees to greet me.

"I can't sleep. Please, what is that sound?"

"Oh, sound?" She taps her finger to her lips and stares hard at the ceiling. "Oh, that! It is his toy. I hear it all day long. I don't even notice. Sheba! Bring it." The dog dutifully brings the

toy to her. It is a round ladybug encased in a plastic ball. "Okay, you take it, and someday, you bring me back a quiet one." She pats the dog on the head. He's leaning against her leg, this giant beast. Somehow, she doesn't fall over.

Oh, I think, as if just remembering. The dogs. The dogs in the house by themselves every single night.

The thing that will break your heart is that these dogs never get over the loss. I saw a picture in *National Geographic* magazine of a big-headed Labrador lying on the twin bed where the family's dead son used to sleep. It might be a stretch, but the family swore he was depressed. The worst thing was that he never quite got over it. You can't go up to the dog and say, "Listen, he's not coming back. That boy who you remember, he got blown up in Iraq."

The other thing about the photo was that the family hadn't moved on either. The room still had his high school posters of bands he liked and the shelves had his textbooks and a few model airplanes. I imagined that his flannel shirts hung in the closets with his shiny shoes and sneakers lined up underneath in a neat row. How can you expect a dog to get over a death when the people around him haven't done the same?

I put my clothes on in a rush, as if I'm on my way to stop an execution. My hands shake and I have trouble zipping up my coat. I jump in my car and zoom across the city from my apartment to hers. It is nothing – takes 10 minutes to drive, 30 minutes to walk if you cut across the Fairmount.

When I open the door to her apartment, the dogs look startled, caught in the act of sleeping. They have not been pacing the night away or howling at the sky, thinking maudlin thoughts, remembering puppyish moments along the Schuylkill running path with Jodie.

Junie shakes herself awake, her collar jangling. Agnes yawns so wide, I can see the back of her pink throat. The meanest thing I have done is to leave them alone every night for how long now? Too long.

I gather their silver dog bowls, their chewed-on leashes, the heavy bag of Purina, as much as I can carry, except for luxurious dog beds, which will have to come with me later. They can sleep on the floor. Or they can crowd in the bed next to me. It doesn't matter. What matters is that they're on their way home.

The Fittest

If your car parachutes off the Ben Franklin into the Schuylkill River, unroll one window and glide like a mermaid toward the surface. If you're dragged by the pull of the tide into the Atlantic Ocean, float on your back to forestall exhaustion and subsequent drowning. Should you fall through a hole in the ice, look upward to find the circle of light that will help you escape. Should someone on the SEPTA subway have a seizure, stuff your wallet or a wooden spoon in his mouth to prevent him from biting his tongue in two pieces. Do not attempt to move an accident victim. He may have a broken neck or spinal column injury and moving him could result in lifelong paralysis and a colostomy bag for him, a lifetime of guilt over putting someone in a wheelchair for you.

The main thing is not to panic.

Don't let anyone into your apartment without first seeing his credentials. If you must let a stranger in, first grab the phone and pretend to be talking to someone on the other end of the line, because then you can always dial 911 if he goes for your throat. Keep a 16 foot distance from him. If he grabs you, go limp. When he loosens his grasp, kick him in the balls or

stomach or try to poke out his eyes. If you can't do any of those things and he unzips his pants, bite down on his penis, even though this will scar you for life. Also: scream, scream, scream, vomit, wet your pants, tell him you have an STD, ask him if he has a sister, explain that you're three months pregnant. Tell him that you understand his rage.

Make yourself seem like a human being.

Accept your fate in the following situations: plane crash, shark attack, a brakeless eighteen-wheeler, buffalo stampede, ice storm in the middle of the North Pole, a sudden fall from a skyscraper, an inoperable malignant brain tumor the size of a pool cue ball. Yes, people have been known to live through all sorts of catastrophes, but do you really want to have a permanent shunt or one side of your head looking like it's been flattened by a snow shovel or third-degree burns covering over 75 percent of your body?

Think about it.

Memorize the steps involved in the Heimlich maneuver in case you're standing in line at Pat's Cheesesteaks and the fat guy near the front chokes on a piece of gristle. If you rescue a person jumping into the river, turn him on his side to drain excess water. Do that mouth-to-mouth, heart-compression technique you learned in high school health class until the paramedics arrive, but refrain from pressing too hard. You could snap somebody's ribs. Ignore squeamishness about pressing your lips to the blue lips of an unattractive person.

This is a life we're talking about here – not a beauty contest.

If a ball rolls into five o'clock traffic, leave it. Find out your allergies as soon as possible. Even though you may be late for a dinner party, don't cut tomatoes with a sharp butcher knife and slippery fingers. Do not blow dry your hair within plopping distance of a bubble bath. Do not climb a ladder in socks,

even if there's a kitten stuck on the roof. Quit reading the book when you're walking down an escalator. By all means, do not spread honey all over your body and lay down in a fire ant pile.

Do not attempt to remove an arrow from your intestines. No one will be mad if you eat the flesh of dead people when you're starving. Don't stick your hand out of the window of the bus to appear whimsical to the man next to you. Stop yourself from petting that drooling Rottweiler outside of Starbucks. He only *looks* friendly.

It's okay to ignore homeless people, especially the young runaways who find strays on frayed ropes to sit by them to elicit pity. Drop a dollar into their baskets without even making eye contact. You are such a good, good person.

If your boyfriend gives you a black eye or breaks your arm, don't cover for him and tell people you ran into a doorjamb or threw yourself on the floor by accident. They know you're too smart for that.

When going from the train to your apartment at night, hold your keys between your fingers and walk as if you have a purpose.

Let your friends know what photo you want to be posted on Facebook should any of these fates befall you. If you let your mom choose the picture, God knows what she'll pick – probably the one of you in braces and Coke bottle glasses and that gingham dress she made you so you could look like Laura from *Little House on the Prairie.*

When entering a large building like Independence Hall, locate all of the exits. They will be in red.

Before meeting up with that hilarious stranger from Tinder, email his stats to all of your girlfriends.

Wait for the traffic light to change to that blinking human form before you cross. Look both ways.

Stay alert. Keep moving. Never, ever let down your guard.

Princess

It's Saturday at 3 a.m. and I'm coming off a hellish shift at Ray's Happy Birthday Bar. It's pouring rain, no taxis in this part of town, and the 23 bus runs about every two hours now. My feet hurt from standing and my mood is black after spending most of the night serving a crowd of out-of-towners – a group of prickish frat boys slumming it and cracking racist jokes. I let them get good and drunk, even send a few shots of Jack their way, and then, when one of the jerkoffs slaps his Am Ex on the bar, I add $100 to the tab. I know they are too drunk and too cocky to eyeball the final tally. Good thing, too, because they leave behind a five-dollar tip and some change. When one of them asks for directions to Washington Avenue to hail a cab to Center City, I send him south instead of north, deeper into darker territory not so friendly to their kind. But hey, they said they were looking for an authentic Philly experience. I am just making sure they get what they asked for.

So I'm standing at the curb, weighing my options, when a car pulls up, splashing filthy rainwater over my sneakers. Now, I know better than to jump into a car with a near stranger,

but it's raining hard, in the way only a summer night in Philadelphia can deliver – appearing out of nowhere, flooding the sidewalks, sending Styrofoam cups and discarded cheesesteak wrappers from Pat's careening in a river of water down the curb. Lightning cracks the sky like the end of the world is right around the corner. And I see from his crag-nosed profile that I do sort of know this guy – he's the uncle of a kid I used to sleep with. Uncle Tony (one of many Uncle Tonys in this part of town). And a former regular at Ray's before Lou, Ray's son and the owner, banned him from setting foot in the place ever again.

He sits in his big maroon Chevy Cadillac, a fat man with a salt-and-pepper crew cut wearing a too-big, shiny Eagles T-shirt. The passenger window rolls down. "Hey, doll," he says. "Get it the car. You're soaked." I hesitate. "Holy Mary, Mother of God, don't be stupid. It's not like I'm some douchebag from Trenton you never met before."

I check the street again. My shirt smells like a cigarette butt after eight hours of serving cheap beer and shots. It sticks wetly to my back. What the hell. I get in the car.

He has the heater running full blast, which I appreciate. The interior is a deep plush maroon and stinks of stale cigars and cheap cologne. "You South?" he asks.

"Yeah, just drop me at Eighth and Morris, and I'll hop out."

A rosary hangs from the rearview mirror with a sad-looking Jesus dangling forlornly on the end.

"Hey, let me ask you something." The car idles. "You hear what happened to my nephew Johnny?" I shake my head. I haven't seen or thought of Johnny in a couple of weeks, not since I kicked him out of my bed. "Smashed by the 147. No helmet, not that it woulda mattered. Run him over while he was on his bike. F-ing SEPTA buses." He drums his pudgy

fingers on the steering wheel. "No chance even for any last words."

"Jesus, sorry, Tony." Too vain to wear a bike helmet. I am starting to remember more about Johnny now. His long curly hair was one of his best features. Though I could be remembering one of the others. They blur together after a while.

"Yeah, well, what can you do?" He doesn't seem that busted up about it. "He left his journals behind though. You ever read them?"

"No." I am starting to think it's time for me to take a pass on the ride and be on my way.

"He ever talk to you about a key? He leave one at your place? I'm wondering, because in his journals he hints a lot about where this key might be. It's the one that opens that garage across the street. Where he stores his bikes, right?"

The car begins to feel a little too warm. I see that I've made a mistake accepting this ride. Maybe a big one.

I grab the door handle. The automatic lock clicks shut. "I don't know what you're talking about, you lunatic. Let me out of here." I remember now why Lou banned him for life from the bar. He'd started a brawl one night about the lack of paper towels in the men's room. After getting no response from Lou, he hurled a bar stool at the big-screen TV behind the bar. He missed the television, but busted the neon Bud Light sign. That was his last night at Ray's. He was crying and wailing, "But I'm a Mummer!" when they tossed him out onto Passyunk Avenue.

"Listen, just tell me where the key is and I'll take you home like I said," he pleads.

I reach in my purse to take out my pepper spray. He lunges forward, and, for a second, I think maybe he's going to kiss me. He takes my face in both of his hands and whacks my head hard on the dashboard. Then it's lights out.

Princess

I wake up to the tickle of something licking my ankle. I'm sitting on a cushioned chair with my hands tied behind my back, feet bound together by what looks like a dog leash, and duct tape covering my mouth. The something washing my foot is a fat brown dog, one of those pugs with the curly tails and popped-out eyes. It wears a fancy pink collar. I jerk my leg. The dog looks up at me, eyes rolling stupidly and blackish tongue hanging out of the side of its mouth. At least my clothes are still on; all except for my shoes.

I struggle against the ties and look around. I've descended into the middle of South Philly grandmother land. My best guess is that it's Anthony's mom's house. It's an old-school Italian living room with thick, pink shag carpet, a blue leather sofa, and a matching armchair covered in plastic. The surfaces are decorated with doilies and throw pillows with fluffy white kittens stitched in needlepoint, along with Afghans, Virgin Marys, and numerous renditions of Jesus – Jesus and a lamb, Jesus on the cross, baby Jesus, Jesus flashing the peace sign, and Jesus looking like a hipster. The best is a picture featuring the holiest of holy – Jesus, John F. Kennedy, and Pope John Paul II. How they got the three of them together for that photo op is anybody's guess. Underneath it all is the trapped-in smell of old lady. Part Jean Naté body wash, part pancake makeup, and part getting closer to death. No wonder Johnny never brought me here. He had mentioned he was crashing at his gran's for a while, but didn't say he was living with an old-fashioned stereo as big as a spaceship, giant fake flowers in an even bigger shiny vase, and a crappy oil painting of the family hanging in a gold frame above the couch: Grandma, Anthony, and Johnny. Another unholy trinity.

I've got to make sense of this somehow before the lunatic returns. I am starting to recall a little bit more about Johnny.

I don't usually chat up customers, but Wednesdays are slow at Ray's. He wore low-slung jeans and a white T-shirt that stretched tight across the muscles of his chest and back.

I was new to the joint – the first female bartender, but I didn't need to prove myself. Lou, Ray's son, was a friend of my dad's. I just wanted a job where I could get paid in cash and stay off the radar of the IRS for a while.

He looked just like all the white, angst-filled hipster dudes you see there or at the Dive or Pope's – in their grungy T-shirts from Circle Thrift and skinny girl jeans with one leg rolled up so that they can get around the city on their beat-up, expensive vintage bikes. Chain wallets, ironic tattoos, and multiple piercings. I can't say that he was any different, except he said "please" and "thank you" when I set the PBRs in front of him and he was writing in a red spiral notebook – like the kind you'd use in high school. His wrote feverishly and I imagined it was a screenplay about a misunderstood twenty-something, or a proposal to City Council for a more sustainable Philly, or song lyrics for his Flaming Lips sound-alike band so that they could get another gig at Johnny Brenda's.

We started talking about what he was writing. He had a rough voice, the voice of a smoker who'd picked up the habit with a vengeance in junior high, though he couldn't have been too far into his twenties. He told me he'd always kept a journal. "I know, I'm a pretentious prick. No poetry though," he added. I asked him what he wrote about. "Deep, dark secrets," he said. He didn't look like he'd lived long enough to have anything worth hiding, so I figured he was making shit up. "I write descriptions about places. Like this dirty little bar and that old man over in the Elvis shirt with his head on the table. I wrote a paragraph about you." He read it to me. He was generous.

I took him home to my latest cheap house on one of those narrow one-way streets without trees – this shitty apartment next to the JC Chinese restaurant. I go to sleep and wake up smelling chop suey. It's the kind of street where you hear Mexican music playing and jacked-up cars revving at all hours. I don't mind. I usually sleep through anything, like a dead person. Junk lines my street – crushed Red Bull cans and empty Corona bottles, dirty diapers, and abandoned condoms. Like the rest of the city, South Philly changes from block to block and I happen to live on one where the shades are always drawn shut with yellow mini blinds and the windows sport signs reading, *Se cuarta a renta*. But the apartment is dirt-cheap, and I have lived in worse places.

Johnny had a bike, of course, and insisted on taking it inside with us. He didn't stay the night, which I appreciated. He came back to the bar the next night. I took him home again. He had a tongue ring, which I also appreciated. This went on for a while, not long, maybe three weeks, and always with that stupid Raleigh bike, and then one night when he wasn't at the bar, I brought someone else home and Johnny showed up at my door, ringing the bell again and again until I answered, and bleated, "But you don't understand. I love you!"

I told him to get real, get lost, and get a new dive bar to hang out in – try the Royal or Pope's – not Ray's anymore. He called me a fucking bitch. I pushed over his bike and he squealed like an adolescent girl, picked up the bike, and pedaled furiously away in his high-top Converse sneakers, never to be heard from again.

Except he *had* come back.

I consider my next move. I imagine the *Inquirer* headline: "Stupid Bartender Murdered by Moron." As if on cue, the moron walks in.

Tony has changed into yet another Eagles jersey. He seems glad to see me awake. "Look, I don't like this any more than you, but I figured we'd get lots more done if you wasn't running loose." His eyes are bloodshot, but instead of smelling like booze, he smells like Old Spice.

He turns on the big-screen TV plastered next to the family portrait and turns it to the classics sports channel, the one that replays old football games where you already know how it all ends and who wins. "Now, I'm going to pull off this tape and it's going to hurt, so I'm sorry about that. Don't scream."

He rips the tape off in one quick motion, taking half my lip with it. I scream. "You'll scare the dog!" he says. The dog is stretched out across the floor on its back, snoring. Tony pushes the volume up on the TV so that Howard Cosell's nasally voice booms out into the room. I am going to die listening to Cosell announcing a bygone two-point conversion. "My ma is down the shore, but she'll be back before too long, so we got to figure this out quick."

Maybe if I stall long enough, Granny'll rescue me. That's assuming she isn't an accomplice in whatever this mess is. I've seen plenty of these South Philly old ladies, sweeping up the sidewalk in front of the house early in the morning with their teeth still sitting in a jar by the bed. Cross them, and they'll cold cock you in a second with the broom or whatever else is handy.

Tony picks up a red spiral journal from the doily-covered coffee table. "Johnny wrote a lot about you. I just need to know where the key is. He writes that he's left it with someone he trusts. Well, I can't find it here, and believe me, I've looked under every doily and cookie jar in the place."

"I barely knew the kid. We maybe hung around once."

He frowns. "Oh yeah? Does this sound like you?" He flips to the middle of the book and reads a description of my apartment

with the rusty kitchen sink and the rats scrabbling in the walls. He describes what I look like in bed and the color of the mole under my right arm. Tony snaps the books shut and pushes up the sleeve of my shirt. "What a coincidence! This shit about you goes on for pages and pages. I know Johnny told you something more about where the key is, didn't he? If I can find the key, I can get to the money, and if I get to the money, you got nothing to worry about."

In fact, Johnny may have mentioned a key of some kind.

He was a chatty Cathy. Problem is I'm not much of a listener. Still, I would've remembered money talk.

"He wrote about you like you was his girlfriend," Tony says, waving the notebook under my nose.

"We were fuck buddies, that's it." His eyes flick to the Jesus on the wall. "We weren't going steady or anything. He didn't hand over his old high school letter jacket from St. Nick's. I don't know about any of this."

"You know the A&M garage across the street from Ray's? He keeps his bikes in that place. You know that?" I nod. "You ever wonder what else he might have tucked away in there? You ever wonder why he was delivering office paper at two in the morning?"

Working as a bartender teaches you pretty quick that people will eventually spill whatever it is that's gnawing at them. All you have to do is wait. And so I wait. And keep telling him that I don't know anything about a key. And wait some more. Repeat my innocence. Then shut my mouth, praying he doesn't beat the shit out of me or worse.

He paces the room. I notice he's not wearing any shoes, just long white athletic socks pulled up to the knees. I suppose we're both shoeless so the carpets don't get messed up. He explains the "sitch." Johnny was a drug courier – some of his friends

were too, but he was the head honcho, the numero uno courier. The drugs were shipped from New Jersey to Johnny's storage place at A&M in bicycle frames. Johnny would then distribute the bikes to his other courier pals to take apart so they could peddle their wares to various eager customers far and wide across the City of Brotherly Love.

I am starting to have a little more respect for the dead kid.

Tony doesn't elaborate on his role. "I was just the connector, mostly, with these guys in Jersey. I never touched the bikes. I never even seen the bikes. I just arranged for the shipments. To tell you the truth, I had no idea what was really going on until the thugs in Jersey contacted me and told me." His voice is stiff, like one reserved for false testimony in court. And then, it seems, Johnny got greedy – maybe he needed some new guitar amps or fancier pens – and he started keeping a portion of the proceeds locked away in the storage center along with the bikes. And then the Jersey guys, these "bicycle distributors," wanted to know where their money had gone.

They didn't want to hear about how Tony couldn't get to it or how Johnny had taken the secret to his grave. They just wanted to get paid, and fast. "They been here twice already," Tony says.

"What does your ma say about this?"

His thick, caterpillar-looking eyebrows fly up in surprise. "She don't say nothing. She just grinds up beans for coffee and gives them cake."

I don't believe him, but I don't say that either. I bet Granny's grown used to the perks the money brought in, the status she earned for the extra church tithes; maybe she even bought a few wigs made out of real hair or new plastic covers for the furniture. "How about if I make you a deal? You let me out of here and we forget about this whole thing. I'll talk to Lou about you being

allowed back in the bar. You know, we'll start with Tuesday night karaoke. You can sing Johnny Cash or Britney or whoever the hell you want. But you gotta let me out of here first."

"They'll be coming back soon," Tony says. He actually wrings his hands, like an old lady. "And now I got you to deal with and no key and no money either."

"I'm telling you, I'll put in a good word with Lou. No problem. I bet he'd even help you out with the money if I ask him nice. And talk to these Jersey thugs. He's a popular guy. People love him."

Tony gives a big long sigh. "Give me a second." He paces some more and then says, "You need anything? Like a glass of water?" I nod and he disappears into the kitchen.

The dog looks up at me as though we are old friends, then jumps on my lap, landing on my full bladder. Her collar jingles. It's an ornate thing with a name tag and other assorted doggie bling. She starts licking my face. "Get off!" I try to shake her from my legs.

From the other room Tony yells, "Get down, Princess!"

A church bell rings from some distant street, signaling the approach of dawn. I recall something else about Johnny. Like every other hipster kid, his skinny, undernourished body was plastered with tattoos. Nothing too strange, no Tweety Bird or names of ex-girlfriends drawn in Gothic lettering. He did have an awful tattoo on his ankle though. I spotted it the first night because of his rolled-up pant leg. A dog. A pug, to be exact.

"What's that?" I'd asked.

"That's Princess," he said. "She holds the key to my heart."

I told him to stop talking like a Danielle Steele novel and take off his tighty-whities already. Which he did.

Tony comes back into the room, holding a glass of water etched with daisies. It looks as though he's reconsidered the

situation. "Aw, shit. Aw, Christ. Look, I really just wanted to talk to you, but you bartenders are intimidating."

I make my face as blank as possible. He sets the water glass down very carefully on one of the doilies. "Listen, you can think about it, but I have to pee," I tell him. "I have to pee right now and if you won't let me use the bathroom, I will piss all over this velveteen cushion. You know how hard it will be to clean? I bet these are antique chairs. I bet this fringe is from the old country. Irreplaceable. How would you explain that to your ma?"

He shrugs, trying to shake off his look of concern. "The dog coulda done it."

"That little thing?" The dog scratches itself, fancy pink collar jingling, and then begins grooming its private parts in earnest. "There is no way the amount I have to piss could come out of that runt. Trust me. I don't know what time it is exactly, but I would guess I haven't used the powder room in a good four hours."

He looks torn, but finally he begins to untie me. I wish the knots were in the front, so I could kick him in his fat face. When I'm free, I say, "We'll work this out." I try to walk casually and not bolt for the door. I close and lock the bathroom door. I figure I have about one shot at knocking him out. I search the room. A toilet plunger isn't going to do the trick, and neither is a plastic lady torso whose skirts cover the extra toilet paper rolls. I could Aqua Net him to death or stab him in the eye with a bobby pin.

I study my face in the vanity mirror. I've got a nice purple shiner and a crust of blood on my upper lip. If I make it out of here, I'm going to treat myself to a real haircut, not one of those ten-dollar Chop Shop hatchet jobs.

Then I catch sight of it in the reflection of the mirror: a heavy-duty Virgin Mary statue with her hands outstretched as

if she's saying, *Don't look at me. It's not my fault.* She's propped up in the bathroom window, surrounded by cotton balls and Max Factor makeup. Hail Mary, full of grace. I tuck her under my arm.

Tony hovers outside the door. "Okay, listen, you'll talk to Ray then?" He sees what I'm carrying. "Hey, what're you doing? Put that back! Ma will kill you!"

I walk into the living room. He follows. "No kidding, don't be smart."

I put a little distance between us and then, with the VM held out in front of me like a bat, I spin around and smack him as hard as I can across the head. The statue stays in one piece. His head does not. He gives a little "Oh" of surprise and touches his temple in disbelief. He staggers and bleeds all over the plastic on the furniture. He looks more horrified about the mess he's making than he does about losing his life. When he sees the blood spill onto his Eagles shirt, his legs accordion and down he goes. I've never seen anyone bleed quite like that. We've had two guys drop dead at Ray's, but neither were bleeders. The cut isn't going to kill him, but it will buy me enough time to get out and make it to the storage space. I'm sure the money is there along with one or two of Johnny's stupid bikes. The Jersey jerks will get to Tony soon enough. Or his own mother when she sees what he's done to her living room.

Hey, I'm not a murderer, just an opportunist.

The Virgin Mary statue lies on her back on the pink shag carpet, staring up at the ceiling, still looking as if she's just an innocent bystander. Except she's not. In fact, she may have just changed my life. Now, I'm not going to start genuflecting and hanging out at the doors of St. John's. I don't believe much in that Catholic shit, but you never know. Maybe I'll even buy a Virgin Mary night light from the Italian Market after I get the

money and move out of my shitty apartment on Morris and into a slightly less shitty one farther west.

I take hold of Princess's collar – rabies vaccine, heart-shaped name tag, and a key. I remove it and slip it in my pocket. I consider leaving the animal. It's not like she'd be much of a watch dog for me. She doesn't seem at all concerned that I cracked Tony in the head and he's now bleeding on the carpet. I look at the dog and she looks back at me with her popped-out googly eyes. She wags her stubby tail halfheartedly as though unsure about the deal too. "You're not much of an accomplice," I tell her. I could dump her on the streets. Some sappy grandma would take her in. Or she'd get hit by a bus just like Johnny.

"All right, Princess, let's go." I pick her up. "You can stay with me," I say. "For now."

On Top of the World

At the age of 35, Hazel finds herself living with her elderly mother in a retirement community called On Top of the World. The front of the subdivision has the name written in a golden scroll over a sun-faded globe, as if to suggest, "Here are all of the places you'll never go."

In the beginning, Hazel told herself the arrangement was only temporary. Her mother had a painful knee replacement, and now walks as if one foot is on the curb and the other in the gutter. She is doing what any good daughter would – taking a leave of absence from her paralegal job in Philadelphia and moving down to Tampa until her mother can maneuver the grocery cart at the Publix on her own. But two weeks have turned into four, and one month into two, and in the meantime, she received a polite letter from work stating that if she doesn't return within another week, they will be moving in a different direction (away from her).

There are moments when she and her mother are sitting down in front of Maury Povich at 4 p.m. with their dinner on TV trays in front of them, and Hazel wonders if maybe she hasn't fallen a bit too far from the norm. She focuses instead

on the good she's doing for her mother, recalling lines from a book she read in high school, "It is a far, far better thing that I do …." She can't remember the title, but vaguely recalls that the speaker was then decapitated.

Not that death is on her mind, but it's hard not to think about it, living in a place where the old people drop dead at an alarming rate. The main sound effect of the community is the wail of the ambulance siren. First, Mr. Baker popped off from a coronary, then Mrs. Enzmann was found prone in her front yard with the garden hose watering her petunias, and just last week, Mr. Markett, whose long-suffering wife has seen him degenerate from Alzheimer's, jumped into the shallow end of community pool. Her mother, on the other hand, seems to have a new zeal for life. One of the youngest residents at age 67, she has started going back to church again, urging Hazel to join her.

"Mother, I'm an atheist," she has reminded her, as they sit in the living room, shoving stuffed animals into clear plastic bags. The creatures are the fruits of her mother's crochet club: six or seven of the residents who get together to make toys for the burn victims at the Shriner's Hospital. It makes them all feel noble, as if they're really doing something good. For Hazel, it's difficult to give the stuffed animals up. She's still getting the hang of crocheting and so it takes her a week to finish a stuffed dog, and by then, she's grown fond of it and doesn't want to relinquish the toy to some stranger with burns over 75 percent of her body, who probably is suffering too much to truly appreciate it anyway.

"Oh, dear, honey, I forgot to tell you," her mother says as they are tying up the tops of the plastic bags. "The Auttersons are coming to dinner tonight with their son. What's his name? Could he be named Lesley?" She taps vaguely at her forehead.

"I don't know, mother!" That's a lie, because Hazel knows exactly who Les is. Mrs. Autterson talks about her son often, gesturing at the giant photo of him she keeps on the mantelpiece, one of those cheesy corporate photos in black and white. But he does have a nice profile, despite a slightly weak chin and slicked-back hair, giving him a furtive animal look, as if he might be a biter. And she certainly noticed when he came to stay with his parents. She has, in fact, taken to riding her mother's bicycle around the subdivision. It's a ridiculous contraption; it looks like a giant tricycle with its three wheels and wicker basket between the handlebars, but it's the only way she can think of running into him, short of offering to deliver a homemade pie to the Auttersons' front door.

"Well, anyway, I thought it might be nice for you to be around someone your own age," her mother says.

"I guess I don't have anything better to do with my time!" Hazel stomps out of the room to her bathroom, slamming the door like a teen. She stares at herself in the mirror, appraising. She looks pale and puffy, the result, no doubt, of gorging on leftover Easter Peeps and Mountain Dew.

Hazel is no spring chicken, that's for sure, but she's still got an okay figure and good teeth courtesy of dear old mom and the orthodontist. She imagines how her mother might describe her if she turned up missing: "Oh, let's see. Dishwater-colored hair, about shoulder length. I think at one point, she referred to it as a bob. Brownish eyes. Slightly upturned nose." Or how the morgue workers might discuss her, should her body be found on the side of the road, like a fallen deer. She imagines them standing over her, two men in white coats, while she lies naked under a sheet on a metal table. Would one of them note the delicate turn of her ankle before slicing her open from stem to stern?

She is losing some fundamental adult quality – this ability to reflect and evaluate a situation. She's like a child again. But if she left, her mother would be bereft! Who would take her to Eckerd's to refill her arthritis prescription? Who would help her exercise her poor distressed knee, a knee that will now have a jagged scar across it forever? "Well, there goes my swimsuit modeling career," her mother had joked.

Who would sit with her at night and help her puzzle out the questions on *Jeopardy!*? "What is desperation, Alex?"

Everything around the house is broken or on the verge of breaking. The light bulb on the front porch needs replacing, and the ceiling fans are making these strange whirring sounds when turned above medium speed – sounds that make Hazel think that one of the blades is going to whir off unexpectedly, causing certain decapitation of her or her mother. The toilet leaks, the bathtub spigot won't stop dripping, and the dryer now has taken to getting their clothes only halfheartedly dry, chugging along and then coughing out the clothes still damp and wilted.

Since Hazel's hiding out, they can't call the community super, Gerald, to fix anything, because that might raise suspicion of Hazel's still being there. She has taken to wearing certain minor disguises when she runs errands, a blue kerchief paired with large Jackie-O sunglasses, a straw hat and blond wig on other days. So far, no one has approached her mother about it, but Hazel knows her days are numbered.

Every time she brings up the idea of leaving, her mother nods, says she understands. "Of course, you have things ...." They both stare into the air as if wondering what things she might have to return to. A dead-end paralegal job? A dying cactus? But Hazel does have things; she has food spoiling in the fridge and acquaintances who sometimes still forward her videos of cats misbehaving. It seems that every time Hazel

makes a feint toward an exit, her mother suffers another minor mishap – a dropped water glass, a misplaced checkbook, a full-blown crying jag behind the thin door of her bedroom – until, finally, Hazel relents. One more week, one more week.

But just yesterday her boss, Mark Becker, called to remind her that her leave of absence ends in one week. She has been gone so long that the picture she has of him in her mind has gone fuzzy. Dark, foxy hair and a mustache. Red suspenders. She'd had a from-afar crush on him for years, but he was unhappily, though dedicatedly, married. She has 10 unheard messages on her voicemail.

"How you doing?" asks Mark Becker, Esquire. She pictures him idly snapping his red suspenders. His mustache makes him look like a villain in an old-time movie. She would like him to tie her to train tracks.

"I'm on top of the world!" she says, winding the phone cord around her arm like a bracelet.

"We'd like you back. I need some help on the Vitullos." The Vitullos' file is bloated with evidence, a divorce that's been simmering for 20 years. Every time they get close to an agreement, one of them unearths new evidence of blame – old love letters, blurry photos, a past-due electric bill.

"Let me think about it," she says.

"Do you miss work?" Her mother wants to know after she hangs up. Does she? Does she miss the days of photocopying discovery for divorce cases? Of making chatter with the other paralegals over gritty coffee? Does she miss riding home on the subway in the dark, surrounded by strangers? As she aged in Philadelphia, she felt herself slowly shrinking into the world of the unseen-by-men. At least here, she gets noticed by the arthritic Mr. Baker and Mr. Johnson. In the city, she has become something of a ghost.

Each morning, Hazel helps her mother with leg exercises, moving her knee up and down and around and then counter-clockwise. Her mother grimaces, but she's a trooper – she's never been much of a complainer, never really been much of a talker at all. Hazel also takes her mother to the community pool, a calm place filled with elderly women doing the breast-stroke sedately across the length of the pool, their hair tucked up in bright plastic bathing caps. They're like an elderly troop of Esther Williamses. Many still have distinct traces of beauty on their lined faces, and their arms are tan and strong. Many of them are widows, having had to learn how to survive on their own without the assistance of their husbands, who seemed not to have the same will to live.

When Hazel's father died five years ago, she remembers hearing her mother call for her from behind the bathroom door on the day of his funeral, using her newly frail voice. Hazel went into the bathroom and found her mother sitting on the closed lid of the toilet, her face made up with too much rouge, her best black dress on, with a pair of pantyhose crumpled in her hands.

"I need your help with these," her mother said. She waved the pantyhose.

Hazel realized that this was one of the intimacies of their marriage, this weekly Sunday ritual with her father kneeling before her mother to put on her pantyhose before church. It struck her that from that moment on, he never would do so again. She pushed that thought down as best she could and bent down in front of her mother to help her with one limp foot after another. Her mother thanked her and patted her on her arm. "You are a dear," she said, her voice cracking. It was one of the few times in her life that she could remember her mother using such a tender word.

As soon as she could, Hazel went singing out the door, promising to return soon, promising to fulfill her daughterly duties at a later date. And now, here she is, years later, forced to make good on that promise. How much time is enough?

She leaves her mother at the library and goes to the tanning parlor. She situates herself on the tanning bed at Tans R Us in her mother's bra and underwear. It's not that she doesn't have her own bra and underwear; it's that damn old dryer that leaves her clothes damp and smelling like mildew. She and her mother are nearly the same size, though Hazel would never think of wearing a bra like this one in real life – it's hefty, manila-colored, offering full gal coverage. Hazel remembers a time not too, too far off when she had her own bras, pretty ones, with rosettes in the center, and she wore them knowing that a man might see her naked.

The tanning bed looks like a space-age coffin with lights underneath it to illuminate the body. She lies down on the bed with her eyes shut and the warm heat thrums through her. The blond woman out front asked her how much color she wanted, and she joked, "Turn it up to skin cancer level." The girl didn't laugh. She just blew a giant purple bubble with her wad of gum and handed Hazel her receipt. Now, in the booth with the manufactured heat hitting her from all sides, she wiggles a little, finding it hard not to think about sex – not like she can even remember the last time she had sex.

That's not 100 percent true. She does remember. In fact, it's a preoccupying thought, one that comes unbidden to her at odd moments. As she pokes at a package of chicken breast in the grocery store, for instance, or when she's brushing her teeth with the electric toothbrush, or when the old dryer starts to clunk across the floor.

George Alfonso was the last one, a married lawyer who practiced litigation and liked to joke that he would sue her if she ever told his wife about the affair. She still has nightmares about him, though in her dreams, he's changed into a doctor who always calls to deliver bad news. "I hate to tell you this, but that leg has got to come off from the knee down," he'll say in the dream. Or, "A mastectomy can be a liberating thing for some women." In real life, he saved his own bad news for just after they'd had vigorous and unsatisfying sex in her studio apartment. He had one hairy leg draped over hers when he announced it was the last time he'd be seeing her. "Why did you come over here? Why did we just have sex?" she asked, sitting up.

"I wanted you to have something good to remember me by," he explained, patting her arm.

The next day, she called his wife and described his penis in exacting detail, how it curved up at the end like a question mark, and the mole on his back in the shape of Canada. The wife demanded to know her name.

"I'm no one," she said. "No one you would know."

When he showed up at her apartment that night, banging on the door, she sat at the kitchen table, squinting at the Thursday crossword puzzle, wondering if she had made a mistake by asserting herself. What if he really were a nice person underneath all of that seeming horribleness?

He kept pounding until one of her neighbors came out into the hall and threatened to call the police. He gave one last feeble pound. She stood on the other side of the door. Maybe, if he said one last nice thing, she might let him in. She peered through the peephole, seeing him distorted, his head a giant blur. "I know you're in there," he said, looking up. Then he left, as they always do.

While lying in the tanning bed, Hazel focuses her attention on Les. She imagines taking him into the guest room where she's now sleeping – the one with the twin bed. Candles, there must be candles somewhere, and then she thinks about what would happen if one of the candles got too close to the duvet and it caught on fire and then *whoosh*! She and Les would be recipients of knitted woodland animals from the Shriner's Hospital. Fine, no candles, it's too hot for candles and so she imagines instead a hot tub or a pool, with willow trees overhead. Les begins strolling toward her in black bathing trunks, but then it seems that she's left out one of her roller skates and he trips on it, lurching forward, cracking his head on the cement lip of the pool, and blood leaks into the water in red ribbons. My God, she can't even have a sexual fantasy without it ending in destruction.

Hazel sits up in the tanning bed, dizzy. She has tremors in her stomach. It's ridiculous, but she's nervous about meeting this strange man who will probably turn out to have a cleft palate or a love of NASCAR.

Hazel heads to her mother's beauty shop, Curl Up and Dye. The lady at the counter first asks her if she wants to get her mustache removed. Hazel touches her upper lip. "Oh, yes. Fix the eyebrows too." In the middle of it, she finds herself worrying when it will fade, or if she will have a reddish upper lip during dinner as if she's just been punched.

When she returns to the library to pick up her mother, she sees her in the new books section. Hazel watches as her mother reaches up on tiptoe to grab at a novel. When she can't get it, she finds a step stool. Hazel considers intervening, stopping her mother, reminding her of the hurt knee. Before she can say anything, her mother climbs up on the stool, strong as a mountain goat, to snatch up the latest Nora Roberts novel.

Hazel ducks behind the nonfiction section. She waits to give her mother time to climb off the stool. Then, she pretends to walk in for the first time. Her mother gives a little start and waves, saying, "Oh, a nice man helped me with the seven-day fiction."

Hazel has convinced her mother it's time to make a big purchase, a new dryer for the tiny laundry room. The current dryer groans when you open it and, as the minutes tick by on the regular dry cycle, the machine creeps slowly across the floor, as if attempting to escape out the back door, until it unplugs.

At Home Depot, she and her mother are debating the finer points of the Kenmore versus the GE when the salesman swoops in. He is a roundish guy with a pleasant face and a short crew cut. "How can I help you ladies?" he says, with a slight bow. "Tell me what you're looking for and I will find it."

She tries to remember how to flirt. She thinks it involves something to do with her hair, her posture. She pushes out her chest. "We're just looking at upgrading what we have." She smiles, wondering if she has anything between her teeth. "You know, something that'll get the job done." He nods. She imagines how she must appear to him. Her hair isn't terrible and she's wearing a clean shirt. The salesman clasps his hands together. "Are you and your partner hoping to take something home today, or do you want to do some comparison shopping?"

With a sinking stomach, Hazel understands how he must see them. Her mother, who still buys her clothes in the juniors section at Macy's, and Hazel, who has taken to wearing her mother's pants with the elastic bands and, on occasion, even draping a forlorn cardigan over her shoulders to ward off the freezing cold of the air conditioning – the gap in their ages has shrunk somehow in wardrobe. A couple.

"We'll take this one," she says briskly, pointing at the nearest dryer. "We'll figure out how to put it in ourselves."

Her mother mews in protest, but Hazel can't seem to stop herself. She must make her escape before she suffers further humiliation.

When Hazel gets home, she finds her own clothes, many still tucked away in the suitcase in the guest bedroom. She puts on a blue V-neck top, to show off her cleavage, and a denim skirt, worrying that it might be too matchy-matchy, too obvious, too like the little engine that could. But fuck it, she can't worry about everything. She has also changed into her own bra, the one with the black lace, though it's slightly damp, but a person only lives once.

The Auttersons show up exactly at 5 p.m. She can imagine them waiting in the car until just the minute before. It's what all the retired people do. You wait for the next event in your day. The early bird special, bingo at the church, the two-for-one coupons in the Sunday circular, the next free meal at a funeral. Hazel finds that she is waiting too, measuring her days out in the same way with library books and crosswords and the occasional Internet porn search when her mother goes down for a nap.

In person, Les's eyes are closer together than she'd thought and his hair is long in the back and crunchy-looking from some kind of gel. She should feel flattered – because he's trying. He and his khaki shorts are making an effort. He shakes her hand, leaving it wet with sweat. "Sorry," he says. "I'm a little nervous." The laugh he gives sounds exactly like he's saying, "*Ha Ha Ha.*"

During dinner, the Auttersons and her mother discuss various people from church who have died or are in the midst

of dying. "Oh, that poor Mrs. Crowley!" says Mrs. Autterson. "The last time I saw her, she looked just as pale as Jesus."

"Pale as Jesus," Les snorts. It's the first time he's spoken all night. "Was Jesus notoriously pale, or are we confusing him with the Holy Ghost?"

"It's an expression, honey," his mother says.

"I don't think these were adjectives found in the New Testament. That fatty bit of Pontius Pilot."

"That beanpole, Joseph," adds Hazel. Les gives her a twitch of a smile.

"These English majors," says her mother, passing around the limp little Caesar salad for the third time. She changes the subject to Mr. O'Connor's bladder infection and the conversation patters on, but now Hazel has a bit more of Les's attention and that makes her both self-conscious and satisfied.

Les takes a sip of water. His Adam's apple bobs, and Hazel considers what it might be like to run her tongue up along it. Salty, maybe.

"So, Les, how long are you staying for?" her mother asks during a pause in the conversation.

"A week?" he says. "A week or so, depending."

"Depending on what?" her mother prods.

"Depending on if I don't hang myself in the garage before then."

Hazel snorts.

Mrs. Autterson clucks her tongue. "He just has to say things like that to ruin everyone's good time."

Throughout dinner, it's Mrs. Autterson who makes conversation with Hazel, not Les, who focuses most of his attention at a spot above her head. As Hazel talks about her life, how she's helping out her mother, how she used to work in a law firm, how she's not sure when she's going to go back, she hears

how it must sound to Les – how pathetic, to be living with her mother, to have no ambitions, no plan.

"Now, how long have you been here?" asks Mrs. Autterson.

"Decades?" Hazel says, taking a long gulp of wine.

"Why, just a few weeks," overlaps her mother.

She sees that Les is looking directly at her. Finally, she has gotten his attention.

After dinner, Mr. Autterson suggests they play a couple rounds of Uno. "No, thanks, dad," Les says. He's sitting on his hands.

Hazel's mother clears her throat. "Why don't you show Les around the subdivision for a few minutes?"

"Around the subdivision? It would take no more than 10 minutes."

Mr. Autterson shuffles the deck again in the expert way he has, bellowing, "Come on, looking for the wild card!"

Les follows her into the kitchen. "Do you really want to see the neighborhood?" She leans her hip against the sink, unsure of what to do with her hands. The Auttersons have the same kitchen. With a few variations, the houses are all laid out with the same linoleum, same rails on the bathtubs to prevent slipping. "If I show you the dryer, do you think you might be able to help me put it in?" Every word she says seems to have some vague sexual innuendo to it. "God, that's like the worst opening line for a porn movie."

Something bright comes into his eyes. Oh, yes, finally, they've hit on something they may have in common.

They go into the garage and she thinks, maybe now, maybe this will be the moment, maybe they can clear a spot away on the hood of the Volvo and do it there, maybe he will grab her hair and push her against the wall in a forceful yet non-rapist

way. Instead, they stand around looking at the bras hanging on the makeshift clothesline. He doesn't make a move toward her and Hazel isn't going to be the first one either; she's learned her lesson the last time she was alone with a man, throwing herself at him while he fended her off with the verbal equivalent of pepper spray by saying, "Oh, I think you're a nice girl and all, but ...."

Les leans against her mother's Volvo. "I've got to get out of here," he says. "Living with my parents is death."

"It's not so bad."

"Have you been to the bank? Have you stood in line behind anyone? It's like we're all on the same death train in a Truffaut film."

Oh, God, he's smarter than her. She loves that about him. He continues, "The cockroaches. I had one land on my face the other day." He looks at her. "You like it here?"

Does she? Yes, she likes things about it. She likes being needed. She should've been a nurse. Is it too late to change professions? Les is still talking – about his parents, about how depressing it is, about how as soon as he gets some money together, he's out of here.

She gestures to the dryer box. "I'd do anything to get this thing installed."

"Anything?" says Les. He actually licks his lips. He leans in toward her.

The edge of the dryer box presses into her back. "Say something nice."

"I think ...." He searches her face, as if looking for a single good feature. "I think you have beautiful eyebrows." He brushes his finger across her forehead. He leans in and kisses her. It's a polite kiss, like you might give someone during a rehearsal for

a play. He pulls away, wearing a puzzled look. "Do you smell something funny?"

"Like gasoline?"

"Like spoiled milk?"

That would be her bra, she realizes. The not-quite-dry sexy bra she wore for just this purpose. Or something like it. "I don't smell anything." She pushes him back against the car, then drops to her knees, banging them painfully on the concrete. She looks up at him, and is relieved to see his eyes on her, completely, totally enthralled. "If I do this, will you do something for me?" He nods, his dear Adam's apple bobbing.

As she unzips his khaki Dockers, Mr. Autterson calls out, "Uno!"

It only takes a half an hour to move the old dryer into the garage and replace the new one. After he's finished, Hazel takes the pineapple upside-down cake out of the oven and brings it into the dining room. They all look up from their cards. Her mother beams. "Now, aren't you two a sight for sore cataracts!" she says.

"What did you think of Lester. Lesley?" her mother asks after they leave. "He seems a little dark."

"I like dark," says Hazel. Her mother says nothing. "Mom, I think I might have to go back soon." She braces herself – for tears, for begging, for the wringing of hands. Her mother looks back at her with watery blue eyes. "Please don't cry."

Her mother sneezes. "I'm not crying. I'm allergic to whatever perfume you've doused yourself in. No, go back if you want. I can take care of myself," she says, grabbing at the edge of the table to haul herself up into a standing position. She wobbles,

almost falls. "Whoopsie-daisy!" she says, righting herself. "See? Good as new."

When her mother goes to bed, Hazel calls the director of the retirement community. He doesn't answer. She leaves a message, roughening her voice up to make it sound older. "You should look into the Johnsons' house. I believe they have a visitor who has outstayed her welcome." She pauses. "And the Auttersons. I think they're bending the rules too."

She hangs up the phone, a wash of relief running through her. She will be able to go and it won't be her fault. She can still be a good daughter.

She prepares for bed, imagining how Mark Becker will react when she returns. She tries out different expressions in the bathroom mirror – pursing her lips, widening her eyes – then leans in for a closer look. Her eyebrows do look good. Mark Becker, Esquire, she knows, will not notice.

In the background, the dryer hums, finally in working order again.

The Disabled

It is just past Thanksgiving, and they've already begun playing Christmas carols at the theme restaurant where Eleanor works. The music streams from the speakers on the ceiling, like a curse from God, until her head feels stuffed with jingle bells and sleigh bells and holiday bells. She is so bloated with pre-Christmas spirit that she feels sick, as if she's eaten an entire plate of Santa-shaped cookies with an inch of frosting on the top. And yet, somehow, the show must go on!

She has been living on her own in the City of Brotherly Love for just under three months in a shitty garden apartment with a leaky ceiling, and auditioned for zero plays. She can't seem to find the time, what with all the old AMC movie watching she must do and the waitressing and homeless people to dodge.

Table 2 would like more ketchup in a white salad dressing cup, please. Table 3 would like several free refills of Diet Coke, some with a lemon and some with limes. Table 5 would like a new husband and, in the meantime, will take her unhappiness out on Eleanor by sending back her calamari first as not warm enough and then saying the plate burned her fingers. Table 6 explodes with rowdy German tourists who will not tip and

table 7 is the angry wheelchair guy, a regular who purposefully juts his chair out in the middle of the aisle, making it difficult to maneuver around him, especially if you're carrying a heavy tray of food filled with super fun holiday appetizers with sprigs of holly, as if he hopes to be doused by chili con carne. He also wants his food prepared in a very particular way and explains that if it's not – if, for instance, the carrots interact with a peanut in any way – he will keel over and need an EpiPen stuck in his neck, which may spoil the lunch of the other patrons. However, he is also fiercely handsome with a square jaw and the chiseled features of a 1940s movie actor of some kind.

Lately, she feels a defiant buzzing in her chest, as if when she opens her mouth, she will release a long string of bees into the air, buzzing in the key of G. So when the wheelchair guy asks her out, she trills, "Yes, of course I would love to go out with you! How about after work?" Why not? She's off at 4 p.m., and what does she have to look forward to except for numerous glasses of cheap wine and the newspaper crossword puzzles from the break room where half of the clues have already been filled in, often incorrectly, by the line cooks? Why not go out with a strange, angry, crippled man instead?

"I'm busy tonight," he says. She stops, confused. Is she mishearing things? "Tomorrow is better."

He cracks his knuckles. He wears fingerless leather bicyclist gloves, white with Velcro at the wrists.

His wheelchair looks expensive, possibly the Bentley of chairs with a black backpack on the chrome handlebars. He has the body of a gymnast – powerful arms and a muscular torso. But his legs. What must they look like?

"What's your name?" she asks, feeling suddenly awkward and giant standing above him.

"Tiny Tim," he answers quickly, unsmiling. She freezes. He says, "Colin. It's an easy joke." Oh, good, he can laugh at himself (even though he's not, in fact, laughing). That takes some of the pressure off. She still feels cautious, makes a note in her order book to pinpoint the phrases she should banish. *Sorry, I'm running late. Gotta run! Quit walking all over me!*

They make plans for later and he dismisses her with a nod, leaving behind an eight percent tip.

On the way home from work in the freezing Philadelphia rain, she finds herself thrilled to have something new to focus on aside from her own failures in life, which she can easily list from A to Z. Did he become paralyzed while trying to save a passel of mewling kittens in a burning building and then become trapped or pinned under a fallen beam? Was it too many drinks at an Irish pub and he ran into a car of singing church choir kids, spending months in recovery, crying to his mother, "I don't want to live! Why couldn't it have been me?" Or maybe it was a debilitating illness, some weird throwback disease that's usually 100 percent curable if caught soon enough. No way to ask politely, that's for sure.

At the wine shop, she drops three quarters into the March of Dimes plastic canister at the checkout. She is such a good, good person.

She skips up the steps of her apartment. If the date goes well, how will she invite him back to her apartment with the three stairs leading to the front door? She imagines heroically throwing him over her shoulder and carrying him. His legs will be thin and small, like those on a Raggedy Andy doll. He will be light, lighter than expected, and easy to carry around.

They go to see a movie full of shoot-outs, high-speed chases, and bad Santas. As he does in the restaurant, he positions his wheelchair in the aisle, so people have to detour around him.

Someone knocks into him. "Watch it, asshole," he hisses. Heads turn. His level of anger is awe-inspiring – it's like seeing a low-burning fire suddenly doused with gasoline – an explosion of flame and heat.

The guy who has bumped him – a burly, testosterone-puffy man in a Philadelphia Eagles jacket, defers and moves away. "Sorry, man."

After the movie, he takes her back to his place. His bed, which does not (thank God) turn out to have hospital side rails, is a queen-sized mattress low to the ground made up with tangled white sheets. She feels her heart thumping in her ears. She is not sure what to expect – hasn't figured out how to ask him what he can and cannot do.

"It works," he tells her. "I might be crippled, but my cock isn't."

She laughs too high and loud, a laugh like a cartoon schoolgirl.

It's not good. It's awkward and embarrassing and she doesn't know where to look. His kisses are dry and formal, his hands inside her panties within the first 30 seconds. He touches her breasts like a doctor would, weighing them. "Your breasts are uneven," he says. "This one's bigger." When she tries to maneuver to a more comfortable position, he says no, there is only one way for him. She has to be on top. She obliges, self-conscious of her deformed, different-sized boobs. His eyes remain shut. "You move," he directs. "You have to move if this is going to work."

She moves and it hurts but she keeps at it, feeling vaguely charitable and not at all turned on, which makes it even more uncomfortable. It takes a long, long, long, long time, and when she tries to vary her approach, his hands clutch at her hips, strong hands, and set her back to his rhythm. She imagines

herself as Rosie the Riveter, doing her part for the boys over there, over there. He crows, startling her, and she realizes it's over. "You can get off now."

She does.

They lay in the dark on their backs. She waits for him to say something like ... what? *Thanks? Good job?* Even a high five would be better than silence.

She is about to ask him what he might rate that experience when she hears his heavy breath turn into soft teakettle snores. Oh, well. A line pops into her head from her first college play. She was cast as Laura, the sad little lame girl who could never find a suitor. Typecasting, she had thought, at the time. Still thinks. "I was not expecting any gentleman callers," she whispers.

She is trying to find her center; doesn't want to feel like she's constantly on emotional tip toes, liable to fly off in any direction like a ballerina at moment's notice – anger, despair, hope! She must grow up, plant her feet firmly on the ground, establish roots, and become like an oak tree.

"Be here now," her movement teacher, Liesel, instructs. Liesel wears her hair in a long thick braid down her back – so long, it almost touches the ground. The braid looks strong enough to climb. And yet Liesel never steps on it while they're doing the nonsense movement exercises that involve them bending and rippling like trees. She reads a long passage from Thich Nhat Hanh about staying in the present moment, in a soft, seamless voice. Outside of class, Liesel speaks with a slight stutter, every word thought about carefully before she articulates it and many of her sentences coming out twice in a row, as if she doubts she got it right the first time, right the first time.

Liesel has a large, encephalitic-like head and tiny, thin arms. Strangely, she also has a soft big round bottom that seems to help keep her more grounded. She has no trouble moving like a birch or an oak or a palm tree in a hurricane. Her bottom-heavy body defies gravity again and again while Eleanor's arms refuse to allow her fingers to graze the floor when they hang over like unstrung marionettes.

She should try harder. She should recognize how fortunate she is to have all of her limbs in working order. She should be running races, vaulting beams, grateful for the use of her legs, the way she doesn't have to think before moving, it just happens.

Liesel finishes her passage and closes her book. Her eyes rest on Eleanor when she says, "And now, stop." They freeze in space and Eleanor tries, really tries, not to imagine how stupid she looks, frozen with jazz hands meant to represent bare winter branches.

She calls her long-distance best gay friend Joseph to tell him about Colin. They met at her ninth-grade audition for *Annie*. At first, Eleanor convinced herself she was in love with him – he could tap dance, he did great imitations of Mickey Rooney as well as Shirley Temple, and he made her laugh until she peed her pants. As soon as he realized she thought he was boyfriend material, he said, "Oh, Dorothy, we have to work on your instincts." He always called her Dorothy, and wanted her to call him Lillian, like the Gish sisters. And yet despite this affection he had to say the words to her, "I love boys. All boys. I love you, but not like that." And she was heartbroken for a day and then she got the part of one of the main orphans, and felt better about herself.

Now, she explains to Joseph that she needs his advice. He already knows it has to do with love, because it always has to do with love.

Joseph is slightly hard of hearing. She tries not to think of it as an affectation. When she mentions that she's dating a guy in a wheelchair, he exclaims, "With no hair?! Like, none?" She speaks louder, saying no, he's disabled. "On cable? What is he, a weatherman?" Their conversations flow much better in person. She confesses to Joseph that she feels guilty because of, you know, her non-disabilities. Also, she explains, he's not even that nice and the sex is bad.

"What!" he yells. "Do you like him or are you dating him because you feel like you should? Are you that lonely?" Yes, she says. He makes a tsking noise. "You need to change your internal monologue. Your interior voice is a Jewish mother going, 'What're you complaining for? At least you have your legs!' Get out more, for God's sake."

Colin invites her to a cocktail party thrown by his ex-girlfriend, Chelsea, at her apartment in Rittenhouse Square. Who lives like this? With real furniture purchased from real stores and not stuff that they've found next to the garbage on their way to work?

Chelsea is beautiful, with a medley of springy red ringlets like a girl from a fairy-tale book. After a few drinks, Eleanor finds herself shivering on the patio alone with the ex, sharing a cigarette. Chelsea stares at Eleanor with slanted almond eyes and says, "I bet you think he just became a dick, right? That his accident changed him from this sensitive, sweet guy into an angry one, right? Is that what you think?"

Eleanor says yes, actually, yes, that has occurred to her.

"Did he tell you he has MS? Or that he was shot down in Iraq?"

"I didn't know he was in Iraq," Eleanor images him – a war hero!

"He wasn't. Those are just the stories he tells. It was a car accident. His fault. Many dead." Chelsea takes a delicate sip of her martini. "He was always a prick. If anything, he's nicer now." She smiles at Eleanor, revealing a row of tiny, straight white teeth like those you'd find in a baby doll. She exhales a long streak of cigarette smoke and they both watch as it unwinds in the cold air above their heads.

Some nights, after work finishes and she drops into her futon at 1 a.m., she spends the rest of her night chasing the orders down in her dreams, with everything larger and more cartoonish than in real life. The cooks move in slow motion, the customers scream about their orders with rivers of color spilling out of their mouths, the floor is littered with banana peels and ice puddles. On those nights, it's like she is working a double shift; no matter what, she can't seem to escape the stress of waiting tables.

She is in the service industry, after all. This means that she is meant to remain cheerful, use a bright voice and say "I'm sorry" 500 times a day, even when she is really sorry zero of those times.

"I'm sorry your chimichanga isn't hot enough," she says to a frowning man in a business suit bursting at the seams. What she would like to say is, "I hope you eat these fried beans and your stomach explodes."

That's one of the things she admires about Colin – he just doesn't seem to give a shit what people think of him. He says whatever he wants and people are so taken aback that they seldom respond to his rudeness.

He rages at everyone while Eleanor watches, in equal parts amazed and embarrassed. The clerk at the CVS who isn't able

to get the Trojans fast enough gets called an obese Slav, the guy in the aisle of the bus who doesn't move out of the way fast enough is rammed in the shins, the hostess with the Southern accent who doesn't understand that he wants to sit by the window is told she suffers from Fetal Alcohol Syndrome. He lashes out at anyone he perceives as thwarting him and then shakes it off like a Lab does water. She realizes that she's waiting for him to do the same to her, but he never even raises his voice. He's unfailingly polite to her, says please and thank you, makes a killer cappuccino with the perfect snowball of foam on top, and lets her sleep in on his giant bed, swaddled in 500 thread count sheets. Meanwhile, she waits for him to decide she's a waste of time.

The holiday gift looms on the horizon – this big weighty thing. They've been dating for one month; what's the anniversary symbol for that? "Grass," Joseph tells her over the phone. "I believe you're supposed to get each other something made of grass. Or corn husks, I forget which."

"That's three months," she counters.

"What I Did for Love" plays on her iPod as she steps on the Broad Street Line on her way to find the perfect Christmas gift for Colin. She feels like shouting it to the people waiting on the platform, come on, people, sing it with me, "Can't forget! Won't regret! What I did for love." This compilation of old songs comes from her high school musical theater days, and she has a whole bevy of them to choose from. It turns out that it's actually true that musicals cheer a person up. Who could feel blue after hearing "A Bushel and Peck" from *Guys and Dolls*? She thinks about mentioning this to Colin, but stops herself, wondering if he might have something negative to say about people who can execute high kicks.

It will ever be thus, she realizes. She will always be checking her thoughts against his possible reaction and imagining disaster before it strikes.

She browses the bins at the Circle Thrift – a hipster-type Goodwill store that tries very hard not to look like a Salvation Army by putting retro clothes on one rack, and hanging up funky ugly paintings of kittens on the walls.

The furniture can be found in the back of the store by the non-handicapped accessible restroom. Eleanor's entire living space has been built from cast-off pieces of this store and whatever she had left over from college: furniture that is more than slightly distressed, bookshelves with bowed sides from water damage, a coffee table with a bum leg held steady by a wad of napkins, a TV stand made of an upside-down packaging crate with "Bombay, India," stenciled on the side. Though the dishes and other items are arranged nicely, they're still mismatched pieces given up by people who have died or divorced or moved on in some way.

They have a giant plastic toilet seat for old people or the disabled. Should she jokingly buy him a hemorrhoid chair? A puffy toilet seat? A stained suede jacket? Something kitschy? She picks up a shepherdess figure with a chip on her finger and no sheep in sight. She has no idea if he would have a sense of humor about it. The shepherdess has dark hair and a row of daises around her head; she looks like a hopeful, slightly deranged Snow White, with one of her cornflower blue eyes half chipped off, which gives her a winking, jaunty look.

The girl at the register wears kitty cat eyeglasses and has her lip pierced right in the center with a giant hoop. She rings up the purchase while still talking to the other girl next to her, a similarly pierced and outfitted girl wearing a peppermint-striped

knit cap. "And like, this guy goes, 'I don't think I should have to pay full price for something that's used.' ... I'm like, 'Uh, it's a dollar forty-nine and you are in a thrift store.' ... Douchebag."

"You get what you pay for," Eleanor chimes in, handing over her five-dollar bill. They both look at her and say nothing. More friends she won't be having. They are not her type, she decides. But she must find some who are.

Maybe there will be a miraculous moment where she'll convince him to try standing, and he will resist, but she will keep encouraging him and he will get so angry that he stands up, still holding onto the handles of the chair, sweat pouring down his face, and then he does, he is able to stand, for just one second. That victory would give him confidence to try it again until the moment when he's standing on his own and she says, "Try to walk to me," with her arms out to him, and he does, like a baby fawn, on wobbling legs, one foot in front of the other!

She does not share these fantasies with Colin and they evaporate the first time she sees his naked legs. They are thin and pale with no muscular definition, and she sees that she may not be able to save him after all.

Before Colin, a long line of waiters paraded through her garden apartment, one after the other, still wearing their black work pants slightly stained with mozzarella sauce and smelling like French fries. They all also had aspirations of something greater – they were waiting tables but they were artists or musicians or poets or actors or comedians. The road to greatness in the arts started first with the blooming onion and grew from there. She needs to find her niche, her one true dream, beyond being able to afford something more than ramen noodles for dinner and to have more than two dollars in her savings account. A balance large enough that she was actually earning interest.

The shift manager, a tall, beanpole-thin guy with bright blue eyes and a prominent Adam's apple, claps his hands in the break room to get their attention. "All right, people, now we've had some complaints among the customers that our attitude isn't right. We need to remember that we're out there to make people happy. If they want extra special sauce, we give them extra special sauce, with a smile. Ladies, if they're a little flirtatious, flirt back – you'll get a better tip."

As Eleanor listens, she replaces the word waitress with "call girl." It's really not that different. They get violated in similar ways: humiliated, degraded, made to feel like they don't matter. The one difference is that the risk of pregnancy is lower. As is the pay. When Rob asks if anyone has any questions, she raises her hand. "If the guy wants to feel us up, should we charge extra or is that on the house?"

"On the house!" Rob says, half-joking.

Her day is again filled with unhappy tourists as "Feed the World" plays on seemingly incessant loop from overhead. She tells one group of five guys that they must be in the wrong place; Hooters is across the road. They think she is hilarious. They leave her a two-dollar tip on an $80 tab. When Colin texts to tell her that he's going to be late, she texts back, "Me too."

After her shift, she goes to the bar and tells Mikey, the bartender she has not managed to seduce, to line up three shots. "How about just one to start," he suggests. He has a two-year-old daughter named Maggie after *Cat on a Hot Tin Roof*. Like her, he is a lapsed actor who still likes to keep ties to the theater community.

Rob, the manager, breezes over. "You know, it's against policy to be up here. We don't want our customers to see the staff drinking."

She waves her black book in the air. "You know how much I pulled in tonight? Fifty bucks. And from that 50 bucks, I had to tip out $25. All my customers have gone home to torture their dogs. None of them are left. I'm having a drink."

Rob stares back at her, blinks. She knows he's not in love with his job either. He has to pretend to care about all of this shit when all he wants is to practice music with his garage band, The Losers of Solomon.

He turns to Mikey. "Make sure it's on the house."

When Colin texts again that he's still going to be even later than he thought, she tries to imagine who he's with, and realizes it doesn't matter. She pictures him meeting a buxom waitress from another themed restaurant – the place where the wait staff is paid to be rude to you. Or someone from TGI Fridays who sang him happy birthday. It could be his thing. Maybe he goes around to restaurants picking up vulnerable waitresses with self-esteem issues.

And so she will have a couple of drinks, flirt with Mikey, who will flirt back even though he's clearly not interested, and that will be that. Maybe on the way home, she'll be gang-raped by a bunch of teens. Probably not. Most likely, everything will be just fine. No musical theater ending with a kiss under an elm with a perfect half-moon hanging in the sky.

She walks the two miles home, weaving only slightly, the music from her iPod now from *Gypsy*. How did that story end? Mass suicide?

She notices a guy approaching – a thin, scrawny white guy with his hat pulled down over his eyes. The tips of her fingers tingle as she wraps her hands around the keys in her jacket and straightens her spine. Be here now, she thinks, in this moment when something is happening.

A light snow has started, and the snowflakes swirl around his head in the streetlight as if he were a sparkling apparition from Christmas Past. She quickens her race by him, but he bumps into her, his hands fumbling at her coat pocket. She pushes away and he comes at her again, this time grabbing her arm to twist it behind her, but she is wearing a too-thin raincoat of slippery acrylic and manages to wiggle away. He rushes at her once more, grabs her jacket, and pulls her toward him, away from the street.

"Get away from me, motherfucker!" she screams. She pushes him as hard as she can and he slips on a wet patch of snow, his arms pinwheeling backward for balance. She kicks out, connects with his stomach, and down he goes on his back. She hasn't thought far enough ahead, doesn't have mace to blind him, and this is the part where she should just run away, but instead she stands over him, still screaming in a voice she doesn't recognize. "You want me to kick you, you dumb shit? You don't touch people like that! You stay away from me!" She moves as if to kick him and he flinches and she sees the circles under his eyes.

"I'm sorry, hey, I'm sorry," he says, crawling backwards away from her. "It was my mistake."

"Good," she says, still buzzing with anger. "You stop that now." She walks away, furious and singing inside.

When she gets home, she unwraps the figurine from its newspaper. It's still in one piece, wasn't broken in the struggle. She unwraps and sets the milkmaid on her wobbly mantel.

It wasn't for him after all. She wanted it for herself. That much seems clear to her now.

What We Learned

In nursing school, we learned how to take a patient's vitals, how to give CPR, how to give an enema, how to calm a patient who is hyperventilating, how to treat a bee allergy, a nut allergy, a poinsettia allergy, how to get a sock off a person with a gangrened foot, how to help someone use a bed pan, how to clean up after a patient misses the bed pan, how to determine if someone is altered because of meth or crack cocaine, how to triage a wound spouting blood, how to bathe a paraplegic, how to bathe a quadriplegic, how to identify the addicts who will break their own bones for oxy, how to start a catheter, how to handle hypothermia to avoid amputation, how to stay alert with handsy doctors, how to buy work shoes that won't raise blisters on your heels, how to nap while standing, how to apply ice to burn victims to minimize scarring, how to turn a body so that bed sores do not begin, how to recover pieces of a face after a dog attack, how to manage a grand mal seizure so the tongue isn't swallowed, how to remove windshield glass from a forehead, how to recognize the sound of a death rattle, how to call a death when the family is absent, how to call a death when the family is in the room, how to clean blood from a dead body

so the family can view it, how to look for signs of sexual abuse in a baby, a toddler, an adolescent, a young girl, an old woman, how to give a rape kit, how to take skin tissue from underneath broken fingernails, how to administer an IV when the veins are tiny, how to evaluate if a person is being abused, when to call DYFS, when to turn and look the other way because there is nothing to be done.

We did not learn how to manage our rage.

Rage

My rage has a color and a shape – it's bright orange and round like an egg. The rage doesn't just happen when I turn on the news. It is triggered by almost any gurgle in my day: a patient whose vein I can't find because she's too skinny, a woman coughing without covering her mouth in the frozen food aisle of Wegman's, a dead raccoon flattened on the side of the road. I feel it in the tips of my fingers, as if I need to squeeze something very hard. As a nurse caring for fragile women and teenage girls (and sometimes teenage boys) who are starving themselves to death, this can be a liability.

Today, I must find a way to make up for yesterday's work outburst.

Bedside manner has never been my strength. Since taking this job five months ago, I've been given one verbal warning, and now been written up once. The verbal warning came after I threw a paper towel roll at Tina T. "Throwing" is an exaggeration. I would say it was more like tossing. Like, a gentle tossing of the roll in the direction of Tina's head. I thought she would catch it, but instead it hit her in the nose, which started bleeding.

If I screw up again, I will be let go. I don't care. Nursing jobs are easy to come by. I know because I've had five in the last two years. Fuck you, nursing is hard.

However, because I don't have another plan just yet, I spend 15 minutes in my car in the August sun, breathing in and out, trying not to get pissed off by the man parked in his giant gas-guzzling Ford next to me, blasting twangy country music for all the world to hear. I open the door fast, banging into the body of his truck. He glances over at me, and I smile and shrug, like, *Whoops!*

Imagine a white fluffy cloud, passing over a blue sky with the relentless summer sun poking through.

I walk through the electric doors of the clinic with slow steps in my padded white sneakers. My other latest self-help thing is to think in terms of gratitude. *Thank you that I can walk. Thank you that only two of the three Tinas are working today. Thank you that I did not get gang-raped in the parking lot after my late shift last night.*

I work with three Tinas. All three grew up in the surrounding towns of rural PA and graduated from Penn State Nursing School. I imagine they have dads who wear camouflage on the weekends and moms who bake meatloaf. Two out of three Tinas have bumper stickers with American flags on them. I'm as patriotic as the next atheist, but do not feel the need to advertise.

My supervisor, Tina B., is a busty blonde with an overbite who brings in brownies on a regular basis. She never eats any of the baked goods she offers, telling us they are made from a gluten-free mix she got at the Publix grocery store (as if we care). When I walk into her office, she glances pointedly at the Mickey Mouse clock on the wall. Each number on the face is a black floating Mickey Mouse head and, on the hour, the clock

plays "It's a Small World After All," which can make you wish you had a hammer.

I have been told many times to walk it off. I try to take this advice, but it never works. I have a full file floating around, the phrases "overly involved" and "inability to separate" written in multiple places. My school record has similar marks in it: "lack of respect for authority," "constant questioning," and "unwillingness to maintain the status quo." AKA a troublemaker.

She waits for me to sit down and then she clears her throat. "How are you liking it here?"

"I love it," I say, staring at her snow globe on her desk. It has little plastic creatures in it, penguins or possibly dancing opossums or tiny rats. I fight the urge to pick it up and shake it.

"Okay, I am glad to hear that because it seems you've had some difficulties adjusting. We like to think of ourselves as a team, like the Three Musketeers." *There are more than three nurses on the ward though.* "And if one of us is unhappy, it impacts all of us." I bob my head, as if agreeing. "Think of this place like a little terrarium. You have one of those when you were a kid?"

"No. We didn't have pets." *We had cockroaches. Our cockroaches had pets.*

"Okay, well, I had one and I loved it to death. It came in this aquarium-like thing, and you had one layer, which was stones, and then earth, and then grass, and so on. Ferns and what not. And the plants only grew if the other parts were working. So the ecosystems are dependent on one another for air, moisture, growth. If one of the things is off, it impacts the whole environment."

I look into the distance, nodding like, *Gee, I never thought of it that way.*

Apparently, that's the limit of her inspirational speaking abilities because she caps her pen and says, "Now, let's problem solve this interaction before the parents arrive." I understand that Tina B. also does not want to be here at 7 a.m. on a Saturday morning. She may wish her humongous iced coffee were not leaking all over her desk. She may wish she didn't have an eggplant-shaped nose and a face only a blind mother could love. *Thank you, universe, that I do not have Tina B.'s genetic profile.* I straighten up as if prepared to listen. "You tell them that you're sorry if your words upset them, and that you've thought it over and realized you need to work on professionalism."

I nod. I've taken out a pad of paper. In teeny, tiny script, I write, "Say sorry."

She takes a noisy slurp of her coffee. "Let's remember that you're here to service the family, and that your first priority is to do so in a calm manner. Your anxiety will only serve to trigger their anxiety."

I clear my throat. I do not say that servicing clients sounds like something a prostitute does. "I wasn't feeling anxious."

"Don't interrupt, please." Her phone rings. She picks it up. "What? Okay, send them in."

"Hello," would've been the professional way to answer the phone. *Hello, this is Tina B. How may I help you?*

After a moment, the parents step in, and for the first time, I realize how tall and gangly the dad is and how small the mother is compared to him.

Tina B. stands and beams. "Welcome, welcome, thanks for coming in. Please, have a seat." She gestures to the white sofa next to her desk, the one with the Disney stuffed animals littering it. They sink into the cushions. The Tigger stuffed animal falls face forward into dad's lap, and he pushes it away.

The mother's purse strap keeps falling down and she keeps pushing it up to her shoulder. "Is everything okay?"

"No, it's not okay," Tina B. says, shaking her head.

The mother leans forward, the strap falling again. "Marigold?"

Tina B. waves her hand. "No, no, everything is fine with Marigold. She's really doing well with her treatment."

This is a lie. After the parents left and she was admitted, we tied Marigold to her bed with soft cotton hand and ankle restraints because she tried to gouge her eyes out with a plastic spoon.

"We are committed to this treatment," the dad says, and he too leans forward. If he were wearing a hat, he would be holding it in his hands.

"Kit, did you have something to say?" Tina B. smiles at me like a person in a car insurance commercial.

"Sure, yes." I put on my best serious expression. "I am really very sorry about how our initial interaction went when you came in. Here at the Wells Fargo Eating Disorder Clinic, we are committed to giving your family the best level of service." I blather on and they look back at me blankly, neither happy nor sad. I sound like a brochure. In fact, I read the brochure cover to cover last night to prepare for this interaction. The tagline for the clinic is "Bringing light into the darkness," which sounds like an advertisement for corneal surgery.

Neither parent responds. They sit, waiting for us to say more. I say more. They nod. Tina B. says some more things and makes hand gestures.

It takes a while for us to figure out that they think they've been called in because their daughter is going to be kicked out. They are not raging for an apology; they are ready to apologize.

Apparently, she has a long history with programs and lighting things on fire, figuratively and literally.

The dad clears his throat. "So you're not asking us to take her home?"

Tina B. says, "Goodness no! We just started her treatment."

"Oh, that's a relief."

We all shake hands and the mother swoops toward me like she's going to hug me, so I bend down, pretending to tie my shoe. A success.

Tina G. has a long blond ponytail and a too-loud voice. She brays when she laughs, but not when the doctors are around – then, she is demure and soft-spoken. Tina G. is really named Christina, and she sometimes goes by Chrissy, but prefers Tina, even though there are too many Tinas already. She has a large Italian family and is always in a fight with her fiancé, Joey. I know it sounds like I'm generalizing, but these are the facts.

Tina T. is the youngest and the easiest to boss around. She just graduated from Penn State with her BSN degree and likes to remind us when we get something wrong. She thinks that I'm old, even though I'm barely over 30. Okay, barely over 34.

When Tina G. turned 25 last week, she brought in a frosted cake for herself in the shape of a parrot. Tina T. jumped up and down, clapping her hands. She said, "Oh, my God, you're halfway to 30!"

I said, "Actually, she's halfway to 50," and took a big slice of the cake from the end piece.

None of the Tinas laughed. I took most of the cake home and ate it by myself while watching reruns of *Dateline*. Spoiler alert for any episode: the husband murdered the wife. The husband will have always murdered the wife.

Rage

My shift starts with an update from Tina G., who is basically shouting into my ear. She wears her hair in that perpetual crunchy state, so that it always looks like it is wet and possibly made of glass, like if you squeezed an end, it would break.

Today, she has a dark stain on her white uniform and yellowish gunk on her sneakers. "It was wild today," she says, tightening her ponytail. "Full moon tonight or what?" She fills me in on a new intake – a young mother, age 32, Caucasian, who is six months pregnant and weighs 94 pounds. For once, Tina G. speaks in a hissing whisper. "She's starving that baby. You can't even tell that she's pregnant. If this continues, the baby will be born underweight and then DFC could be called. Doesn't she get that?"

Except we don't take babies away from moms who are just starving themselves. They have to be co-contaminated. That means they have to be starving themselves and injecting heroin. Or starving themselves and smoking meth. Or starving themselves and in a Christian rock band.

I enter room 102. "Hey, I'm Kit, and I'll be the nurse on duty today." The mother looks and me and throws up, just bile, and maybe the juice they gave her this morning. Tina G. is right; she doesn't look pregnant, she looks a little bloated around her abdomen, like she's had a big dinner, though the bones in her arms are thin twigs, and her face has that insect look they get when they are in starvation mode – wide and dry, the lashes and most of her hair fallen out.

She wants her phone. Now. "I'm expecting a call from my pediatrician."

I look at her chart. "Dr. Marks will be informed that you're here. We've already reached out to her, so she'll call us."

She slaps her skinny little thigh so hard it will likely leave a hematoma (translation: surface bruise). "She doesn't work for this place."

"We have an affiliation, so she might turn up to take a look at you." She shuts her mouth. I take her blood pressure and ask her if she's in any pain.

"No, no pain." I watch in amazement as her stomach moves and realize that it's the baby. Her skin is so taut and her body so thin, I can almost see the tiny fist jutting out, like, *Save me!* She says, "I hate when it does that."

"Yeah, I'm sure that feels weird."

"It feels like I need to poop when it does that."

What I'd like to ask her is, "Did you not want this baby that you're calling an 'it'? Was this not part of the plan?" But I button my lip and make sure she has what she needs before I leave the room.

I go back to the nurses' station to get Tina G.'s notes. Husband is out of town, and the neighbor called an ambulance when the woman collapsed on the front lawn doing yoga, and then the family was implored to admit her. History of depression and bulimia, but no psychotic episodes, unless you count the starving-your-baby thing.

The right thing to do would be to call social services. That's if you're not worried about keeping your job. I do it anyway, making the call with my hand over the receiver, telling lies, telling the truth.

Next, I wrangle with the new intake whose parents I (sort of) just apologized to: Marigold. She's 5'9" and I was right about her weight: 92 pounds. She's beautiful and concave, like a gorgeous alien thing that has landed among us. She is a ballerina/aspiring model whose agent has told her she needs to lose five more pounds. What does he care? The industry needs

women who look like pieces of art, all corners and sharp angles, collarbones that look like you could rest your drink on them. Her teeth are perfect and straight, her hair like a wave down her back, eyes blue and wide with long lashes, a living deer with legs as thin as my arms.

I am new to the job, but not new to nursing, so I say, "Well, you know, let's get you checked out and comfortable and we'll see where we are." I have already taken her vitals, and given her a new set of hospital-wear in extra petite, a child's-sized gown with the tag ripped out because these girls, I'm learning, want to fit into the smallest of the small. They want to be a size negative 15, as long as that's the tiniest. They would like to wear baby onesies if at all possible.

I ask her when her last meal was, and she says, with a laugh, "That sounds like you're one of the apostles. My last meal was wine made from blood."

I like her and feel like I can relax a little, be myself a tiny bit more than usual. "We haven't gotten to the substance abuse questions yet."

"Oh, god, do you even know how many calories are in alcohol? It's a waste."

"Last time you ate though?"

She taps her finger to her chin. "What day is it?" She's pretty, which shouldn't matter, and she shouldn't be, because she only weighs 92 pounds, but she still has her hair, and a fine coating of extra animal hair along her arms that comes from starvation. The body starts to grow it to keep you warmer. This should tell you that, sometimes, the body knows better than the brain. "Don't believe everything you think," is a bumper sticker I would buy if I could commit to one.

She refuses the grilled chicken. She picks it up and throws it in my general direction. I don't duck, and it hits me on the cheek, and then lands with a splat on the floor. I page the kitchen to ask for an orderly to bring up another chicken breast. Marigold folds herself up in the chair like a piece of elaborate origami, all elbows, knees, and sharp chin. You could see how she would make a Kate Spade purse look irresistible with it covering her entire tiny body.

"I hate those shoes," she says, chewing on a hangnail. She has no implements in the room to hurt herself, so she uses her teeth to tear at her skin. She thinks she can turn herself invisible, because that would have saved her a lot of trouble with her ballet teacher. Or her choir director. Or her dad. On the other end of this program, he waits. Here, I could add a statistic about how girls who have eating disorders are often trying to disappear because they were molested. Or the stat about how if you are raped or molested once, your chances of being abused again double. It does something to your mind and your body. It makes you into a different creature, one who is more like a jellyfish, easier to see through and manipulate. But Marigold is not a wilting flower; she wants to gnash her teeth at everyone who comes in contact.

When the second chicken arrives, she spits at it. "I don't want this fucking piece of fucking disgusting fucking animal meat they're calling chicken." We both look at it lying on the plate, this unappetizing beige-ish hunk with grill marks in it. "Would you eat this?"

My nurse self should say, *Yes, of course. It's filled with nutrients to make you healthy again so you can play a doll in* The Nutcracker. My real self says, "It looks gross."

"Thank you! It is gross. I'm vegan. I told them that."

We could negotiate a different piece of food, but it's not about the piece of food, it's about the consumption of it. "Okay, well, you have to eat it or I've been directed to administer an IV." They all hate the IV. It makes them feel out of control, all these disgusting, fat-inducing calories pouring directly into their veins. I hate the IV too, because it's a temporary solution aimed solely at the body, not the mind. "Cut it up into as many pieces as you want."

"With what?"

She is not allowed a knife, especially after last night. "Use your canines. You can make each bite as small as you like, but you have to eat it."

"How many bites do you think it will take to finish this chicken? Is this like that old lollipop commercial?" She says, waving the piece of meat in the air.

"How do you even know about that?"

"I wasn't hatched yesterday, not like this poor chicken. I bet they kept him in a cage and he didn't even have enough strength in his legs to walk. I bet the legs would fold right over if he tried to stand on them."

"Can you eat the pieces and talk about Harvey while you do it?" I know from her intake notes that Harvey is her ballet teacher.

She pinches off a tiny piece of meat. I look away as she puts it in her mouth and swallows it like a pill. "He has a blue dog."

"What's the dog's name?"

"Blueberry. So original. I know, it's funny, because he doesn't even like blueberries, but it's this little white dog and they dye it blue." I see from the corner of my eye that she has taken another bite, with a grimace of disgust.

What I've learned so far is that you can jam these girls with nutrients, force-feed them. You can give them calming mantras

and therapy around positivity and how they have their own journey to go on and they will still not eat. They can lose all of their hair, grow a pelt on their backs, find it difficult to sleep because of the jutting bones in their back, and they will still not eat.

It occurs to me then that they may be enraged too – some just handle it differently, turning it inward, not outward. That's the problem.

Marigold keeps talking and tucking away bites, but only when my eyes are averted. When she's finally done, I look at her face, and her clean plate. I clap. "Ta-da," she says, giving me jazz hands. "Now you can leave."

I have forgotten my lunch, and so browse the shared refrigerator in the nurse's lounge. You might have guessed that working with starving people makes food have new and terrible associations. Most of the nurses avoid talking about dieting around the patients but seem unable to stop themselves from counting calories.

Since I started here, I've lost 10 pounds, mostly through the atmospheric osmosis of general panic around food.

Most of the rest of my day is spent shuffling around in my too-big uniform, doling out meds. The Tinas have all decided they'll deal with extra small, even though they're all clearly medium or bigger. But they seem to prefer to have to suck their stomachs in all day, to go home with button-hole indents from the pants, to be bursting out of the tops. I would like to bring that up to Tina G., because I feel like it goes against code, not to mention decency and sets a bad example for our starving patients who are nothing if not body conscious. Instead, I say nothing.

The orange man is on the TV in the hospital lounge again, his ass-like pucker of a mouth spewing hate. You keep turning

the channel, and he keeps popping up everywhere like a villainous marionette. I find the remote and change it to the travel show. A gondola floats by, and the voiceover narrator says, "Even on these peaceful waterways, navigation can be trickier than you might expect."

My shift is nearly over. I have managed to make it through the day without getting into any kind of additional trouble. Over the last 16 hours, I've had to repeatedly wipe the ass of a young woman who has ingested 45 diuretics and won't stop shitting water – on the bed, on me, on herself. I was not gentle. I threatened a diaper in a low voice. She threatened to tell her parents. I hissed back that she could lose her phone privileges. She agreed to sit on the toilet, even though she said it hurt her butt. This is probably true; she was all flesh stretched over bones. I have checked on Marigold, checked on the pregnant woman who is reading a book called *What to Expect When You're Expecting*, as if she were a normal pregnant woman.

Last on my list is Janice, a woman who has been here for about a week. She's no-nonsense, doesn't like small talk. Me neither. We get along fine.

I check her vitals while she talks on the phone. She's holding a cup of water and taking small rapid sips like she's about to run a race. I put the blood pressure cuff around her tiny arm, and she drops the phone. She says, "Goddamn–" and then she lets out a loud burp. Her eyes go wide, and she hiccups. The hiccup becomes a sharp cough and then we watch in amazement as a fountain of blood spews from her mouth.

"Oopsie," I say, reaching for a wipe. She coughs again and another river of blood gushes out, onto her gown and the bed. Her eyes go wild with panic. She tries to talk but gags instead. Her teeth are covered in blood, and then her arm jerks away and the cup flies across the room.

I push the red alarm button. She grabs my arm with strength that doesn't seem possible, her eyes on mine, hand squeezing. "It's okay," I say, though it is definitely not okay. My mind scrambles for a reason. A burst stomach ulcer. A ruptured esophagus. Organ failure.

The room swarms with people – Dr. Patel, two residents, and Tina T., who is supposed to take over for me at the end of my shift.

Dr. Patel is a handsome Indian man in his early forties. He wears funky purple glasses and is good with the patients, friendly but not flirtatious. Now, he becomes very focused, very fast. He's calm in executing orders for drugs and in making sure her airway is clear.

I keep hold of her hand though it has gone limp. Dr. Patel is feeling her stomach, trying to locate the problem, but the heart monitor tells us what it is. It's beeping like crazy. This activity, combined with the seizures and the blood, means she's going into cardiac arrest. I don't need to suggest this, because the next moment, the monitor flatlines and the paddles are charged and then Tina T. pulls up the patient's gown. Tiny body, no breasts, her bones protruding from her chest and collar, she is a sliver of a human. I can't imagine now how she had the ability to talk to me a moment before.

Another eruption of blood explodes from her mouth, landing on my face in a hot rush. I think I'm okay, but then when I blink, my left eye blurs and burns. I rub at it while looking with my other eye for something to clean the blood away.

When Tina T. sees my face, she says, "You need to flush that immediately." She pushes me toward the bathroom.

The heart monitor buzzes. I splash cold water on my face. I rub at my eye. A flash of pain needles through my head. More water, and it's still burning. I peer into the mirror, seeing a

blurry face, and try to move more carefully, opening up the burning eye and reaching for my contact, which has moved up to the corner of my vision. When I finally get it out, it's got a speck of blood on it. I look back in the mirror and see my own eye, puffy and red, unfamiliar.

I drop the contact, turn the taps on full force, splash my face again and again. My eye is ribboned with red lines and a single red dot. My rational mind names it – subdermal hematoma. It's not dangerous, only if the woman is HIV positive, which is unlikely. I stumble back to the room, covering my bad eye with my hand.

In the blur that is the room, I see bodies bent over Janice, and at first, they look like ghosts, all in white, moving toward her like something I remember from a dream. They are trying to start her heart, but the compressions and the paddles are violent. The action seems medieval even though they're sur-rounded by equipment.

Dr. Patel swears and asks for the paddles again. Janice's eyes have rolled back in her head, but the snap of the paddle on her chest causes her body to seize off the bed, as if levitating or freeing evil spirits.

As we fail to get a pulse, time grows taffy-slow, stretchy. Every minute down is a minute away from survival.

The monitor gives a weak bleep, and then stays flatlined. They charge and apply the paddles again, Dr. Patel doing compressions in between. A snapping noise like a twig breaking means he has likely broken one of her ribs with the force of his compressions. Bones get fragile without nutrients, so it can't be helped.

They apply the paddles. Nothing on the monitor.

They do it again.

They do it again.

They do it again.

Each time, I feel a surge that's like the electricity going into her body. Each time, she lifts up and then falls flat.

They do it again, and the monitor blips. The heartbeat is thready, short. We stare at the slow lines moving in blips. Dr. Patel turns to Tina T. "How long has she been down?"

"Forty-seven minutes." She keeps her tone neutral, but the twist of her mouth tells me that this is a very bad thing.

"Too long." He thumps his head with the palm of his hand, three times. He has some kind of tick – he has to do things in threes. "I'll call the family." He does an about face, nearly colliding with me. "If you do not mind, please clean up the body."

"And that's how Monday goes," says Tina T. in a shaky voice. She's looking for another gown, one that isn't stained with dark red blood. I grab a gown from the cart outside the room and hand it to her. "Thanks." She tries to smile and lets out a sob.

"Oh," I say. I am having trouble seeing and have one hand covering my eye.

"Sorry!" She swipes at her nose. "This is my first one." She gestures toward the bed, toward the body. Janice is not a person anymore. With that much time elapsed, her brain activity will be nil.

The doors to the elevator are just shutting when Dr. Patel steps on. He nods, his funky violet glasses glinting. As the doors shut, he says, "The apnea test will show us that she no blood flow to the brain. The woman." He presses the button for his floor three more times.

"No chance of recovery?"

"She can be a donor if the family agrees," he says. "One good thing, I guess." Our reflections in the elevator doors are wavy, as though we are underwater. "I should not have kept at it," he

says. "I should have stopped to compressions. Now, the family is suffering because they think she will live." I've never witnessed this particular thing before: a doctor admitting a mistake. The elevator dings again, and the doors open to the ICU floor. He nods and strides away, a real human person.

I feel something in my body, not rage, something else – it's harder to identify, it's something I struggle not to let in. The anger, I realize, is just the cover.

In nursing school, we learned how to take a patient's vitals, how to defer to doctors, how to swat away pharmaceutical salesmen/women, how to give CPR, how to administer an EpiPen, how to wash someone's ass, how to give an enema, how to help a patient who was hyperventilating, how to dislodge a penny from the esophagus, how to administer mouth to mouth, how to read if someone was altered because of drugs or biology, how to triage a gaping wound, how to evaluate if a person was being abused, how to pinpoint an alcoholic, how to bathe a paraplegic, how to bathe a quadriplegic, how to identify PTSD, how to gauge a person's true pain level (a person will always say it hurts more than it does), how to remember the chronics, the ones who came in for drugs versus treatment, how to irrigate a wound, how to treat hypothermia, how to quickly dress burn victims so as to minimize scarring, how to call a death, how to put a face back on after a dog attack, how to manage a seizure, how to take someone out of shock, how to wrap a clean a body before the family sees it, how to clean a wound, how to clear an air passage, how to look for signs of sexual abuse in a baby, a toddler, an adolescent, a young girl, an old woman, how to give a rape kit, how to take skin tissue from under fingernails when someone was attacked, how to staunch a knife wound versus a gunshot wound, how to give quick stitches if the doctor isn't available, how to take out stitches, how to give a shot, how to

give an IV, how to temporarily set a broken bone, how to push a bone back into place when it's come out of its socket, how to treat a bee allergy, a nut allergy, a poinsettia allergy, how to work with homeless patients, how to breathe through our mouths, how to get a sock off a person with a gangrened foot, how to stitch up a superficial wound, how to put teeth back together, how to set a broken nose, how to help someone vomit or use a bed pan, how to clean up someone after he was unable to get to the bed pan, how to turn a body so that bed sores would not begin to diamond across the skin, how to recognize the sound of death rattle in the throats. No one ever taught us how to manage the grief.

When I finally leave the clinic, it's 3 a.m. and my contacts are stuck to my eyeballs, and the right one still feels damaged.

The subway car is mostly empty, except for a man sleeping fully laid out on two of the cars, his body made compact, his feet hanging over the end. The rocking of the subway car can be like a cradle, lulling, and the conductor leaves him alone.

At the South Street stop, a guy gets on, eyes glassy, hair wild. He assesses the car, sees it's only me, sitting with my backpack on my lap, knees together, still in blue scrubs.

He walks to my end of the car and sits across from me, all the other seats empty. I stare at the sign above his head, "See something, say something," the newest anti-bullying campaign meant to keep people safer while also creating a greater paranoia in this Big Brother way: God is watching.

He says softly, "Hey, lady." He's leaning forward, hands dangling between his legs. Hey. Lady." I move my gaze to him. I can't smell alcohol, but he's altered, that's clear by the dullness of his eyes and his slow speech. Altered or not, he is bigger than me and stronger. "You all alone this late, huh?"

He's leaning even further forward and I know, just know, that he's about to unzip his pants and take out his member. It is too late, and I am too tired, but I get a jolt of energy, thinking about our patient who died, the one I didn't even know how to save.

I feel a tingling in my fingers and at the base of my neck. I stand up, ready to move away. He stands up too, at the same time, and reaches for me. I spin away, a dancer's pirouette I didn't know I had in me, and at the same time, this other part of me is reacting in a surprising way, my arm is coming up and in one motion, I have swung my bag at his head, upwards, and hear it connect with his face with a dull sound. He steps back. I swing at him again, connect again, feeling the weight of the bike lock in the bottom of my bag and the satisfying way it hits him in the temple. He staggers, sits, puts his hand to his head. It happens in three seconds and he's bleeding, a trickle of blood, down the side of his face.

I say, "You should get that looked at," and move away down the car, open the door at the end, step between the speeding cars, and into the next one, which is populated with a half dozen late-shift workers talking about their boss.

I sit near but not next to the people. I regret nothing. The rage is warm and glowing, safe, like a cage.

The Eyes Stay

They said his brain might be dead. He can't speak or open his eyes, but his heart still pumps blood. She, the mother, is crying and blowing her nose into a scratchy piece of toilet paper in the emergency room next to the body of her son, Brian. Her husband, the father, stands like a soldier, his torso unbending, nodding, "Uh-huh, I get it, yep, I hear ya," as the doctor gives them the news.

"He failed the Glasgow coma test," the doctor says. He has dark circles under his eyes, this doctor, and he should really have a nap. They should all be allowed to put this on hold and just lay down for a minute.

"The glass blow test? Was he able to blow into a tube?" She, the mother, can't make heads or tails of it. It's really too loud in this place. On the other side of the curtain, two nurses chat and it sounds like they are clamping together bed pans or something. She will write a letter to someone about this when she gets a minute to figure it out.

Brian's knee jerks and he sits up slightly. It's a miracle! "Doctor, did you see that?" She turns to him.

He takes her fluttering hand. "I did see that. They do that sometimes. It's called 'posturing.'"

Grotesque. This whole thing is grotesque, and she really needs to be going now. She was in the middle of something before this, something important involving eggs. Brian looks absolutely fine, except for the bandage around his head with a dime-sized drop of blood in the center.

Is that his brain leaking out? She can't stop these thoughts.

Next, they are in the waiting room, and it comes back to her, what the doctors did before. She clutches her husband's arm. "Did they put a Q-tip in his eye or did I dream that?"

None of this seems very scientific.

The doctor returns, carrying a clipboard. He clears his throat.

"Is Brian dead? Is he Brian-dead?" She corrects herself. *"Brain-dead?"*

Her husband laughs. Surprised, she laughs too and looks around. This has got to be a joke.

The doctor does not laugh. He waits for the moment to pass and then says, "As I said two hours ago, there is no blood flow to the Brian – the brain."

Then, they are all laughing and it feels like they're in the middle of a very, very, very bad dream.

The doctor explains how the donation would work, in rehearsed, brochure-like terms. "He has a healthy heart. His organs could save the lives of up to seven other people ...."

Another woman steps forward. She is thin, with straggly brown hair and wide eyes. She wears a badge that reads "transplant coordinator." This reminds the mother that she has geraniums that need to be re-potted. They'll die otherwise. "It's the chance to do something good," the coordinator says.

The mother remembers now – when she was little, her dad, a pharmaceutical salesman long since dead, kept a plastic head

on his desk, a gift from some doctor or another. The brain and skull were illuminated separately, as were the eyeballs with their red, thread-like veins. The head had blue eyes.

(Brian's eyes are brown. With a blown pupil.)

The head on the desk horrified her. It glowed in the dark. Sometimes, she would dare herself to stand in the doorway of the office with the lights off and stare at the gleaming white skull until it seemed to hover in the air. This was how she went about improving her courage – forcing herself to stay still for 10 seconds, 20, one minute, inching closer, daring herself to touch the plastic head, even as she was imagining it coming alive, its teeth suddenly snapping down on her fingers, breaking bones. Brave girl to endure it all.

"Could we be there? Could we be in the OR when you make the first incision?" She has adopted the lingo of the medical staff, a survival technique, *I am one of you, I can relate*, and most of the vocabulary she must be pulling up from episodes of *MASH* she watched as a kid. Triage, incoming, sutures.

"We don't advise the family attend. If you want some time –"

She interrupts, "Will they take his eyes?"

The transplant coordinator looks at her, and she must see something in her face, because she quickly says, "No, they don't take the eyes. The eyes stay."

"Oh, good," the mother says. A rush of fear blows through her chest, whooshing through to the tips of her fingers, making them icy cold. When Brian was a baby, she used to hold his warm and sleeping body close to her face and place her lips against the soft spot in his skull, fearful he might break. "Then, oh, okay. We should do this, don't you think?" She turns to her husband, who is both nodding and shaking his head. She straightens her back, switches gears, back to the coordinator. "Yes," she says. *Yes.* It is the only word, so far, that makes sense.

A Good Thing

We start the day by going over the list of the dead. I'm new to this job as a transplant coordinator, and I find myself continually shocked by the many ways you can die. It makes me afraid to leave the house in the morning, to cross the street, to walk around in socks. I keep waiting for the story that ends, *And then the patient fully recovered and walked out of the hospital with just a slight limp*. It never once happens.

The receptionist distributes rolls of all the viable brain-dead in the Tri-State area. This week we have two gunshot wounds (one accidental, one self-inflicted), one motor vehicle accident, a suicide via hanging from a NordicTrack machine, and one helmet-less bike messenger flattened by a car on the Walnut Street Bridge.

Alison, a large woman with a hangdog face and tiny hands, talks about her case – a 16-year-old boy in North Philadelphia who heard gunshots, stuck his head out his apartment window, and was struck by a stray bullet. The family had lost another son in a shooting two years before.

I consider moving to South Dakota and farming the land. I would raise good-natured beagles and drink only green tea.

Alison met with the dead boy's family for over two hours while they argued back and forth about what the boy would have wanted. Finally, the patient herniated and was declared brain-dead. The family consented to donate all but his corneas.

"What did we learn from this case?" asks Andrew Clarke. He's the director. He has a rugged, pockmarked face and blue eyes. I imagine he'd be excellent in bed, persuasive and reassuring at the same time.

Alison looks at the ceiling. She's been at the hospital for 24 hours straight. There are dark circles under her eyes; traces of prettiness swim in the tired lines of her face. "We learned to stall the family until the patient throws a clot," she says.

We clap. I'm grateful for all of it – these people who make jokes and speak inappropriately so that we can get up and do this again the next day.

Training lasts two months.

Words and phrases we're taught not to use when dealing with the donor family: *harvest, excision, cadaver, organ procurement, dead as a doornail.*

Words we do use: *saving the lives of others, donation, transplant*, every form of *to give*. We talk about the patient in the past tense – *What would she have wanted?* – even as the blip of the heart monitor persists in the background.

We learn to compartmentalize our feelings. I picture giant pieces of luggage stuffed with body parts: a bowling bag with a head in it, a trunk holding a torso, a golf bag filled with legs.

Before we face real people, we practice the rhetoric of donation through role-play. One day I'm a mother of two who has lost her husband in a car crash late at night on I-95. I get carried away as the grieving widow sobs and exclaims, "But he was so young!"

My partner, Jesse, pats me on the back with his fat, soft hands. "There, there," he says.

The instructor, a tall man with bangs, advises us to take a five-minute break. He comes over and asks if I'm okay. "You were very convincing," he says. I thank him. He asks if I can do it again for the next group of trainees. Of course. Of course I can.

We take numerous classes: Empathetic Listening, Donor Management, Donation after Cardiac Death, Donors without Heartbeats, and Ways People Die in the Bathroom. "You don't want to know," I tell my boyfriend later.

We're sitting in the living room in the dark, watching cars blow up in an action-packed thriller involving a foreign invasion. He turns down the volume. "Let me guess. You fall off the toilet and hit your head, right? You slip in the shower?"

Yes, those are some of the ways. I don't mention the others.

A newborn is thrown into a porta-potty by his anxious young mother.

A guy ODs over a urinal at Locust Bar his first time shooting up.

A woman falls backward through a glass shower door because the water is too hot.

A man cuts an artery shaving.

He says, "Would you rather watch a movie with kitties in it?"

I say, "Yes, please," and he changes the channel to Animal Planet. But what I really want is for him to keep asking me questions.

Later that week, I'm at my boyfriend's end-of-summer work party, stuck in a group of accountants who think that wearing a cartoon tie makes them whimsical. Most are drinking martinis.

I'm standing at the edge of a small knot of them when a tall woman with impossibly shiny hair turns to me. "And what do you do?" she asks.

I tell her I'm into organs. At first, she thinks that means I play an instrument, so I begin with the most recent story: a family on vacation from China whose five-year-old son fell off the edge of the LOVE sculpture while his dad was taking a photo. They stare at me like I'm a monster. Maybe I am. I can't get enough of this stuff. I try to explain that in every story, no matter how ghastly, something funny happens, or something odd.

"Yes, it's hilarious that their child died," spits the lady with the glowing hair.

"Not that. The odd/funny part was what the father said after the coordinator explained brain death to him. He didn't speak English very well, and he nodded and nodded and then said, 'Yes, yes, I get it. We want brain transplant!'" No one laughs. "I didn't mean 'funny' like funny ha-ha; I meant 'funny' like awful funny."

I want to tell them that you have to talk about it this way; otherwise, you'd lie down on the floor and never get up.

Much later, after I've had my fourth glass of chardonnay and I'm finishing up a story about a girl whose parents refused to donate because they thought their daughter would snap out of it, a man with thick sideburns and an upturned nose announces, "Well, I for one don't want some guy letting me die so they can transplant my organs. No, thank you! That's what they do. They just take everything, before you're even dead."

The other guests nod or stare into their drinks.

They know about organ donation from TV shows like *ER* or *Dateline* – the transplant recipient who begins to act like the dead donor, the doctor paid off to remove the kidney of a perfectly healthy kid, the boy who receives a baboon heart. I know this, and yet I still can't quite believe it – I can't believe they believe it. "Yes, we want every last thing," I say. "Even your

eyeballs." I fish the olive out of his drink and pop it into my mouth. "Mmm. Tasty."

My boyfriend pulls me into the kitchen. "Hey, listen, maybe you should switch topics. You know, try talking about the weather. And not about how it relates to a fatal car accident, if you can help it." He gives me a tight, angry smile.

The hostess enters the room and sees that we're busy hating each other. She says, "Whoopsie-daisy!" and swivels away on her heels.

"Maybe we should make up conversation topics on index cards," I suggest, barely slurring, "and you can hand them to me as the evening goes on."

"Great idea." He takes my arm and steers me out the door, his grip hard against my elbow. *Good*, I think. *Maybe tomorrow there'll be a bruise.*

I want to be more giving to him. I leave him little sticky notes in the medicine cabinet. *Don't forget your umbrella. Looks like rain.* Or *2 good 2 B 4 gotten.* He doesn't mention them. I want to give him something of myself: my eyes, my fingers, my heart. Instead, I mop the bathroom floor and check out books for him from the library, mostly about the American Revolution.

After my last day of training, I present him with a bicycle helmet. "Just wear it." He shakes his head. "Hey, try not to worry about your hair. Worry about your brain being splattered on the sidewalk outside of a Starbucks. Think how embarrassing that would be." I strap the helmet on my own head. "Look, look – you'll be the envy of all of your friends." I try to explain that he has no idea how dangerous the world can be. Bricks fall from the sky. Ice is slippery. You can be at a bar having a nice conversation, then say the wrong thing, and some burly construction worker can hit you over the head with a Heineken

bottle. "These are matters of life and death. You should pay attention."

He says, "You were happier when you were an RN at that doctor's office. Remember those days? Remember when you always wanted to take my temperature?" At one time in our relationship this would've been a come-on. Now he gives me a look like I'm a defective purchase he wants to return. "I think I liked you better then."

I lie on the floor in front of him, still wearing the helmet. "I think I liked me better then, too."

He turns on the TV, to a rerun of *Law & Order: Special Victims Unit*, and politely asks me to move.

At our work Halloween party I count one Terri Schiavo, two blood bank operators with fake blood splattering their clothes, several ghosts, a few zombies, three vampires, and a cat. We're a scary bunch. My boyfriend has consented to go with me – a rare occasion. I parade him around the room, introducing him proudly as if to say, *Look, look, this is the person who tolerates me!*

He's dressed as a Holstein cow – the same costume he's worn for two years running. I go as the Bride of Frankenstein. We stand by the punch bowl spiked with vodka. I've made a mental list of conversational topics to use with him – ones that don't involve blood thinner or dead children.

We all drink too much and get swept away by the karaoke. Andrew, the director – dressed as a caveman with a single, thick eyebrow drawn across his forehead – croons "Living on a Prayer." His eyes are squeezed shut with sincerity. It's the same look he bears when speaking to families, and the expression I imagine him wearing during sex.

I realize I'm staring at Andrew and turn instead to my boyfriend. His cow horns are crooked. I straighten them. "I find you udderly attractive," I say, knowing it sounds unconvincing.

He gives me a side hug.

I'll go on at least 16 cases with a seasoned coordinator before I'm set free to convince families on my own. My first time out, I'm paired with Bryan.

The case is an eight-month-old girl whose mother accidentally left the baby carrier on top of the family SUV, then backed out of the driveway, still talking to the child she thought she'd clicked into the car seat. Halfway down the block she braked at a stop sign and heard a thump. She assumed at first that a neighbor's garbage can had tipped over. Then the truth of what occurred rose with appalling certainty in her throat.

You think this story is an urban legend; you've heard it before, or something similar. But here's the thing: it really happened. It happens and worse: a drunk father who accidentally runs over his son with his ATV, a hunter who mistakes his brother for a stag, a girl whose hits her twin sister in the head with a lacrosse ball.

While we're waiting for the neurologist to declare the baby brain-dead, another call comes in on Bryan's Blackberry. Thirty-four-year-old Caucasian male, hit by a car while biking to work. I wonder how I would feel if it turned out to be my boyfriend. I find myself blushing at the thought. How selfish I am. Why must everything relate back to me? And yet I imagine the funeral scene: me as the stoic girlfriend, his family caving under the grief. I try to work myself into tears, as I was able to do in training, but can't seem to muster up the correct emotion.

And of course it's not him. It's someone else's boyfriend, someone who's not as lucky as me.

After the baby is pronounced, Bryan and I go into the waiting room, where the father paces. The mother, hysterical, has been heavily sedated. We talk to the father about donation. He nods and looks back and forth between our faces with a look of

complete bafflement. "Yes," he says when we're finished. "Yes, if she can save another baby, then yes. Do whatever you need to do."

He wants something good to come out of this tragedy – anything, anything, one good thing.

The baby has a full head of black curls like her dad. Her eyes are shut and rimmed with blue bruises. She resembles a baby panda bear. She is impossibly small and pale, and I want to wrap her up and hide her in my coat, take her home with me, and pray for a miracle.

Initially, we're hopeful. The doctors work hard to keep her heart beating so she can be a donor, so we can give the family something. They pump her body full of blood thinner to maintain her for the operating room. But she arrests. All her organs become toxic, unusable, worthless.

And she dies, and no one is saved and my head empties of reason. The father shakes my hand with a blank look on his face. It will take some time for the truth to sink in.

I walk all the way home in my sensible black heels, hoping for blisters as penance for being one of the living, for not having to survive without someone I love.

I go into the house, where my boyfriend is sitting at the kitchen table doing a crossword puzzle. He's wearing his glasses, which reminds me of when we first met. He brought his mom into the doctor's office because she couldn't stop hiccupping. He wore his glasses then, too, and I thought, *What a sweet guy. He loves his mother.* He looks up. "How did it go?"

"We lost the baby," I tell him.

"Well, have you tried looking under the sofa?" He glances back to his puzzle.

I open my mouth to tell him what happened and then shut it again.

I go upstairs. He's plugged in the radio again over the bathroom sink, just a few feet from the tub. I unplug it, wind the cord around the center, and stow it in the closet behind a mountain of towels.

I lie on our bed, hands on either side of my body like a dead person. I begin listing parts of the anatomy, beginning with the letter *A* and working my way down the alphabet: *aorta, bronchial tube, cranium, duodenum.* This is how I distract myself from thinking about what I should do.

And then, just in time for Christmas, it's my turn to go on a case alone. They give me a black beeper. I might be called once on the shift, twice, three times, or never. The day burns bright with just a slight chance of snow. I pray this means no one will die today. Tomorrow, okay. But please not today.

My boyfriend has called in sick to work. He perches on the sofa in his droopy gray jogging pants, playing a video game that requires him to shoot people with a semiautomatic machine gun and drive a sports car. I sit next to him. "What's the point of this game?" I ask.

He can't answer because he's concentrating, speeding down a twisting highway in Southern California. He's explained to me that the game is an exact replica of Los Angeles and the outlying areas, down to each building and street. Just like real life.

I nudge him with my foot. "How do you win?"

"Damn it!" We watch his car careen off a cliff and plunge into the water. Seconds later his man surfaces, unharmed, and begins swimming toward shore. "You don't win."

"Then why do you play?" I don't state the obvious: that his video game hero would've been an organ donor a hundred times over by now – because at some point, my God, I have to shut up.

"It's a rush." This is what he wants our life to be like – one long, fun-filled adventure after another with no real casualties.

The beeper goes off an hour later.

I call the office. Marla, the receptionist, gives me the details. Couple involved in a car accident, sideswiped by a truck whose driver had been awake all night trying to make a noon delivery to New York. The husband has superficial cuts on his neck and chest. Doctors are working to save the wife, but she has an internal bleed. I ask the questions I think I'm supposed to ask while putting on my hat and shoes. I attempt to zipper my coat and realize my hands are shaking.

Marla tells me to call if I don't think I can handle it and she'll send in another coordinator. She tells me I'll be fine. This is my first conversation with her, and she's managed to calm me down in a way I know my boyfriend never could.

"Leave the light on for me," I tell him. He nods. I waver by the front door. "Goodbye, then."

"Good–" he begins, but stops as his car plummets off yet another cliff.

I see the truck driver who killed the woman, sitting in the waiting room. He's a mammoth of a man in red flannel, a John Deere cap tucked back on his head. His eyes are wide, and his face is a picture of raw disbelief. When he sees me, he stands, taking off his hat.

"I didn't mean it," he says.

"I know," I say.

The rush of people swooshes around us – nurses, a little boy wailing, families arguing. A TV mounted near the ceiling broadcasts close-up after close-up of beautiful soap opera actors, their artful faces bearing a whole range of recognizable expressions: sadness, joy, jealousy, triumph, fear.

I ask a nurse if she can find an open bed for the trucker, so that he can lie down for a while. She says okay and he follows her obediently, like a large child.

The surgeon greets me as I walk into the ICU. He's an older man with graying hair and deep-set brown eyes. I'm in luck: he's one of the good doctors, one who's treated transplant recipients in the past, not one who calls us "the death squad."

He explains the situation. No hope of survival for the wife. She hasn't taken a breath on her own in two hours and has failed two apnea tests. The CAT scan shows no cerebral blood flow. I nod. "Okay, okay."

He knows it's my first solo case. "You can handle it," he says.

I take a deep breath and go into the patient's room. The husband sits beside her bed. My training has taught me that the dead look dead. They don't appear kind of dead or somewhat dead. Even as their chests rise and fall because of the ventilator, there's something missing in them.

The woman's dark hair is pulled off her face with a headband. Around the room her family and friends have left flowers, balloons, stuffed animals, as if she were a kid having her tonsils out. One of her eyes is half open. If I pulled up the lid, I'd see the pupil blown out, filling the white. In slide presentations during training, it looked like something from a scary movie – the eye of death, one might say, if one were given to such dramatizations. Her other eye has been covered by a white bandage, giving her a slightly jaunty air.

The husband is tall and handsome with stubble on his chin. He's been told that there's no chance of recovery, no miracle on its way. He's seen the nurse put a cotton swab to his wife's eye and watched as it didn't blink or move. "We were only married for a year," he tells me. "We just moved into a new house. We haven't even hung up the pictures yet."

"I'm sorry." Instead of dispensing the platitudes we've been taught (*You can give the gift of life! It's your time to make a difference. One dead wife equals seven others saved!*), I listen to him.

I listen to him talk about his wife, Lena, for a long time. They met in a dive bar in Northern Liberties. He thought she'd be a one-night stand, but he stayed that night, and the next, and the next, and then he moved in his stereo and that was it. They were married in Hawaii by a priest with a lisp. They have a fat golden retriever named Jack. He pauses, staring off toward the wall. His eyes are clear and blue. "How am I going to break the news to Jack?" he says. His gaze turns to me. "Maybe I should tell him to sit first?" His laughter comes out in a burst.

I say, "Maybe you should remind him that he's a good boy?" We're both laughing. It's hysterical, this laughter, and a blessing.

The doctor hovers in the doorway. It's time to go. I ask the husband if there's anything he wants to do before we take her to the operating room.

He doesn't hesitate. "Could you find me a brush or a comb? Her hair is a mess. She would hate that." I get him a brush. We set her headband on the dresser beside the bed. I hold her so that he can reach the back of her head. He brushes her hair with careful, clumsy strokes.

We don't talk about donation. The husband has already consented. I don't have to convince him of anything. He knows what she would have wanted. He knows what she would have said.

When he's finished, he puts her headband back on. I remain quiet, though I know they'll remove it in the operating room. "You're doing a good thing," I tell him.

He nods and I leave him alone for a moment, not because I'm generous but because I can't stand to watch them say goodbye.

I follow the transplant recovery team into the OR. The woman has become "the body," "the chest," no longer the person, the

wife, Lena Dixon. They wrap her in clear plastic, cocooning her. The nurse swabs her with iodine and the room fills with the smell of it.

The surgeon picks up a scalpel. His eyes flicker to me as if checking whether I'm okay. I'm okay. Everything is A-OK. He makes a long incision from throat to stomach. Another doctor cracks open the sternum. The chest bone is difficult to break; sometimes they have to use a saw. The surgeon snips the aortic valve, delicately, his pinky raised, and then I see it. It's bigger than I thought it would be – twice the size of my fist. Not red, not beautiful. A purple and black muscle, a wonderful and horrible thing, still beating.

The rest of the transplant surgeons do what they need to do. The heart will be placed in a red cooler and flown via helicopter to a different hospital where another family waits. The lungs are trickier and may not be usable. The liver might go to a local woman, the kidneys to two other people. Skin tissue for burn victims. Corneas for a blind person. One life to save seven others.

It's a good thing. It's a good thing. It's a good thing. I repeat this to myself while the nurse sews the empty body closed with neat black stitches.

It's 4 a.m. when I stumble through the hospital's automatic doors. My legs tremble from standing for so long. The parking lot is deserted, the moon just beginning to fade as streaks of orange and purple flood across the sky. The start of another beautiful day.

The porch light is off, which shouldn't matter really since it's already dawn. I fumble with the keys for a long time before I unlock the front door.

I pull off my shoes and notice a hole in my tights. This makes me think again of the black threads across Lena Dixon's

skin, how the nurse stitched her up as though it were a normal procedure, and not the end of something.

I drag myself upstairs to the bedroom and stand over the sleeping shape of my boyfriend. His arm is thrown up over his head as if to shield himself from an attack. He seems younger; in sleep he doesn't have to arrange his face in any particular way to prepare for what I might say next.

He was dear to me once. At least, I think he was.

In training we learned the many reasons people say no. They say no because they look at the body and can't believe their son/daughter/husband/wife/brother/sister won't snap out of it. They say no because they understand that doctors make mistakes, or because they hear the word *coma* and believe there's a chance their loved one can be saved. Because they still have hope. They say no because they met someone who knows someone whose brother was in a terrible car wreck but made a slow recovery and is now bagging groceries at the local supermarket. They say no because they can't bear that their son's dog will outlive their son. They say no because they raised this child, fell in love with this face, remember with clarity how he used to move around in space, his habit of gesturing with his hands when telling a story. They say no because to say yes would mean accepting death.

I sit at the kitchen table and make a list. The sun creeps across the floor as I write. *Replace the tangle of cords beneath your computer. Buy new batteries for the smoke alarm. Sidewalk salt for when it's icy. A waterproof radio for the bathroom. Duck-shaped stickies for the bottom of the tub* .... I write until my hand aches; this is the last good thing I can do before I leave.

The Bluest Skies

I hear him before I see him. Everyone in the ICU does, this one long moan of a word, "Shellyshellyshellyshellyshelly."

I check in first with the head nurse, Joyce – I remember her from last time. She is not a fan of organ donation and calls us the Vulture Squad. When I first met her, she gathered herself up and said, "I'm going into the earth the way the Lord brought me in. Intact."

I said nothing.

What I wanted to say was "Oh, yeah? Well, unless you're cremated, your internal organs will be removed by the mortician and placed in a silver basin like so many slippery fish. Then, formaldehyde will be pumped into your veins by a number nine needle. A dab of super glue seals your eyelids shut so that they don't pop open for the viewing and also because, guess what? Your eyeballs have been removed. Your hands will be shaped into a prayer position, because otherwise, they will curl up into your palms due to rigor mortis."

These are the inside thoughts. They come out in our Monday morning quarterbacks with other transplant coordinators, because they understand. We sit around and talk about who

died that weekend, and how, and whether anyone was saved. In training, I distinctly remember a PowerPoint presentation by the county coroner called, "Ways You Can Die in the Bathroom, Part 1."

I am deferential to Joyce. She is accustomed to doctors who barely register her presence. I don't lean on the counter like an overly friendly representative from Pfizer. I stick with what I think will make her talk. "I was at HUP last night. I wish that you could have seen this nurse. She wasn't sure how much dopamine to administer on this nutjob who shot a nail gun through his foot."

She glares, but is compelled to answer, "Well, that depends on the body weight, doesn't it?"

"That's what I said." We both shake our heads. I don't make a joke about how the kid's name was Jesus and he was practicing for Easter Sunday. That's for a different nurse, one who doesn't have a gold cross swaying between the wide white sea of her uniform.

I've brought her two Kit Kats from the gift shop because I tucked that bit of information in my head from the previous aneurism case. I hand them to her, saying, "I don't like chocolate." She looks up. She doesn't say thanks, but she doesn't say no thanks. Now, it may be easier with her the next time I'm called out to talk to a family after their kid hangs himself with a bit of nylon.

All this from the one business marketing class I took in college called Knowing Your Audience: How to Seal the Deal.

I'm familiar with Jefferson's ICU and so many others like it in the City of Brotherly Love. Slick white floors, whooshing doors, a murmur of whispered voices and the occasional shriek from a bleeder. The last time I was on the sixth floor of Jeff, we had a gunshot wound from a drive-by: back of the head,

21-year-old white male, and screen positive for crack cocaine. His organs turned toxic before the family could consent. They dawdled and prayed and fucked around and his heart went south and no one was saved and everybody died. We all went home and some of us coped by watching the entire first season of *House of Cards*.

Before approaching the room, I get details on a call with John, the transplant intake coordinator. He wears a headset all day, like an air traffic controller. I imagine that he would be generous in bed – would touch your thighs with light fingers, testing, *Is this okay? How does this feel?*

This patient is Caucasian female, age 24, found unresponsive in her kitchen, slumped next to the stove with a gaping head wound, likely from a hammer of some kind. One apnea test and one scan. Zero activity. Not even a trickle of blood flow to the brain. "And the next of kin?"

"Well, there's your problem. She was an aged-out foster kid, no close family, so your guy is the alleged perp." John pauses. I hear him tapping. "Oh, but it looks like she's negative for drugs."

"Say again?" I hear a low murmur: *Shellyshellyshelly.*

"You got to ask the husband for consent."

"You mean the hammer-wielding guy?" An intern walks by, pushing a lumpy gurney containing what might be a load of laundry or might be a corpse.

"His name is Joseph. Short for 'I Killed My Wife and All I Got was this Ugly T-shirt.'"

I'm not having a great month. Two consents, two denials. One of the two denials was a dead baby, and those are hard to get "yeses" for. You have to go to the parents when they've just learned that their two-year-old, Michaela, who was found face down in the neighbor's above-ground pool, is now officially

brain-dead. Good news is she's a perfect match for a baby in need of liver transplant in Peoria!

I thank John and hang up, searching for a strategy.

A uniformed cop stops me at the door in the ICU. "You from that gift place?" He has dark blue eyes, and bulging arm muscles. I do not imagine what he would look like naked, but I do note that he has thin wrists, which my mother said meant he would be a better kisser. Something to do with evolution.

"Gift of Life, yes. I'm a transplant coordinator."

He sizes me up. I stand a little straighter. "You guys move fast, huh? You really scoop them right up."

"We have to move fast. Just like you." Here is where I could launch into my story about how rare brain death is and how there are thousands of people on the waiting list and some of those people die every day. Here's where I could say, "Your loved one could save the lives of up to seven people today." That's what we learned in training, but to me, it sounds like a bad advertisement: "Buy one, get seven free!" I can see from his blank stare and crossed arms that a different approach is needed.

"I have her DMV record. She's an organ donor already, but we still need someone to sign the papers." He gives me a look like, *So?* "That's a dead girl in there. She won't be talking. I know you want to get the guy in for questioning, but I need him to sign some forms."

He squints at me. "You watch a lot of cop TV?"

I quickly scan his badge. "No, Officer Patterson. My dad was a highway patrolman." The lie pops out, fully formed. "In Nebraska. He saw a lot of car fatalities, not so many murders because it was a small town, but plenty of people who went through the windshield or shot themselves in pickup trucks."

"He come home and talk about it over potpie?" He senses bullshit.

"It was a hard job." I pause. "I just need 10 minutes with him. Ten minutes, and the next time I get a hit-and-run with even a tiny clue, I'll call you ASAP. No matter what."

"You saying you don't normally call me?" He keeps his eyes on me, ignoring another gurney that flies by with a squeaky wheel.

"No, I'm saying I'll call you first. Like, on speed dial, if that were still a thing. That helps your numbers, right? Mine too."

"I need to bring him in. I can't question him here." He's looking at me like maybe I have something to offer.

"Ten minutes, and then you can have him." I smile in a way that I hope is firm yet professional yet flirtatious. I've been practicing.

"Don't try to use your feminine wiles on him."

I flutter my eyelashes, and turn to the side to show him my chest, which is not an insignificant thing. You have to use it all. You have to use your whole body. "I would never."

I've made a few calls already. There's a girl in Hartford, same blood type (B positive), status one on the heart transplant list. She's tiny, 95 pounds, but so is the body, so the heart should fit. We take measurements, consider cavities. There's also a lung recipient one county over, who is probably getting the call right now like from the movies, "Drop everything and get to the OR!" A kidney patient in Delaware. Another in New Jersey. We give it all away: eyes, skin, bones. Reminds me of a game we played in gym. "Heads, shoulders, knees, and toes."

But first, I have to get consent.

Room 202 is not filled with family or Mylar balloons with Ziggys on them or bursting bouquets of flowers. It's just the bed and the body and the sound of the heart monitor, that deceiving blip that makes families believe there is hope. At work,

we have this plan to create a heart monitor with a "booing" sound.

The rosiness of her cheeks and the warmth of her skin – it's an illusion. *Shellyshellyshelly* is a corpse.

There's a man bent over in a chair. He wears a white T-shirt with what looks like spaghetti sauce spotting it. It takes me a second to reconcile that the spots might be her blood. Why they didn't let him change in the last 24 hours is not a question I can answer. His face is dark red with the strain, and he's got that prison/gang-banger bristly crew cut and the blue ink of some badly done tattoo snaking up around his neck. He keeps saying, "Shelly, Shelly, Shelly, Shelly."

I take a quick glance at the body, and then away. Her head is wrapped in gauze and she has a tube coming out of her mouth attached to the ventilator that's breathing for her with big asthmatic pumps.

His eyes are puffy, bloodshot. "Joseph," I say, careful to use his name. "Is there someone else you want me to call for you? Your mom? A lawyer?" Your probation officer? I don't suggest.

"I want out of here." He rocks, pulling the shirt up higher on his back. "I want to touch her face."

"Okay, I know you do. I'm sorry this is so hard right now."

"What the hell, lady. Are you some kind of social worker? A woman priest? The priest already been here."

My beeper goes off. It's the other hospital in Hartford, looking for a heart update.

I step outside of the room. In an ICU in Connecticut, the unnamed girl with B positive blood is being hooked up to machines. She's 1,500 miles away, waiting with her family. Danny, the living organ coordinator, tries to find my soft spot. "She's a swimmer. She's 15. She wants to go to the homecoming dance."

"Oh, really? Well, I wasn't going to push very hard, but I will now so she can slow dance with her summer crush."

He tries again. "She has two dogs." I say nothing. Two seconds later, I get a text with a photo of a gray terrier with whiskers out to here and a black Lab, both scrunched in next to her in this hospital bed. The line below their picture reads: "Say hi to Gracie and Sam."

I go back to the call. "Stop with the dogs."

"How will the dogs feel if this doesn't work out?" he asks. "They'll probably be taken to a shelter and put down immediately." We had a fling once upon a time at a national conference on non-heart beating donation. I seem to remember he was very ticklish around the armpits.

"I'll do my best."

I return to Joseph, who has gone silent. The heart monitor beeps in the background, and the murmur of overhead calls can be heard, but that is all. Her legs are tiny branches under a white blanket. I try not to look at her head, to see if anything is leaking through to the bandages.

After a little more negotiation, the cop lets us move to the grieving room. This is where the ICU sends families to cry and shake their fists at the ceiling. I take Joseph there not because I want to give the guy some peace. It's because I need get him away from the body. With the body in his sight, he will never consent.

We sit in a room that looks like a combination chapel/board room, with boxes of Kleenexes and donated flowers on the tables, alongside daisies with wilting petals and bright "get well" cards. Outdated magazines with ripped covers are strewn about, mixed in with kid books like *Are You My Mother?*

"What if she wakes up while we're in here?" Joseph asks. He's pacing a bit in the small room, turning around on himself. I want him to sit still.

"She won't." I don't say, *Because you killed her*. "You want something to drink?" He doesn't answer.

He finally sits with his hands folded over his face.

I sit too. The chairs are cushioned. I start to feel like he does – worn out, confused. That's the problem with empathy; it can put you on a bad path, one where you aren't able to do your job. I shake it off.

He starts hiccupping. I teach him a trick where you bend over from the waist and take three huge breaths. Hiccups are really just your diaphragm getting caught in a weird loop. You have to give it time to get back on track. He does as he's told. By the look of his eyes, he is going on no sleep for at least 24 hours and possibly coming off an opioid. The strange thing is that he smells good, like Irish Spring soap.

We sit in silence until the hiccups stop.

On the muted TV hanging in the corner, Wolf Blitzer's huge white head of hair fills the screen. The world keeps happening around us.

I get him a Coke from the vending machine because I keep lots of change on hand and because I know that's what he'd ask for if he could think straight.

"How much did the doctor talk to you?"

He turns the soda can around in his hands. He shrugs. Big, boxy shoulders. He could've been so many other things. A bouncer, for instance. I mean, let's not get carried away. "No blood flow?" He says it like a little kid with a speech impediment. His face is getting redder and redder, even though he's not moving.

160

"Tell me something about her. What kind of music did she like?" I use the past tense on purpose.

Old school Guns & Roses. "She's got eyes of the bluest skies ...," he says. (With a blown pupil), I add silently. Favorite ice cream? Rita's Water Ice. How'd they meet? Kensington High together. She was a sweet girl (was). She never liked to party, and she hung out with the right people. They got married because what the fuck, why not (his words), and it was almost always good. Almost always.

I could see the attraction. You could find yourself watching just his lips move, knowing that you're dating a cliché, this guy on a Harley who gets in fights at the Ray's Happy Birthday Bar. You know he will end up in jail or dead, but that's part of the attraction. When you're with him, you are living. He will have bruises on his body, hip bones jutting out that you want to kiss, and puckered scars on the back of his neck, just below the collar where teachers can't see them, where his dad put out a lit cigarette (be more original, Dad!). He will like to go down on you, any time, any place, and he will hold you in place, worshipping. You know that you are meant to save him. He is misunderstood, and you are not like the others. You see how he gets around babies, all soft and mushy. How could a guy like that be bad inside? He doesn't use his fists; he uses whatever else he can get his hands on because he is not like his dad, he believes. He would never hit you like that. That's how he thinks.

Or so I imagine.

I'm trying very, very hard not to look at the wide face of the clock on the wall. It's a timing thing. The organs will start to turn bad if you leave them too long. She could throw a blood clot any second and flip into cardiac arrest. It's the same for the people on the other side, the bodies waiting to be saved.

I have a creak in my joints, a distant ringing in my ear like a dinner bell, an occasional eye twitch. My knee bones will have to be replaced by plastic someday; I can feel it in my joints.

He starts a story about a carnival they attended in Fishtown. It feels like we're moving in slow motion. I lean forward until I'm almost touching him. I say, "You're a good person. I see it. And there is a way you can make this better."

He shakes his head. His face is wet and I can't tell if it's sweat or tears. I hand him a Kleenex. He looks right at me then, his eyes a vivid green framed by dewy eyelashes. You can see what he looked like as a little boy. You can almost picture him in cowboy pajamas watching whatever horror show went on at his house when he was little. Best not to think about that. "What's going to happen to me?"

I say, "I don't know." Because honestly, I don't. And because whatever will happen next to him is not going to be good.

He rubs his wrists and starts to murmur her name again.

My palms itch with an urge to push this forward, thrust the pen into his hand, get consent. I force myself to go slow. My back bristles, knowing that the cop is going to rap on the door soon. He's given me time with the alleged perp, but he wants to move, start the processing, the endless paperwork that both of our jobs are really about. People reduced to short sentences on a form, "alleged perpetrator seems agitated."

"Donor body viable for heart, lungs, and liver, negative for kidney function."

I'm supposed to make sure he understands brain death. If I could, I would draw him a picture, because frankly, I'm a visual person. I would make a big, wide, onion-like shape to represent the head. I would leave lots and lots of white space to illustrate the lack of brain activity. I would draw black Xs where the eyes

should be and a tongue sticking out. I would draw the stem of the neck, as if the head were decapitated. I would draw a line to show the blockage of blood to the brain, and then arrows representing how the blood can no longer get past the brain. No blood, no thought, no life.

Instead, I take his hand with its wide clean fingernails. No scratch marks at all. He could be innocent. I whisper to him, "I know you didn't mean it. This is one way she can stay alive."

It's like he didn't hear me. "I just want to fucking lay down." He puts his head on the table like a kid.

"This is the last thing." I take out a pen. It's a Bic, nothing too pretentious, nothing with anything on it that could be some other impediment, like a religious affiliation or a Pet Boys logo when they work at a local shop. I keep my eyes on his. "Sign here."

He sits up. He clutches the pen. He wants me to tell him it is okay. I need him to sign the form. I say, "It's okay." I wait. He looks at me, squinting, as if he thinks we've met before in some other nightmare. Maybe I remind him of someone too. I can't tell if that is a good or a bad thing.

The cop raps on the door. The kid jumps, spilling soda in a wide pool on the table. He drops the pen. My phone beeps, angry, exacting, the buzz of the transplant coordinator waiting in Hartford.

"One minute!" I call out. I sop up the wetness with a napkin.

He grabs my hand again. He has a strong grasp and it makes my pulse throb in my neck. It is a grip that could snap an arm bone like a pencil. "You pray for her?"

I nod, relaxing my body so he loosens his grip. "Yes, of course."

He signs the form. He presses hard on the pen, concentrating, and I don't have to worry about it not bleeding through in

triplicate. "Let me go tell them you need another minute with her." I place my hand on his back, and feel taut muscle through the worn T-shirt.

My guess is he doesn't get what he just did – how he just consented to all of the tiny boxes I previously checked, including the removal of bowels, skin, bone. Did you know that one skin donation can save up to 5,000 burn victims? I made that up. It's more like five people. And tissue can be used to reconstruct breasts after cancer. That is a fact.

His lack of understanding could be a problem later, but probably not. Where he's going, he won't have much of a voice. No one is looking out for her either, so that's really the end of it. For them.

I go to back to Officer Patterson, who leans against the reception desk while Joyce types away on her computer. I note that one of the Kit Kat bars has disappeared, the orange wrapper jammed under a file folder marked "confidential." Next time, I will bring her up-to-date magazines for the waiting room, the good, trashy kind like *People* and *Us* and *Cosmopolitan*; ones with headlines like, "25 ways to excite your man using just your mouth."

"You done with him?" The cop cracks his knuckles. I'd like to take him back into the nurse's linen closet to get to know him better among the starchy smell of the over-washed sheets and wilting pillowcases.

"Yes," I say. I could add the part about how he wants to see her. The last goodbye. But time .... It's brutal. I shove the forms into an envelope and make my way back to the body.

I go into the hospital room, where it's still quiet. I take the temperature. I have gotten the medical history from previous hospitalization records and bloodwork, so we know she is

cancer free, and also so we don't put a pair of HIV positive lungs in a 14-year-old boy and kill him.

I check the blood pressure. It's steady.

A few seconds later, the wail comes from far away and then moves closer, like an approaching fire engine. *Shellyshellyshellyshellyshellyshellyshellyshelly!* I catch a blur of white through the square hospital room window. He seems to be right outside the door, ready to kick it in. I brace myself. "Shelly!" Shelly is dead. He done killed her. The sounds fade away until they are gone.

It's the best thing. If we opened the door, he might fling himself on the body like something from a bad TV show, disconnecting the wires. I've seen this happen and worse. Pretend she is a five-year-old named Brenna and then pretend you are the father who accidentally ran her over with your SUV. On that case, the cops said, "He's not going to survive the year."

I look at the body. I avoid the face, because a brief glance says that though it may have been pretty once, it is now a puff of purple skin and burst blood vessels. The eyes are closed, but if you peeled back the lid you would see a blown pupil, a big black hole, and behind that big black hole is no brain activity.

I tap the fluid line giving her veins nourishment. There's a water jug with a straw in it and a moving table in case she wants to write a letter. There is a robe on the back of the door and a porta-potty seat in the bathroom next to a button you press if you've had a fall. She won't be needing any of these things.

Do I pray? No. I do not.

Instead, I wash the face with warm water to remove the dark smudge of makeup under the eyes and the traces of blood dotting her forehead like freckles, careful to not touch the bandage or the tube helping the body to breathe.

Her hand has blood in the cuticles. The nails are a bubble gum pink, and I don't imagine how she might have had them

painted this weekend, chatting with the other people at the salon, maybe thinking about how much he would like it. Maybe she was a lousy tipper. Maybe she made fun of the Korean women who ran the place. Maybe I wouldn't have liked her at all. Shelly.

I pick up her hand. I close my eyes and squeeze. I know she's dead. I know it. But I wait. Only when I feel nothing can I breathe again.

I call the transplant surgeon. I schedule OR time. I phone my counterpart in Hartford. He is grateful that this is moving forward, his voice wrung out and low. "You owe me big," I remind him.

What happens next is a roller-coaster ride. The residents arrive, all purpose and sound. They bundle her up, and sweep the entire rolling bed out of the room to surgery. The machines roll behind her with the same efficiency, all moving together in a kind of dizzying, clunky harmony.

Before you know it, we stand under the bright glow of the lights in the surgical theater. Shelly's head is separated from her body by a white curtain like something from a magician's trick. The anesthetist hovers near her head, bowing low, so her lips move just above Shelly's hair. She whispers something. That's her thing. Me, I like to watch the body.

You may think that surgeons are exact, like artists, moving in tandem to Bach's Fifth Symphony playing through speakers. This is not true. They are more like mechanics. Their job is to get inside of you and that's not always easy. To access the organs, they must saw through the bones of your sternum and ribs. I've seen a surgeon ask a resident to climb on the table and push with his knee. The crack of the breastbone sounds like a branch breaking clean in half; shotgun loud and mixed with the sweet smell of bone dust from the buzz saw.

I can almost hear the whir of the wings of the helicopter descending on the roof. What they do is take the heart in a little ice cooler, the kind you might bring to a tailgate. They will pack the heart in ice. You have 24 hours before it dies for good. Once the heart is secured, they will pull into the blue sky again, off to the next hospital with another body on wait, this one alive, hopeful.

For Shelly, it happens all at once. The clean scalpel line, a red river of blood, a breaking branch and then –

The surgeon moves his fingers with precision, sweat making a star-shaped splotch on his surgical cap. His hands go inside the chest, and he looks down while the nurse uses suction, and then out it comes – the heart, still beating. It's the size and shape of a small eggplant. It's a live, moving thing – purple and red and beautiful. In a moment, the surgeon will clamp the veins shut, but the heart will continue to pulse for several seconds, even after every other connection to it is gone.

My hand flutters to my chest. As always, I feel a stab of surprise. It beats.

This Belongs to You

She was my 57th client. I remember that because the house number was 75 Leipzig Street, and I thought that it was significant that the numbers were reversed. Back then, I was always searching for signs, making meaning out of birthdates and billboard signs, license plates and fortune cookies.

I worked for 20 years as a professional organizer. I'd seen hoarding before; that was my job. You must imagine that my own house was as neat as a pin. And it was until Margaret Pieman. After her, I let things stay where they fell, began to like the towers and the path I wove through to make it to the microwave or the recliner where I slept after my bedroom was overtaken by cast-off clothes, stuffed animals, jars of jam, black umbrellas turned inside out by the wind. But I am getting ahead of myself.

Margaret Pieman, age 67, lived in a three-bedroom ranch in Fort Worth, Texas. When I first got out of the car, the sun reflected off the windows and I thought, *Oh, wow, this is beautiful,* because the whole house was lit up like it had a halo around it. The windows were blocked off with blankets, so it was impossible to see inside.

She met me at the front door, beside a faded sleigh with Santa at the head of it, his mouth open as if he had just finished a string of "ho ho hos." Nine plastic reindeer lay on their sides, looking like they had fallen into a sudden and deep sleep.

Margaret shook my hand firmly, a tough grasp with hands in gardening gloves. She said, "You are not going to believe this."

I thought, *Yes, I will.* I'd been to the house of a gentleman the month before who kept every single store receipt since he was 15 years old, who wore a diaper. He could no longer make his way to the toilet because the hallway was blocked by boxes of fly-fishing magazines. A jar of dentures earned a privileged space on a bookshelf stuffed with Russian newspapers. That is one example. At the time, I thought it was a tragedy.

"Put this on." She handed me a football helmet, then strapped one on herself. "Don't let go of my hand," she said. She looked me in the eyes, and I thought, *Why, she seems sane,* because by then, I had decided that the people who hoard were insane.

We went inside. I had my mask with me, in case there was a smell. Bug spray in case there were roaches. Cell phone on speed dial in case one of us tripped over boxes and tipped head-first into a collection of broken shells. But I was not prepared for what happened when she opened the door.

First, the smell. It is true that I have smelled sewage before, many times. Human feces, animal waste, food rotted past the maggot stage and well into fly development. That is what I braced myself for, the odor of decay and neglect. Instead, what I got was cinnamon and yeast, like baking bread. It reminded me immediately of my grandmother's bakery in Jersey City.

Margaret gripped my hand, saying, "Don't be afraid, I won't let you fall."

I moved forward in the pitch black and heard the roar of a roller coaster so loud, I ducked, thinking that a track ran above

us, then the jingle-jangle of fun house music, mixed with the murmur of people talking, as if we'd stepped into a crowd. It reminded me of a family vacation to Atlantic City from 35 years ago. We kept moving forward in the dark. It was like being plunged into the bottom of a cave. But I could feel this very particular bite of wind on my face – a brisk wind, cold, the slicing type only found on New England cliffs, where I had been when I was 15 or so. That was the summer I fell in love for the first time with Haskell Jenkins, a weird name, a weird boy, a weird family. Best kisser in my life. I hadn't thought of him in forever.

Margaret said, "Get ready." Like a blind had been released, light flooded into the room.

"Oh," I said. "Oh, my God."

At first, it looked like a typical hoarder's property. A sea of seeming garbage, random objects, piles of clothes, worn cardboard boxes with caved-in sides. But when I got over the initial and familiar shock of the hoard, I noticed that everything in the room seemed familiar to me. The broken clock looked like one that belonged to my great-grandmother. The china dolls whose heads I could just see peeking from a cabinet across the room – they didn't belong to anyone I knew, but I remembered them from the doll museum we visited when I was 12. The dolls frightened me, because their eyes were mostly painted on, unblinking. A seagull in a cage from the boardwalk in 1987. The square desk of my fifth grade English teacher, Mr. Calise. The red dog collar from our collie, Bolt, who got hit by a car.

"It's all here," Margaret said. "Everything you can remember. I saved it for you."

That whole day and into the night, I wandered through her house, marveling at the collection of things from times and places I had forgotten.

Now, my house is like hers. I go to yard sales. I save bits of paper I find blowing across the street. I collect chess sets with broken knights, stacks of playing cards whose aces are missing, photo albums of strangers, knives locked up tight in wooden boxes. I have a system. I was a professional organizer, after all, so things are kept in categories. Mostly, I'm just guessing what they mean, why they might matter to someone else. Waiting for that person to arrive and find the things she lost.

Advice to the Love Loin

(Dedicated to a contestant on *Jeopardy!* who incorrectly solved the puzzle)

Dear Matilda,

I write to you because I know you understand the artistic temperament and how difficult it is to function in the nine-to-five world. Sometimes, when I'm in meetings at work, I have an overwhelming urge to stand up, pull my shirt over my head, and run screaming from the room. This usually happens when we're on the second to third PowerPoint presentation, but the urge can be brought on even by certain phrases, such as "low-hanging fruit," "drill down," or "it is what it is." When I start to feel this way, I look around the room to catch the eyes of the other people sitting at the conference table, but no one seems to find anything wrong with the situation. They nod or add their own suggestions to "crunch the numbers" by "EOD" to check on the "ROI." Am I alone in feeling that we're wasting our lives on these meaningless things? Should I just accept the quote unquote status quo? Or should I chuck it all and go to graduate school to follow my dream of writing the great American novel? Please advise quickly; we have a two-day retreat coming up at the Sheraton Conference Center and I'm not sure I can stand another Myers-Briggs analysis (I always come out as INFJ). Signed, Stuck in a Cubicle with Nowhere to Turn

Dear Stuck,

We call this life. Get used to board/bored meetings. And more bad news – graduate school will have its own set of wa-ter-in the-ear irritating words and endless classes that test your ability to sit still and behave. You will find yourself lis-tening to PhD students whose teeth seem stuck together when they speak of Nietzsche and Derrida as they argue the mean-ing of those very words in the sentences you mentioned. Your head will begin to feel heavy, as if filled with sand. You'll sleep with the wrong people (poets) and wake up hungover and late for the 8 a.m. Rhetoric and Composition class you must teach to bewildered freshmen who begin papers with sentences like "Since the beginning of time, mankind has loved Downy fabric softener ...." You will try to write the great American novel and find that you only have one narrow story to tell: the one about not fitting in. And my darling, that has already been done.

My advice: accept your fate, get your paycheck, be nice to others, and above all, don't take your shirt off in a meeting. At the same time, you must also pay attention, take notes, ask questions, and consider alternate scenarios and then: go home to your tiny little studio apartment and write about it. Spill it all and be as mean and critical of yourself as you are to others. In that way, you might start to feel like a real person. In that way, you might become a writer. But you will never escape the feel-ing that you are alone, because you are. Just like the rest of us.

Fear of Turning into a Cliché Faster than a Rolling Stone Gathers Moss
Dear Matilda,

I've been single for the last, oh, 25 years of my adult life, and just recently, I've started to realize that I'm exhibiting alarming symptoms of the single old maid trope.

For example, my hem lines are unraveling and I find myself drawn to quirky hats set at odd angles on my head – purple fedoras with plumes, tams with a fist-sized red pom-pom on top, and just recently, a top hat that I keep on my dresser. I like to see it first thing in the morning when I wake up, as I can then pretend I've spent the night with a man-about-town after a night at a formal dance, a man who has perhaps just stepped out to buy croissants and cigarettes.

I've also begun collecting cats in startling numbers. It puzzles me how one stray cat begets more cats – as if they have a party line somewhere, an invisible tin can that stretches between my house and the nearby alleyways. One will show up on the doorstep, and then three others follow, not to mention the mama cats that give birth to robust litters in the coat closet behind my rows of increasingly unfashionable shoes bought at thrift stores.

The drinking is mainly under control and I'm still bathing regularly, though again, strangely find myself drawn to bathing rather than showering – taking these long, skin-puckering bubble baths with my hair wrapped in a turban, listening to Aretha Franklin belt out "Respect" on continuous loop.

I bet I know what you will suggest – get out there and meet a man! Go online and set up a few dates! Well, I have done this, but I keep doing things on these dates that I know will turn them off, talking intermittently about my cats and celebrity problems I've read about in *People* magazine. Sometimes, I even cry a little before we've gotten to the main course. I almost never have a second date, and as my phone remains silent for days at a time, I feel a twinge of relief. Thank God I don't have to shave my legs anytime soon. Thank God, I don't have to put on eyeliner and hopeful underwear. Thank God there's a Shirley Temple marathon on TNT.

At the same time, I'm worried about my behavior – is it inevitable to become quirky and undesirable once you pass a certain age (45)? Also, how much worse will this become, because there hasn't been a book written about a single woman past a certain age who didn't turn into a sociopath or a harpy? Is that the next thing, or can I just remain in this constant state of awkwardness among married and partnered couples, all of whom seem determined to set me up with Mr. Right, who often just happens to be this other single guy they know? Please advise. I have stuff in the oven I need to get out for movie night. Signed,
When Will I Start Giving the Evil Eye to Young People in Love?

Dear Evil Eye,
    Two years.

Single, Confused, and Starting to be Concerned about the Flea Situation
Dear Matilda,
    I have been broken up with this guy for over a decade, and yet I still dream about him on a regular basis. It's the same dream. We're about to board a Greyhound bus, and at the last second, he is late, or stuck in the bathroom, and I get pushed on without him, and he isn't going to make it. We're about to be separated forever and it feels like I'm going to a death camp without him or he's being left behind in prison or some such version of that scenario.
    In real life, he lives across the country and I haven't spoken to him or seen him in years. Well, that's not exactly true. I have seen him; he has just not seen me. Two years ago, I had to go on a business trip to a neighboring state, and I made a detour to his state (not that far away – like three hours by train). I found

out on Google maps where he lives, and I went to his house, or rather, I went near his house or by his house a couple of times. Just to be clear, I didn't go up to his house, it's not like I looked into the windows at night and saw him eating dinner or playing with his children. But, well, no, I waited until they were all asleep and then I found the key in one of those fake rocks and let myself in the back door.

Let me tell you, my heart was in my throat. Mostly I was worried about the embarrassment of being caught – like, what would I say? What would he think of me? To be on the safe side, I wore a really cute dress and kitten heels and this sparkly black cardigan, I mean, no one who saw me could or would consider me a thief, more like someone who'd made a wrong turn and forgotten where she lives. Anyway, I looked around his kitchen, opening up cupboards to see if he was eating the same cereal as always (yes, Frosted Flakes) and I picked up and held his yellow coffee mug with the smiley face on it. I gave him that mug one year and he still has it. That must mean something, right?

I went into the bathroom and sniffed at his bath towels for just the shortest period of time and then I started to get even more nervous b/c I was pretty tired and so I worried I might fall asleep in the bathtub or something and be discovered in the morning by his beautiful wife, who I've seen too but never formally met, though if I'm to be completely honest, I did make an appointment to have my teeth cleaned by her, she's a dental hygienist and I paid for it out of my own pocket, just to get a closer look at her.

She was very good at her job, very gentle, and barely made my gums bleed and I could smell her perfume, this light, fruity scent, and imagined what it must be like for him to smell her and then I wondered if he left me because I didn't smell right,

if maybe I might have kept him if I had discovered the right perfume, the right clothes, the right job, the right attitude, the right background. If only I had been her, instead of me.
Signed,
Am I Crazy?

Dear Crazy,

No, you are not. We have all done this – wished for the past back, wished we could be someone else. My advice to you is to check out the real estate listing in their neighborhood to see if you can purchase rental property nearby. Once you've moved in closer, you will have ample opportunities to run into the love of your life at the grocery store, the community center, his own guest bedroom closet. You may consider other ways of insinuating yourself into his life, such as becoming an elementary school teacher where his children attend or giving them music lessons. You might turn up as a temp in his office or the auto mechanic at the Lukoil on the corner. Do whatever it takes to win him back, even if that means turning your life inside out or becoming a different person entirely, someone who is lovable by sheer force of will.

Our Boys

We were worried sick about our boys.

That summer in the City of Brotherly Love, a series of heinous rapes unfolded in quick succession as straight white college boys were sexually assaulted by a female perp. Most of the boys were just over the cusp of adolescence, their narrow chests beginning to sprout whorls of light hair, reedy voices moving up and down the vocal register. Did the attacker like the way they looked? Like the way they rough-housed at soccer practice? The way their young muscles undulated under their jerseys and the sweat trickled from their handsome brows? Was it their pheromones that attracted her, the scent of young sweat, not unlike the smell of horses?

We could only imagine.

It was our job – no, our duty – as Philly's finest special victims unit to solve these outrageous crimes before another boy was hurt. We couldn't figure it out – nothing like this had ever happened. We'd seen crimes before, of course – break-ins, robberies, stolen baby carriages, runaway buses, horses gone wild, an explosion of the feral cat population, Ponzi schemes, adultery, small animal sacrifices, but nothing, nothing like this. We'd

heard of guys having their asses grabbed, yes, we'd heard our fill of dumb jock jokes, we'd written down complaints of wolf whistles, cat calls, chicken clucks, and other general harassment, but nothing that crossed the line into physical contact.

It worked like this: the victim would be out drinking at a local bar in South Philly, places where hipsters typically hung out: Pope's, Tattooed Mom's, Ray's Happy Birthday Bar, Low. He'd stumble to the back alleyway to pee, and she'd strike. The victim would feel a cold hand clasp his balls, a voice hiss in his ears. All of the victims remained paralyzed as she instructed them to put both hands on the wall. She used warming lotion (K-Y jelly, we guessed. Too many pharmacies in the city to target who was buying the stock in bulk), and touched them until they ejaculated, often on the bricks they had been emptying their bladders against moments before.

We tried not to think of the crime as avoidable. We tried not to judge the fact that victims were hanging out at dive bars in a seedy part of the city, drinking with their buddies, wearing stretched white T-shirts that showed off their triceps and biceps, skinny jeans from Urban Outfitters that tapered just so along the ankles, sneakers with a thick sole that gave a lift to their asses.

You focus on their behavior and appearance and you forget that nobody goes for a pitcher of Bud and two-for-one curly fries imagining he'll end up confused in an alleyway, his limp dick hanging out of his jeans, asking the one question every rape victim asks, "Was it my fault?" When you take that question apart, you find one more: *could I have prevented this?* The answer is an emphatic no, and also a quiet yes. Yes, maybe they could have.

At first, the victims didn't report the crimes. It wasn't until one brave dad stepped forward that similar assaults came

to light. His son had been acting strangely. He'd quit lifting weights in the garage, stopped drinking protein shakes. He took to wearing bulky sweatshirts and high-rise jeans belted tight at the waist. Refusing to make his picks in fantasy football, listening to Kenny Chesney for hours on end. "It's driving me nuts," said the dad. Dad had been handsome once. You could see it still in the squareness of his jaw, slightly hidden by drooping jowls. How he used to be fit but now sported a few extra pounds in the middle, a potbelly he kept sucking in as we talked.

Once the story broke the media gave her a nickname immediately: Jerk-off Jane.

More victims came forward. We talked to the boys in soft voices, offered them energy drinks and Butterfingers from the vending machine. We asked them if they wanted to speak to our male detective. They were embarrassed, of course, because their bodies had betrayed them. None of them could give us specific details. In recounting the incidents, their tongues turned clumsy, unwieldy, as if someone had fed them peanut butter.

Do you remember what kind of lotion she used? Some said it smelled like peppermint, others said lavender. One said sandalwood with a hint of cinnamon. *Did you see her face? Any distinguishing marks?* A very few had caught a glimpse of her face, but none described her in the same way. One said she looked like Cameron Diaz in *There's Something About Mary* and another one said she looked like Drew Barrymore in that film where she keeps forgetting who she is. *Fifty First Dates?* Or was it *Fifty Fist Dates?*

Everything now was colored with dangerous sexual innuendo for the victims.

We asked them instead to write down what happened. *Could they do that?* Yes, they could write down some of the details,

but when they put pen in hand, all they could draw were stick figures of people illustrating what had been done to them in these primitive, cave painting ways.

Only one consistent detail: her hands. We brought in a sketch artist. Unfortunately, the perp had all of her fingers and no distinguishing tattoos or jewelry. Her nails were clipped neatly. No polish. One of the victims insisted she had that thing his mom got – what was it? That thing where they paint only the tips?

"A French manicure?" Barbara suggested. She was our oldest detective, a squat woman whose throaty voice betrayed a lifetime of Virginia Slims and hard gin. Over ice. With a slice of lemon. We knew each other so well by then.

"Yes, a French manicure." The sketch artist quickly put together a composite. We all agreed it wasn't much to go on, but it was all that we had.

Then, things turned darker. Rugby, a 20-year-old male, Penn student majoring in global supply chain management, was found wandering around the farmers' market, barefoot, his GAP T-shirt torn at the collar. His eyes were wet pools of tears. Blue, like the ocean. Rugby was the first to report that she'd threatened to cut him, "down there. Near my junk," he said, a catch in his throat. It was only by a stroke of luck that a bus boy from the bar happened to step out into the alleyway and she bolted. This suggested that simply humiliating the boys was no longer enough. She wanted blood.

When Rugby came to the station, Amber, our lead detective, approached him as one would a skittish stray. Amber had eyes of blue steel and a body to match. But she knew how to handle the boys. "Rugby, it's okay. You're safe now. No one is going to hurt you." She poured him a glass of Gatorade, tried not to notice the delicate bob of his Adam's apple as he gulped it down. "Would you rather talk to a man?"

He shook his head, eyes cast down, long eyelashes near-ly touching his cheeks. It killed us to see our boys like this. "She, she followed me outside of Tattooed Mom's, and she ... I ... She ... I ... She .... At first, I thought she needed help looking for her kitten or, I don't know, but then I –" He burst into big, heaving gasps.

Lieutenant Randy Washington, a well-muscled blond who kept his pants tight, but his demeanor professional, stepped up to the boy. "Listen, I have a rule I go by, and it's something my dad taught me. No matter what the problem is, there's no reason a woman should be asking a man for help. She should ask another woman. You got that?"

The boy nodded, blinking back tears. He told his story. He'd gone out to take a piss, but tried to stop when she appeared. She was quick, pushed him forward, one hand pressing a knife to his throat, the other clutching his balls. "You move, I cut." He stayed still. She kept him there, facing the wall, and began touching him. She had some kind of lotion – "I don't know what it was, it was warm, it, it, it, it, it, it, it, it, it, it, it, it, it, it felt good – I couldn't stop –" Rugby rested his head on the interrogation table where one of our perps had used an earring back to scrawl "Johnny's a Slut" in tiny letters.

"Who can we call for you?" Amber asked, her hands balled into tight fists.

He sat up. "No one. Don't call anybody. I don't want anyone to know."

"It's not your fault, Rugby. You didn't do anything wrong." We refrained from adding, *Except for pissing in a public space, which is technically a Class A misdemeanor.* Hadn't he been through enough?

We gathered outside of the room. We had a lot of questions. "You buying this story?" Amber asked, turning in a circle.

"Why did he run from the scene? You think he's doing this for attention? Anyone run a toxicology?"

We all agreed there was a high percentage that he was lying, because – well, we couldn't think of why he'd do that. For attention, maybe?

"Rape kit first," Barbara said, blowing her nose into a handkerchief with a loud honk.

Amber and Barb went by Rugby's house to speak to his parents. They pegged the father right away for a martyr. His eyes were puffy and red from crying, and he was wringing his hands like an old fisherman. He insisted that his boy hadn't even been at Tattooed Mom's. No way his son was out at a bar. He was underage. He'd never do that. He was a good boy.

The dads. They always saw their kids through rose-colored glasses.

Barbara pulled the mom aside when she got home from work, exhausted, smelling vaguely of gin. "You mind if we have a look at his room?"

"Be my guest," the mother said with a sweeping gesture, knocking over a vase of peonies.

Barb and Amber followed the mother into the boy's bedroom. It was all done up in navy and white stripes with a sailboat trim. Trophies for swimming, baseball, lacrosse, water polo, but strangely, no awards for rugby. A collage of photos of him and his college buddies tucked into the edges of the mirror. Pictures of a dog wearing a jaunty blue bandana. Chew toys. "Tell us about your son," Amber said, sitting on the edge of the bed. "Tell us what his dad won't say."

The mother squinted at them, evaluating. Then, she sighed, running a hand through her dark, silver-threaded hair. "He was a bit of a showboat," she acknowledged. "He was also girl crazy.

And he fancied himself a hipster. We asked him to stick to sports bars, stay with his friends, but he said he liked the vibe at Tattooed Mom's."

A slobbering, giant-headed retriever bounded into the room, nuzzling at their crotches. He had a wide feathery tail and a dangling scrotum that looked as heavy as cue balls.

"Down, Buddy!" When the mother wasn't looking, Barb gave Buddy a swift kick in the nuts.

Once the story broke in *The Inquirer*, we had no choice but to manage the fall-out through a press conference and a series of community education initiatives. Our graphic designer created a poster that read "Pee Safe. Stay safe." We posted the flier on cork boards next to band announcements in bars, in gym locker rooms, over missing cat photos on telephone poles. It was slow getting the word out. Which was fine by us – it's not like we wanted the whole city to know that we were dealing with a serial rapist and all we had to go on was a couple of discarded scrunchies and one too many college boys who would never be the same. Probably. Actually, we thought, it wasn't that big of a deal. But still.

We went into to the college campuses to educate the boys on how to avoid the assaults. We had a PowerPoint outlining the locations of the attacks, and tips for not tempting the perp. Pee with a buddy, watch out for one another, don't wear soccer shorts that have easy access – it sends a message, right or wrong. We gave the boys whistles to wear around their necks like collars.

A crew-cut dad with a giant moustache argued that his kid should be allowed to wear whatever he wanted, that wearing gym shorts doesn't mean he wants to be forcibly given a hand job. "I mean, look at him!" We looked at him and at the other boys. They pulled their T-shirts down over their bellies, faces burning, wiggled in their seats, tugging at their low-slung jeans.

We bit our tongues. We didn't point out that in the tighter versions of their shorts, you could see the outline of their dicks, the mushroom-shaped head, or the cloudy clot of their balls.

We took the Penn football cheerleaders aside before practice, all of them women except for Jeremy, in his tight stretchy pants and glowing white wristbands. We sent him to fill the water bottles. "You got brothers?" Barbara asked.

"Yeah," a high voice yelled from the back. "She's got a brother and he is smoking hot." A sports bra sailed through the air, hitting Barbara square in the face.

They'd understand all too clearly when some guy they met at a sorority party cried rape and their whole life was destroyed because a needy bro thought they were more than just hook-up buddies. We'd seen it happen. Well, actually, we'd never seen it happen, but that didn't mean it wasn't a possibility. A rep for rape could keep you from so many things – a job as a law enforcement officer, for instance, or a judge, maybe. Possibly even president of the United States.

Secretly, we imagined it would only get worse before it got better.

With no solid leads, we decided to set up a sting operation. Lieutenant Washington, perhaps too eager to please, volunteered immediately, his hand waving as if hoping to be picked for prom court. We didn't have the heart to tell him that he wasn't attractive (or tall) enough, didn't have the requisite physique to be tempting to her. When the others weren't looking, Amber slipped him a 20 percent-off coupon to Gold's Gym.

We settled instead for Brandon, this kid from the IT department. He was young and tough, grew up on the hard streets of North Philly, yet somehow looked as though he'd been raised in the best private schools in upstate New York. *She's tricky*, we warned. *Be careful.*

Barbara gave him a condom, for no reason at all that we could think of.

"I got you," he said, trying for an awkward high five. We looked the other way, certain now that we'd made a mistake.

The plan was simple. We'd send Brandon to Tattooed Mom's, where the attacks had happened a half dozen times before, where the bathrooms were disgusting and the alleyway was easily accessible. We dressed him in khaki Dockers and a polo shirt. We argued with Barbara about whether or not he should pop the collar. She favored yes; we mostly said no. "She's got a type," Barbara insisted. "She likes the collars up."

We gave Brandon a pair of mirrored sunglasses to wear backwards on his head, enough hair gel to tame his wild locks into crunchy-looking Styrofoam waves.

You're good to go, we said, punching him on the shoulder, pinching his cheeks, pretending to grab his ass. He was scrumptious really. Enough vulnerability in his mouth to be alluring along with the heady smell of Tommy Hilfiger shower gel. We found ourselves leaning in and then, no, shaking it off.

We were not like her.

Brandon sat for three hours in the dark bar, drinking lager after lager, going outside to piss a half dozen times. She never showed. We ended up listening to an increasingly more intoxicated Brandon sing every possible Billy Joel song on the karaoke machine. When he started "Angry Young Man," for the third time, we called it a night.

Brandon was devastated. "Is it me? Am I not handsome enough? Too skinny?" He gave us a pained, shattered look. "Am I not attractive enough to rape?"

"Naw," Amber said, glancing away so he wouldn't see she'd noticed something about plain about him, a bit too ordinary. "You're perfect just the way you are."

She bought him one last beer and a shot of JB. He took it well and didn't even say no when she insisted on driving him home. She watched him walk up the stairs to his row house, his shoulders down, the glasses still on the back of his head, looking back at her as if pleading. She did not sit idling in the car wondering what he would do if we knocked on the door, if he would answer in his bathrobe, hair wet now, free of gel.

Like the rest of us, she'd been down that road. It only led to heartache and broken promises. The perp, that's where our attention needed to be.

Some of us had sons, yes, and daughters. Who should we worry about more? Our sons were more careless, prone to car chases down one-way streets and skinned knees from skateboarding feats at Rittenhouse Park. We bought them kneepads and shin guards, darling jock straps shaped vaguely like speculums.

But how well did we really know our daughters? Our daughters were taught to respect boundaries, to open doors for old men, to leave a 20 percent tip or more, even when the service was subpar. Who's to say they weren't tempted in dark cars behind bowling alleys with their high school crushes, the moon hidden behind fast-moving clouds? What might they do in the dark, tempted by the flash of checkered boxer shorts above denim, or the tight stretch of ab muscles, rippling across their stomachs, the scent of sea breeze aftershave mixed with lacrosse-induced sweat?

We started smoking again and drinking more. We cursed our ex-husbands when they arrived bearing plates of Sloppy Joes and wings, as if attending a tailgate. We built a pyramid of Pabst Blue Ribbon cans underneath our poster of Justin Bieber, the Calvin Klein years, and then knocked it down with a

swift left hook and a ball of yarn. We slept around carelessly. We were haunted, chased, tortured, and titillated. Most shamefully, we dreamt of young college boys, romping like puppies, drowsy with hormones and smelling of whole milk. We woke in a sweat, our sheets tangled in our legs, the cats aghast at the foot of the bed, looking at us with glowing yellow eyes like, *What's the problem?*

It did get worse. Much worse. We heard of copycat jerk-off assaults in D.C., Baltimore, Boston. Taylor Swift released a song called "You Knew I Was Trouble" that went straight to number one on the country and pop charts. We saw the beginnings of pornography fetishizing the white male as liking forced hand play, even as their anguished faces told another story. Barb caught her niece arranging naked Ken dolls in provocative positions. Our boys were running scared, considering community college only, refusing to pledge Kappa Alpha for fear of being roped into a night of binge drinking that ended in salty tears and misgivings.

And then, a break.

Rugby showed up at Amber's apartment, wearing a tight white T-shirt and soft gray jogging pants. The porch light backlit his head, making his dark hair glow like a halo. "What are you doing here?" she asked, taking off her reading glasses.

"I needed to see you." It was raining and he shivered. Goosebumps raised on his sculpted biceps.

She let him in, poured him a drink, and threw him a towel. "Don't drip water on my nice floor." She offered him a sweatshirt. He shook his head. He took a sip of whiskey, shuddered and gasped. "What's going on?"

"I think I know something," he said. "It's freaking me out."

She suggested he calm down, take a moment, do some deep knee bends or squats.

"I know you're smarter than me," he shrugged, wiped his nose on his sleeve. He looked like a little boy.

She told us later that she wanted to grab him by the shoulders and shake him, just to watch his mouth open wider, so she could get a look at his tongue. But she was a professional, goddamn it. "What is it, Rugby?"

"Well, it's that we all have Labs."

"We checked the majors of each victim. Most are business, political science, or global supply chain management."

"No, not labs like science. Labs like Labrador retrievers."

She remembered now, all of the dog hair on the victims' windbreakers. "Go on."

"I didn't know all of the guys who were attacked, but I recognized some of them from the dog park. Not friends of mine, but I'd see them every other weekend or whatever, or picking up after their dogs on South Street. Then it hit me – we all own the same kind of dog."

"What does that matter?" She was distracted. She tried not to stare at the Cupid pout of his mouth, the way he shook his hair to clear it of the rain.

"Our vet. I think we all go to the same goddamn vet!" He cracked then. He started to cry, to take her plastic fruit out of the centerpiece and throw it around the kitchen. "I need an answer! I need this to be over! I can't live like this anymore."

She slapped him. Hard. His hand flew to his cheek, eyes stunned blue orbs. She apologized. She hadn't meant it, but Mother of God, he needed to quit being so hysterical. He let her hold him. She whispered cooing calming words, lullabies from his childhood featuring anchors and stalwart little boats into the curls of his hair. "Shh, it's okay, come here."

She told us later that she gave comfort the only way she knew how. With her hands. Hands that were meant to soothe

sweating brows, to knead bread, to untie knots in hoodies, to twist the neck of a chicken for Sunday dinner.

While leading him to her bedroom, Amber looked at her hands. Capable of so much love, and so much violence. She laid him gently on the covers. In the dark, she moved with care, touching only when and where he allowed her to. She got a faraway look in her eye when she described the way he startled when she touched him, as if it burned. How she found deep valleys of scratches on his thighs likely made with the sharp blade of a pair of scissors. That he whispered he wished he had the courage to take it further. These details – what did they matter? She assured us that eventually, he offered himself up to her. Our boy, this boy. Him.

We tracked her down easily after that. Her name was Kimberley Cotton, and she ran her own veterinary clinic on Arch Street across from the Betsy Ross House. The Standard-Standard Vet Clinic, it was called. She emerged from the back room, wearing a doctor's coat, and carrying a squirming white rabbit. "Ladies," she said, holding the bunny tight. "What took you so long?"

We brought her to the station. While she was in our custody, we searched her clinic. Her records confirmed she had our victims as clients. Brad, Chad, Tad, Dave, Brett, Alex, Christopher, Brock, Blaine, Blake, TJ, JT, and yes, Rugby. Every single one of them. A survey of her stock also showed she was well lubed; bottle after bottle of lotion was found lining the cabinets of her shelves.

She wore a faint slash of dark lipstick. Height could be right, if she wore sensible heels. She had a foxy look – pointy nose, hair pulled back into a pink scrunchie. We looked at her hands. Her fingernails were cut short but painted in the French manicure style the victims had mentioned.

"We have reason to believe you were involved. Evidence saying it was you."

She coughed into her fist. "Oh, okay, but can they pick me out of a lineup?"

We excused ourselves. All we really had was circumstantial evidence. We wondered if Rugby might be able to identify her from a hand test. We couldn't get prints because the first 10 victims hadn't come forward until after the others were reported, and the ones who did speak up were too ashamed to have their dicks powdered.

Before questioning her further, we decided we needed a positive ID.

We argued how to best handle identification. "Should we do a hand lineup?" Barbara suggested.

Amber nodded. "Sure, I mean, yeah."

Do we need to do the hand motion?

You mean, like, get what – a banana?

Barbara turned to Lieutenant Washington, who was taking notes. "Randy? You think that's a good –"

He shook his head, his mouth a thin line of disapproval.

All right, then, just hand and vocal recognition. *What were some of the things she said to them?* We made a list. The only boy who was available was Rugby. He appeared right away, looking at us with a yearning expression we couldn't stomach. Amber avoided eye contact, tossing her plastic cup of water toward the trash can. Missing.

During the lineup, we had six women, including our main suspect, hold out their hands. Next, one by one, they stepped forward, reading the words off the index cards we'd given them. "Oh, yes, you're such a good, strong boy. Yes, good boy. Good, good boy." When the suspect read her card, she did it in a monotone, hardly any enthusiasm. Rugby shot up out

of his chair. "Number three," he said. "That's her. She's the one."

We returned to Kimberly, and let her know she'd been identified. We got down to business. *Tell us about the boys.*

"What about them?"

"All of them owned Labrador retrievers," Barbara said, a note of impatience in her gravelly voice.

The vet snorted. "It's a lack of imagination. They feel like they're supposed to get these big dumb dogs to match the big dumb dogs their dads grew up with. And then they don't have the time to walk them or give them the care they need and so the dogs get rowdy from neglect. I love dogs. I don't love the boys who own them."

Amber slammed her fist on the table. "But why? Why did you do it? What turned you into this creature?"

"You want me to say that my daddy left me when I was a baby and my mother's parade of boyfriends molested me in the swimming pool? You want me to confess that I was unpopular in high school, humiliated and teased by beautiful male track stars? None of that is true. I grew up in the burbs of Boston. My parents loved me, and they are still married. I was a cheerleader in high school and also took jujitsu. No man every touched me unless I wanted him to." She smiled then. She had a gorgeous smile, and a dimple tucked into her cheek like a stitch. She leaned back in her chair.

Barbara wasn't convinced. "You never once made a play for one of these guys? Maybe got rejected a time or two?"

Kimberly sat back. "I mean, they're into blondes, I guess." She sighed, plucked at her dark hair. Then, she leaned in again. "You want to know the truth? I did it because I could. They're such easy targets." She narrowed her eyes, gestured for Barb to

come closer. "I felt like they belonged to me, you know what I mean?" She might have winked then. It was either a wink or tic, but either way, she seemed to have no remorse.

We had our confession. We were all a little tired, dazed. Even Kimberly seemed exhausted. "Look," she said. "You mind if I use the bathroom? It's been a long day and I stopped at Starbucks twice."

Sure, yeah, we're not animals here.

We let Brandon take her back to the lady's room, told him to watch the door.

How she managed to escape through the tiny square window was not anything we could explain. Nor could we figure out who had forgotten to put bars on the bathroom window of a police station, for God's sake.

She left us one final message, scrawled in lipstick across the bathroom mirror. We saw it the moment we walked in. "Grab 'em by the balls." It seemed like foreshadowing, the red words an ominous precursor to what, we could only imagine.

Amber raged when she learned of the escape. "You left her alone?" She threw her mug of chamomile tea across the room. Lieutenant Washington rushed to swab away the growing stain.

We were silent, finally, even Barbara. We had nothing more to say.

She's still out there. She's moved on to another town, maybe the Windy City, a place where Midwestern farm boys go to chase their dreams of love and fame. On the streets, the boys are more gullible, and also more irresistible with their sunburnt, open faces and trusting demeanor, smelling like fresh hay and dime store aftershave.

She's coming for them. Our boys.

Curb Appeal

Jenny is thinking it might be time to make a move. She's been in Philadelphia for six months working (unsuccessfully) as a real estate agent. Because she used to be a child movie star known as Jenny Darling, strangers often stop her on the street to ask why she looks so familiar. The same thing happens when she's meeting a new client to show them a house. "What's your name again?" asks her newest one, a woman who shows up to the first house in scrubs. She does something with hospitals and needs to be close to Jefferson Hospital. She has large circles under her eyes, like a vampire. *I work with organs*, she had said, by way of introduction, waving her hand. "Is it Sander-something? I feel like we've met before."

Jenny nods. "I get that a lot." People are fascinated with child stars. They always want to know the dirty details: if she was offered cocaine at a fifth birthday party, if her costars were lecherous, if she knows any secrets about DeNiro. It's exhausting. "You may remember me from one of the missing children's specials on *America's Most Wanted*," she says.

"Oh, shit, no way!" The woman reaches as if to pat her arm, and then changes her mind when Jenny dances away. "Well, at least you were rescued. At least they found you."

"Oh, no," Jenny says. "They never found me. I'm still missing."

It's not a complete lie. She *was* in several movies, including one about a child stolen by her daddy and taken across the country in his pickup. And another about a piano teacher with Tourette's. And the one about the murdered child beauty pageant contestant. That was her favorite. For hours while they shot the scene when her body was found, she lay prone on the floor, the hem of her skirt flipped up to reveal just the slightest hint of her white little girl underwear. The movie people stood around her, adjusting lights, testing camera angles, and she played dead until someone finally noticed and said, "Could someone tell that little girl to get up?"

Another man with a deep voice said, "Check her pulse," with zero emotional expression.

She didn't move a muscle until a woman who smelled like lemons leaned over her and whispered, "Honey, we're done with the scene. You can go home now."

But she still didn't move, pretending to have fallen asleep, just to see how long it would take before someone might come to help her up off the floor.

Before moving to Philadelphia, she lived in a series of crappy studios in New York, doing voiceover work when she could find it, pinging from job to job. Some of the time, she taught aspiring kid actors how to deliver lines like "Hey, Mister, is this your dog?" with the right amount of lisp-age. She also took classes. Lots of classes. Currently, she is only a few credits shy

of six different careers: a chiropractor's assistant, a flower arranger, a web designer specialist, and a nurse's assistant.

But then, suddenly, New York had become overbearing. Too much jackhammering, too many sweaty people on subway cars, too much anonymity, and a too-small studio with only a stand-up shower.

In Philadelphia, she accidentally became a real estate agent. The problem is that she's not very good at it.

For example:

At 2 p.m., she meets Dave, a bejeweled film producer and chronic gum chewer who has flown in from L.A. to look for a shooting location for his next film. When Jenny first arrives, he is standing on the patio with the cell phone glued to his ear. He waves at her to hurry up and open the door, which she does, slowly.

He walks in, still talking, making deals, breaking deals. He raps on the basement door with his hairy knuckles, opens and closes the fridge, and checks out his hair in the hall mirror, turning this way and that. He tests the garbage disposal without turning on the water. Finally, he snaps the phone shut. "Fucking movie people," he says. "Never happy, you know what I mean?"

"I know."

He sniffs the air. "What smells like mildew? Is that coming from the walls?"

Jenny realizes that the smell is coming from her; more specifically, from her not-quite-dry blouse. She has taken to wearing her clothes slightly damp, due to a faulty dryer in her own home – one that requires several cycles to dry a sock. "I don't smell anything."

He squints, really looking at her for the first time. "You in the business?"

Jenny smiles, which she knows makes her used-to-be signature dimples more pronounced. "Why do you ask?"

But he has moved on to the bathroom. "This place is okay, but I need a lotta, lotta space for this project." He fishes a purple wad of gum from his mouth and throws it at the garbage can. He misses. His phone rings. He steps into the foyer. "We're done here, doll. I gotta take this call."

"Oh, okay." She is disappointed to realize that he doesn't recognize her at all. "Wait, one second." She peels the gum off the floor. "Don't forget this," she says, dropping it into his hand.

Her mother calls later, after Jenny has had time to unwind at home, which specifically means after she has eaten a handful of Ritz crackers and downed two glasses of wine. "Have you heard from your father?" her mother asks. Jenny says no, even though she has. It was not an amicable divorce. Many dishes were broken, many tears were shed, and many soap opera scenes were performed with Jenny as the audience. "I'm thinking about a visit to Philadelphia. All of this sunshine is depressing."

"I won't be here!" Panicked, as if someone is watching her, Jenny looks around her living room for a large piece of furniture to hide behind.

"I haven't even said when I wanted to visit."

"Oh, no, it's just that I'll be filming for the next several months." Her fourth lie of the day. A new record. "I got an offer for a show."

There is a pause. "It's not an adult film, is it? Because if it is, your career will be in the toilet forever." Jenny does not remind her mother that it has been over and done since she was 12. "Succeeding is not as easy as it seems."

Jenny's mother should know, since she spent five years in New York working to make it big, and, when she finally did

– landing a job as the main model for Maidenform's full-figured bra line and seeing her silhouette and torso on tags in department stores all across the country – well, that was when she met Jenny's father and gave it all up. "I don't regret it, honey," she has told Jenny on many occasions. "Those days in New York were the happiest ones of my life. And then, I married your father and I had you … and those were some great days too."

Jenny scrambles for a plausible lie. "It's a reality TV show called *Training Babies.* Former kid stars teaching up-and-comers how to nail an audition."

"Well, that's a start. But don't embarrass yourself, honey. Don't act like the Lindsay Lohan, if you can help it."

"Mom, if I was going to act like the typical child star, I would've developed a substance abuse problem," she says, taking a long sip of her chardonnay.

"Maybe you could try representing a product like that Valerie Bertinelli and her Slimfast."

"I'm not fat."

"You could *get* fat," her mother insists. "If you really wanted to succeed, that is." There is a pause. "I'm joking, Jenny."

"Thanks for your help, Mother." Jenny hangs up, feeling drunk and defiant. She jams the cork back into the wine bottle and heads out the door with her laundry basket tucked under her arm.

She heads to a two-story row house in Fairmount that has been on the market for 10 months. She is able to get the code for the lockbox by pretending she wants to show it. "Thank you so much," she says to the receptionist, using a British accent.

This house has real curb appeal. In it, one could imagine giving dinner parties (if one could also pretend that one knew how to cook something besides microwave Lean Cuisines), or

cozying up to a rich attorney in front of the mosaic fireplace, or just simply walking from room to room, admiring the Jacuzzi tub, the charming retro touches, the wainscoting, the lack of the cracked plaster Jenny has in her rental.

She pads around the rooms in stocking feet, sliding on the newly redone cherry wood flooring. Three bedrooms, one bathroom. Perfect for a new family with room to grow. Or a single woman with an indeterminate future. Something always seems to be broken or nearly broken in her current abode – the aforementioned dryer, the alley door that swings open on windy days, the leaky roof that the landlord has told her will cost $10,000 to repair. She has learned to live with buckets on the floor.

In the basement, she finds the dryer, a brand-new Amana. She pushes her damp clothes into its bowels. Then, she goes back upstairs, where she has seen a row of robust dusty wine glasses winking at her from the built-in glass cabinets in the dining room and a single bottle of red wine, its neck covered in dust. The rest of the evening flashes by like mini movie previews – reclining in the Jacuzzi in her underpants, finishing up the wine and tossing the bottle with a flourish over the back fence, watching several minutes of ... what? Was it *Sophie's Choice* or the other one about the concentration camp with the girl in the red coat?

She wakes up on the floor. Sunlight streams in through the windows, making it hard to see. A white face hovers above her. In a blink, she recognizes the woman with the clipboard as a realtor from a competing agency. She realizes that she is still clad in her underwear and a T-shirt. The rest of her clothes remain downstairs.

"Oh, thank God." Jenny sits up. "Thank God someone came. I think I had another one of my seizures."

The real estate lady wears a silky blouse with a huge bow at her throat, like she has just stepped out of a turn-of-the-century play. "You need to vacate the premises. I don't know what you think you're doing here, but this is highly unprofessional." She suggests that the next order of business might be a call to her boss.

Jenny's eyes well with tears. "Okay," she says, her voice trembling, only a little, a hint of a wobble. "Okay, I understand." She forces a hiccup.

The agent is having none of it at first, but then her eyes soften, and if it were written in a script, it would actually give the direction "eyes soften." She says, "I'm the one who should be crying. I can't move this property to save my life. Someone died in here."

"Really?" The agent spills the story, an apparent carbon monoxide poisoning due to a bad contractor. "How many died?"

"All of them," the lady says. "They all died."

It makes Jenny feel sorry for the house, with its perfect wooden beams and hardwood floors. It is not the house's fault that the person who installed the oven was high on meth.

The agent must see something in her face, because she goes into professional mode. The entire gas line has been replaced. Jenny goes to the kitchen, opens the fridge. This is new too, all of the plumbing has been reinstalled, the investor who bought it thought if he gutted the place and put in all new fixtures, no one would remember the deaths. But they do.

The house is like a stage set. None of the furniture belongs to the dead family – it has all been removed and replaced. The new Jacuzzi in the bathroom has never been used (well, not by anyone but her). The fruit in the salad bowl? Fake. At the same time, when she turns on the faucet, real water spills out. Real cold air flows from the fridge.

"Why, may I ask, are you dressed this way?" The agent crosses her arms over her bowed chest. She has very long fingernails, painted bright red.

Jenny considers the distance between the basement door and the agent. If she sprints, she could probably make it down the stairs, grab her clothes, and barrel toward the front door. The lady could do damage with those claws. "I –" She can't think of a plausible excuse. She decides not to try on any voice. It's wearisome, pretending to be someone else all the time. "All of my clean clothes are downstairs."

"You did laundry here?" the woman shakes her head, though her perfectly coifed bob does not move, and for a brief second, Jenny wonders if possibly this woman is wearing a wig. Why? A bad haircut? Chemo?

"My dryer is on the fritz."

"Unbelievable. Not to be believed!" Jenny hangs her head. "Hurry up. And don't think I won't be calling Dawn about this." The agent's phone rings, and she actually snaps her fingers at Jenny while taking the call.

Jenny descends into the lower level. The basement itself is the only negative aspect of the house. The owners haven't redone it, and the ceiling is low, with flaking, sagging walls and a dusty cement floor that has mysterious bumps in it, as if it were built over a children's graveyard. Though the owners have a dehumidifier running, the room is still damp and smells like mildew. For some reason, this makes Jenny feel better.

She piles her clothes into the hamper. On the shelf next to the dryer, she sees a plastic leg. It takes her a minute to realize that the leg is attached to a doll, not a human being. She pulls it out and finds a perfectly intact Shirley Temple doll circa 1960, wearing the white and red polka dotted dress she wore in *Baby Takes a Bow*. Her sausage curls have lost their spring

and she has a minor chip on her cheek. She might be worth thousands of dollars on eBay provided she doesn't have spiders in her head. Or not much at all.

Jenny quickly gets dressed. Shirley seems to be staring at her, though her blue doll eyes are going in two different directions. The real-life Shirley Temple (Black) did well for herself, getting out of the business and becoming an ambassador to China or some such country. Now there's a child star who really made something of herself.

She takes the doll off the shelf and tucks her into the bottom of her laundry basket, concealing her telltale curls with a dish towel. Together, they make their escape.

Cast of characters: the boss, Dawn Wiggins, real estate agent, 42 (though possibly lying about her age), attractive, with a scratchy voice and high heels, who would be played by a younger Jane Fonda. Peggy Johnson, 83, kind face, thin older woman given to wearing ponchos dusted over with cat hair. She would be played by a character actress – Angela Lansbury (if Angela would be up for such a role). Her boyfriend: currently an invisible amalgamation of Bradley Cooper and Lloyd Dobler from *Say Anything*. The movie producer would be played by someone who wears a long ponytail and snakeskin boots, someone completely unlikable from the first glance, these walking sharks, these wheeler-dealers.

When her bathtub first started leaking, she put down towels. It was manageable. It was too much of a hassle to get in touch with the landlord, who lives in North Jersey and isn't great at returning calls. Or maybe he is dead. She rented the house and never heard from him again, though her monthly checks kept getting cashed. When the dryer started shooting sparks, that's when she thought maybe things had gotten out of hand.

Without the dryer, she couldn't make sure the towels were not constantly sopping wet or that she didn't walk around smelling faintly like a wet dog.

The next day, Jenny meets with Peggy/Angela Lansbury who wants to move to Clearwater to live with her son, Edward. She is frail with sharp, marble-blue eyes. Jenny gives her about a year or two before she falls and breaks her hip, particularly if she stays in this rundown house with the cracked basement steps.

But here's the thing: Peggy has a cat problem. Not just a few cats, but dozens of cats, possibly in the high twenties. To give her credit, the house is as clean as it can be for a cat hoarder. Peggy has made sure to place a litter box in every corner, and water bowls and cat food bowls all over the place, but wherever Jenny turns, she is met with a cat. The top of the fridge? Cat. The thing about to pee in her purse? Tomcat. Those throw pillows on the bed? Actually cats. "I would like to stay, but I can't afford the mortgage," Peggy says. They agree to put the house up for $175,000 – enough for Peggy to have a little savings for the rest of her dwindling years. A steal, really, for whomever buys it. And the cats. The cats come with the house. Free!

Jenny does not mention to Peggy that she will not be putting that clause into the home description. If the house is sold, she will find a nice no-kill shelter. Or a nice kill-kill shelter, whatever is quickest.

Peggy is no chump though. "I want to be sure these cats are okay," she emphasizes. One of them meows over her words and two others answer back, a call-and-response chorus. It would be cute if there just weren't so many of them and if Jenny could stop imagining them crawling over the corpse of their owner and nibbling on her long earlobes.

She grabs Peggy's hand, and is surprised when Peggy grasps it back, her fingers strong and icy. "I will take care of it. Of them, I mean. I promise."

It's like the pivotal scene in *The Missing Girl* where the woman playing Jenny's mother asks the sheriff if he will go to the ends of the earth to find her daughter. "Yes," he said, his bristly mustache quivering. "Yes, ma'am, I will." And he kept his word. But her character died anyway. That was her last movie. It made under five million and was only distributed to a small number of theaters. A big disappointment for all.

Selling properties requires the same talent as acting. You pretend to care, you act as if you are on their side, like you don't mind if they buy the goddamn house or not. *Take your time! Don't rush into it. Of course, I'd be happy to make that ridiculously low offer for you. I agree that windows should not have plastic shades! Yes, why is this door so rectangular?*

Later that morning, she meets up with a mother-and-daughter duo, set on finding a house to accommodate both of them. The daughter, who has the echo of her mother's face, makes jokes about wanting a place with an attic. "I need to find somewhere to place the old lady."

The daughter wants to see yet another house in the art museum district, a house that she can't afford. She's already looked at over two dozen places in the last month. But she and her mother want to see every available property. They want to see the broken-down homes in Port Richmond and the mansions surrounding Rittenhouse Square. "How about if we just look at houses within your buying range?" she has suggested. Oh, no, oh, no, they want to explore *all* of their options, even those that aren't actually options.

Today, as happens almost every time, the mother is at first delighted – look at the lovely cherub staircase! The charming four-paned windows! The two-flush toilet! Then, she starts having doubts. How much closet space is there in the office? What side does the second bedroom face? Will the sun be in her eyes every morning?

The daughter tries to intervene, her voice tight as a wire. "Mom, no place is perfect."

"Don't make us leave you in the basement!" Jenny says, wagging her finger at the mother, trying for a comedic tone.

"I've seen your face before," the mother says. "Do you also work at my bank?"

No, she tells them. She used to be in the public eye. For a brief instant. A long time ago.

"Wait; were you that girl in the Mrs. Butterworth commercials from the sixties? The one with the glasses?" the daughter asks.

"I don't think I was born then."

They keep guessing until finally she names a couple of her movies. The mother gasps. "Oh, my God, really? You've gotten so …." She stops.

Jenny jumps in before she can say more. "So … fabulous? So tall? So much better looking?" They all guffaw, but the awkwardness lingers. Her guess is that she no longer looks like the adorable, baby-faced Jenny Darling of yesteryear, but no, she does not want to know what they think.

If she's not careful, she will burst into a show tune and really bring the house down. She suggests that they move on, even though they haven't seen the basement yet. After all, this isn't really what they had hoped for, is it?

After the appointment, Jenny returns to her cubicle at Benevolent Real Estate to check her email. Her boss, Dawn, calls

her into her office. She is a bright and cheerful thing, not unlike stage moms Jenny has known and not loved. "How's it coming, darling? I'm just wondering here because y'all haven't had a closing yet. I'm keeping my eye on you for a sale this month." She winks, her eyes heavy with mascara. "You think you can close a deal for me, sugar?"

Of course she can. Absolutely! In fact, she's expecting an offer to be written up by the end of this week or sooner.

Dawn's eyes turn back to her iPhone, and so there will be no further sharing. As she opens the door, Dawn's head pops back up. "Oh, I forgot to tell you! I couldn't sleep the other night and so I turned on TBS and there you were in that film about the runaway girl and her talking poodle. You were just the sweetest thing!"

Yes, she was. She used to be, anyway.

On the Broad Street line, Jenny thumbs through a discarded *U.S. News and World Report*. In the obit section, she sees a name she recognizes. She begins reading. Blair Winfield (not his real name) has died at the age of 62 (not his real age – five or so years have been shaved off, following Hollywood's industry standard). Blair Winfield, who played her dad in a movie she made when she was five years old. Her second movie, she can't recall the title (yes, she can, she's being modest. It was called *Family Way*), but the two of them were in a lot of scenes together. Mostly, she remembers him carrying her on his back in between shots while they were waiting for the scene to get set up. A nice, nice man. He always had gum and he taught her how to blow bubbles, a skill that came in handy when she had to play a young softball player in *Far Afield*. He died of esophageal cancer, and the photo in the article is an early headshot, showing his strong profile, a profile you might want on a coin.

Curb Appeal

They hadn't spoken in 15 years, not since she left the biz, after their last film together, the one where the director told her mother that Jenny needed to have her legs broken and reset so she would be less bow-legged. As she remembers it, her mother seemed to be nodding, ready to take down the number of the bone-breaking doctor. It was Blair Winfield (née Winooski), who stepped in and said, "A bit extreme, don't you think?" And sent a grandfatherly wink her way, one that rang almost sincere, even though she'd seen him use it in a scene before.

She wonders why no one called her for a quote about Blair Winfield. "What did he mean to you?" asks an imaginary interviewer.

"He was home to me," she would say. Home. Home is a movie set. Most of her scenes took place in kitchens and dining rooms with plastic fruit in bowls and how they looked so real, she once bit into a pear and chipped her front tooth. The shelves held empty cereal boxes and rows of cookbooks that weren't books at all, just the spines of books. All of the rooms were two dimensional, with no real plumbing or working fixtures, but the camera lights were always warm.

She remembers another made-for-TV movie where she had a small unnamed role, something like "Baby Sister." They had to do one scene multiple times and it required her to hold back the tears while her "parents" were fighting. She had to do it again and again and again because the adults kept messing up their lines. But she was able to bring the tears to her eyes without letting them spill over the edge, every single time. In each scene, her "mother" hugged her and whispered in her hair, "It's not your fault." When the director finally yelled "cut," the woman playing her mother walked off set to smoke a cigarette. When Jenny walked by and smiled at her, the woman's eyes passed over her as if she were a piece of furniture.

Later, Blair Winfield pulled her aside. He smelled like spearmint and reminded her of her grandfather. Or a guy who had played her grandfather in another movie. She wasn't sure anymore. "You're talented," he said. "But I don't know if it's good for you. You can always do something else."

A small door opened in her brain and she realized, at the age of 12, that her career could be over. And so she stopped acting and nobody died. Her father stopped speaking to her, but no actual person died. Something else was lost, and she's never been able to figure out what (or who) that was.

Instead of going home, she shows up at Peggy's. The house is still on the market, but Peggy doesn't seem to mind. Peggy opens the door with a piebald cat under her arm, asking no questions. They sit at the kitchen table, drinking tea.

"Do you miss it?" Peggy asks suddenly. Peggy is the only one who knows about her past, and it's not because she told her, it's because Peggy remembers her films. Peggy, in her mid-sixties, divorced from the second used-car salesman, realizing that she would never have kids. "That was when she got the first cat. I get it. I know they are substitutes." But she went to a lot, a lot of movies, and saw some of Jenny's early work, the toddler days, the elementary school days. "Do you ever think of going back?"

"I don't *miss it* miss it."

"Let's watch a movie," Peggy suggests, and they retire to the tiny living room, where she pops *There Goes the Neighborhood* into her DVD. Suddenly, there Jenny is, age seven, with her dimples and her precious knobby knees (that the makeup man purposely coated with dirt). How weird is that, to see herself as a little girl with freckles across her nose? It's not a big part, but it's enough, a few scenes, and she's watching herself run to her (fake) dad with her arms outstretched, the corniest scene of

all, and a strange hiccupping sound erupts from her throat. Oh, wait, she's crying. It's not like .... It's just weird to see herself as a child. That poor little girl, whose dad ran off without saying goodbye, what a terrible thing to do!

"That is so sad," she says. "That's why I'm upset; it's a pretty sad story."

Peggy hands her a Kleenex. A wiry striped cat jumps on her lap, another one has settled on top of her feet, and the third, a calico, could easily serve as a neck rest were she to tip her head backwards. But it's not why she's sad. She's sad for herself, for the little kid that she was, sad for feeling like she doesn't really have a place of her own.

On the set, the actors had many ways to prepare for a scene. Jenny uses them now, right before she starts her open house. She thinks about her character's moment before. This is called method acting, something she read about in college. To appear pregnant, one must go ahead and get pregnant, for example. To appear to want to sell a house .... She can't quite figure out what that requires.

Her character's moment before is that she has just come from an amazing date with an amazing man, and she is so carefree and happy that she only sees the good in everyone, like Mary Poppins. Jenny keeps her eyes closed, breathing in, breathing out, humming a line from the "spoonful of sugar" song.

When she opens the front door, she says, *Hello!* With such cheerfulness that the woman waiting nearly drops her coffee.

From there, they breeze through the house, and she is enthusiastic, pointing out the wainscoting, the new teardrop lamp, the polished floors, while at the same time, listening to the woman's concerns, or pretending to listen, no, she's listening,

she is in the moment. She is breathing, she is present. She says, "Sorry, what was that?"

The woman wants to know about the neighborhood – is it safe? This lady, she's wiry and thin, her hair still wet from the shower, but tightly wound, a spring. "I'm looking for someplace safe," she reiterates. "For me and my dog."

"Safe? This is Philadelphia. None of us are safe." This makes the girl laugh, and Jenny wonders if maybe she can use this technique, this odd impulse to say what she really thinks.

The next day, Jenny goes into Dawn's office, determined to confess her transgression before the other real estate agent tattles. But as she's about to speak, Dawn tells her that Peggy's house just sold. For more than expected. To the movie agent with the gum-chewing problem. "You're kind of good at this," Dawn says, her head tilted to one side, evaluating. One of her huge hoop earrings almost touches her shoulder. "You need to try to be more authentic though. You come off as sort of a phony. Stop doing that."

On an impulse, Jenny tells Dawn that she's considering making an offer on the house where the children died, the place where she did her laundry.

"You're still renting?" Dawn's eyes are wide. She nudges the sleeping golden dog with her foot. "What're you, crazy? Make an offer. Now. You'd be a fool not to." She sounds like a character from a Dickens remake.

Those words echo back to Jenny throughout the day; she can never shake bad dialogue. *You'd be a fool not to ….*

"Oh, one last thing." Dawn reaches into her desk. Her business cards have arrived. She hands them to Jenny. Jenny is certain her name will be spelled wrong, but when she checks, no, it's there. It's her birth name, not the one she used as a child.

This one is her real name, with all of the confusing vowels and difficult pronunciation. "That's you, right?" asks Dawn.

"That's me," she says, incredulous.

Jennifer Saunderwoszki, real estate agent.

In the end, she scrapes the money together to buy the house and after she does the walk-through and finds nothing terribly wrong and after she has moved in, and after Peggy has forced her to take one of her cats, she sits, in her new old house, staring out the window with a fat orange tiger on her lap.

Her next role will involve a woman who has friends. Perhaps not close friends, perhaps just book club-type people she sees once a month, but this is what will happen next: a dinner party. There will be Peggy, the wiry girl (if she feels safe), Dawn with her two orphan dogs, and the organ lady. It will be a going-away party for Peggy and an introductory party for everyone else.

The end.

Cue music, roll tape.

Dear Man on Page 56 of the Banana Republic Spring Catalogue

I see you lounging against a biscuit-colored shale rock in your gabardine, three-button pants ($69.95). You wear a slight frown, as if pondering the answer to a difficult riddle (why is the writing like an albatross?). Your face, butternut brown, tips slightly to the imagined sun against a perfect baby blue, cloudless sky. Everything about the picture is perfect: your etched profile; your wind-tossed, longish hair: the short-sleeved, 100% cotton shirt with three buttons undone to reveal the deep cleft of your clavicle. I imagine perhaps that off the beach, you love dogs and surfing; you drink, but not too much; you like a rough kiss once in a while; you perhaps take yourself too seriously, but that I can overlook. You have the unreal perfection of the illustrated covers of the romance novels my Aunt JoAnne read and I discovered in her closet the summer before eighth grade. (What could I have been doing rummaging around in her closet in the first place? Looking for just these books, the fat paperbacks with covers set always in what I considered the olden

days, back then, never a cover of a woman in a pair of wool knit trousers and cashmere matching cardigan in ballet flats – I see you too, page 68. Perhaps you and 56 whisper to each other when the catalog is closed and shoved into my book bag, forever separated by a mere 10 pages.) I read those novels with the pirates, the captains of ships, the Lord of the Manor, always the brooding type, and his conquest, because we always had to be captured, cajoled, jerked out of our impertinence by their arms a bit, wrestled into giving in to their bubbling, overwhelming desire on a bed of soft autumn leaves or a down comforter mattress in the Captain's chambers deep in the belly of the ship. *Yes*, I thought. Yes, this is what love is like – I need a man named Raphe or Geronimo, a noble savage to half-rape me into ecstasy, and submission, while still learning a little something himself about humility. A slap would likely be required. At that age, you never think about afterwards – in the books, there is no afterwards, just the next chapter with the awkward after-sex lack of conversation and stickiness left out, it leaps right to the next day, with the conquered and joyful maiden whistling and swinging a bucket down a dirt path, her hair be-ribboned like the thin young girl on page 103 with the khaki shorts and V-neck T-shirt. Back at school, I looked around at my male classmates in their ill-fitting corduroy jeans, Metallica t-shirts, graffitied sneakers, and couldn't imagine standing on the deck of a sailboat with any of them (page 33) or riding a stallion across the great meadows of Ireland (from *She Takes a Village*). Nor did I see them in the high school boys loitering outside of the parking lot next to their parents' cars, cracking jokes and getting each other into headlocks. Where were these mythological creatures? Sometimes, sitting staring at Steve Bencusky's perfect neck in Mrs. Gustafason's social studies class, I could almost convince myself that Steve had another side – and, since

he was on the swim team, it wasn't that big of a stretch. He did have the daily discipline to make morning practice every day, but we never talked, me being of the invisible tribe in middle school, with a flat-chested body and big glasses that made me appear to be squinting. Which is why I still turn to you, page 56. Or page 78, the safari spread. Or page 54, the man straddling the bicycle built for two, a wide smile, teeth straight and frankly dangerous looking, as he careens down what appears to be a treacherous path, shirtless, but with a white-billed cap tossed across his blond curls to keep the sun off his Roman nose. On the back of the bike, we have a straw picnic basket with the top of a champagne bottle peeking its head out, and perhaps the hint of strawberries. On the bike behind him with her feet carelessly off the pedals as if she has lost control totally, is the girl from page 56, and it surprises me to see her there, though I am pleased that they have found one another at last and don't have to carry on waiting and wondering when the other will arrive.

Whistling in the Dark

On our third date, just after we've clinked glasses at this lovely Italian restaurant in a strip mall, Tad leans forward, his tie narrowly missing the flame from the candle on the table. He whispers, "Do you have a rape fantasy?"

I put down my $8.99 house wine. I look over at his soft feathery hair, glowing in the light of the mini chandelier dangling over our booth. I liked his online profile because his username didn't have "daddy" or "69" in it. I liked that the photos didn't show him holding the line of a dead fish he'd hooked or the bloody antlers of a deer he'd shot. I liked that he didn't post a picture of himself where another body had clearly been cut out. I liked that he had asked me lots of questions – where I grew up, what Netflix series I'm into, my shoe size. He seemed safe, an ordinary guy with slight limp who lived at home with his mom. "Of course, I have a rape fantasy," I say. "I have many. Which one do you want?"

He clutches his napkin. I begin.

In my most common rape fantasy, I am startled awake from a dream about auditioning for a part in *Annie*. I've forgotten to

memorize the lyrics for "It's the Hard Knock Life," so it's really a stressful dream and almost a relief to wake up and find myself pinned to my bed by a strange man. I can smell him (armpit sweat, pastrami), but I can't see him, because I have those light-blocking drapes from Bed Bath & Beyond. He presses a sharpish object to my jugular vein. I can't tell if it's a knife or a fork or some other utensil. "Don't move," he says. He garbles something else. I can't really understand him because he's wearing a ski mask. I squint for details to tell the police later. Husky voice, thin wrists, possibly a lisp. I have read a lot about how witnesses do really badly in lineups, so I'm trying to pay attention.

He pushes my knees apart, but what he doesn't know is that I've been taking Zumba classes for the last three months and so my leg muscles are super strong. I trap his legs with mine and flip over, a trick I learned in Girl Scout camp to earn my Rape Readiness badge. He hits the floor, scaring the cat.

This buys me enough time to grab the bedside lamp and bash it against his temple. While he's out cold, I bind him up with a bungee cord and pantyhose. I wait until the last second to remove his ski mask. I'm shocked to discover that he's handsome, in a creepy kind of way, with a matt of gelled blond hair, as if he prepared for the rape like you would a date. Turns out that what he was holding to my throat was a pair of tongs.

The second he comes to, he starts to cry. "I'm so sorry," he says. "This is my first time. I have thought about doing this for a while, but I never imagined it would go this way."

He looks a bit like my cousin Johnny, who raises ferrets and can never hold down a job. "Well, you tried, at least. That shows initiative."

"I'm such a loser!" he says, and if he could hit himself in the face, he probably would.

"You could try something else."

He shrugs. "I'm not interested in anything else."

We chat for a while. I untie him, and we sit cross-legged on the blue and white afghan my grandma knitted. It's meant for the burn victims of Shriner's Hospital, but I got it instead. My rapist wears one red sock and one brown sock. "I've been watching you," he says. "Well, watching this block of apartments. It's better," he explains, "to have options."

"Oh, okay, so I'm not the only one?"

"No, but you were my first choice."

I want to ask why, but then it might seem like I'm fishing for compliments. "Who are the other ones?" I say, feigning indifference. "The redhead lady?"

"I thought about her but she has a pit bull."

"Don't worry about him. He's such a submissive. He's all show." Secretly, I am pleased to be singled out.

"But let's figure you out," I say. I encourage him to take up a hobby like kickboxing or sword swallowing. "You could be so much more," I tell him, which is one of my favorite lines from the movie *Pretty Woman*. It's that scene after Richard Gere's character has fucked the prostitute, played by Julia Roberts's character, and they're both lying in bed in the afterglow of paid sex.

He says, "Thanks, and uh, get your screen window fixed, will ya?" We both laugh at that, and, for a second, it seems like we might hug, but then both think better of it. I let him out of the apartment, lock the door, and the run to the window to watch him move away down the sidewalk. I lean out on the windowsill, and the moonlight throws him into bright relief. As he's crossing the street, I yell, "You forgot your ski mask!" He turns to wave back at me and doesn't see the semitruck coming, and it flattens him. It's sad but not tragic, because they're never really rehabilitated, not really.

Tad has ordered another drink. He takes a quick sip. "That's very specific," he says. "You're in the arts, right? You like to make stuff up."

I am wrestling with the menu. It's one of those huge glossy kinds with photos of the dishes, chunks of mysterious meat smeared in cream. "Oh, my, what to choose?"

He clears his throat. "I can't tell if you're kidding or –"

"I'm not kidding," I say. I like the way his hair looks in the candlelight, as if it's standing on end. "I have others."

The doorbell rings and I decide to answer it because I am expecting a package from Amazon. It's a sweatshirt. I don't really need it, but it has a funny saying on it ("I wouldn't be caught dead in this sweatshirt"). Because it's a delivery I'm expecting, I open the door. In this fantasy, sometimes, it's not a delivery guy; it's the creepy man with the ponytail who lives below me. Or my ex-boyfriend, Shane. Or that new hire from IT who I said hi to once.

The point is not who rang the bell; the point is that I answer the door. I answer the door and I let the guy in and he tries to rape me. I open the door and he wedges his big khaki UPS thigh in to push the door open even farther. I answer the door and he puts a pistol to my temple. I look out through the peephole and go, *He looks familiar*, and then I open the door and he breaks my nose with his fist. When it happens, a part of me thinks, *Did he do that on accident?* Because I know this person and he never seemed violent to me.

I answer the door and it's a cop. He says, "Ma'am, there have been a series of attacks in your neighborhood. Are you aware of this issue?"

I say, "Uh, no."

I'm not going to let him in, because you can't trust anyone, but then he says, "I need you to identify some photos for me. It could help us catch this guy before he rapes again."

I open the door.

The next part is where I know I am going to be raped in my own home, so that I will have to move, which is another undiscussed consequence of rape. "Got rape?" Should be the slogan of a moving company specializing in helping women after an attack.

In this rape fantasy, I have a can of Mace. I aim it at his face and spray, but nothing comes out, because guess what? I've had the Mace since 1997 and it has expired. Like, who checks these things? You can only be so vigilant. I drop the Mace and try that thing where I pretend I'm having a seizure. That doesn't work because I keep hitting my head on the linoleum. When he pins me to the floor, I try to get ahold of his balls, but he's got one hand protecting them and the other one covering my mouth. I took a self-defense course once 10 years ago, but nothing sticks. There's no ready acronym for how to defend against rape like PUSH IT IN (pull under slash howl irritate tug ingratiate [k]neel). I just know I'm going to end up in the trunk of a car, where I've also been told that there are ways to escape. You're supposed to kick out the taillight and pray that a cop pulls the guy over, or you're supposed to somehow drill a hole through the steel of the car body and get your hand out so you can wave to the people behind you. Well, and if the guy is going to tie you up with ropes, you do this thing that horses do when they don't want the saddle on their backs – you puff out your stomach and body, so the ropes will have slack later, but is this something you can do with your wrists and ankles? Swell them up by sheer force of will?

Other strategies: I tell the rapist I have AIDs and brain cancer. I shrug. I'm like, "Go ahead, do it. I'm going to die anyway. I hope you don't catch what I have." I pee my pants. I shit my pants. I foam at the mouth and roll around on the ground making barking sounds. I yell, "Fire!" I yell, "Incoming!" I say my name over and over and over again to remind him that I am a human person. I tell him my dog just died and I can't take one more bad thing. I pretend to be dead already, unless, keeping one eye slightly open, I determine that he's into that kind of thing. I fight like hell, I use the heel of my hand to break his nose. I gouge out his eyes with my car keys, though wondering, do eyes gouge out or gouge in? I don't fully understand the eye gouging part.

I possibly don't blow the rape whistles because it's really loud and seems super dramatic. I act as though I like it, encouraging him, "Oh yeah exactly that, this is what I've always wanted." We call this one the reverse psychology approach since they always say rape isn't about sex, it's about power and control. If I tell him I want to do it just like this but with me on top, he might lose his erection. And then he might slash my throat, but maybe not. FYI, except for the pretending to enjoy the assault (I came up with that one on my own), the rest are all techniques I learned in junior high.

The appetizer plate is empty, except for the empty shrimp exoskeletons. You have to be careful how you eat things around men. Like, for example, with the shrimp appetizer, I don't eat it like I would at home, which would be to wantonly suck the shrimp out of its shell with a slurping noise. Instead, I bite into it and pull discretely to remove the dead shrimp – anything to avoid being viewed as some whore would just go down on you in a second.

Felicity, the waitress, comes over. "Have y'all decided what you'd like for your main course?" I tell her that I have, and order the lasagna.

Tad goes, "Uh ...."

"He'll have the spaghetti Bolognese," I say with a wink.

"I hope you don't think that all men are like that." He leans forward. He reaches for my hand, sees my face, and grabs a piece of bread instead.

"Oh, I know that," I say. "You're mostly decent folk. It's just that we women have to be careful, because it's almost always someone you know."

Tad says, "I meant to compliment you on your cardigan."

"Thank you," I say. For this date, I confide, I've chosen a conservative outfit. You want to look pretty, but not slutty, because if you are raped and/or murdered, that will be all anyone talks about. *What was she doing in that cut-off shirt and those short denim shorts? Why did she have on so much black eyeliner, not to mention the push-up bra and stripper heels?* I usually opt for sensible shoes from Clarks, though they make me look a social worker. A social worker with a trust fund. I keep the makeup minimal, only because it's so exhausting to put on makeup every day.

If my rape is going to take place on a first or second date, I've likely worn a pair of nice jeans and a cardigan. I'll have on decent underwear, on the off chance that we end up liking each other. For this date with Tad, I'm wearing peek-a-boo black lace but also athletic socks so that I can give myself a chance to pause before I go too far.

If I get raped after a late night at work, I'll be wearing a straight skirt and button-up blouse, and comfortable flats. It will probably be my boss who does it. His name is John Smithsonian.

If I am raped on an airplane, I'll have on stretch pants and a comfortable shirt and cardigan. The rapist will most likely be the bearded guy I'm sitting next to, the one who wants the middle seat, whose arms and legs keep spreading out while I try to condense my body into a smaller and smaller space until I am more or less suctioned up against the tiny window. In these moments, I imagine someone outside in the air, looking in at my face pressed there, mouth in an Edward Munch silent "oh" of despair.

If I'm going to get raped at a church, it likely means I'm either attending a wedding or a funeral, since I don't otherwise find myself in church. I'll be easy to catch then, because those events always require heels and I'll be forced to take itty-bitty steps. If the best man is going to rape me at the wedding reception, he's probably seen my dance moves and knows I have some coordination but not a lot, and that I have had several glasses of wine and so will be easier to get into a small broom closet. Just tell me there's a puppy in there and I'm yours.

If I'm going to get raped at a job interview, I've likely got on a two-piece suit – jacket and skirt and dress shirt from Ann Taylor Loft, or else jacket and dress and high heels. I will be more susceptible to being caught at that point too, because really, who rapes someone at a job interview? Would it be in the restroom and instigated by someone from the maintenance staff? Or would it be like in *Fifty Shades of Rape* where the millionaire interviewee finds me beyond perfect for his S&M fantasy and so follows me into the bathroom?

If I'm going to get raped on TV, it could be any number of shows, but most certainly I could be Victim #1 on *Law & Order SVU*. I've already been raped because it's a whole show about rape.

In this episode, we focus mostly on the perpetrator and somewhat on me, if only to determine if I am lying about the rape. Even though this happens in fewer than one percent of rape cases, the show portrays lying as occurring half the time. Sometimes, I'm a gymnast, or a missing teen, or a Syrian prostitute, or a patient with Alzheimer's, or a beauty pageant toddler, or a drunk sorority girl, or a retarded girl from a group home, or a girl with one leg who has gone missing (the girl, not the leg).

The only thing to know about this show is that there will always be a twist. It's not who you initially think it is. The rapist is really ... the twin brother, the sister-in-law with a basting tool, the handsome married cop, the ex-husband's new boyfriend, the gynecologist, the dentist's son, the drippy guy who didn't fit in. That is the rape fantasy of television where all of the perps get caught, and the rape is part of a larger scheme, not an act of violence so common that it has its own series.

Tad has folded his knife and fork neatly over his plate. His napkin, too, is crushed into a tight ball on top of his unfinished meat sauce. He's looking beyond me, into the restaurant, eyes searching.

"Well, I think we should call it a night," he says, almost standing.

"Have a seat," I suggest *not* in a mean way. Just firm, with authority.

He flinches just as Felicity appears at our table. "Dessert, anyone?"

Tad excuses himself and hurries towards the men's room. Felicity leans over the table. She wears a tight black T-shirt that accentuates her breasts. In white cursive letters across the front, it reads, *Eat at Hot Mama's*. "Look," she says, "I can tell you guys are on your first date."

"Third," I say.

"Okay, third. He seems like a nice guy, but I just want you to know he comes here a lot. With dates, I mean."

"Like how often?"

"Once a week?"

I fake a chortle, which isn't easy to do, chortling. "Oh, whatevs," I say. "I don't even know if I like him."

I tell her about this time I was at a frat party. My friend had had too much to drink and she vomited on herself, but I got there the moment before the guy, Tim Thompson, was able to rip off her clothes. I threw the DEK paddle at him and it winged on his head, knocking him from the bed, and my friend and I got away. In the fantasy, we told everyone about the attempted rape. We don't call it sexual assault, which sounds like someone got a little rough during sex. We tell our neighbors, the minister at church, the local paper, the police, our parents, CNN. And the rapist gets kicked out of his frat, and is going away for a long, long time and justice is served.

Except that didn't happen. Not quite like that, anyway.

He's back from the bathroom and his face looks fresher and also redder, like he splashed water on it and patted it dry with a scratchy paper towel.

I tell him about what's really on my mind (since he asked), which isn't so much a fantasy as it is something I can't get out of my head. I'm in high school sitting next to my crush, John Dubos, in the front seat of his dad's purple Chevy Impala. Instead of taking me home after seeing *The English Patient,* he's taken me to the high school parking lot, which looks different in the dark, like an entirely new place. I can see the glow of the bleachers in the dark and the Y of the football field goal posts like other men standing in the field, watching.

He puts the car into park and says, "I've been waiting all night to do this." He lunges for me, his tongue down my throat, his hands on my brand-new cashmere baby pink GAP sweater, and I try to imagine it is romantic – his desire for me is such a huge, unwieldy thing, like the love in the movie where the two characters must have one another on a sandy beach before the guy goes down in a puddle jumper plane and gets burned within an inch of his life. They don't go into details, but you can just imagine his skin peels off as easy as skin off a grape. I'm trying to imagine this as something from the movie, but my thigh is wedged against the gear shift and my skirt is twisted up. A drop of John Dubos's sweat plops on my forehead. He pulls at my hand, bringing it to his khaki Dockers (also from the GAP?) and before you know it, it's out, this thing I've never seen, but only read about in romance novels, where they never describe it like this. This looks vaguely like the sea anemone we studied in Mr. Moon's biology class, with its wavy white stalk. John pushes me against the door so my head bangs against the glass. His hands are up my skirt and I'm thinking, *Oh, god, what kind of underwear am I wearing?* Having not prepared properly for this moment of my de-virgin-izing, I'm blushing to think that they're the kind that go all the way up to the waist. He doesn't seem to care, because off they go, ripped in half, and he's panting like some kind of animal in pain, puffs of air coming out that smell like popcorn. He's saying, "You like this? Huh? You like this?"

And I do not like it, but I like him, and I want him to like me. Which is why I don't exactly understand the next thing I do. I reach below the sea anemone and grab the sac there, again like some kind of creature from underwater, a jellyfish maybe. I squeeze the jellyfish as hard as I can. He goes still and then lets out a shriek as high and loud as a whistle. He rocks away from me, doubled over, knocking his lovely head against the steering

wheel. While he's recovering, I yank open the car door and start running. I am happy I wore Keds because I can sprint out of the parking lot without looking back. In school on Monday, and forever after, he avoids me and I think, *Maybe we were meant to fall in love and I ruined it.*

It's late and the restaurant has emptied. Tad says, "Did that happen to you?"

I might be attracted to him. I could bring him home. It would probably be okay. "Who's to say?"

The check sits on the table. Tad clears his throat. "I get your point of view. I get it. I have sisters."

"You do?"

"Yeah, and I worry about them all the time." He shakes his head. "I think … I wonder if I've ever …."

"Oh, you have," I tell him. I have folded the red paper place-mat into a flower shape, the kind you can open and close with your fingers. I present it to him.

He takes it and it nearly catches fire on the now dim flame. Just to show him how progressive I am, I let him pay the bill.

I pat my lips with my napkin and ask to be excused. He says, "What? I mean, yeah, you don't need my permission."

Instead of going to the ladies' room, I slip out the back door of the kitchen into the alleyway, where the bus boys are smoking near the dumpster. "Hey," I say.

"Hey," they say.

Here is where I could have a fantasy about an almost gang-bang rape where we end up instead playing dice and talking about what we were like in middle school. We're not all that different, I think, holding my keys laced between my fingers. I whistle a show tune as I walk – this is another one from *Annie* – to show anyone who might be watching how not afraid I am.

How to Get Rid of an Elderly Dog

First, don't get a dog. Do not attach yourself to any sentient creature whose life you have to manage. If your dog is old and sick, his eyes filming over, take him to a nearby forest. His ears will perk up, like they used to do, alert to the chattering squirrels in the treetops. Wear rain boots as you walk him deeper into the woods. Find a gentle stream and set down his favorite toy, a blue monster that quacks like a duck. Say, "good boy!" Then turn and run as fast as you can. Because of his eye problems and his crooked hips, his jaundice, his yellowing eyes, tongue half out, it will be hard for him to follow, though his nose is 10 times better than yours, so be sure to spritz yourself with Dog Off to confuse him. Jump in your car. Do not look back.

Avoid that person you love or could love. Instead, read about love in books where the endings make sense. It can happen that you love someone and that person doesn't love you back. Or you could love a man or a woman, and this man or woman could love you back, but not for your entire life – they go crazy, they blow themselves up with a terrorist bomb, they jump off bridges. He teaches yoga and is surrounded by nimble young

women who can hold downward dog and plank for way longer than you. Remember when you tried plank that last time, your arms trembled, and you folded over on the mat in under seven seconds? Yes, the yoga teacher may love you now, but he will certainly fall for that woman in the back of class with the long braid. Her name is Mogwina and she reads Thich Nhat Hanh and understands tantric sex. She's able to have multiple orgasms just from penetration. And you? Well.

If your elderly mother asks you to move in because she's afraid of falling down the basement stairs, get online immediately to find a caretaker at *careformoms.com.* Look, there's Marta who loves crossword puzzles and making toast. Or Lucinda, who will listen to your mom's long (and inaccurate) stories about life with your stepdad, who is 10 years dead and good riddance. For an extra $24.99, you can even do a background check. Or not, they look reputable (make them more horrible). Marta wears a summery dress she made herself and Lucinda holds what might be a stuffed animal or possibly a real live kitten. One more, like three sisters. Seem pretty awful. You don't even have to talk to them on the phone. Email them her address and pin a note to your mom's shirt that reads, *Please help me log in to Netflix.*

When you get home, the dog is waiting for you. He made it back. Somehow. Miraculously, like Lassie. He is not whimpering and wagging his stumpy tail, eyes full of love and shining. Clean up the mess. Take his head in your hands. Look him in his milky eyes, the ones that follow you everywhere, interested in whatever you're doing. Putting on your shoes? Wherever you're going, he'd like to go too.

Hold his head in your hands. Hold him close. Say to him, You were a good dog. Say this to him every day to remind him and yourself. You were a good dog. You were a good dog. You were a good dog.

Acknowledgments

Gratitude to all the writers and friends who encouraged me, gave brilliant suggestions, called me out when I was faking it, and reminded me that I can sometimes write a good sentence. I appreciate Rebecca Zhuraw, my thesis advisor at U-Penn, who asked me to think critically about how my stories were inspired by other writers. Thank you to Lydia Yuknavitch, who read some of the nurse stories at Tin House workshop and taught me to find the patterns and connections lurking in the stories, as well as to Chinelo Okparanta, who read a draft of the collection and pushed me to see how the stories worked together. To Molly Gaudry, from the Yale Writing Workshop, who challenged me to find the depth in my characters. Thank you to Lisa Kastner, at Running Wild Press, who has always been supportive of women writers and who has a mutual admiration for Brad Pitt (she knows what I mean). Thank you to Alison Hicks from the Philadelphia Wordshop, Carlin Romano, and Akashic Press. I'm very grateful to the Edward Albee Foundation, which gave me time to work on a novel that became several of these stories—which also reminds me to thank Raluca Alba, Lindsay Haber, and John Hulme, three particularly brilliant writers who also said, *Keep going*. Thanks to my friend Alex Dawson, who is always positive and encouraging and tells me to shine. Thanks to Joyce Carol Oates for her tough critiques that have made me push myself, and who sent cat pictures exactly when needed. Same goes for Warren Frazier, whose brilliance always improves the work. Thank you to Carolyn Williams and Rutgers

Writers House, who gave me the space and inspiration to write. Thanks also to Laura van den Berg and the Key West lit writers with their spot-on critiques. And many thanks to the literary journals who read and accept and reject short stories and do the hard work of slogging through writers' stories every day, in particular Nancy Pearl, who saw potential in these pages. Oh, yes, and thank you to the City of Brotherly Love, which gave me the best material.

Rubbertop Review, "Our Boys," Fall 2024

Running Wild Press Annual Short Story Anthology, "How to Act," Fall 2022

North American Review, "The Double Negative Boyfriend," Spring 2020

"Rage," winner of the *Solstice Literary Magazine* annual literary contest, May 2020

Ariel's Dream, "Dear Man on Page 56 ..." April 2020

StoryQuarterly, nominated for a Pushcart Prize, "Whistling in the Dark," December 2019

The Minnesota Review, "The Bluest Skies," December 2019

Cagibri, nominated for a Pushcart Prize, "Animal Shelters," July 2018

Thin Air, "How to Get Rid of an Elderly Dog," December 2018

Mortar Magazine, "Jane Err," 2017

Strangelet Press, "Jane Err," 2016

Per Contra, "On Top of the World" (published as "The Visitors"), 2016

Women Running Wild: An Anthology, "Curb Appeal" (published as "Real Estate"), 2017

About the Author

Aimee LaBrie's short stories have appeared in the *Minnesota Review*, *Iron Horse Literary Review*, *StoryQuarterly*, *Cimarron Review*, *Pleiades*, *Beloit Fiction Journal*, *Permafrost Magazine*, and others. In 2020 her short story "Rage" won first place in *Solstice Literary Magazine*'s Annual Literary Contest, and her novel in progress won the Key West Literary Seminar Emerging Writer Award. In 2007, her short story  collection, *Wonderful Girl*, was awarded the Katherine Anne Porter Prize in Short Fiction and published by the University of North Texas Press 2007. Her short fiction has been nominated three times for the Pushcart Prize. In 2012, she won first place in the *Zoetrope: All-Story*'s Short Fiction Competition. Aimee works as a senior program coordinator for the Rutgers English Department and teaches undergraduate creative writing for Writers House at Rutgers. She lives in Cranbury, New Jersey, with her husband, son, and two very ridiculously cute dogs, Millie and Wyatt.